ALIEN
ENTANGLEMENT

Panspermia to Kali Yuga

K. PAUL GOMEL

PAGE PUBLISHING, INC.
Conneaut Lake, PA

First originally published by Page Publishing 2020

ISBN 978-1-64628-163-3 (pbk)
ISBN 978-1-64628-164-0 (digital)

Printed in the United States of America

Dedicated to our parents and their generation of elders, both here and gone. Their altruism was boundless, their fortitude legendary. We know you all continue to bless us with memories and watch over us.

Two possibilities exist: either we are alone in the universe or we are not. Both are equally terrifying.

—Arthur C. Clarke

RUNNING SILENT

She had never seen the planet to which they were heading, yet strangely she was ecstatic to be returning there. After all, this was the place she always considered as home!

Keenly monitoring the planet, all excited to be approaching a place for which she had a strong yearning, she flicked some switches and waved her anthropomorphic hand over the screen in order to increase magnification. It was no use. They were too far away. *Patience!* she thought to herself. The radio waves coming from there was shocking to her. This planet was not advanced enough, at least not according to the reports. Arrival there was targeted to a specific time period, which was a short distance and a shorter time from now. Although arrival this far in the future did not make any sense it could, however, partially explain the presence of radio activity—perhaps her people had modernized and developed since the last report was compiled.

She could not communicate with the planet of the spacecrafts' origin. Communication to and from there took a great deal of energy to process in the vehicle, despite the fact that it was gigantic. Summoning up the amount of energy to traverse the distance to the home planet could leave it devoid of energy and therefore vulnerable and defenseless. Communication had to be kept to a minimum, in case of dire emergencies only. Plans could not change spontaneously—she had her instructions, and she had to obey them to the letter.

A New Place

Ironically, the stark beauty almost breathed life into this barren and inhospitable place. Standing at the threshold of the airlock portal on the lander, John absorbed what he could of this infertile beauty. It was not always like this. Way back in the past there were salty oceans and presumably an atmosphere which inexplicably, over the millennia, had disappeared. His time here was limited, and his purpose, ostensibly, was to make this place habitable. So he immersed his thoughts into the dusty landscape, enjoying its hostile beauty. He could not have imagined in his wildest dreams that the monotony of this planet, seemingly devoid of any surface water, could be this captivating. Even after years of practice in a simulator, nothing could prepare anyone for the real thing. That particular natural shade of redness was impossible to duplicate on a planetary scale and certainly not with the sun at this angle—just prior to dawn. This particular shade of crimson reminded him of the outback in Australia, when he had visited there several years earlier to practice the steps he was about to undertake. Involuntarily he inhaled deeply as if to absorb more of this scenery. Not only was this the dawn of a new day, but this was also the dawn of a new era—the determination of mankind to make increasingly frequent trips to this place. The eventual goal was colonization—at least that was what was being relentlessly communicated to the populace. It was easy to mislead the public. The media obligingly took care of that with round-the-clock coverage of anything related to space travel. People want to believe, so they did; they want to be brainwashed, so they were. This was just a stepping-stone. When John had heard of the real intention of developing lengthy space travel for humans he did not hesitate in volunteering. Another deep breath and the realization slowly dawned on him that there was no way he could delight in the natural fragrances of the planet. Truly experiencing this planet would remain as foreign to him as the truth would be to the masses, for now.

A small minority, the restive religious zealots, could not fathom this travesty—the audacity of establishing a colony on another planet. Their stance was that we are meant to be on the planet where we have evolved—forever. Only John and a handful of very important people knew the truth. If only the fanatics knew the true purpose of making this journey. But they were immersed in their respective religions, unable to see the big picture. Presumably they were afraid that if a colony could be set up elsewhere, the pursuit of "the truth" would matter less; their importance would diminish. Thus, they would lose their power, power that had taken generations and multiple millions of lives to consolidate. After all, there is a fine line between true altruism and the semblance of altruism to gain power and control over fellow beings. The masses needed preachers as much as the preachers needed the masses. They were not about to give it up easily. Besides, their stance was that the colonization of another planet, albeit the closest one, was not a trivial task by any stretch of the imagination. The physical trauma of travel was nothing compared to the mental torture one would need to endure if the first settlers had to permanently exist in an enclosed environment. The zealots argued that mankind was not meant to leave Earth.

Continuing to aspirate normally now that the stunning views settled into the back of his mind, John realized that the sterile odorless O_2 was being supplied to him from the oxygen tank strapped to his back—just like the constant stream of sanitized information that was disseminated to the public. He allowed himself a wry smile at the analogy. Despite minute quantities of oxygen being pumped out by the O_2 generators installed on Mars for just over fifteen months, there was not nearly enough here to sustain multicellular life. At some point in the future, hopefully, there would be no need to carry air on his back. Then he would be able to delight in the natural smell of this place, the odor that contributes to the ambiance of any place. John hoped that someday he would be able to come back and experience that luxury. But that was left to fate. He was one of the very few who knew of the next planned mission. That mission could be the final mission to anywhere and for anyone.

John's mind briefly wandered over to the status of Deepak, one of his crew. He was an expert in anthropology, sociology, and linguistics. An ideal candidate for meeting new intelligent life. Like the rest of his crew, he was unaware that this was a dry run for the true mission. His background in military intelligence made him an ideal candidate for the mission to come. But his expertise in sociology was the reason he was shortlisted for this mission. To everyone else, including himself, he was selected for this mission to mollify the people opposed to colonization of other planets. However, coming out of the hibernation apparatus, he had suffered a heart attack. Only with the expertise of Nicole, the ex-military surgeon, did he manage to survive. Nicole and Kristen, a biologist, had together brought him back from the brink of becoming the first human corpse in space. Per plan, all except Kristen had remained on the orbiter. John radioed, "How is he doing?" to which he received the response from Nicole, "He is stable, and his bio is slowly returning to normal."

This was certainly an unexpected event, but it served to highlight the team effort of this crew and Mission Control to stabilize the first space patient. Luckily, they had aspirin on board, but it was not carried for this purpose—although it worked fine as a first aid blood thinner. Deep, as he was known to his colleagues, would need to be replaced since any future space missions could prove fatal for him, if indeed he survived the journey home. The next mission called for a longer period of hibernation.

His attention back to the scenery in front of him, John noticed that there was thin red dust being kicked up by the generators which were slowly pushing out oxygen. The dust was very light, the consistency of confectioners' sugar. With the early morning sunshine streaming through, it created this particular hazy feast of crimson colors for the eyes. No human had observed this view. Indeed, no human had set foot on this planet before—John would be the first. As he stood transfixed, literally at the doorway to a new planet, the headset crackled, jolting him back to reality. "Commander, if you wait there for another minute or two, you will see the most spectacular sunrise anyone has ever witnessed."

Standing and waiting for the sunrise, John wondered if the natural atmosphere that was once present here had been burned off through the runaway greenhouse effect. Or was it that it had reacted with the iron on the surface and been absorbed by the planet itself in the process of oxidation? Could the planet itself hold the atmosphere that once surrounded it? If that were the case it would be a situation where the planet gave and sustained life, if there were life here in the past, and the planet also took it away. In his thought process, he decided to settle at the comfortable answer by surmising that mankind would find out in due course, but it may be too late for him. Humans would make sure that this planet would become habitable, but it would take several decades. Originally there was debate whether the atmosphere being generated should be oxygen or carbon dioxide. Finally, after thorough testing of the soil, it was settled that O_2 would be the first step, as it was theorized that CO_2 was the reason for this planet becoming a dusty wasteland. Whether this thought process was scientifically accurate or not was immaterial at this juncture. He was an astronaut, and he had work to do. He could not let these tangential thought processes ruin his concentration.

MONITORING MISSION

About eighteen months before John and his crew departed for Mars a secret mission was launched. It contained powerful lights and video monitoring cameras of all kinds and powerful transmitters to transmit images from those cameras back to Earth. That was it. The true purpose of the mission could not be revealed to the populace on any account. The public were told this was a mission to test the new fusion engines, the same ones that took John and his crew to Mars and which would power the next mission. In a way, this was true. But, in the dark depths of space, what the powerful lights were meant to illuminate and what images the cameras were supposed to capture and send back could not be revealed. No one, not even the organizers of the mission, knew what the images would contain. All they knew was that something was erratically approaching Earth.

Minor Adjustments

Arrival was determined to be at a specific time, but also a specific place at the target planet. The meticulous calculations were performed before they had departed their planet and were loaded on to the onboard systems. The plans called for major time adjustments to happen at a point far from the arrival location. As the proximity to the target planet increased, minor adjustments would be made to ensure arrival at the exact predetermined time. To the person monitoring the target planet there was not much to do except to periodically check and make sure that the computer was making the proper adjustments automatically and at the appropriate time (rather like an autopilot). She had to manually approve the adjustments in the automatic system before they took effect. These systems were specifically designed that way because an organic brain made better decisions than automated systems. A brain has better "feel" for the environment whereas an automated system is hard coded with "yes" or "no," "do" or "don't." Automated systems lacked the evaluative process in coming to the right decision especially if the answer were to lie in between the simple "yes" and "no." For instance, what if someone was not a friend but also not an enemy? Her organic brain was entrusted to monitor the potential dangers which could harm the crafts or its hibernating occupants.

In the ample time she had when the masters were hibernating, she decided to do some background research on the planet to which they were heading. This was not the first trip there, but she was not a member of the previous missions. She noticed from the corner of her eye, which had a bigger field of vision than a normal human eye, that a menial robot was scurrying away with a task which she had previously assigned it. The absence of mental

15

activity told her that this was a menial robot which had no organic matter. She mentally instructed that robot to stop. It obediently stopped as soon as it processed the telepathic command. It had no choice—all robots were designed to pick up mental signals. She assigned it another higher-priority task—to which it obeyed without question. It would complete the original task upon completing this higher-priority job.

She had noticed that the radio waves from the target planet were increasing. Had the people who had planned this journey miscalculated? Were they arriving at a different time to what was calculated before they left their home planet? A quick check revealed there were no errors in the calculations. So why was there so much radio activity from a primitive planet?

A detailed check of the parameters which was input into the computer before they left also revealed that the data was correct and did in fact call for arrival further in the future than on previous occasions. The reason for this far a jump into the future was due to a problem with the current stock—they assumed that the brains of the natives had not had enough time to develop. So they programmed the ships to come at a much later time, assuming a few thousand years of evolution would enable the inhabitants of the target planet to evolve. Calculations indicated that this much radio activity was indicative of a civilization that was about 30 percent developed as compared to their own.

It was exciting for her to be going to a home she had never seen. She had to do more research on the target population. When the robot came back with the memory she wanted it to fetch, she instructed it to load it into the system. She will have to remember to return it before her masters came out of hibernation; otherwise, she would have hell to pay. No need for further detailed instructions since there was just enough intelligence built in for it to take high-level instructions. The dumb robot obeyed and inserted the memory device in the appropriate slot. Without further instruction, it went back to doing what it was doing before being interrupted. The cyborg started studying the documents on the memory device with her superhuman eyes and occasionally turning the page with her tactile fingers with enhanced haptic feedback, more advanced than the hands with which she was born. Still she would give anything to have her original appendages back.

PANIC

Almost all the surface water had evaporated, all the iron exposed to the unrelenting sun in this dusty hell of a place had oxidized—giving the dirt a distinctive bloodred tinge. The dust wafting just aboveground before slowly settling back on to the surface was due to the exhaust vent of the O_2 generators being pointed slightly at a downward angle. What little moisture that was left on this planet was mostly frozen below the surface at the poles and not easily visible since it was covered over by multiple layers of red dust. It did "unfreeze" periodically, but no one knew why or when. John's gaze shifted to the spectacular mountain a little distance in front of him. It was the cause for him performing cartwheels in his mind. It was majestic with the highest peak and the broadest base of any mountain known in this planetary system. Of course, from his vantage point he could not appreciate the full enormity of the mountain. This was not like a traditional mountain that he had seen. There were no jagged peaks or rocks strewn all over from past violent outbursts or even snow at higher elevations. There were no dangerous crevasses where you least expect them. This was a gentle gradient from the base over miles of terrain all the way to the peak. Countless years of outpouring of magma without violent eruption had ensured that the peak and the base were separated by more than ten miles. The lack of erosion due to natural forces had ensured that the mountain was relatively smooth on the surface. John imagined that if he were to stand at the base, he would not be able to see the peak. The cause of his unbridled elation was a combination of the sun, Mount Olympus in front as well as the wisps of dust in the background. As the first rays of sunlight peeked over the silhouetted mountain and refracted through the wisps of crimson dust it created an image unlike anything that was observed by anyone. It was like peeking through a kaleidoscope—with no repeating patterns.

John knew that there was an ulterior motive to waiting. The enormous shadow that the mountain was casting was still enveloping a large area where he needed to work. Presently the lander was situated in the shadow of the enormous mountain, in almost complete darkness. As the sun rose, the target area would be bathed in soft reflected sunshine, making his work that much easier. Direct sunshine, even the early morning rays, would be brutal due to the lack of any atmosphere. However, his life-support system strapped to his back would amply be able to cope. In response to the last instruction John nodded, mainly to himself since no one could see his nod. The one team member who accompanied him in the lander was busy subconsciously executing all the routine tasks that were practiced a multitude of times before embarking on this journey with great alacrity. The other members were in the Deep Space Explorer (dSE)—the intraplanetary vehicle currently in orbit of Mars—from which the lander had egressed to make its way to the Martian surface. But as the commander and leader of this mission it was incumbent upon him to be the first to step out onto this alien and hostile planet. A nagging thought came from the back of his mind. He was so busy marveling at the beauty of this landscape and other thoughts about future trips, he had forgotten his rehearsed lines as he took the first steps onto the surface. Suddenly he was gripped with panic. He had thought about it and researched it and prepared for it a multitude of times. Now suddenly his mind was blank. It was not that he was nervous, but too late; the sensitive machine strapped to him as part of his life-support equipment had already picked up this momentary panic. It had sensed his elevated heart rate, blood pressure, chemicals in his blood stream and his brain activity, compared it against the baseline stored in the database and had transmitted the telemetry millions of kilometers away to Mission Control. Literally, within seconds of his fleeting panic attack, the headset came to life and a very concerned voice inquired, "Captain, are you okay?"

John's first thought at hearing this was *That response was fast.* Reassured that he was in good hands, calmly he responded, "Yes!

I was momentarily alarmed that I forgot my lines." Then thought to himself—everything but the thought process is being monitored. Even the brain waves could potentially be monitored. But, other than some rudimentary information gleaned from the wave patterns that the brain generates, there was no way yet to interpret that into meaningful information. The only reason that the brain was being monitored was in order to develop some future technology that could correlate body chemistry with what the brain was subconsciously doing. Other than this potential anecdotal science that was in its infancy, there was no technology to interpret signals from the brain at the telepathic level—at least not that the humans were aware. Unbeknownst to him and anyone else, they would all find out in the next mission.

In order to lighten the mood, the headset crackled again. "And we got excited that perhaps you had seen something with two heads and six legs running across the dry, barren landscape."

Exuding the epitome of calmness, and his biochemistry returning to normal, he quipped, "As a matter of fact that two-headed being with six legs is called Marvin and is asking for directions to Jupiter. It says that they believe our arrival will trash their planet. Strangely, he appears to be wearing a helmet and is about two inches tall."

After a brief chuckle heard through the headset, it crackled again, this time with words "Are you okay, Commander?" The tone was serious which elicited a muted response, "Affirmative, I panicked for a second when I thought I forgot my lines. But I am good now."

The headset came on again. "Your bio is returning to normal. Hold your position, Cap'n, we want you to see the sunrise. We intend to experience that vicariously through you. There will not be another one for at least another Martian day, but you will be long gone by then. It will be a shame for all of us if you missed." That last sentence was said with more than a modicum of sarcasm. All that talking was intended to bring John's biometric readings to normal, or as close to it as is possible on a foreign planet. After a pause, presumably while making a note of the readings, the voice continued, "After observing the sunrise event you can step out and utter the words you were practicing. Maybe that will persuade Marvin and his people to stay back a little longer."

Again, the captain nodded, knowing full well that the nod would not be seen by the people communicating with him verbally. Ostensibly, the task for this trip was very simple—change some replaceable parts in the O_2 generators. These generators had arrived preassembled in private unmanned spacecrafts contracted to the space agency. It had taken multiple missions—three in all, as there were five generators. The first mission carried one—a trial. The two subsequent ones had carried two each. They were landed by remote control and turned on from Mission Control. They were all colocated near one another, so a single person could service the units in one extravehicular activity (EVA). This work would not take very long. The information being disseminated was that these were the first baby steps for colonization. Looking at them and the progress made since they started pumping out O_2 it was obvious they were too small. Clearly these machines did not have the capacity to generate enough O_2 for humans to breathe. This mission had a far deeper purpose than just to service these generators.

Of all the crew who made this journey through space, only John knew that there was a secret motive—a purpose beyond what was communicated to the rest of the crew and to the public. Some of the crew would accompany him in the next mission, but they did not know it yet. Indeed, they did not know that there was a next mission, which was already in an advanced planning stage. John was sworn to secrecy—the information was too sensitive for the population of the world. When he was chosen as a potential candidate to captain this top secret mission, he could hardly control his excitement. With what he saw of his existing crew, he was sure not one of them would hesitate in the slightest to volunteer for the next one. In his mind, he had decided to refer to the top secret mission as the "big one." That way he could give the project some substance—and refer to it by a name that only he knew. If he were to inadvertently blurt out to anyone what he was thinking, no one would know the reference, even if they were aware of the big picture. This mission, however, was a dry run to test some of the procedures, technologies, and theories for the "big one."

John was thinking back to how this whole thing had started. The reason for the "big one" was because a random and inconsequential mistake had led to the potential discovery of some comets heading toward Earth. Working through the proper channels, the information made its way to the department of defense. A few weeks passed, and slowly this information, like so many others, blinked out of the collective consciousness of the public. This is exactly what the department had wanted, without fuss render this information obsolete. Only that in the internal workings of the government it was classified as top secret and was very much active. The authorities could not be sure—comets do not travel in formation. The objects approaching were too hard to spot, and when they could it was only a fleeting glimpse. These objects were blinking in and out of existence—mostly out. It was unclear why, but one safe speculation was that natural debris in space was causing it. No one could ever argue to the contrary. Contact was next to impossible to calculate, but it was deemed to be several decades from the present time, in typical government vernacular, subject to revision. The trajectory of the objects, it was broadly speculated, would take them close to Earth. Clearly more research was needed before unnecessarily panicking the public. But just in case these were belligerent visitors, preparations were surreptitiously being made to welcome them or destroy them before they got too close. In his mind John was certain that these were not comets or asteroid. He was not privy to all the top secret information, but common sense told him that these things were too big for asteroids and comets this size do not travel in groups. His next mission could be his last. He could be one of the first humans to die in space as a result of aggression, if Deep managed to survive the return back to Earth. In fact, there could be a lot of firsts, first man to be killed by alien hands, first man to not have a burial as a result of there being no Earth... He decided to stop day-dreaming at this point.

After the government had pulled out of the near-Earth-orbit supply/maintenance program some twenty or so years earlier, the private companies had taken over the development of efficient delivery of material to orbit. In private hands and with healthy competition they had progressed the space travel technology in leaps and bounds. So much so that space travel had become routine, almost as routine as flying—for a very limited group of super wealthy individuals. The well-heeled could afford the thrill of travel to near Earth orbit, experience weightlessness, and come back. These trips were planned on an almost weekly basis. This had developed to very fast travel across continents. This, in turn, had helped the government agencies by allowing them to focus on developing other technologies necessary for long interplanetary journeys. Initially they had the Orion program for deep space travel. Then, using the private advancements, they had launched new and faster vehicles. One of the technologies being tried out during this mission was the HySleep. This was a dry run for the "big one." Everyone on this mission were guinea pigs for many new technologies—HySleep being just one of them. There were two women on this mission—they needed both genders for the "big one." However, here and now on this alien surface, it was the job of the commander of the mission to take the first steps on Mars. John was ready—now that he had recollected his line that he was going to state as he disembarked from the lander.

PROGRESS OF SENTINEL

Chand, the Mission Control leader on the ground, inquired, "What is the status of Sentinel?"

Sentinel was the name of the mission that was launched ostensibly to test the new fusion engines. In fact, it was a craft loaded with lights and cameras.

Since this was an unmanned mission, a small staff of five scientists were needed to manage this project. However, they still had to provide periodic progress reports to the controller, whose job was to monitor this as well as the manned mission to Mars. Drew responded with, "All systems are normal. We again tested 'lights, camera, and action,'" he laughed as he said this, "and everything is normal. I mean, everything came on, and all we could see was nothing! Except Sentinel itself."

That was to be expected. The lights were powerful but not strong enough to make a difference in space. Chand responded, "What is the R-day?" R-day was short for revelation day, as in all will be revealed when the unmanned mission reached its destination. The answer was succinct, "On target, R minus 735 days"—meaning, they had to patiently wait 735 Earth days for the rendezvous.

The unmanned craft was already in flight for a few months. Satisfied with the answer Chand shifted her attention to the more pressing issue, the manned mission.

HIBERNATION

In the sinister-looking cloaked crafts approaching Earth everything was quiet. The life-forms were all hibernating, except for the robots, which were silently and methodically carrying out maintenance tasks exactly as was assigned to them by the cyborgs. Most of these robots were completely devoid of any organic matter. They were just dumb machines only capable of taking telepathic instructions. The thinking robots were of a higher rank and provided direction to the menial robots while the real masters hibernated. The thinking robots were responsible for specific levels of this immense and multilevel space-faring vehicle. Each had a team of menials to assist. However, all the thinkers were in constant communication so as to coordinate their activities. This coordination was not very important now, but was critical when everyone was at their battle stations and this battle-ship was waging war.

Thinking about meeting humans on the target planet, she realized that she would be unrecognizable in her current form. But there was nothing anyone could do about that now. All her missing parts had long been incinerated. How would she introduce herself when she meets a human? Best approach is to simply announce her name—Lela. She thought about it for a while, and she settled on just identifying herself by her name. Having never seen a human from the target planet, she wondered if the humans had a similar way of differentiating one another, by giving one another labels. There was only one way to answer that question—meet one. Her anticipation level was growing exponentially. She had an additional task—a task that no one gave her. A task that she assigned to herself—that was to save her kind. She had to figure out a way, but that could wait. There was ample time.

Again, she noticed robot wheels whirring in the distance, carrying out its newest responsibility. She called it back and gave it an additional task of returning the memory chip. It would not fail or forget—it was programmed to carry out whatever tasks her kind or her masters gave it. This technology was simple and effective, but there was no intuition—that is where she and her kind fit in.

STARK BEAUTY

Deep in thought, he was sharply brought back to reality when the first shards of light harshly penetrated his retina. What unfolded thereafter was spectacular. John increased the blocking intensity of rays on his visor to the maximum setting, so that he could see without being blinded. Still day-dreaming, viewing this marvel of natural beauty, John wondered about his ancestors. How would they react to such a sight? They had their share of adrenaline highs—the captains and crew of so many sailships exploring the unknown world. He knew that he could trace his lineage directly back to the British explorer Captain James Cook. But the intervening generations since James Cook had shown no inclination for adventure. Somehow that particular gene for excitement had resurfaced in him, Commander John Cook, and he was always the happiest when traveling, intercontinental or especially interplanetary.

The headset came to life. "John, did you get a glimpse of that?"

Jokingly John responded, "A glimpse of what?"

After a momentary pause, for the joke to develop in their minds thousands of kilometers away, Mission Control responded, "We saw it on our monitors and it was fantastic. I am sure some of us shed a tear or two marveling at that natural phenomenon." A second later they continued, "Or was it because of staring directly at the sun?"

That lightened the intensity of the beautiful event a little. "Anyways, time to move before the Martians come calling. You know what to do, you have the replacement parts in your bag of goodies. Better get going before a dust storm kicks up."

Without further banter John stepped out and started down the extended ladder, the other end of which was on the Martian surface. He noticed that the broad pad at the base of the ladder was not visible—already covered in dust. As John stepped off the last rung of the ladder he spoke, "This journey, the first of many, will further the understanding of the purpose of life," a veiled reference to the next mission—the "big one." As he started walking toward the generators an ephemeral thought went through his mind, was this entire planet now part of United States? If the United States manages to make this planet habitable, who owns the rights to this alien world? How would the territories on Earth be able to carve up the virgin territory on Mars? It was a fleeting thought. He had work to do, and he needed to focus.

The walk was easy in gravity about a third of that on Earth. The heavy replacement parts he was holding was a fraction of the weight here. He covered the distance from the lander to the generator in quicker time than he had anticipated. His progress was being monitored on Earth by Mission Control. As he approached the first O_2 generator he noticed that it was larger than he had estimated. He looked back and noticed that the lander was smaller from this distance. Suddenly he felt a chill. He was alone on this lifeless planet. If any of his life-support systems failed he would not be able to make it back. Then he realized that there were redundant systems in his life-support equipment. He had trained on Earth with one or more systems purposely programmed to fail. The chances of failure were very remote. Then there was Kristen, a very capable biologist, who was on the lander and would not hesitate for a moment to run out and rescue him. Being on the lander, she was already suited up. That momentary chill must have triggered some chemicals in his body which was picked up by the monitoring systems.

The headphone came on, "John, are you okay, we see an abnormal elevation of adrenaline."

Calmly he responded, "I am fine, getting ready to replace the filter."

The response was "Roger that, proceed with caution. Take your time and be careful." That last part was redundant. This was a simple task, there was nothing dangerous he was doing, so there was no need to be overly cautious.

Seconds later he reported, "First one completed, moving to the second one."

As he was leaving, he noticed a slight discoloration on the exhaust vent of the O_2 generator. He went closer and turned on the flashlight to illuminate the shadows. If he had not turned on the light he would have missed the fact that the discoloration was almost imperceptibly a different color to the red Martian dust.

The headset came on again. "Cap'n, you have not moved for about thirty seconds, what are you examining?"

There were cameras on the O_2 generators as well as on the lander. The latter one was trained on him. Mission Control was monitoring his progress audibly as well as visually. However, where John was looking was not in the range of any camera.

His concentration broken, he responded, "I noticed some dust at the exhaust vent, moving on to the next one now."

He serviced the second, third, and fourth ones, noticing the same discolored dust on each exhaust vent.

"On to the last one," he announced. The final one was a little more in the shadow of the mountain. The sun did not catch it as much as the other three. He continued, "On the exhaust vent on the previous four I saw identical discoloration. Confirm that there is not supposed to be any dust in the exhaust vent." It made perfect sense as dust could cover any part of the generator but not in the exhaust vent. The O_2 being pushed out would also blow the dust away.

Mission Control realized what he was saying, and as he reached the final generator, they instructed, "Commander, after you complete the maintenance work, take a swab of the exhaust vent and put it in your bag that you used to carry the parts. Don't touch it."

The part replaced, John turned on the flashlight. The surprise almost made him drop everything he was holding, including the flashlight. Almost immediately his headset came on. "Cap'n, we noticed a dramatic elevation in your adrenaline levels."

Even before they could formulate a question, John spoke, "The discoloration is a deeper color tone than the red dust." He ventured even closer and noticed that there was a slight variation, even in the small area that he was viewing—a sure sign of variations in the life that took hold in this small unfriendly oasis. Immediately he continued, "This is not dust! Bringing home a sample." Carefully not touching the sides of the vent even with his heavily gloved hand, John took several swabs and placed it in his bag.

More Missions

Chand received a report that Deep was stabilized and everything else was normal. The work on Mars was not important. What was more important was to test the new systems in the spacecraft. Her thought shifted to the next mission—a mission that would take the crew much further and therefore would be much longer in duration. It would also be much more demanding for the human crew and therefore more dangerous—much more dangerous. Although, if the Sentinel mission was successful, the danger would be drastically reduced. Therefore, all the missions currently in progress and in planning were intimately linked.

VIGILANCE

The cybernetic organisms in the craft were mostly machines. Only the most important aspect of them, their brain, was organic matter. This way their creators eliminated the need for complex circuitry and programming. They had found that the neural networks of organic matter simply could not be artificially replicated no matter how hard they tried.

The cyborgs in the spacecraft were monitoring the space all around them for signs of any kind of activity; they were concerned that their enemy would show up unexpectedly—not from Earth but from the same direction and time from which they had come. They were being chased. The lead cyborg in the crafts approaching Earth had detected objects leaving Earth's gravity. At first, she was surprised. No one on her craft had predicted this. However, she decided not to wake the hibernating superior officers to communicate this fact. Due to the energy needed for the round trip she decided not to communicate this with Mission Control back on the home planet. Each communication of that intensity exposed them to their pursuers by signaling their whereabouts as well as depleting the craft of energy, which may be needed later for escape. Besides, this was not a catastrophic event, so, in her judgment, it did not warrant this commitment. It also took a while to recover from the outpouring of the resources to send and receive signals in time and space.

The cause for her concern, the satellites in Earth orbit, could be the result of some eruption or natural explosion or even a meteorite impact—although that possibility appeared unlikely as the orbital patterns of the satellites appeared regular and equidistant from the surface. An explosion would not scatter debris into orbit, much less in orbits of approximately equal time period. If by a remote chance

32

there was a meteorite impact, their journey would be a futile effort. They did not embark on this arduous voyage to visit a wasteland. All their past work would be futile and a colossal waste of resources and effort.

Coming back to reality, this was exciting for her. Lela was coming home. She took a step back to turn around, and the wheels on one side locked. She almost fell, but the artificial gyroscopic mechanism enabled her to extend her arm and balance before hitting the floor. She will need to have one of the menials carry out maintenance on her left-side ambulatory mechanism. Then she realized that she was an organic brain encased in a metal body—the people she was hoping to meet on the target planet would not recognize her. One problem at a time, she thought to herself. There was no one to listen even if she voiced her thoughts, not that she could. She would first go and get some rest. After all, she still had a brain which needed periodic breaks.

Journey Back

Due to his excitement, before he knew it he was inside the lander—the natural chemicals in his body altering his perception of time or perhaps just making him ambulate quicker than he would normally. A quick check at his lower extremities as he ascended the ladder revealed that everything below his waist was covered in red dust. He hoped that this was just dust and not any foreign pathogen. Once safely ensconced inside he was subconsciously going through disrobing his newly designed nanotechnology-based lightweight space suit, which was also being tested for the first time, while his mind was processing the possibility of having found alien life. If he had found new life, it would be ironic as the next mission, the "big one," was pretty much guaranteed of discovering new intelligent life. He was not allowed to speak of the "big one," and, he assumed, until the test results were conclusively proved or disproved he would be asked not to speak of the "dust" he had just picked up from the vents.

The voice of Kristen in the lander sounded in his headset, "John, fifteen minutes to power up the thrusters—re-orbital maneuver in twenty. Start your pre-sequence checks." Kristen, a marine biologist, was a candidate for the "big one," although she did not know it yet. Like the other crew members on this mission, she had heard the communication between John and Mission Control. Being in the profession that she was, the possibility of finding new life-forms in the depths of the ocean was her expertise and passion. Now, with the possibility of discovering new extraterrestrial life-forms, she had to exert her utmost willpower to focus on her tasks to re-dock with the orbiter. She was looking forward to some lab time with the Martian dust. Sure, there would be other scientists clamoring to get a piece of this excitement. Hopefully she would be one of them. Having care-fully and properly secured the dust in a biohazard container, she con-tinued with the task of lifting off and returning to the mother ship.

Twenty minutes later a whooshing sound, gradually increasing in amplitude, was audible to the two occupants of the lander. This was accompanied by gentle, but increasing in frequency, vibration of the craft. A quick peek out of the window showed the craft enveloped in a cloud of red dust. A few seconds later, a better bird's-eye view showed a slowly receding planetary surface, but the red cloud still suspended in the low gravity like an apparition. About an hour later, John and Kristen were reunited with the crew of the mother ship—the Deep Space Explorer (dSE).

Aboard the dSE, Nicole inquired, "So what do you think? Did you see it? Do you think we found something that could alter our way of thinking about ourselves?" Of the six crew members who were selected for this mission, only Nicole was a physician. Like the rest and unbeknownst to her she, too, was targeted for the next mission.

Nicole was looking directly at Kristen when she asked the question. She knew exactly what Nicole was implying. If indeed the dust that John collected showed some primitive life, it would be a monumental discovery. The very thought process of humans would inexorably be altered. To date humans had assumed that all life existed only on Earth, although most scientists knew that this was not entirely true. Now, if there was a positive indication of life on another planet, humans may not be that unique after all. Kristen responded, "No, John had already enclosed the dust in his bag. I did not want to take any chances by opening it and potentially inhaling it. Who knows what pathogen it may contain? I took the sample from John and immediately hermitically sealed it. I don't know if the sample has survived, but I hope I get a chance to work on it."

Nicole, being the resident physician, had tasks to do to pre-pare for HySleep. Especially with a gravely unwell astronaut, she had to decide what to do with Deep. Dispensing with formalities was encouraged as long as the hierarchy was respected, Nicole had to inform John of her plans for Deep. "John, we will put Deep back into hibernation for our trip back. This is the safest course of action, and the lower metabolic rate will reduce the stresses he would experience otherwise."

Astonished, John did not allow her to complete her thought. "But wait. I am not a doctor—Would that not cause a problem for him?"

Nicole continued, "I am suggesting that we put him into hibernation with the rest of us. But the rest of us will be woken up when we reach Earth orbit. I spoke this over with Mission Control while you were down on the surface. They are okay with the plan to transport him under hibernation to the ground. There, we take him to the hospital, and with the best resources present, we can wake him up. They will have all the equipment and personnel needed at the hospital and would be able to deal with whatever comes up. This is the best course of action. We will wake up as planned—in Earth orbit. He will wake up once we reach the ground—in a hospital."

Chand, at Mission Control, was monitoring this conversation. She was the ground crew team leader and a "special" friend of John. Although they had tried to keep things discreet, there were rumors of their special friendship. Right on time Chand cut in, "John, we [she said 'we' with emphasis clearly implying that they had discussed it at Mission Control] are okay with this arrangement. In hibernation, it is highly unlikely he will suffer any further events. We are making arrangements to transport his hyperbaric chamber, in its entirety, to the lander which will bring you all back on land. Once in hospital he will have the best care." She was known for her precise brevity.

John looked at Deep who nodded approvingly. There was no hint of worry on his face. In fact, he was very composed. A quick glance around and John saw that everyone except Nicole looked at ease with the plan. With the patient appearing unconcerned, John was okay with the course of action. That is the best they could do under the circumstances.

John beckoned Nicole over to the side, out of earshot of Deep. "You seemed concerned?"

Still deep in thought, Nicole responded, "No, not concerned. This is the best course of action for him. I was going over the steps in my mind to reprogram his hibernation module so he is not woken with the rest of us—I don't want to get this wrong. If I do not do this right he may not wake up. That is what is worrying me. I will need to refer to the manual stored on the onboard computer."

John encouraged, "That is a good idea. Besides you are here for your abilities, I am sure you will do it right." Then as if to pre-emptively prepare for Deep getting worse, John continued, "Know this—no one could have done this any better than you. Your best effort is as good as it gets."

With those words of encouragement John commenced attending to his duties to exit the Martian orbit and Nicole set about her task of reprogramming Deep's hibernation module, with her fingers crossed and hoping for the best—this was not a trivial task.

The "big one" would start soon. Secret preparations for it were in an advanced stage of completion. The last thing remaining was to put a check mark against some of the newly developed technologies. In fact, it would be very reasonable to state that the entire Martian mission could be attributed solely as a dry run for the "big one." Indeed, it would not be beyond the realms of possibility that the entire space program was privatized in order to develop these technologies that would enable the "big one" to materialize. It was crucial that the next big mission take place—essential for the survival of mankind.

"Five…four…three…two…one—we have ignition…," was the next thing that the crew heard over the speaker system in the dSE. Mission Control was controlling the initiation of the return by firing the chemical rockets. The hibernation was approximately timed to coincide with the firing of the motors. The chemical rocket motors would come on for about twenty-five seconds. After providing the initial thrust the journey would be completed with the aid of the new fusion-powered drive. After the initial thrust was over, silently each crew member took turns to get off their seats to change into the specially designed hibernation suit. The suits were comical to look at and even funnier when worn, with wires and hoses coming out of various areas. However, it served a serious purpose, which was to facilitate the survival of the wearer. The jokes already dispensed with during the journey to Mars, no astronaut made any comment on what appeared like a Halloween suit. Also, Deep's condition made the atmosphere somewhat somber. Instead, they silently got into position and waited for Nicole. As each crew got into position for hibernation, they wished Deep their best and promised to see him once back on Earth.

Once in position, each member could individually self-connect the wires and tubes. However, in this case, the presence of Nicole meant that she would check each connection. As the last action before hibernation, she would connect herself. She, being a trained doctor, was part of the team which developed this technology and was as knowledgeable as anyone about the hibernation physiology of humans.

The hibernation machine to which they were attached could be turned on or off from Mission Control. The last set of instructions heard over the speaker system was "Good night and see you in a few months!"

The journey back was uneventful and predictable—the best-case scenario. Several new systems and components were success-fully tested on this manned mission to Mars, not least of which was the new Quick Transition Suits (called by its acronym QTS). These lightweight climate-controlled suits replaced the bulky ones of the past. They could be worn or taken off without help, hence the name "quick transition." Getting into and out of hibernation twice, once on the way there and once on the way back, also proved highly success-ful. The health problem that Deep had suffered was unpredictable. It could happen to anyone and at any time. It was also a risk everyone was willing to take. The main purpose of testing HySleep was to see if the crew could independently function without any help from the Mission Control personnel. In this mission, the crew had to execute without a hitch getting in and out of hibernation, using only the onboard equipment and no external help from Mission Control. If the crew had trouble with the HySleep unit during the next mission it would be a very bad scenario. A rescue mission would be out of the question. In that aspect, the heart attack, unexpected as it was, served to confirm that the crew could function independently. Finally, the new engines were tested. The fusion-powered engine technology was the spectacular advancement of the last ten or so years. This was the one technology which made long journeys possible. The next mission where these technologies, and a host of others, would be exercised was much longer than this short trip to Mars.

APPROACH

Once the Sentinel mission reached its target, it would send pictures back to Mission Control. The next mission would send people to the same location and possibly make contact in space. The plan was to get as close to the approaching objects as possible, turn on the lights, and send the images back to Earth. Monitoring systems indicated that the Sentinel craft was approaching its target.

Chand was called to the Sentinel Mission Control. "How are we doing?"

"Ready for some illumination," the mission operator voiced with a smirk. He was referring to light as well as knowledge. He continued, "We had sent the code a while ago. If everything is normal we should be receiving the images shortly, I would say within seconds."

Chand and the others in the Sentinel Mission Control waited patiently as the seconds ticked by. Seconds became minutes, and when a few minutes passed, Chand spoke, "Is there a problem?"

The operator checked his instruments and responded, "This is unusual. We should have had images by now. I am checking our systems, and I will send a diagnostic code to the Sentinel. But it will be a while before we know for sure."

Chand, assuming it was a minor glitch, responded, "All right, I have a meeting in a few minutes. Keep me apprised of the progress." She was already leaving the room as she finished her sentence. Clearly, she had a lot on her mind and on her plate.

RESEARCH EARTH

Just as the Sentinel mission was meant to research the approaching objects, Earth was being researched by the occupant of the approaching craft. Continual monitoring of space for potential activity in all directions revealed no unusual movements. There was nothing coming toward the veiled juggernauts which were headed for Earth. What was at first unusual were the tiny objects leaving Earth but mostly staying in close orbit around Earth. A few had traveled farther, but none of them coming in the direction of the approaching crafts. That changed recently when one tiny speck was heading straight toward her crafts, but she was certain this miniscule object posed no harm. The sentry cyborg decided to continue monitoring but not to alert anyone else. There appeared to be no danger from these objects. They were so tiny that the highest resolution imaging was needed with considerable processing on the computer to detect tiny gravitational and light perturbations to even notice their existence. Even if one of these objects from Earth started heading toward the crafts, she decided that she would not alert anyone—unless absolutely necessary. After all, she was heading home, a home she had never seen. If any of these tiny specks approached her she could take care of it herself.

Where she and other captive humans were born there were rumors about Earth, mostly rumors of freedom—freedom which Lela and her kind did not have. She had wanted to experience Earth at least once in her lifetime. Maybe she could help the rest of her people who were in the same predicament and possibly future generations of captives. What was confusing her was why her superiors had decided to go to Earth this far out into the future. As a cyborg, she was not privy to all the information. But in the time available before her masters awoke from hibernation, she was determined to find out by scouring the vast internal archives. She had ample time. She sent out for more memory containing details about the target planet recorded in previous missions. Lela was specifically looking for the ones that contained the relevant data about the people on the planet where her ancestors were captured. The menial cyborgs were dumb. They just took orders. They would not remember the repeated trips to fetch memory from the archives. If they were to be questioned it would be a one-way conversation as they had no memory to remember even the basic tasks which they had executed in the past. Lela allowed herself a chuckle at the mental image of this comical scene of interrogation.

THE "BIG ONE"

The space shuttle program was superseded by a new program—officially called Exploration of Space for Peace and Knowledge (abbreviated to ESP). ESP was responsible for the development of a new vehicle—what was remarkable about it was that it was a reusable vehicle. It was smaller than the shuttle but had more room inside the cabin to move around comfortably—due to the absence of supporting structure to harness scientific equipment or other items to carry into space. This new vehicle, although multipurpose, was mainly built as a human transporter. The room available was equivalent to a medium-sized commercial jetliner. Launched from a specially built airplane, it was launched at high altitude. The rocket booster would be fired soon after separation and would easily reach orbit. The new vehicle was used in the first Mars landing by a human. Commander John Cook landed and took the first steps on Mars. There was capability for two or more of these Deep Space Explorers (dSE), as they came to be known, to be linked together in space to double or triple or even quadruple the available space. More importantly, with multiples of these dSEs linked together, there could be four times the engine power and fuel to traverse vast distances. They could also be unlinked in space to be used as individual reentry vehicles or left in orbit for use in future missions. A total of seven dSEs had been ordered, built jointly by two major American corporations.

The first such mission was a trip to Mars, a single vehicle configured to carry a crew of six. It also carried inside the cargo bay (set up specifically for the mission to Mars) a landing module for the trip to the surface of the planet and back. The return was uneventful. The journey back down to the surface was flawless. All the astronauts took the hibernation process well with no ill effects, except for Deep.

43

Other than the heart attack he had coped with the rest of the journey well enough and been taken to hospital. Under constant care he was recuperating well.

As soon as the quarantine period and the debriefing sessions were over, Kristen tracked down Chand. Chand was the mission manager, responsible for everyone involved in this project—including the astronauts. Chand was known for her speed—speed of thought, speed of talk, speed of decision-making and not least speed of ambulation. She normally walked at such a pace that people joked that no one would be able to keep up with her and speak at the same time as they would soon get out of breath. Kristen had to literally sprint when she spotted her walking toward her office at the far end of the massive Mission Control center. Kristen reached her just as she turned into her office. "Chand, I need to ask you something." Although no slouch Kristen was out of breath, Chand's reputation was real.

Chand almost knew what was about to come. "Hi, Kris." Chand had a nickname for Kristen. Chand economized even in her usage of words or syllables. If she could walk faster or communicate quicker she would gladly do so. As Kristen finally took the final steps to reach her, Chand continued with, "What's up?" softening her demeanor with a broad smile.

Between deep breaths Kristen managed to get out the words, "I was wondering about the sample we collected. I would like to be part of the team looking into that." Kristen was very well-conditioned—a prerequisite for any astronaut. Besides, Kristen's background as an expert swimmer, scuba diver, and someone capable of deep-sea diving in submersibles meant that she had to maintain a high degree of fitness throughout the year. She must have sprinted down the long hallway in order to catch up with Chand. The offices where space program is managed can be gigantic. Due to the expert-level fitness Kristen's pulse and breath were normalizing quickly.

Chand was a supremely capable woman—hence, she had risen through the ranks of NASA. Now focused on the potential aliens arriving, Chand had been given the task of setting up the entire personnel program to enable this final push to meet them. She had to set up the Martian mission without revealing its true purpose—that to dry run the next mission. She had succeeded thus far. Her scope included everything but the hardware. Any and all technologies were at her disposal. While setting up this mission she had gotten close to one particular astronaut. Some of her closest friends at work had suspected this, but no one could confirm it. Generally, the joke among colleagues was that no one was fast enough to catch up to her, let alone have a relationship with her. So when the innocuous gossip started everyone agreed that it stood to reason that the relationship would be at work. All were happy for her since more than a few times her superiors had quietly expressed concern that there was no one else in her life. Although there were no specific rules, office romance was not encouraged, due to obvious emotional entanglements in an inherently dangerous occupation. In this case on one was going to raise hue and cry about this. Her response to Kristen was "Yes, about that. We have an exciting new mission coming up. You know about the mandatory meeting today. After you attend the meeting you can decide. Until then hold off on getting too excited about the samples."

Generally, such comments are precursors to a "no" answer. Somewhat disappointed but maintaining her composure, Kristen responded, "I was really looking forward to working on those samples. You know I have the background and I am qualified to be there with those scientists." Kristen was referring to her doctorate in marine biology and ecology and her vast experience in working and classifying extremophiles—the creatures found in extremely hostile (to humans) conditions.

Chand could not say much at this point. She did not want to spill the beans to anyone before the meeting. She was one of four individuals on the base who knew about the next mission—all of whom had taken the oath of secrecy. But that secret would be a little less of a secret after the meeting—the crew would know, but they would also be prohibited from revealing anything outside the base. In the most persuasive tone she could muster, she responded, "Believe me. Just hold off till the meeting. I can guarantee that you will not even remember the samples by the time the meeting ends."

What could be more important than the potential discovery of an alien species? Before Kristen could recover from that thought, Chand turned around and walked away.

The ground support staff was also invited to the mandatory meeting. This was the occasion were everything would be revealed and at the same time all would be sworn to secrecy. Indeed, as the final preparations began, most if not all the team would be sequestered to the base. At this meeting, it would become clear why some of the ground-based Mission Control staff had been practicing communicating with artificially induced audio lag, mimicking communicating over distances greater than any human had traveled. To the bewilderment of the ground crew there were many such exercises that they were carrying out. That would become clear by the end of the meeting. At this gathering labeled as "all hands on deck," the plan was to announce the next mission, the one John had labeled as the "big one." There was work to be done, and time was short.

The astronauts who had made the trip to Mars would be invited to make this journey. In addition, a new astronaut would be announced. Ken would replace Deep who clearly could not take any further part in any space or physically intensive activities. The advanced welcoming crew, as they were called, would journey to the edge of the solar system to rendezvous with the approaching objects. As yet no one was certain what these were, just that they were not natural. The replacement for Deep was an equally literate professor with similar educational background—except for the fact that he was in peak physical shape. However, the one major problem was that Ken had never been to space. Not an adrenaline junkie, he was even uneasy of flying a commercial plane. New to the team, he would have to undergo an accelerated training program to prepare himself as best as he could prior to the launch date. The others had trained together for years and would help him prepare. This was an obvious weak link, but the calculated risk was that the others could compensate for him. His credentials were excellent, and for reasons only known to him, he had accepted the offer to join the spaceflight program when the officials had approached him at his university.

The meeting commenced and ended soon—Chand was speaking at a pace normal to her but fast to everyone else. Chand was right. By the time the meeting was over, not a single person could talk about anything other than the imminent threat and the next mission. Not that there was any lack of enthusiasm, Kristen was the first to accept the invitation. Although it was made abundantly clear that this could be a one-way trip, depending on what they found and how friendly they were, there was no hesitation from anyone. Surprisingly, Ken had raised his hand to accept the mission almost as swiftly as Kristen.

MISSING SENTINEL

The small Sentinel mission team was gathered in a meeting room when Chand walked in at her usual brisk pace. At most times, she had a number of things on her to-do list, but her walking demeanor only heightened the air of a person with too many things to juggle at the same time. Without wasting time and even before taking her seat she inquired, "Good afternoon, all. So what is the status of the Sentinel?" She was not expecting good news, having heard before that there was no response from the satellite sent to take pictures of the objects.

The mission operator spoke up, "Unfortunately we have no contact with Sentinel. We have tried everything, but it is just not responding. This is very unusual as we have so many redundant systems built in. But none of the systems is responding. It is as if it had encountered some space debris and disintegrated."

This meeting was more to officially communicate the next steps as opposed to discussing the problem at hand. In that regard, there was nothing Chand could say except, "We were relying on these images so we could make plans when the manned mission reached those objects. Without those images, we are literally going into the unknown. We are basically blind."

That was a rhetorical remark. Everyone present knew it. She continued, "The higher-ups have told me that the manned mission will go ahead as planned. They and I want you all to do whatever you can to get it back online. Use any tricks you have up your sleeves to get something. Otherwise, we are going in blind, and that could be dangerous for the team going up there." She ended with, "Good luck!" and departed.

IDEA FOR A PLAN

Her research concluded that extrapolations based on automated heuristic algorithms designed for predictive analysis revealed rapid human evolution of the DNA during a certain critical period of time. Then relatively little change thereafter. The small craft that had left Earth and traveled to the nearby planet had not gone unnoticed by the cyborg. When she looked this up in the material she was researching, she found that this level of technology was within the threshold of the predictive algorithm—although on the very high end of the scale. At the low end, the inhabitants would only be able to move around on the surface of the planet using automated means. So this gave her some idea that there was some amount of sophistication. Her form, the artificial body that encased her organic brain, would not be alarming to the humans whom she was desperate to meet. That fact alone gave her some level of solace.

Based on her assessment, the craft that had left Earth was tiny and the technology it contained was primitive compared to her craft. Judging from the size of the craft that had left Earth, the humans were no match to the capability of her captors. The population of Earth had progressed as predicted by the algorithm. The creators would be pleasantly surprised because that meant there was an increased opportunity to quickly find the right candidates and depart quickly. That meant that there was little chance they would become easy targets to their main adversaries on foreign soil. The second reason, she found in the material she was reviewing, was key to her masters who designed the ecosystem. The inhabitants of the ecosystem had to be completely unaware of their creation or the reason for it. They had to be unaware to prevent contamination in the inhabitants' thoughts. The last batch, it was assumed although not verified, was contaminated due to some unknown reason. The speculation for the contamination was that somehow the inhabitants started believing in superior beings.

The last stock was not completely malleable, and considerable effort had gone in to train them. This was not acceptable, and the thought was that the brains had not evolved enough. Some, like her, were clever enough, but that was not the case in most specimens. This is why, she guessed, they were asked to go to a time further along into the future than the last trip. The hope was the natives' brain had more time to evolve. This was the population from which her masters wanted to harvest.

She was upset at all this. Although her superiors had created this race, this was no way to treat them. She had to put a stop to this barbaric behavior; she had to come up with a clever plan, a plan that would not raise suspicion with her masters or the humans whom she would encounter. If either knew that she was planning something, her plans would be jeopardized. Due to the way they communicated, she could not even think about the plans in the presence of her masters.

Another key item she had uncovered from the archives—once the craft landed, they could use the electromagnetic forces of the planet to effect communication not only from within the craft but also from several ancient structures scattered about the planet meant for the purpose. Communication with the home planet was very energy intensive. In space, the only source of energy was what was available within the crafts. However, once landed, the electromagnetic forces of the planet provided unlimited and undiminishing supply of energy to send and receive communications. She read in the archives that this is what was used in the past. So for her plan to be successful she should prevent any communication with her masters' home planet for as long as possible. The indecisiveness of her master, whom she had carefully evaluated, would help her in her cause.

LAUNCH

In the meeting when the "big one" was revealed, every one of the crew had volunteered without hesitation. The objective was exciting as well as dangerous. But more to the point, humanity depended on the success of this mission—although the definition of success as it related to this one was ambiguous.

In order to conceal the true purpose of the mission from the general public, it was labeled Titan Explorer (TE). Due to the potential ramifications, they had to maintain the secrecy for as long as possible. They could not reveal the fact that aliens were approaching Earth till it was absolutely certain. Otherwise, there could be pandemonium. Titan is the largest moon of Saturn and also the second largest moon in the solar system. Ostensibly this was going to be a mission to explore Titan. Preparations had begun; six of the seven dSEs were in position for the long journey. At the appropriate time the last dSE would transport the TE crew of astronauts to the cluster of dSEs that had been built up over several months. After transporting the astronauts, the last dSE would return to Earth and could be used as an emergency rescue vehicle. The six dSEs were arranged in a grid pattern, three on top and three below. The bottom row was positioned so that the underside was facing the underside of the top row. In effect the bottom row was upside down. However, there is no upside down or right way up in space. In this two-by-three grid pattern, the dSEs at the ends of the top row were connected to the corresponding ones in the bottom row with hollow metal cylinders. In addition, the outer ships in each row were attached to the middle ship at the side using similar metal cylinders. This way, the astronauts could walk from one dSE to the other without the need for special EVA clothing. The middle two ships were not connected to each other; those two were connected to a cylindrical module. This module was brought to the International Space Station earlier and was separated and moved to the TE cluster and attached in between the two middle dSEs. The purpose of this module was to house the bridge and serve as the main housing for the astronauts. The seventh dSE was left on Earth, in readiness to bring the astronauts back—if they were lucky enough to come back.

The veil of secrecy that the agency had maintained had worked. Seemingly this journey was to Saturn to further explore its rings and its moons. Hence, even the name, Titan Explorer, was meant as a misdirection for the general public and foreign governments. The true purpose of the mission would be revealed well after the launch. The need for this surreptitious behavior was not shared by all at the space agency. However, all objections were mollified when the potential consequence of announcing the possible existence of aliens to the public was considered. The cargo in the hold of the dSEs was disclosed as the usual scientific equipment, probes to send down to Saturn, life-support systems, etc. However, some important items were not mentioned at all. These happened to be weapons systems, both laser and nuclear, and lots of fist-size balls filled with electronics. The idea being, at those distances, they would need some kind of a booster for the signals from Earth to traverse space all the way to the dSEs and back. These electronics-packed small round objects were intended to boost the signal strength of the radio communications. The so-called probes packed into the hold were nuclear devices, bombs measured in megatons. There was nothing better available. If the nuclear bomb did not work, the last and ultimate possibility was to crash the dSE into the alien craft in a kamikaze-like mission. The mission crew was aware that this could potentially be their last mission, although the kamikaze option was the last option. Some questions had come up regarding the cost of the project, the benefits to mankind, the safety of the crew, etc. These questions were successfully deflected with the usual rhetoric. If only they knew the real reason.

All the media scrutiny and the intense questioning were parried by citing the useful ramifications of investing in space. In reality, there had been useful spin-offs from all the investment made over almost eighty years. Other than our understanding of the universe which was immeasurable and on which no one could put a monetary value, there were also many direct benefits. The controlling of the fusion reaction process ensured that there would be no need to burn fossil-based fuels or even fission-based fuels. This resulted in a cleaner atmosphere and no problems of disposal of highly radioactive spent fuel. But all the accrued benefits may be moot depending on what the crew would find with the Meteorite Group or MG as the approaching alien crafts became euphemistically known. They acquired this label more for secrecy than anything else. The government authorities did not want the news about the alien spacecraft to become public, so calling them Meteorite Group would not raise any suspicion of alien activity, even if the information became inadvertently disseminated. The ground staff was strictly asked to refer to the aliens with this moniker.

To the media they also cited other benefits such as new medication which was developed for the long journey. Until now, hibernation was not a possibility. However, the new medication kept the astronauts in semi suspended animation till it was time to wake up. This drug was called HySleep for hibernation/sleep. The drug put astronauts to sleep, and more importantly reduced the metabolism so that minimal energy was expended during the slumber. This was as close to hibernation as technology would allow. The effects on being awakened were nothing more than feeling disoriented and groggy for a few hours, feeling ravenous, and not being able to sleep for about forty-eight hours after being woken up, till the circadian rhythm was reestablished. The inability to sleep for forty-eight hours was only if the astronaut was asleep for more than a few days. Feeling hungry was natural. The crew had to adopt a similar practice as is done before surgery, no food for twenty-four hours prior and to empty the bowels. Of course, the crew was provided liquid nutrition through tubes inserted into the stomach in order to stay alive while hibernating. A specially designed computer carefully controlled the amount depending on blood pressure, pulse, breathing, brain wave patterns, etc. If any individual's reading crossed a predetermined threshold the computer woke them so that corrective action could be taken manually. In addition, the hibernation chamber was equipped with mechanisms to eliminate pressure sores. The computer even monitored the brain wave patterns partly to measure the accurate dose of the HySleep medication and partly to determine if there was any danger to the individual. Of course, there were backup systems, in case the primary systems failed. All this data was monitored via telemetry by an Earth-based team at the control center, which, as usual, was done around the clock. The team on Earth could, if required, override anything programmed into the computer.

This technology had been used for the ride to Mars and back with no ill effects, except the unfortunate and unforeseen heart attack that Deep suffered. It was eventually diagnosed as a congenital issue which was impossible to detect or foretell. The computer did all the work to keep the astronauts alive and comfortable till they were woken up from their enforced slumber. The only reported effect was that the semi-sleep/semi-wakefulness state created an environment for lots of dreams, some pleasant and some not so pleasant, depending on individual disposition. With all the nutrition coming through liquids, albeit slowly, there was an occasional need to empty the bladder. This, too, was monitored by the computer and, via a small dose of a specific medication, relaxed the bladder muscles. Each astronaut was attached to a gender-specific tube which kept them comfortable and dry during the sleep. No one on board was allowed to have long hair. It would be a mess coming out of HySleep, and also there was potential for it to get caught in the space suit and cause a slow air leak.

Inexplicably it was proving extraordinarily difficult to accurately estimate the distance of the alien crafts. The primary reason for this difficulty that everyone had concluded was that there was some kind of cloaking technology being deployed. The other reason was that this was being purposely being done to confuse the humans. In reality neither synopsis was accurate. The time before the aliens reached the outer planets of the solar system was calculated at two years and eight months. At approximately two years and six months after launch from Earth the plan for the dSE cluster was to slowly start turning through 180 degrees so that when the crew woke up, they would be heading back to Earth. When the turn was complete and the crew awakened from HySleep-induced hibernation, they would be able to look out of the side window and see the MG. This rendezvous point would be somewhere in the vicinity of the orbit of Pluto, although the dwarf planet would only be visible in the distance. Then the plan was to manually navigate, using hand controls on board, as close to the MG as possible and observe them. Boarding the MG was a possibility, if they could visually find a way to board. Technology used in the Mars lander was used to build these small EVA vehicles. Some of the weapons included in the cargo were handguns, rifles, and other small explosive devices such as shoulder-launched grenades. They could be fired from a mount placed in the air lock chamber, and the person firing had to be suited up in an EVA suit to avoid asphyxiation.

Through one of the panoramic windows in the approaching spacecraft the mission crew noticed that the six dSEs were already attached to one another, in configuration for the TE mission. For the sake of convenience, the letters TE evolved to mean both the mission as well as the cluster of six dSEs, depending on the context of usage. The maintenance crew had one task to perform before the astronauts could go into HySleep—to start the fusion engines. When the TE mission crew began their final approach to the TE cluster, they saw the maintenance crew was busy at work. Jets and thrusters were used to slow down and move the dSE close to the TE cluster so the astronauts could jump ship. As they got closer the pilot of the dSE transporting the TE crew announced, "We are in place. You can commence the EVA." He added jokingly, "Please check your overhead bins and under the seat and take items you brought along. Otherwise, they will be returned to Earth and can be found in the lost and found at the control center, if you are lucky." It seemed that the dSE pilot, too, was unaware of the true nature of this mission.

The TE mission had a crew of eight astronauts, one commander of the mission, one doctor, one biologist, one linguist, and four euphemistically labeled engineers who were also weapons experts. All had undergone extensive training, in total secrecy for the last four years with no one, except Commander John Cook, being aware of the true purpose of this mission. The other seven only found out about the true nature of the mission soon after they landed from the Martian mission, about six months ago. When they found out about the rendezvous, no one backed down—the mission from the very start was a *go*!

PLANS

The lead cyborg, Lela, had come up with a plan that was foolproof—maybe. She would not do anything for now, so that her superiors would not be able to sense her intentions to compromise the mission. If she did not have that thought running through her mind the superiors would not be able to read her mind. All she had to do was to communicate it to the other two cyborgs on board with organic brains. Although she was the highest-ranking cyborg on this mission, the other two would not need any convincing. Everyone like her, including the ones who did not make this journey, were vehemently against this kind of fate for her race of beings.

She looked at the monitor and, almost subconsciously, used her haptic hand to approve another minor adjustment. Adjustments, based on calculations by the onboard computer, were continually approved by the cyborg not only to arrive at the correct millennium but also to throw off their pursuers. One of these minor corrections was to make a slight leap toward the tiny speck that she had noticed earlier. This speck was still some distance away, but it was heading directly toward her crafts. The purpose of this tiny craft was unknown to her, but she had to take care of it. So, although it was hardly visible, a quick correction in time enabled her to jump to a location close to the craft. A quick remote check revealed that it was devoid of any organic matter—it was so small, it could not contain any life. After that, it was the simplest of tasks to capture it and store it in one of the storerooms in her craft.

THE JOURNEY

Having completed the short space walk from the transport ship to the TE, one of the astronauts for the long journey, Bharat Solanki (Baz), read the instrument panel and indicated, "John, we are all on board. The fusion start-up can begin."

Baz was one of the engineers who had a master's degree in astrophysics and space science, was a trained weapons systems expert, and was very adept at hand-to-hand combat. He had expertise in anything that fired projectiles at high speed such as guns, rifles, propelled grenades, etc. Indeed, he had tried out for a covert operations program which included rigorous physical and mental challenges in a team-based environment. He had been selected and had accepted the offer to serve his country. When his commanding officer had told him of this opportunity to travel into space, he did not have to think twice. The astrophysics background and military training were significant reasons to offer him a chance to try out for the mission. Other very capable soldiers were also given the chance, but Baz always had an advantage, provided his attitude was right, to get the nod due to his education. Never in his wildest dreams did he imagine that his combat training could potentially be used in deep space.

John checked the main panel and responded, "I see that, but just give it a second till everyone settles down. No need to hurry. We have a long period of sleep ahead of us."

Baz, having worked in a similar role for the Martian mission, quickly realized that there was no point creating unnecessary stress for the crew this early in the mission. He succinctly stated, "Roger that."

All eight astronauts for this mission were gathered in the command module, the label they chose for the cylindrical module that was moved from the International Space Station. For Ken, a recent substitute for Deep, this was the first exposure to a weightless environment. With a panicked look in his eyes he was flailing his arms and kicking his legs in order to move closer to something solid to which he could anchor himself. With an amused look the others were observing his antics. Eventually he pleaded, "Can someone please help me get down?"

John, for whom gravity-free conditions were second nature, expertly moved over to where he was floating and helped him down, but not before he could hear Ken sardonically mutter something to the effect of, "I cannot wait till I get into hibernation!"

John then announced to the crew, who were now gathered around the control panel, "As you know we have controls in all the individual dSEs. However, this module is the master, and while this is active, controls in all other dSEs are inactive. The advantage this module provides is that a carefully controlled spin will be induced to mimic gravity. This being the center of rotation, in this module gravity will be almost normal. However, if you go to the extremities of the dSE, gravity will be slightly different. You will need to compensate for that." Then smiling ear to ear he recalled the hapless Ken floating just moments earlier. "But, as Ken demonstrated, we do not have gravity yet, so please refrain from any sudden movements lest you upset Ken."

Ken rolled his eyes as everyone burst out laughing. He was seen mouthing something that appeared to be "Very funny," but it could have been some other two-word sentence.

Greg floated over and reassured Ken, "Don't worry about it. We were all like that the first time around. You will get used to it."

Reassured, Ken started to relax a little. His facial muscles relaxed, and there was even a hint of a smile. He responded, "Thanks."

Gregory Thomas was a British-born pilot in the Royal Air Force who became interested in space and wanted to become part of the space program as an astronaut. To accomplish this, he went back to school at the later age of twenty-five and subsequently graduated with a master's degree in space science in just one and a half years. He then worked in the European space program but was disappointed to see that there were no manned missions in the offing. So when the opportunity came up, through some contacts in the US space department with whom he had formerly exchanged ideas, he grabbed it. That was seven years ago. Hard work both on physical fitness as well as engineering got him selected to the Titan Explorer mission. His Air Force training and his interest in martial arts made him an ideal candidate for this mission. His fitness regimen included Tae Kwon Do, in which he had achieved third-degree black belt. He was an expert at close quarters combat.

Noticing that everyone was at ease now, John continued, "The way it works is this huge cylindrical module that has been 'liberated' from the space station has been placed in the middle and attached to the grid of dSEs. It was constructed and brought into space specifically for this purpose. When we blast off, we will induce gravity by turning the whole cluster in a circular motion so that the whole array will turn at a speed to generate approximately one g, same as on Earth. As you can see, the master controls are here and they are identical to what you would find in each dSE. In addition, if you look around, you will see that there are eating, exercising, and general lounging quarters." John was beginning to feel like a real estate agent—he thought that he best stop before making a fool of himself.

There was support staff still present on the TE—completing their final checklists. Space technology had come a long way in a short period of time. Launching for a major mission from space was a different prospect than launching from the surface of Earth. While the support crew assigned to work inside the TE cluster was finishing up loading the final essentials, the external crew was preparing for the start of the fusion reaction. The first step had been completed. That was to connect the ships to the solar array to get electricity to control the plasma. The ships were slowly maneuvered into place so that the dome could catch the sun's rays at the correct angle and start the heating process to initiate the fusion reaction.

Greg had moved Ken over to a window so he could see what was going on outside. But Ken had turned away. Instead he was looking at items inside the command module. The rest were observing with astonishment at what was unfolding outside.

"Use the sun and some lenses to start a mini sun—very neat," Baz proclaimed. He continued, "The ease with which they are maneuvering this craft is a testament to privatizing the space program in the early 2010s."

Near Earth space walks were done efficiently and quickly as compared to the cumbersome space walks of the past. The lightweight suits, now a standard issue for any space activity, helped by providing the wearer a wider range of motion. These suits were just one step removed from wearing work overalls on Earth. When the external support crew completed their tasks, they would retreat to the dSE that had brought them to the TE cluster and then return to Earth. The final preparations for the long journey would be done remotely.

The all clear was issued from Mission Control. Fusion was about to start. All the preflight checks were taking place. Each crew member of the TE mission had an assigned specific preflight task. The doctor, Nicole Goodman, had gone over to the HySleep module and was checking the systems. Although this was done remotely, she was doing a manual process check. Due to the extensive training, she was very familiar with the connections and tubes and was checking to see if anything had worked itself loose with the vibrations during blastoff from Earth.

Within a few minutes, the first of the reactors had started.

"Commander, the fusion has started on unit 1, proceeding to unit 2," echoed the intercom system in the command module from one of the support crew at the SCC who was assigned this task.

"Copy that and standing by for unit 2," came the reply from John.

"I don't hear anything. Shouldn't we at least feel something?" Ken, who was standing next to John, asked in a surprised tone, wondering if the first engine had actually started. He was expecting some sort of vibration or noise from the fearsome fusion reaction.

"Well, you won't," Baz chimed in, "there is enough isolation from the reactor units. The reactor domes are perched up on the end of a rod, and there is sufficient damping to prevent any vibration. Besides, sound does not carry through the vacuum of space." This being the first time Ken had been to space, everything was new to him. He did not know what to expect, and he was not taking the emptiness of space very well. That is why he was not gazing out of the windows. The weightless floating was something that was disconcerting him more than he had expected. Despite the Earth-based training, there was nothing to compare with the actual experience of being in space. Although he could still back out and return back to Earth with the support crew he was determined to carry on. It was too late for any replacements, and he did not want to negatively impact the mission. Perhaps after gravity was established he would feel better.

"Oh! And by the way," Baz continued looking at John, "Greg, Manny, Thor, and I will now go and check the special systems." John nodded in agreement.

Ken, Clare, and Kristen were with John at the command module. Although John was busy keeping an eye on the progress, the rest had no prelaunch assignments. They were watching the starting up of the reactors. Except Ken—he was holding on to something like his life depended on it and not daring to look through the window. The oldest and the most experienced space traveler was John, at forty-three years, with many missions to his credit. Except for Ken, everyone else had been to Mars with John. Due to the heart attack to Deep, Ken was brought in as an eleventh-hour replacement. The accelerated program was clearly not sufficient. Kristen and Nicole had been on the mission to Mars with John, in order to experience the actual working of the HySleep system and to prepare for this mission. Baz was sent because he was the second-in-command and needed to establish a working relationship with John and the rest of the crew. Baz's task was to watch and learn from John, the commander of the mission, so that there was redundancy in case John became incapacitated. There had to be redundancy at all levels. Sometimes two stages of redundancy had been built in. The mission could not be jeopardized under any circumstances.

Ken Salazar was recruited from Yale University where he was a fully tenured professor. Originally from Canada he was married, but had no children. He was the only married crew member and like the rest of the crew was in the age range of thirty to forty-five. He was chosen not only because of his physical prowess—he was a fitness fanatic. He was chosen to replace Deep because of his deep understanding of various cultures from around the world. From a young age Ken was interested in languages, both ancient and modern. After graduation, he lived in various countries around the world so he could learn firsthand about languages, cultures, and societies. His parents were wealthy and were willing to sponsor him on these journeys because of his interest in learning. This experience enabled him to provide his students a cultural background on any of the languages he was able to teach. He believed this would provide the student with a better, more immersive, and richer educational experience. He was also the director of a foundation set up by his parents which promoted global cultural understanding. They believed understanding others was the pathway to a peaceful world. Growing up he lived in various countries in South America, Europe, and Africa as well as Middle East, India, China, Japan, and the Oceanic countries. He not only learned languages but also picked up the local cultures. He later researched on the roots of languages, writing his dissertation on the possibility of *one* root to all of Earth's languages. His special interest was to research on ancient dead languages and, unbeknownst to anyone, would prove to be very useful.

When government officials had come up to his doorstep, he had initially thought that it was a joke. Upon realizing they were serious, his first question was why him. Initially his answer had been, "No, there is no way I am going into space. I don't even like flying!" When they explained to him why he was one of just three or four candidates in the world, one who was indisposed and the others too old for the rigors of space travel, who could make the journey his jaw dropped. Their criteria had been someone who knew diverse languages, was physically in top condition, knew cultures and history of cultures, was not married, and did not have dependents and finally someone who would may need to communicate with a species not found on Earth. That last criteria had clinched the deal, no matter what his reluctance was to flying. Although the informal guideline about marriage was violated, Mission Control was willing to compromise to get the best candidate quickly rather than trying their luck waiting for the exact match and wasting more time.

"Unit 2 started, proceeding to unit 3," echoed the speaker in the command module.

"Copy, proceed to 3," John replied.

"How long did that take, John?" Kristen was wondering. She was sure that the second one took a fraction of the time.

Kristen Sinclair, a marine biologist from Australia, had graduated from Stanford with a PhD in marine biology and ecology and was working on the scientific reclassification of deep-sea creatures found in the very abyss of the oceans. She was most interested in studying organisms that survive in what we consider hostile environments. She had been to the deepest trenches in special submersibles meant for the purpose and was therefore used to spending a lot of time in confined spaces. At those depths, where there is no sunlight, it is difficult to differentiate day from night and up from down. Therefore, in some ways it mimics space—Kristen had thought of the similarities between the two for a while. In each case, the outside environment is hostile. However, in space, there are no creatures that glide by. Moreover, space is empty as compared to deep water, which is dense and at very high pressure. In the submersible, which is comparatively much smaller than the TE cluster, there is a lot of vibration from every moving part as well as vibrations due to the tremendous water pressure trying to squash it. The command module in the center of the TE cluster, which had no direct link to the fusion propulsion system, there was complete silence and was devoid of any vibration.

Standing at five feet and four inches, Kristen was most interested in how organisms survived in hostile places. She was petite for her height, making her ideally suited for spending time in confined spaces such as mini submarines. Normally with dark, thick and naturally curly hair, it was cut short for the space travel. Not easily flustered she had a calm and soothing personality, which made her suited for space travel. Almost anyone could get along with her from the moment they met her. She had taken a course on the possibilities of various kinds of life-forms that may exist. However this was nothing more than speculation since no one had observed anything extraterrestrial—not even a microbe. There was nothing more than one basic college course available since there was no material available to teach effectively. Even that one course kept referring back to deep ocean volcanoes and other inhospitable places where specially adapted multicellular creatures—extremophiles—not only exist, but also thrive. But the largest ones are nothing larger than an average crab. When the call came, she jumped at the opportunity at doing something extraterrestrial. The potential for this mission was special. There could be a highly developed and intelligent life-form on the MG which could rival or exceed human capability. Her knowledge, training, and demeanor made her almost ideally suited to be on this mission. She was also the only one adapted to space travel, not only because of her experience spending long periods deep in the ocean in tiny vehicles but also because she spent even more time in decompression chambers after resurfacing. One way to cope with the monotony was to do meditation, which came naturally to her. She did not realize why pulling herself deep into her consciousness came to her that easily. She would find out when she met the aliens.

John was busy pressing some buttons and moving some switches and at the same time speaking in the communicator. At the end of his short burst of activity, he answered Kristen, "It always takes longer to start the first one. They use the heat from the first reaction to speed up the process for the second and subsequent ones. We will be on our way in a matter of four or five hours. Within six hours we will be in the HySleep chamber. I cannot wait for the HySleep. I am famished." John, like the others, had to fast for the long sojourn so that there was no solid matter in his stomach. Naturally he was hungry.

Baz, with the other three engineers Manny, Greg, and Thor, were checking the weapons systems that were stowed away in units 1 and 4. These units were in diagonally opposite corners of each another. In order for the rotation to be smooth the weight distribution needed to be balanced. Units 1 and 4 had the heavy equipment, nuclear explosives, shoulder-launched grenades, etc. There were other smaller weapons in the other units. However they were mostly handguns, rifles, and other drilling equipment in case drilling was necessary to gain access to the alien MG cluster. One of the units was almost completely filled with identical fist-size balls—packed with electronics.

All four of these engineers were almost of identical build, ranging from five feet eleven inches to about six feet one. Manny and Thor were recruited from the highly secretive SEALs program. Manny had Mexican ancestry, and Thor was a second-generation Scandinavian. Thor was the only one where the decision to send him was not unanimous. Thor had a reputation of having a "shoot from the hip" personality, making snap decisions which, to his credit, were more often right than wrong. Being of Scandinavian origin, he had bright blond hair and naturally he also had blue eyes. His physique was envied, by men and women alike, and didn't do anything to dispel his "bad boy" image. However, his other credentials were more than impeccable. Calling it a calculated risk would be an exaggeration, based on his mastery of all things related to electronics and communications it was decided that he be selected. Everyone who makes it into the Navy SEALs has a special aptitude, both physically and mentally; however, these two along with Baz and Greg had shown special aptitude in spaceflight as well. They were the first of a breed of engineers who were recruited to protect mankind from aliens—true aliens.

The final crew of eight was shortlisted from twenty-one trainees. They were selected as much for their abilities as for their interaction with one another and their collective capacity to be comfortable in small and confined spaces. They had to work synergistically by augmenting one another's strengths while compensating for one another's weaknesses. Although the cluster of six dSEs had ample room, the total square footage was larger than three single family homes combined, there was no possibility of going outside for a walk or to cool off in case there was a heated argument. With the amount of time they would spend together, cabin fever was almost a certainty. Therefore, the mental makeup of each selected astronaut was critical. Their personality was carefully studied by experts, they spent countless hours in training in cramped spaces, and their mental makeup was carefully tabulated. The trainers had experience from past missions to select crews that amplified one another's capabilities without rubbing one another the wrong way. Each had to be motivated, capable in their areas of specialty, be able to discuss with a cool head under stressful conditions, and go with the majority decision or the commander's decision without feeling slighted or belittled. They had to understand and keep in mind that internal conflict during the mission could be fatal not only to themselves but also to the entire planet they were protecting. The leaders who put this team together, comprising of several individuals including Chand, were confident that they had assembled the best team.

An hour later, Baz, Manny, Greg, and Thor returned to find the other four still in the main command module. Nicole Goodman had earlier run diagnostic tests on all the life-support and hibernation systems. Everything worked flawlessly. She was an Army physician and had treated many conflict-related injuries. She was a West Point graduate, which meant that she was very capable both mentally and physically. In physical prowess, she was nearly on par with most of the men in her graduating group and well ahead of all her female alumni. She had chosen to help the wounded soldiers and veterans in the Army by training to become a physician, if necessary even to go to the battle field. However, thankfully there were no major conflicts, so her only experience in the war area was to help refugees in conflict-torn areas who had very warlike injuries. She had seen some gruesome wounds and had treated them, innocent victims of political conflagrations.

Her capabilities extended beyond her profession. She also had outstandingly remarkable looks. She would not look out of place on a modeling runway. So believing that she was a doctor was difficult for most people. Her remarkable bedside manners made convincing people that she was one of the best physicians even more difficult. Blonde hair with a slight hint of redness, radiant blue eyes, and standing at about five feet five, her smile lit up a room even on the gloomiest of days. It was as if she had an internal lighting mechanism—a bioluminescence. Wherever she went it was as if she was wrapped in the aura of an angel. Her smile could melt the heart of even the most cynical person, and if that did not do the trick her calming voice certainly did. Being a team player most women also found her to be very amenable. Always eager to help, she was a remarkable person and ideally suited for this mission. Even if her expertise was never called into action her presence and aura alone had the power to mollify any frictional situation. There could potentially be many of those in an enclosed spaceship housing eight adults. In the military, she had a nickname Bio, as in bio-Nicole—a double entendre for biolumines-cence and being a doctor (biology).

It was carefully chosen that the build of the two women was similar to help with various aspects of protective clothing and facil-ities for biowaste collection and disposal. Similarly, the men were of similar build, although they were taller, ranging from five feet eleven inches to six feet and one inch.

Baz announced, "All weapons systems are accounted for. They are secure, and we are ready for the final launch. I did wonder about all those small round things the size of tennis balls occupying almost an entire dSE…"

John, who was checking something on the main console, heard the question. He was the only one of the eight who knew the pur-pose of those round objects. While still at work he absentmindedly answered, "Oh! Those things. They are relays." When there was a stunned silence he looked up at a puzzled-looking Baz. Then he looked around, and everyone had an equally quizzical look about them.

He was forced to explain. "You see, as we get further and further away from Earth the communication will take longer and longer—partially because the signal gets weaker as the distance increases and partially because there is background radio interference. We cannot amplify too much, or the sound we want to hear gets too distorted." Everyone nodded. They all knew that fact.

John continued, "When we are close to the turnaround point, the maximum distance from Earth, signals could take as much as fifteen hours or more. So, each signal to and from Earth needs to be boosted and have a lot of error checking and redundancy built in, which takes a lot of processing time and causes further delays in communications. We do not have the luxury of not communi-cating clearly because the penalty of not understanding and having to retransmit could be more than a round trip of thirty hours. We may not have that kind of time. So to compensate for that, during the outward journey, at predetermined distances, a ball will be automatically ejected with zero velocity relative to Earth. This means it will stay where we put it for a very long time—if not forever. These are powered by internal batteries and what little sun's radiation is available in space. These balls will be used to enhance the transmissions between Earth and us. This should increase the efficiency of communications and make it clearer without the static and hiss you normally get when signals are weak. This is simply to aid in the communication process. It will not significantly speed up the communication time. Radio signals travel at the same speed, but the signal will be strong—hopefully. It has never been tried before, so we are the first ones. By the time we wake up, there will be none left on board, so there will be more space for us to stretch our legs—not that it is very cramped now."

That was a more detailed explanation than Baz expected. He agreed and responded, "Yeah. There is ample space now, but a little more never hurts." Immediately another thought occurred to him. "What will happen to them when we are done with this mission?"

John anticipated this question and was ready with the answer almost as soon as Baz had finished asking. "Well, they will be there for any future missions that we or someone else may undertake. Eventually they will succumb to the gravity of the closest planet and crash into it, much like most of the millions of asteroids that are free-floating in space. They will burn up on reentry if they encounter an atmosphere around the planet or become embedded in it if the planet does not have an atmosphere."

Everyone appeared satisfied with that answer. Over the next four and a half hours the rest of the engines were started. There was nothing much to do for the astronauts except watch and wait for each fusion dome to erupt into a bright light—indicating that the reaction had started. In order to break the monotony of waiting, Ken, who was in space for the first time and had not seen these fusion engines up close, made the comment, "This is remarkable, and it looks spectacular with that bright bluish light coming from the reaction. Looks like a giant light bulb. Fascinating!"

Due to his background Baz understood the process very well. In addition, he had taken pains to understand how the whole thing worked, especially when he had accepted this mission. It was important for someone to know the inner working of this machine, in case emergency repairs were needed far from Earth—not that much could be done by an individual in the proximity of such high temperatures. But still, for Baz, it was interesting subject matter and good to know just in case a simple fix could save a lot of trouble. Baz decided to take on Ken's comment as a question and answer it to distract Ken from his predicament. They had all noticed the unease in Ken's voice, and the way Ken was behaving led everyone to believe that he was at a high state of anxiety. Gravity had not been initiated, and Ken was rooted to one spot, not moving at all and holding on as if to prevent him from floating off into space. Clearly, he was not comfortable. If Baz explained the technology at length to Ken he could attempt to distract him from his distress. Baz started, "Well, since we have some time, let me explain. As you know we have had a miniaturized nuclear fusion reactor for well over ten years. There are various versions, but this one uses a version of hydrogen, called deuterium, to fuel this fusion reaction which we carry in cylinders on board this craft. A helium isotope called helium-3 which we mine from the moon, is also carried on board for the same purpose. The temperatures required to start the fusion reaction is achieved through an array of solar panels and mirrors focused to a point." Baz was pointing at a reflective surface near the vehicle in which they were standing. Ken assumed that the dome that was being worked on was in the focal point of the mirror.

Baz continued, "In space, it is surprisingly easy to increase the temperature in this manner. The intensity of the sun's rays in space is much higher than on Earth as there is no atmosphere or pollution here to dilute the rays. Yet, as you can see the whole process is cumbersome. We have to blast off into space from Earth using the same old chemical rocket technology. But once we get the dSEs here the crew can maneuver it to a position close to the solar arrays and mirrors."

Then Baz realized that he had to provide a background of how the mirrors got to where they were. He continued speaking tangentially, "The solar arrays and mirrors had been placed in orbit for this singular purpose. These had been transported into orbit by numerous previous missions specifically for the purpose of initiating the fusion reaction. Each mission carried a segment of the solar array or the mirrored surface and like a giant construction set attached together to form a circular disk. The mirrored disk acted as a heater to start the fusion process, and the solar array generated enough electric current to manage the plasma thus generated."

Baz stopped for a moment to take a breath and let the information digest with Ken. He noticed that Ken was beginning to relax a little, so he continued, "It is critically important to keep the dSE in a precise location, so that the mirrors are pointed exactly at the reactor contained in the dSE. If the dSE deviates even slightly and its bare metal is exposed to the focal point of the mirrors, the heat would melt the metal and put the crew in a life-threatening situation. In order to protect the inhabitants of the dSE from the heat generated from nuclear fusion, the reaction is designed to take place in a dome which you can see is attached to the dSE by means of a telescopic boom. The location of the dome ensures that hardly any heat generated from the reaction is conducted to the fuselage, hence keeping us safe. Additionally, the plasma generated from the heating of the gases has to be contained within the dome by means of a system of electricity and magnets—another critical requirement. If the plasma came in contact with the sides, the heat would melt the container, which would be catastrophic. Therefore, it is vitally important to keep it from touching the sides of the container in which it is housed."

The others noticed what Baz was doing. In fact, the speech was so effective that everyone had settled into their favorite weightless corners and was intently listening.

Another short break to catch his breath. Baz could not wait too long before he continued—he had Ken's attention. Ken was visibly less tense now. So he continued as soon as he was able. "Initiation of the fusion reaction is a complicated process involving three major steps. Once the dSE is in orbit, as a first step, it is required to be maneuvered to the solar array. As you can see, we are already past this step. Extravehicular activities (EVA) are needed by the maintenance crew to attach a cable from the solar array to the dSE. The solar array provides electrical power to the dSE. This electric power along with magnets keeps the hydrogen plasma from touching its container walls and prevents it from burning through the vessel. It also provides additional heat to augment the heat generated by the mirrors. Once the first step is completed, the second step is to raise the dome from the cabin of the dSE. This is then locked in place above the dSE. The dome is located on a telescopic boom which I mentioned earlier ensures hardly any heat generated would be conducted to the fuselage of the dSE. The third step is to carefully move the dSE a short distance, using the built-in thrusters, in front of the mirrored disk so that the energy from the mirror is focused exactly on the dome. Then the variant of hydrogen (deuterium) is introduced into the dome through pipes in the telescopic boom. This gets heated up by the sun's rays being focused via the mirrors and the electric heat, enough to start a fusion reaction. The dSE will then be decoupled from the solar array to become a freestanding interplanetary vehicle ready for its mission. That is what we are waiting for now, and it should happen soon."

Baz glanced at Ken and noticed that he was completely relaxed. Ken was completely focused on what Baz was saying. Baz continued, "The fusion reaction is self-sustaining, the same way the sun sustains itself. The reaction produces heat, and 'new' hydrogen injected from the cylinders gets heated up and produces more heat, and so on. The volume of reaction is controlled by the amount of hydrogen introduced. Once the reaction starts, there is enough power to generate all the electricity needed to energize the magnets which kept the plasma in place. In addition, carefully controlled magnetic pressure squeezes the plasma from all directions so as to compress it. This makes the reaction even more intense and fuses the by-product of the deuterium fusion, namely helium, into higher and denser elements which are ejected from the exhaust manifold. This is a form of ion drive, but more effective since it achieves acceleration quicker than the ion drive in its basic form."

Baz was now hoping that the work of starting all the reactors was nearly complete. He was running out of material, and he did not want Ken to slip back into an agitated state. He continued slowly so as to use up more time, "The fusion reaction creates tremendous number of particles, photons, electrons, neutrons, protons, etc., which are channeled out of the back like the exhaust of a jet engine. This is done with the use of an exhaust manifold, which, until the initiation of the reaction, was tucked away in the cabin. As the reaction started, the commander of the dSE remotely, with the aid of computers, moved the manifold into position so that one end of the manifold is against the vent in the dome containing the fusion reaction and the other end exhausted at the back of the dSE. This is what John was doing and is doing as the final one or two domes are initiated." Looking at John, Baz asked, "How many more to go, Cap'n?"

John subconsciously said, "We are on the final one."

Baz muttered, "Oh good," under his breath then quickly looked around to see if anyone had heard him. No one had or at least no one acknowledged that silent remark, so he continued, "Okay. So as I was saying, once the manifold is in place a small door in the dome will open to vent the exhaust particles into the manifold and eventually to the back of the dSE—very much akin to the exhaust systems in automobiles. The path of the hot particles also needs to be controlled with magnets so that it does not touch the sides of the manifold. There is enough power at this point to be more than sufficient to provide engine thrust, energy to keep the plasma in position, as well as for all other life-sustaining functions within the dSE. Some of the power is used to generate a magnetic field around the space station, which keeps the occupants safe from the solar radiation. Much like how the Earth deflects the sun's radiation. Some of the power is used for other items on board such as to recycle air, to extract moisture from all waste products, etc., so that fewer supplies are needed to be carried and thus reduce the overall weight. Of course, the laws of entropy dictate that there will never be a completely self-sustaining biosphere. Everything will diminish over time. But with sufficient planning and enough supplies on board, this is not a concern for us. If the deuterium runs out, the reaction will stop. At that point, only battery backups will be available for a limited time—until the batteries ran out. Then, in this hostile environment, sustaining life would be impossible—resulting in the death of the occupants. But don't worry, scientists have done their work, and we will not be running out of anything."

Ken was nodding and actively listening. Presumably he was now completely unaware of where he was. Baz continued, realizing that he was coming to the end of this particular subject of commentary and hoping that the final dome would be completed soon, "As you can see, once the reaction is started, the dSE looks spectacular with fusion reaction burning brightly, a bluish color, and clearly visible through the metal-coated transparent dome. When detached it looks like we are moving with a giant light bulb over our heads." Baz noticed that Ken was actually relaxed enough to smile.

A glance outside and it was the turn of Baz to breathe a sigh of relief. Outside the dSE, their work completed, the nonessential crew, Baz noticed, was slowly retreating to their safe confines. They would retreat into a module that would take them back to the space station where they lived and worked in shifts of six months. A different crew had already attached two traditional rocket booster engines so that the initial push would provide the instant velocity needed to gather speed, then the onboard engines would continue to accelerate the TE cluster. The firing of the boosters and the initial control of the fusion engine would be controlled through computers and ground-based support staff, who monitored the progress day and night, and reprogrammed the various components as necessary.

Just as Baz was about to start a new thought process the speaker crackled. "Countdown to the first stage, please prepare for the rockets to fire in five minutes."

"Take your seats and buckle in for the initial thrust," John announced. "This will be a one-minute burn, and the rocket engines will then be jettisoned. We will be on our way." Each crew member had their assigned seating depending on where and how the controls were situated. John and Baz were behind the controls, which were in the middle of the control module. Directly in front of them was a reinforced glass window, much like an airliner, only that the window was much larger. There were cameras that could project images on the window and monitors on the side in case the outside shutters needed to be closed, in case they encountered space junk, or if they wanted to protect themselves from the aliens when they reached the MGs. To the left and right of the console were the HySleep chambers, four on one side and four on the other. At the back was the rear window. A big reason to have these large windows was to prevent the feeling of claustrophobia—studies had shown that large windows prevented what is commonly known as cabin fever. This window, too, could be closed. Also in back there were cots, rooms, toilets, "showers" which were in effect moist towels, and a dining area. There was lighting that illuminated the whole command module, but could be turned off for "nighttime." There were also separate lights for all the individual crafts that formed part of the cluster.

Things were proceeding fast now. Soon they would be on their way. Gingerly Ken was helped to his seat. As soon as Mission Control noticed that everything was clear and the astronauts were safely belted in their respective seats they started the final checks. John heard the announcement, "All systems within tolerance levels," to which he responded, "Roger that."

"Final countdown," the announcer on the ground was heard saying, "ten…nine…eight…"

"Ignition started, all systems are *go*! Three…two…one…full thrust and blast off for Titan Explorer. Good luck to the crew and Godspeed."

John started to acknowledge, "Roger—" He did not have a chance to complete. The surge of acceleration was instantaneous, and he was pushed back into his seat so hard that his lips, with the rest of his face, got flattened, and momentarily he appeared to be quite literally grinning ear to ear.

To Ken it was somewhat disconcerting that there was a surge of acceleration, but there was no noise. Almost immediately he realized that sound does not travel in the vacuum of space. But the telltale vibration from the force of the rocket thrusters revealed to him that they were indeed rapidly gaining speed. He could not move any part of his body. In order for some level of comfort he moved his eyes from left to right and noticed that everyone was pinned back in their seats but were otherwise calm. Other than that, there was no other sensation of gathering momentum. Looking out of the large windows in the front he noticed that nothing was changing. He realized that the vast distance to the nearest star and no reference point close by, he likened it to the feeling of taking off in an airliner during nighttime with the windows closed. Everyone feels the surge of acceleration, but nothing else changes. By the time he had processed this information the viselike grip of acceleration abated and vibration stopped.

"Successful separation of booster engines, initial thrust achieved. John, prepare for HySleep," announced the ground control staff member who had counted down.

"Roger that." John announced to the crew on board, "This is it. There is no turning back now. It is time to get changed for HySleep." He noticed that everyone had an anxious expression, so to relieve the tension he mentioned, "Just imagine, when we wake up, we will be heading towards Earth." That seemed to do the trick. The palpable apprehension appeared to subside. The circular motion to generate gravity in the modules had been initiated soon after the booster separation. The computer was slowly increasing the rotational speed with the use of thrusters. The rotational acceleration would stop when about one g was attained. Thereafter, due to the lack of friction outside, the rotation would continue indefinitely. Any minor adjustments would be seamlessly controlled by the onboard computer. Gravity was coming back in the TE cluster slowly, and the astronauts did not have to fight the tendency to float anymore. But since the full rotational speed was not yet achieved, any kind of movement took less effort than on Earth. This would not be the case for long. Within half an hour the required rotational speed would be attained. However, Ken was already feeling a lot more comfortable than earlier.

Due to the length of the trip, each individual had their own separate private area where they could store their essentials. They were allowed to bring a very limited amount of personal items so as to personalize their space. This individual space was no bigger than a tiny changing room. Only a curtain secured at both ends made this private. It was an unwritten and unsaid understanding that no one violated the privacy—except in emergencies. Everyone dispersed to their changing room to change into their custom-tailored clothes for HySleep. They had to change into comfortable clothing specially made to attach to the HySleep unit. The inner garments were gender-specific and custom-tailored with tubes attached to strategic places. Over this went the HySleep suit. The tubes in the special underwear let liquid waste to be expelled. The HySleep suit relieved pressure points to prevent bedsores. It also kept the individual ensconced in the correct moisture/temperature environment.

Nicole, the physician, would be the last to hibernate. Her task was to assist everyone else first and make sure that all the monitoring equipment were properly attached. Not that it was a difficult job, any one of the crew could do it. However, she was the doctor, and so she had taken it upon herself as one of her duties. She was one of the first to emerge from her changing area, followed by Kristen.

"Did you apply the diaper rash cream? You do not want to be fighting aliens with itchy private parts," Nicole joked. In fact, this was a serious question. The elevated moisture in case the "liquid" did not drain completely led to rashes, similar to what babies get. This was easily and effectively overcome by passing dry air in through the tube and also with the use of creams specially formulated to last more than a few hours.

Kristen gave a wry smile. "You don't think we are going to battle, do you?"

"I guess time will tell. It will be about two and a half years before we are awoken, but it will feel like last night that we went to bed. You will not feel that you have aged because you have been err… resting during the whole time. You will be hungry though."

"Two and a half years of not eating is enough to make anyone hungry," Kristen joked.

"Well, there is that, but also these HySleep modules have been designed so that a few weeks before wake-up time, the pressure inside gradually starts decreasing. This is essentially a hyperbaric chamber. The pressure decreases to a point equivalent to being up on top of a mountain at an elevation of about three thousand meters—about ten thousand feet. This increases your red blood cell count, so when you wake up, you do not feel as weak as you would otherwise do. That adds to the hunger, although the liquid nutrition compensates—

there is nothing like solid food. When you start the HySleep process, the pressure is high so your red cell count decreases, to go with the decreased metabolic rate."

"I guess it has all been carefully thought out." Kristen did not know the medical details. Other than her previous experience the only technical details that she was aware of was what she had heard in passing and read in popular media.

"In addition, these electrodes gently jolt you periodically so that during hibernation your muscles do not atrophy too much."

During the conversation Kristen had climbed into the HySleep chamber, and Nicole had carefully attached all the electrodes and monitors.

"Okay, Kristen, you are all done. Pleasant dreams, see you when you get woken up. Are you ready?"

Kristen nodded, and Nicole pressed a button which closed the lid of the HySleep chamber. Kristen saw Nicole wave goodbye to her before moving to the next waiting person, about three feet away. But Kristen did not hear what Nicole said as the HySleep module was already working and she was lapsing into deep hibernation.

Movement was becoming more difficult; Nicole figured that gravity was approaching one g. One by one, she had helped get everyone into the HySleep chamber, using her best bedside manners, making small talk with each as she went about her self-imposed task. She reminded everyone that, after this extended length of hibernation, upon waking it was normal to feel disoriented and hungry. She made it a point to mention that it would take a few hours to regain full mental faculties and reminded them not to panic. Also, she reminded them, upon waking, to fight the urge to eat lots and quickly although they would be ravenous. About an hour later, all were in the hibernation chamber and fast asleep. She took a moment to look around. She scanned the entire module. It was large and resembled images that she had seen in movies. She could take a moment to really absorb the entire view inside and outside the TE cluster. Now that the gravity was at one g, it almost seemed like she was in a large airplane. It was almost eerie. Suddenly the loneliness made a shiver run up her spine. Almost immediately she realized that she was not alone. There were strategically placed cameras on board, and the ground crew was actively observing what was happening on deck—that somewhat comforted her. There were various teams constantly monitoring the various aspects of the ship's function as well as monitoring the telemetry of the human functions. But for now, they had maintained radio silence.

She looked out of the large window and saw stars in the distance. It was a fantastic view. The number of stars visible was so much more than on Earth. She realized that the view from Earth is obstructed by the atmosphere and the pollution, so much so that the density of stars seems far less than it actually is. From space, the view is clear, literally as far as the eye can see. She tried to see if she could spot the MG, but there were too many stars in the background to be able to distinguish with the naked eye. Besides, because they were spaceships, there would be no light coming from them that was powerful enough to register to the human eye even with the use of powerful optical aids. Dark ships in a dark background, like finding a black cat in a totally dark room. She couldn't resist a small smile at that analogy. She felt relief that her anxiety level was slowly abating. Going into hibernation at a high level of anxiety, although not dangerous, is not a pleasant experience due to the susceptibility to nightmares. If you go in relaxed, the scientists had indicated, the dreams would be pleasant.

She looked out of the rear window and could see Earth. Although it was not apparent, the Earth was receding slowly. She thought that by the time she looks out of these windows next, in about two and a half years, she would be looking away from Earth. If the Earth were visible to the naked eye, it would be from the opposite window as the TE would have turned around. However, the MG would be visible through the side windows. She looked around the cabin. There was a common area for dining, relaxing, lounging, and exercising. There were various enclosures and cupboards containing food, clothing etc., each individually labeled and appropriately located around the perimeter of the command module. As she was scanning the scenery around she was jolted to the present when her stomach rumbled. She was hungry. She had to plug herself into the chamber and go to sleep, just like the others. She gave a final wave, a thumbs-up, and a smile to the camera as if to say, "Everything is okay," and stepping into the chamber, she connected herself to the various wires and tubing. She knew that she would be safe, with the ground crew monitoring every aspect of the ship and the hyperbaric chambers around the clock.

By the time she closed the lid from the inside, she was already feeling sleepy—whether it was due to hunger, or due to the fact that it had been a long day or the fact that she knew she had to sleep, she did not know which. She was thinking that the mind is a powerful device. It can be made to do anything humanly possible. The psychosomatic condition of the mind telling the body it has to do something will make the body do just that. The mind can tell itself through self-suggestion, hypnosis being one of them. Her mind was telling her body to sleep, and therefore her body was tired and the mind was feeling sleepy. She was thinking. The mind is almost as if it was a separate entity to the body. The mind remains sharp even when the body is not capable due to aging. One can have out of body experience, some Hindu mystics can do it at will, and often do to get closer to a state called realization.

Her mind had no time to make any more connections, tangential or sequential. The chemicals to make her sleep were now flowing in her body. She was thinking how or what the state of realization was and whether an encounter with their target would be anything like the supposed realization that some people are supposed to have experienced on Earth. She had always been skeptical. With those thoughts lingering, she went into hibernation. No time for any conscious brain activity. From this moment, all the activity would be involuntary, coming from the subconscious, like dreams. At the same time, the protective shutters to the front and rear windows were slowly being closed.

HOSTILE CRAFT
APPROACHING

The lead cyborg, Lela, noticed the new craft, as she had noticed all other craft leaving this planet. The unusual thing about this craft was that it was larger than the others, although miniscule compared to the one she was in, and was coming toward the spaceship in which she was traveling. It was also brighter, just like the one she had seen sometime earlier. That one had gone to a nearby planet. The most unusual thing was that this craft was not the usual enemy. It was coming from Earth—a planet toward which she was heading. She had a chilling thought. Had the race unexpectedly evolved to become belligerent, and were they equal in technology and strength to her master's? Quickly she dismissed that thought although thinking along those lines made her happy and also a little sad. Happy because there could be war out here in space and if the beings coming toward them from Earth were strong enough they could destroy her crafts. Or at least the Earth beings would be able to destroy them once they arrived closer to Earth. She was also sad because if they were destroyed before they landed she would not be able to see Earth.

This craft was coming from a place to which she had special attachment, even though she had never been to Earth. Suddenly she had another frightening thought. What if the enemy had colluded with the Earth creatures to travel in space in an attempt to destroy her crafts? But just as suddenly that alarming thought subsided—the enemies, if they had a hand in helping the Earth creatures, would provide a higher level of sophistication than the approaching craft would seem to indicate. The enemy would never have a hand in making the humans more powerful. On the contrary they would do everything to make the humans less potent. The worst-case scenario, she could destroy the Earth craft as easily by merely thinking about it. Merely using her thought she aligned the weapons systems to follow the trajectory of the approaching craft—just in case.

Still there was no need to alert or awaken anyone.

THE AWAKENING

The plan was to awaken the physician, Nicole, first. This was in case anyone else needed medical assistance during the revival process. If the doctor herself needed aid, then she would be able to call home and get the necessary assistance. If she was too weak to call, the next crew member trained in first aid, Kristen, the marine biologist, would be revived remotely from Earth. In addition, Baz, the engineer was also extensively trained in the first aid process—multiple layers of redundancy. Here in space, this far from Earth, it was necessary for the crew to have cross-training to be prepared for the unexpected; that was their motto—expect the unexpected. The crew had to be self-reliant, self-sufficient, and self-aware even though they had support from the Earth-based staff at Mission Control. From Earth, only so much could be done. The hands-on work would all be done in the spaceship.

Although there were various electrodes attached to the hibernating body to keep muscles active, when Nicole woke up, she felt very weak. Not every muscle could be electrically jolted in order to stave off atrophy. Whether this was the case or whether it was extreme hunger, this was the first time that Nicole or anyone on board had hibernated for this length of time. Tests were conducted on volunteers on Earth, but it was in a lab-type condition and not for this period of time. She was dreaming of floating in space when consciousness slowly came back. The breathable medication that kept Nicole in an almost unconscious state was slowly reduced till there was nothing flowing through the tubing. Slowly, what was in her system wore off, and she was ready to be awakened. The speaker crackled. "Good morning, Doctor, how was your sleep?" It was a voice she recognized. It was the control center physician, Dr. Diaz, who had spoken. Was it in her dream, or did she really hear the voice? Slowly consciousness came back, and Nicole noted that she had heard the voice coming from the onboard speaker. But she was too groggy to answer. She took a few seconds to orient herself and realized that she was in the hyperbaric chamber. Slowly, she regained her thought process and realized that she was not dreaming—this was real. Indeed, she was not dreaming of floating in space. She was actually floating in space. Only floating was not the condition. The spaceship was traveling at tremendous speed, albeit there was no sign of velocity. Everything was quiet, just as it was when she entered the HySleep chamber. She moved her head which was on a pillow while still prostrate on her back. She glanced at the rest of her body and saw various wires and tubes still attached, just as she had done when she connected herself and gone to sleep. The speaker again crackled. "Good morning, Doctor. How are you feeling?" Mustering tremendous energy she tried to utter some words, but it came out hoarse and garbled. "I arrrrm feerrrrliinng…" She gave up, figuring she will try again in a few minutes. Although it took a while for the sound and images to travel the vast distances, aided by the electronic relays deployed automatically on their outward journey, Dr. Diaz heard what he wanted to hear. He knew that she would not be able to speak so soon. He wanted to see if she was registering what he said. He would try again in a few minutes.

After a period of time the speaker activated again. "Doctor, please unhook yourself and open the hyperbaric chamber. There is no need to speak now." Nicole was unaware of how long it was between the voices she had heard, but this was a different voice, a female voice, possibly an engineer encouraging Nicole to start moving and exercise her dormant muscles. "You will feel better once you start moving around." She was going in and out of consciousness, but she complied, without saying anything. Everything was happening in super slow motion. She could feel her throat was still hoarse and dry. She would feel better once she drank something. After unhooking herself she opened the lid of the chamber and gently put her feet on the floor. "Stay there for a minute, till you get your balance back," said the same female voice. Nicole thought she must be moving slower than a sloth for the voice in the speaker to be instructing her directions. Nicole knew that she could not stand up right away; otherwise, she would fall. As a doctor, she knew the inner ear will have to adjust first. It was a good thing that there was gravity in this craft. Otherwise, it would take a lot longer to adjust.

She did not know how long, but a few minutes later, her mild dizziness subsided and she tried to put weight on her legs to stand up. Surprisingly, this took more effort than she had anticipated. At least she was not dizzy anymore.

"Doc, take one step at a time and walk close to the edge of the ship supporting yourself against the walls. You can prevent a fall in case you feel dizzy," came the gentle reminder of the female voice over the speaker. Obviously, the cameras that the ground crew was monitoring were working, and they were watching her every step. There was a delay in communicating, but time was not something that Nicole was conscious of at this stage of recovery from an extended hibernation. Nicole felt like saying "I know" but decided against it. It would not come out right. Instead she nodded, making a deliberately exaggerated gesture so that the cameras could pick up the movement of her head. She had to move blonde locks out of her face, which indicated to her that her hair had grown back while she was hibernating—it will have to be cut again. She decided to try her next words only after imbibing some liquid—water. There was a tank of recycled water that was available replenished from the waste products.

Gingerly Nicole went up to the galley, holding on to the sides of spaceship, taking one deliberate step after another. It seemed like an eternity to walk the short distance to the galley. She noticed that she was famished, but water had to be the first thing that needed to go down her throat. She had received instructions on how to prepare the packaged food for consumption when she was in training on Earth. Upon reaching the galley, she instinctively went to the cabinet where she knew the food would be found. Each cabinet was labeled, and she had to find the one marked "First Food." She had to locate this specific cabinet to find the proper first food, a highly nutritious mixture packaged in very small quantities. Due to the prolonged time that the stomach had not received solid food, it was imperative that food be consumed often, but in very small quantities, to prevent toxic shock. This was the only cabinet labeled "First Food." Still she had to make sure by visual confirmation. It was difficult to focus. The eyes had been closed for such a long time, just like a person cannot focus on an alarm clock or anything for that matter, immediately on waking in the morning. It takes a second or two. Nicole, being a physician, knew this and did not panic. She looked up at the camera and pointed to the cabinet where she knew the first food was available. The ground staff knew where and what each cabinet contained. A few minutes later the speaker came on, "Doctor, that is the correct cabinet. You can take one packet only at this time," said the same female voice. Nicole did not need reminding that she was entitled to only one pouch now, but Mission Control was being careful. She could almost hear the relief in the female's voice. Nicole thought, *They may have realized that, although I have to overcome some physical challenges, I am thinking properly and all my mental faculties are intact.*

When she sat down at the galley and had some water and ate the contents of the pouch—five or six morsels of the mixture, she felt much better. The food was not prepared for taste, but that did not matter. When you are that hungry, you relish every bit. She knew it was nutritious and would help her, and that she was initially allowed small quantities only. Normal food intake would resume in about forty-eight hours. Until then she and the others were allowed small quantities of food but at shorter intervals. She took her time to chew, not only due to extreme weakness but also to savor the food in the mouth and get the saliva flowing again. Eating slowly has the effect of making one seem full with less food. *More people should practice eating slowly, and there will be less of an obesity problem*, she thought then immediately remembered where she was and realized there were more pressing issues at hand.

Finally, she summoned up enough courage to speak. "I feel much better now," she announced, still a little hoarse. It was much clearer than the first words she spoke which, she thought, even she would have had trouble understanding. "Doctor, sit there for a few minutes. There is no hurry," proclaimed the female voice, clearly relieved that Nicole could now communicate with words, not gestures. In the silence that followed, Nicole looked around and saw out of the front portal. Slowly the realization dawned on her that the front and back windows were now open. *They must have sent the signal to remotely open*, she thought. The view was exactly as she remembered at the start of the journey some two and a half years ago. Complete blackness of space except for the band of stars that made up the Milky Way. On either side of the band there was complete blackness except for the distant stars and galaxies. *We have traveled two and a half years and at this speed and are still nowhere close to the nearest stars*, she thought. She looked out of the rear portal, but this view was different. Whereas at the start of the journey was a clearly visible Earth, now there was almost nothing except for some very distant stars. However, there was a bright star in the distance which she assumed to be the sun. Being this far from home she suddenly felt lonely—the same feeling she had had just prior to hibernation. She realized that the craft had probably left the solar system, beyond the orbit of Eris, the last recognized planet, albeit a dwarf planet. She realized that if anything were to go wrong, at this distance, there was no hope of rescue. Of the eight in the ship, she was the only crew member to be aware of a special cabinet, which contained, among other items, some capsules that would, as was described to her, "prevent unnecessary suffering." She knew exactly what it meant. She felt wetness on her cheeks and realized that they were tears. Was the long-term hibernation playing tricks with her conscience?

As if the ground crew could tell what she was thinking the female voice in the speaker said, "All systems are functioning properly." They wanted to bring her back to reality and get her to start her normal routine as soon as possible to take her mind away from the loneliness of space. "If you feel stabilized, Doctor, you can move around and get your heart pumping. Be careful and walk where you have support, along the edges of the craft," said the female voice. Nicole stood up and walked, initially taking small steps and slowly gaining confidence. After about fifteen minutes she felt confident enough to walk unaided although she was close to the perimeter walls—just in case she lost balance. She asked, "How long before the next crew member wakes up?" She longed for company and wanted to talk to someone there—not through a microphone and speaker. There was no immediate answer. A few minutes later she asked again, "When does the next crew wake up?" She waited again with increasing anxiety. After a while the female voice in the speaker announced, "Doctor—that should be in about ten minutes. Remember that the signals take some time to traverse space. No need to worry, we are here and can hear you loud and clear. We are also monitoring you visually. It takes a few minutes for your voice to reach us, so we have to communicate with the delay in mind." Nicole realized that she must have sounded panicked when she had asked the question a second time. She had just woken up, and it would take time for her to think straight. With the fog lifting from her mind, this was the first time she had attempted having a meaningful conversation with Mission Control—up until now it was mostly instructions. She had forgotten that they were so far from Earth that two-way communications would take much longer than normal. "I remember, no worries," she announced.

Ten minutes later Kristen was woken from her enforced slumber. But for Kristen, Nicole was close at hand to assist. Nicole had already prepared the water and the first meal and kept it on the table, ready for Kristen. Next to it was Nicole's second meal—they would dine together as it was approaching time that Nicole also ate. Nicole went through the routine, making sure to provide instructions only and not to ask questions, so Kristen would not need to answer before the water and food was consumed. Finally, when Kristen had finished, Nicole asked how Kristen felt, and the terse response was "Weak but better than ten minutes ago."

"Don't worry, I still feel weak and I came out of the chamber a few hours ago. But the human body is a remarkable system. It quickly adapts to stimulus. You will rapidly feel better. When you can—try and walk around slowly, to get the cobwebs out of your system." Kristen nodded and complied. With company and elapsed time Nicole was also feeling better, both physically and psychologically.

About an hour later Kristen was walking around unaided. It had taken less time because Nicole was there to help. Soon, John would be woken. But before that, both Nicole and Kristen changed

ALIEN ENTANGLEMENT

into their regular clothing, which was a standard-issue jumpsuit that was more practical and functional than fashionable. It was approaching almost five hours since Nicole had the first food and about three since she had the second helping. It was time for the third course of another five or six bites of food. Kristen could have her second course with her, and they would both eat again with John after he was woken up.

As Nicole was chewing the food, Kristen asked if there was any news. "All systems are functioning normally," indicated Nicole. Kristen shook her head. "No, I mean from Earth."

"No, I did not ask that question." There was silence after that while they finished their second course. It did not take long since the quantity of food was small. Kristen was surveying out of the front, rear, and side portals, presumably noticing and feeling the same way that Nicole had when she first woke up. Thinking why Nicole had not inquired about any information from Earth, she was starting to get herself worked up. As if they were reading her mind, the speaker came on, "We will give you an update when all have woken up. That way we can inform everyone at once," said the female voice. Kristen looked at Nicole quizzically. "There is a time lag before our voice reaches them and their voice reaches us," indicated Nicole, which did not elicit any more questions. That comment from Mission Control also helped ease Kristen's mind

John was next to be woken up. Nicole and Kristen felt a sense of relief as John did not feel any new or different ill effects of the slumber. He had the same reaction that the first two had when they first woke up. This time around, however, Nicole did not have to do all the work, with Kristen helping with the food preparation and assisting John to the galley and answering the questions, the answers which Kristen had recently learned. When he was able to speak, John asked the same question as Kristen, "Any news from Earth?" Kristen indicated there was none from Earth, however, "The craft was functioning perfectly." As Nicole and Kristen before him, he went to all the windows, port, starboard, fore, and aft of the spacecraft. He noticed that nothing was discernible except for brilliantly speckled stars in the distance. "You know this is the farthest that anyone from

89

Earth has ever traveled," he mentioned to Nicole and Kristen. "It is very exciting, and I must admit, a little scary too," he added and felt butterflies in his stomach. It was either excitement or he was still hungry, he couldn't tell, possibly both. He continued, "We are practically out of the solar system, or should be by now if things are going per schedule." After a moment's pause to gather his thoughts, he added, "We have been traveling at about five hundred thousand kilometers per hour, for the best part of two and a half years. That should put us just beyond the mean orbit of Pluto. Pluto is a dwarf planet, and although there are three other dwarf planets beyond Pluto, and of course, there is the Kuiper Belt, I personally consider going beyond Neptune as leaving the solar system. I cannot be sure whether or not anyone else agrees with me. We are certainly in the vicinity of Pluto." His thoughts were beginning to get more coherent, and he decided to stop speaking in case he was disconcerting the others.

Kristen said, "Wait a minute, at that speed we should be well beyond the orbit of Pluto!"

John responded, "That would be true if we got to five hundred thousand kilometers per hour almost immediately after we blasted off. But we took time to accelerate to our current speed. We took a lot of time since the acceleration was so slow. We were in hibernation while we were accelerating. That is why you don't recall it, and that is why we are not farther away from Earth." Kristen nodded. Clearly the mental faculties were slowly coming back.

The plan was to rouse each crew member one at a time. In case someone needed assistance the one available doctor aboard could attend to that person while others were still in hibernation. There was no need to take unnecessary risks. Besides, there was plenty of time, and a few extra hours of hibernation would not matter at all. The plan was to start waking the crew members about eight weeks before manual maneuvering was to take place. At that point, the TE spacecraft would be well into its slow 180-degree turn to start heading in the same direction as the MG—back toward Earth. All this was computer programmed, with manual override from Earth, if necessary. It was all pretty straightforward programming. The only difficult part was to do the final adjustments so that the dSEs were close enough to dock with the alien MG. In the plans that were meticulously drawn up and refined several times, there was no scenario where it would be acceptable for the TE to dock with the alien craft. There was too much that was unknown and there could be a danger of deadly pathogens—even if the aliens were not belligerent. They would get close enough to dock but not actually dock—even if it were technically possible. The actual transfer of personnel from the TE to the alien craft would be accomplished using a specially built craft. There were two of these craft loaded on board, called rovers—each capable of carrying up to four individuals.

At this distance, the sun appeared small and weak. The only light illuminating the inside of the dSE was from the internal lighting in the spaceship. This far away, most of the sun's rays and heat had dissipated into space, very little of either reaching the dSE. Just like on Earth if they could see one of the other planets in the solar system, it would be due to the planet reflecting the dim sun's light. However, due to their position relative to the sun, they would only be able to see the outline of the planet from the front portal. In order to view the non-silhouetted planet, they would have to be almost parallel with or in front of it. For that, they would have to view the planet from the rear portal. However, the spacecraft was navigating a course that did not take it close to any of the planets. They could only see the lonely denizens of the solar system at a distance if the timing and positioning of the dSE was correct. Being at a distance from some of the massive planets was fortunate as the crew did not have to compensate for the massive gravity these giants of the outer solar system wielded. The lack of any large objects in the proximity provided for an eerie atmosphere, as if submerged in the depths of the ocean with nothing around but almost total darkness.

Baz was the next to be roused from hibernation, Nicole doing the honors of awaking him. He took a while before being able to stand up and walk slowly to the galley. He ate some meal that was readied for him by Kristen. During this time John was at the control panel studying the data as best as he could. His visual acuity had not completely normalized. Like the others his eyes could not focus on near objects. The close things such as lettering or words on the monitor were not completely discernible. He thought it was similar to the drops opticians use to dilate the pupil in order to examine the retina. It was comforting to know that the ability to focus on close objects would eventually come back, after a few hours. John was not worried about this since he had experienced it before during the trip to Mars. "How are you feeling, Baz?" he inquired finally. "Like a hangover, but without the headache," came the curt reply. That was sufficient conversation for now until Baz recovered some more. Baz did the same routine as the others, walk gingerly to each window to observe what was visible and see the space around him, this being the farthest from Earth any human had been. Finally, he spoke and the question was familiar, "Any news?" The answer was familiar also, "No news other than the craft is functioning normally. We will have a briefing once everyone is up and able to think coherently and hold a conversation."

Manny, Greg, and Thor were next, in that order. By the time Baz had brushed off the cobwebs and started asking questions, four hours had elapsed, six if you count from the time Nicole had first opened her eyes. Last to be roused was Ken. By this time, Nicole, Kristen, John, and Baz were moving with alacrity. They had almost completely got their natural rhythm back. They all had completed their second meal and were each performing their tasks, or at least looking busy. Nicole was busy with Kristen stowing away the medical equipment and shutting down the hibernation units, John and Baz were checking and discerning the readings on the control panel, and Manny, Greg, and Thor were in various stages of normalcy. By the time Ken was up and about, seven and a half hours had elapsed, almost an entire shift by Earth standards of normal working hours.

The support crew on Earth, however, worked two twelve-hour shifts per day as opposed to three eight-hour shifts. This was done in order to reduce the communication issues between different sets of support personnel from different shifts. Each shift had to provide information to the next so that the work could continue smoothly, and this event, called the turnover, occurred every twelve hours. The turnover took anywhere from thirty minutes to one hour. This way, the transfer of shift could occur between the same two individuals.

If the shifts were of eight-hour duration, this would not be the case since there would be a third individual. The teams were designed so that maximum synergies could be achieved, and teamwork was the key concept for this endeavor to be successful. The crew on the dSE would, however, have to work around the clock, taking catnaps when time allowed and working through exhaustion, if necessary. The survival of Earth and its population of humans, depended on the success of this mission.

COMMUNICATION DILEMMA

Lela had completed her research. She had found that the inhabitants of Earth were hybrids, created from two or three sources. The source was not clear—in fact, the only thing clear was that it was top secret and was not on any memory device on the spacecraft. She was also unable to determine how the Earth beings communicated. If she had to guess, she could surmise that some of the natives could communicate like her. *It would be a reasonable assumption*, she thought to herself, *because of a small contingent of people who had a hand in the creation of the natives had stayed back in one of the previous missions*. Those who had stayed back were kings, and they were charged with training the people they had created. She assumed and hoped that she would be able to communicate with the Earth beings. She would find out soon—there was a craft from Earth heading in their direction.

She then silently cursed to herself; in her excitement and anticipation she was focused solely on what was in front of her. She had not checked the view from other cameras monitoring other areas of space around her. She quickly changed the display to show the view from the other cameras to check for the enemy pursuing them. Previously there was no indication of them. Now there was a small blip on the scanner. This by itself could be anything, a comet, meteor, tiny planet, or a planet fragment—no need to panic yet. If it was the enemy, currently they were far away, too far for concern. She will have to keep an eye on it to see if it was gaining on them. She needed to focus all around, or her plan would fail if their enemy chasing them caught up with them. However, she could not wait for the craft in front to close the vast distance.

Voice from Earth

When Ken, the last one to be awakened, had his second meal, the elapsed time was about nine hours since Nicole had woken up. She had worked efficiently and almost continuously, albeit with the help of the other crew to see that everyone was safely awakened and fed. She did have time to rest and relax a little during the time that the others were helping the newly roused individual. Nevertheless, it was still tiring work—however, a sense of deep relief enveloped her. Her major task was over. Indeed, the relief was sensed by all, now that each knew that the other was safe and well on their way to a state of normal functioning. No one had moved away from the command module to explore any of the other parts of the spacecraft. No one had even suggested it. Everyone had to be in full view of one another in case someone had some unforeseen side effect and needed medical attention immediately. This was especially true for Ken who had never experienced hibernation. Everyone was deep in thought, in their own world when suddenly the radio came alive. "Good morning, ladies and gentlemen." No one aboard knew whether it was day or night at the control center, but they had been asleep and were now awake, so "Good morning" was an appropriate greeting. The female voice on the radio continued, without pause, "We are ready to provide a briefing, if all of you are up to it. Remember that at this distance, the radio signals for audio as well as visual are delayed. Please account for that when you speak. You will get used to it in a few hours, after we have had a few exchanges."

John stood up and looked at one of the cameras monitoring the command module. He was the commander of the mission and therefore would take ownership of communicating. There was no set protocol. It made logical sense that he be the one to speak since everyone speaking at the same time would lead to chaos. As commander, John would make all onboard decisions. Protocol dictated that the second-in-command, Baz, would take over if John became incapacitated. Everyone else had equal rank, with all medical decisions logically being left for Nicole and all linguistic decisions being left for Ken, if and when it came to requiring their subject matter expertise.

"We are ready, Mission Control. As you can see we are all up and almost back to normal functioning. Ken was the last to be woken up, but I think his faculties have normalized…That is a scary thought," he added jokingly to relieve the monotony. That seemed to do the trick. Everyone on board laughed, perhaps more than the joke was worth. They all had worked together for several months on Earth in preparation for this trip, and some good-natured ribbing had become part of the norm.

A few minutes passed, everyone knew about the delay, but it seemed longer than expected. They were almost losing interest. Finally the female voice came on, "My name is Sarah, and I am the communications supervisor as well as the communications voice. I will be the one speaking with you for now. My shift mate is Tracey. When I am off shift she will have this responsibility. Between the two of us ours will be the voice you hear for close to 100 percent of all communications." Ground control had used women to provide communications because the female voice is of a different pitch and clearer over radio communication. It can also be more soothing. Most electronic systems, whether using real voice or electronic voice, always used a sound range in the female voice spectrum. "After this communication is over, please go to the individual dSEs and check the contents. Our telemetry readings indicate that the spaceships are functioning normally. However, we cannot see or monitor the contents. There is nothing like visual verification." Sarah continued without pause, "As you may have expected, the TE is well into its turn. At the moment, you will not be able to see the MG through the windows because they are obscured by the opaque walls of the main module. However, if you go to one of the dSEs, you will be able to see them, depending on where in the rotation cycle the dSE happens to be. It will take approximately 238 hours to complete the turn. At that point both you and the dSE will be heading in the same direction, towards Earth." This seemed to elicit a collective sigh of relief from the astronaut crew. The thought that they would soon be heading toward Earth, not away from it, was an enormous relief. Sarah continued, "Their velocity at last measurement has remained constant. However, they are traveling approximately 34,500 kilometers faster than you. So we will have to increase our speed. You will have plenty of time to slow down before reaching Earth. We will adjust your speed relative to them from here. In fact we have already started to speed you up. However, the final maneuvering will be done on board by you, John. You will have to use the thrusters to move the dSE close enough to send a boarding party to the MG to take a closer look. This is a lot of information. I will await your questions." The speaker went silent.

This was exactly per plan, and John and everyone had been briefed in great detail about the procedure, so there was nothing new. He spoke, "What is the news from Earth? Was there anything that happened in the last two and a half years that we should be aware of? Over to you." He echoed all the crew's thoughts. He did not need to ask each member what to ask.

There was silence while the signal traversed the vast distance, aided by the small electronic relays deployed on their way to this point to reach Earth. Everyone waited patiently, eagerly, expecting.

"We are all here, as is Earth. The usual events have happened, volcanoes, floods, hurricanes, tornadoes, riots, in various parts of the world. It is not worth going over those events. It is the usual stuff." It had been decided not to trouble the astronauts with the mundane details of the usual events. "All the countries on Earth are basically the same as before. Countries with a space program and monitors have detected the fact that this mission was not heading in the direction to rendezvous with Titan, the original reason given for this mission. We have covered it up by saying that there was a malfunction in the dSEs and that we are taking corrective action. That has satisfied them for now. No need to go into the details. When you get back, you will find things to be almost exactly the same as when you left them. All your families are fine, and they have been briefed that you are all safe." Sarah purposely kept it vague, and to add a little pep talk she added, "You will be heading back to Earth soon. Let's get our jobs done safely and get this over with. It will be over before you know it." It was also decided early on during the planning stages that there would not be any pictures relayed from Earth. Although the technology was available, all unnecessary equipment was removed to save weight. Moreover, they did not want the astronauts to get homesick, longing for Earth. It was one thing going to Mars, just a few months away, and traveling for about two and a half years to the outer reaches of the solar system. This was, after all, the farthest anyone had traveled from Earth. They wanted the crew of the TE to be completely focused on the job at hand—at all times. The safety of Earth was at stake.

"Understood…over to you," John replied. There was nothing much to do. The spacecraft was navigating itself, with slight adjustments from Earth. It would take about two weeks before he had to do anything, maybe longer.

"You have some time to rest and recuperate. Suggest you use the time to walk around, get some exercise, check out the equipment, see if you can make visual contact with the MG, and basically get stronger after that long sojourn. We will be watching you, and if you have any questions, just ask, there is always someone here. Over." That last sentence was added on purpose in order to comfort the crew, in case any of them were already longing to be anywhere but there.

John responded, "Roger that!"

SLOWDOWN

Finally, the craft from Earth had arrived to a visible (to the naked eye) distance from the alien ships carrying the cyborgs and its other crew of robots and hibernating beings. It had taken a very long time for the spaceship from Earth to turn around. Now both the cyborg's ships and the ship from Earth were heading in the same direction—toward Earth. The cyborg saw that that the technology to build the ships was several generations old compared to theirs. In fact, to assist with the rendezvous she had ordered her crafts to be slowed down and also applied imperceptible gravitational assistance to the Earth craft. She was allowed to make these minor adjustments while her masters were hibernating.

She was determined to make the occupants of the ship from Earth make contact with her. She had realized that there would be a communication issue. She would worry about that later. If things did not go well and the approaching craft showed belligerence, she could destroy them easily—the weapons were already trained on them. She had not and did not have to tell anyone. No one would ever know that a spaceship from Earth had arrived and was destroyed, en route to Earth. If things went well, she would capture the humans and bring them to her masters. If she had to destroy the human ship, she would somehow have to engineer the euthanasia of Earth also—to prevent further suffering.

CONTACT

On the dSE, everything was automated. The ship was navigating by itself without any input from the crew. The software was running flawlessly on the computer systems—or so it appeared. Minor corrections, if necessary, could be radioed directly into the onboard computer from Mission Control on Earth. As the intention was to get close to the alien crafts, the onboard systems were only checking for proximity to the alien craft. It was not anticipated, and so there were no checks built into the computer to see if there was an external force, helpful or otherwise, acting on the dSE. So no one realized that there was an external force being exerted on the dSE—to bring it closer to the alien craft. The human craft was exactly where the cyborg wanted them.

On the dSE the days passed with little or no meaningful activity. Anticipating lengthy periods of inactivity and in order to avoid going stir-crazy the crew was encouraged to load into the computer as many ways of passing time as they could. They were in the form of electronic games, books, music, movies, self-help courses, etc. This had no weight, and there were lots of memory to load everything the crew wanted—to last a very long time. There were many monitors where they could either view or play individually or collectively. On some occasions, they watched movies, and on other occasions they played electronic games, either with one another or against the computer. There was also a lot of information loaded about the various unusual life-forms on Earth, both marine and terrestrial, as well as some of the defunct languages and communication systems of the past. There was ample computational power on board to support each member even if each one chose to do a different activity at the same time. Every day at certain times each member was required to exercise on the treadmill as well as with the punching bag. This was mandatory, in order to keep themselves in shape—they may need every ounce of strength in the near future. Some friendly sparring to keep their close quarters skills sharp was part of the drill. They had decided to dine together to build and keep a sense of camaraderie—this provided an opportunity to communicate and prevented anyone from being isolated and get into a mental state where they would do some harm to themselves, to others, or to the mission. John, ever the leader, thought of various mental games to simulate what they may encounter. In addition, they collectively discussed various circumstances that may arise and various options to handle them. In addition to this, they formed a routine to check and recheck various critical items.

During one of the sightseeing forays into the extremities of the craft, Ken noticed an object in the distance and toward the front and side of the craft, reflecting the weak rays of the sun. Orbiting around it were three moons. "What is that? It looks beautiful," he commented.

"Oh, that is Pluto," came the response from Baz.

Ken, rather surprised, asked, "I did not know Pluto had moons?"

Baz, who had knowledge of the solar system, accepted the invitation to speak. There was nothing much to do anyway. "Charon—that is what the biggest one is called. It was not discovered till much later, only in the 1970s, I forget the exact year. If memory serves it was 1978. The other two are Nix and Hydra. All are named after Greek mythological characters." Baz continued, "If you look closely, you not only see the three largest moons, but also some smaller ones. These were a chance discovery in 2015 by the New Horizons mission that was sent to Charon in order to study it. At this distance from Earth, it is extremely difficult to detect the smaller moons. These tiny ones are too small to be named individually. Charon is only about six hundred kilometers in diameter, and Nix and Hydra are between thirty and forty kilometers in diameter. The others are even smaller. No point naming every piece of rock that we discover."

After a short time when no one picked up on his lead, Baz continued, "We had no idea of the unnamed moons till a probe was sent to Charon to study that satellite in greater detail." Ken nodded with increased interest but a quizzical expression, trying to figure out where Baz was going with his thoughts. Soon it became clear when, after a moment's pause, Baz continued, "All those years ago, when they spotted the alien craft, they must have been very fortunate. We cannot be sure how big the alien craft is, but I bet it must be at least twenty or thirty times smaller than the smallest moons we have found."

No one had thought of it from that perspective. There was a better chance of finding the proverbial needle in a haystack. In fact, there was a better chance of finding a needle in all the haystacks on Earth piled into a single heap.

Baz was referring to the fortuitous event during the Cold War, decades earlier, that the alien ship was detected. Ken was a replacement and a new member of the crew. He was brought in to replace Deep who had unexpectedly developed health issues when coming out of hibernation during the training mission to Mars. The mission leaders could not take any chances, so they had brought in Ken as an eleventh-hour replacement. They had accelerated his training program and had eliminated briefing him on some unessential items. One of the areas which was compromised was the history of how the aliens were detected. Ken exclaimed, "Oh! I did not know that we have known about the aliens for more than fifty years."

Seeing that Baz wanted someone else to pick up on explaining to Ken, Kristen jumped in. "Like Baz mentioned, it was a lucky happenstance. From what we were told, a newbie signal operator made a mistake in repositioning the newly developed radio telescope. The telescopes were being deployed as an early warning system for incoming hostile missiles. Luckily, he was also an amateur astronomer. When the telescope, now out of position, was turned on he discovered some faint images where there should have been empty space. He immediately reported his finding, and it went all the way up to the president. The White House decided to keep it quiet since, at that time, there was no means of reaching this distance in manned craft and they did not want to panic the public. Years of development later, here we are...", she let that sentence drift as the rest was obvious.

The rest of the crew knew about this. Ken responded, "Fascinating!" There were many questions Ken had, but they were mostly about the alien craft. He knew as much about those as the others, which was basically nothing. He did not want to think or ask too much about them. He knew that the answer would include the words, when we get closer to investigate." Lack of enough time to acclimatize him to a weightless environment made him very uncomfortable to even think about it. His travails just before hibernation were still fresh in his memory. If only the others knew how uncomfortable he was before gravity was introduced to the dSE. He had put on a brave face, and for the most part, it had worked.

Neither Ken nor anyone else pursued this subject, so gradually everyone went about whatever they were doing before.

After a while John mentioned excitedly, "Well, this confirms it. We are officially out of the solar system, because Pluto is in front of us." And as his reason to believe so, he added, "Well, at least at this point, we are beyond the rocky inner planets obviously and beyond the gas giants too. In my mind, everything beyond the gas giants are debris, despite the fact that they are orbiting around our sun. They may someday coalesce to become a planet, but are not so at the moment."

"Well, I don't think so," commented Baz. "In my opinion, the last dwarf planet is Eris, which by the way is more massive than Pluto. Then there is the Kuiper Belt. If we had traveled beyond the Kuiper Belt, we would have left the solar system. Everything going around our sun must be considered as a satellite of the sun—"

"Yes, but there are lots of rocks drifting in space," John interjected. "We need to draw the line somewhere. Lots of people consider a rounded or spherical celestial body as a planet since it has enough gravity to round it off, like the Earth or Mars or even the moon. If you consider that to be a definition of a planet, then Pluto is round so it has enough gravity, however," John continued as Baz was about to cut in, "it fails in the other criteria that it has not cleared the area around it of other debris. None of these dwarf planets have done that as evidenced by the numerous small rocks that populate the Kuiper Belt. Once these rocks and ice boulders have succumbed to the gravity of Pluto or Eris or some other planet and formed a larger planet, then it could be considered as the end of the solar system. Therefore, they are not planets, and so I maintain that we are out of the solar system."

The friendly banter continued for a while. The crew had plenty of time after their daily mandatory activities of checking and rechecking to make sure that everything was in working order, especially the weapons systems, the recycling systems that provided them with water, the generators, etc. They also practiced getting in and out of their customized space suits as well as exiting and entering explorers docked in the dSE without actually opening the bay doors and egressing the dSE. Of course, without opening the door, they only got as far as getting into the explorer. They practiced this over and over till they were able to do this almost blindfolded. They practiced getting in and out of the extravehicular activity suits to make sure that every clasp was locked properly, the helmet was screwed on as it should be, and the oxygen tanks and battery packs were connected to provide oxygen and to power the wearable electronic devices. The suits were designed to be worn without assistance. Therefore, each crew member was supposed to be able to wear one and also disrobe out of the suit when they were back on board. There were two explorer vehicles that were on board one of the dSEs. These were designed to function independently, untethered to the main craft. Each of these explorer vehicles could carry a crew of four, piloted by one individual. Baz and Thor were trained in the maneuvering of these, although the rest of the team were given theoretical instructions of how to use the controls. When the time came and John had moved the dSEs as close as he could, the explorer units would be deployed to make a closer inspection. The time was approaching for this event to happen, in just a matter of a few dozen hours.

Activate Plans

She noticed that they were coming to investigate. The cyborg gave the orders for the portal to be unlocked so it could be opened from the outside. She knew it was safe to do so. It was time to put her plans in motion. Fortunately, there were very few of her kind on board—all except two of the other robots were menial, designed to just take orders. They were incapable of reasoning, remembering, or replying other than a few words such as "yes" or "no."

EVA MISSION 1

After their sleep/wake pattern became normalized after the lengthy hibernation they took turns to keep vigil, in case immediate action was needed. There were at least two crew members monitoring the gauges and visually checking the MG to see if anything had changed, especially if they had changed course toward them. The MG was still visible through the aft window of the ship, which meant that the alien crafts were still behind them. However, since the MG was traveling faster, by the time it was ready to do manual maneuvering they would be on the starboard side right next to the TE craft. The TE craft was slowly accelerating to match the speed of the MG.

Pluto and its moons were still visible but not from the starboard window on the right anymore, but from the window on the rear of the dSE. Also visible, albeit just barely, was the MG. However, since it did not reflect much light, presumably by design, it was difficult to be spotted with the naked eye. When it first came into view, there was considerable excitement. Everyone gathered to the closest window and took turns to look at the MG. However, their excitement soon abated when they realized that nothing more than a faint outline was visible. Even with magnification, it was difficult to see much due to the low light and a nonreflective surface of the MG. The alien craft looked like a ghostly comet speeding toward Earth from the heavens.

"I can't be sure, but it looks like they are all of similar shape and size and have a broad base and are narrower at the top." Kristen was speaking to no one in particular. Everyone had gathered to the same vantage point to view the MG through one of the windows in the outer extremities of the craft. With the blackness of space and the dark color of the MG, its shape was barely discernible. "If I had to guess it looks like a pyramid," Kristen continued. "This shape has four equilateral triangles meeting at a vertex, and a square base. It appears that the top is narrow and the base is wide. This gives me the impression that the shapes are based on the tetrahedron shape," she said. After studying them some more she continued, "I can positively confirm—there appears to be more than one of them. They are flying in formation—I cannot tell how many are there." That was a piece of bombshell information. From Earth, it was difficult to tell if there was one or many alien crafts. From a distance, the individual units could not be differentiated—they appeared as one craft. The proximity revealed that there was more than one traveling in close formation. As to how many there were could not be determined—it was more than five, perhaps as many as seven.

Astonished, John exclaimed, "What? Let me see." Everyone took turns observing from Kristen's vantage point and realizing that what she had observed was true. Astonished and with a myriad of questions popping up in the mind of each individual, almost before the previous one completed, they went to their favorite location to process the information and be ready for the direction from Mission Control.

Finally, Kristen spoke, "Did you notice that the surface appeared to be kind of rough, not smooth. It was difficult to visually judge the distance from the spacecraft or how large each one was." Then she said something that everyone was expecting, but when they heard the actual words confirming their thought, it gave everyone goose bumps and sent a chill down their spine all at the same time. Kristen said, "These are almost definitely not natural. They seem to have been constructed and launched by some alien entity." If the previous information about there being multiple crafts did not have enough of a conversation-killing effect, this latest statement had it—even for Kristen. No one spoke for a while. However, all conversations aboard the dSE were designed to be picked up by the microphones aboard and relayed to Earth.

The instruments indicated that they were about twenty-five thousand meters away, but the readings were fluctuating, as if the instrument attempting to measure the distance could not get a firm reading, much like an autofocus camera that is unable to bounce its signals off an object to get a good measurement of the distance. Therefore, the lens keeps rotating clockwise and counterclockwise in an attempt to focus. *That is about sixteen miles*, John figured out in his mind, once the group had returned to the main module. When John was able to maneuver the TE craft closer, they would get a better idea. There was more than one pyramid in the MG, and they were arranged in a geometrical pattern. Although the crew could not count all of them at this distance and with their angle of view, they were able to just about see three. There almost certainly were more, hidden from view from this angle.

Finally, after what appeared to be an eternity after the latest revelations, the speaker came on. "John, you take manual control and bring the TE as close as you feel comfortable, before launching Explorer 1 for the first close rendezvous," announced the female voice in the speaker. Interestingly they had not opened the conversation with the latest news of multiple craft.

The female voice continued, "Your window of opportunity is small since the MG, per our calculations, is traveling faster than you. You will not have too much time to manually adjust and deploy the explorer. Time is of the essence. If you notice them speeding away from you, you will have to make the decision to fire the high explosive weapons." They all knew what it meant—the nuclear devices— however, she did not have to say it in so many words. "We do not want to take any chances. While you were in HySleep, we took the precaution of readying the last of the defense mechanisms, which are currently in geostationary orbit around the Earth, ready for activation, but hopefully it will not come to that. The weapons on board will have to be deployed at least to blast them off collision course with Earth. Your job will be more difficult as there is more than one MG, but ultimately it does not matter how many there are. Our jobs remain the same while we continue to process the information here."

Mission Control was right. The job remained the same, only it was that much more difficult as there are multiple alien craft with which to deal.

That last set of instructions brought about a sense of foreboding in the crew, especially the non-engineers who had hoped to at least learn something of the alien crafts. The engineers took it in their stride. They were trained for this eventuality—they were formerly soldiers. John was already gently nudging the spaceship to the right in order to get closer to the MG. "They are not going that much faster than us," Ken mentioned. This made everyone follow his gaze. Ken was at the window on the right looking at the alien crafts, and it looked like although the human craft had gotten closer to the alien crafts, the change in speed of the MG relative to the spacecraft from Earth was not dramatic.

"Either we have speeded up sufficiently or they have slowed down or both," he continued.

"Probably both," came the response from Baz. John was busy firing the thrusters in tiny bursts, each burst nudging the humans closer toward the alien crafts. He had to take extra care that the human spaceship did not float into a collision course with the alien craft. As he nudged closer, the full scale of the alien crafts became more apparent. "There are eight of them. I can see them all, I think," Baz mentioned. He elaborated, "One in the top row, three in the middle row and four in the bottom row. If you connect them with imaginary lines, they form a pyramid. Each one of them is roughly in the form of a pyramid. For some reason they like triangles," he added. "Each is massive, probably as big as the great pyramid of Giza, in Egypt. And, by the way, they are not traveling faster than us."

The control center on Earth heard all the conversation that had taken place, only it was delayed. The onboard speaker came to life. It was like a disjointed conversation because Baz had uttered those words a long time ago. "We are now showing that the alien craft and your craft are traveling at about the same speed. The only explanation we have is that they slowed down. We believe they are aware of your presence and are monitoring you." That was another chilling revelation to the occupants of the TE. Thus far there had been no sign of life in the pyramids, no communication, no radio transmissions, nothing. Although no one verbalized it, the astronauts had settled to an uneasy comfort of assuming that the MG was devoid of life. The chances of life in the pyramids were fifty-fifty. Believing that there was no life was far more agreeable than believing that there was life. However, this information from Earth seriously questioned that assumption and brought them to reality—there was work to be done. She continued, "Has there been any signal from them, any radio transmission, any light, or anything else that indicates that they have tried to contact you?"

John, as was becoming normal, responded first, "None whatsoever, all outwardly signs indicate that they are running silent."

Nicole asked the obvious, "If they appear to be monitoring us, do you think they can see us now or at least feel our presence?"

That was an interesting question. No one at this point was able to answer that question, and no one attempted. It was scary enough to think that they were monitoring the occupants of the dSE. They could be monitoring with capabilities that were as yet unknown on Earth. It was getting close to the time where four of the crew would board the explorer rover mini space vehicles and approach the alien craft, but which of the eight pyramids would they choose? Although the explorers were airtight, the crew would have to suit up and use the oxygen cylinders attached to the suits. Depending on the level of activity, each member had about two hours of breathable oxygen and about thirty minutes of reserve. This depended entirely on the level of activity, since vigorous activity meant using more oxygen. The weight of the wearer also played a part on how much oxygen was consumed. A larger person consumed oxygen at a higher rate. Most importantly, the disposition of each member played a large part—a calm individual consumed oxygen at a slower rate than a nervous individual. Therefore, each crew had practiced, on Earth, being calm and relaxed even in a tension-filled environment. Once detached from the mother ship, the rovers would lose the artificial gravity induced by rotation on the TE. This is because the circular rotation would be stopped by firing thrusters on the rovers. The four chosen by Mission Control were two engineers, Ken the linguist, and Kristen the marine biologist. John announced, "I cannot get this thing any closer. Prepare for a closer encounter with the pyramids." John would continue to navigate the spacecraft, Baz would be monitoring communication with the exploration team, and Nicole would stay on board with Thor. That meant that Manny and Greg would go with Kristen and Ken.

The speaker came on again. "Although we have no good basis for recommending this, we feel that you should first go to the alien ship nearest you, which would be the one of the four at the bottom of the eight-unit cluster. We have agreed to name them, from our point of view, number Pyramid One at the top. Two, Three, and Four the middle row, from left to right. And Five, Six, Seven, and Eight in the bottom row, again from left to right. In this scenario, Two in the middle row and Five in the bottom row would be the farthest, and Pyramid Eight would be closest to you. Do you copy that?"

John responded very enthusiastically, at last there was something to do, "Roger, copy that."

Mission Control responded, after the normal delay to which everyone was getting accustomed, "The only reason for selecting Pyramid Eight is we do not know the alien's disposition and if you have to make a hasty retreat, Eight is closest."

John responded, his enthusiasm unabated and on the other hand fully realizing that the words would get to Earth much later, "Copy, we will go to the closest one, Pyramid Eight."

Everyone understood.

During their routine checks and setup of equipment in the period when they had plenty of downtime, Manny and Greg had already placed the necessary close-combat weapons as well as larger explosives in both Explorer 1 and Explorer 2. They were going to use Explorer 1 for this mission, so Kristen and Ken loaded items they would need. Each had a small bag. All four suited up and got into Explorer 1. All the necessary and final checks were performed, then Manny said, "John, we are in place and ready for the sightseeing trip. We deploy as soon as the hatch opens."

John acknowledged, "Roger that, opening hatch. Good luck." All four on board had intense and mixed emotions. Ken had one additional concern, which was dealing with zero gravity. On the one hand this was a significant occasion, and on the other they did not know how this encounter would end. They had repeatedly practiced everything except for this part. Moreover, the designers of the alien crafts were obviously intelligent, but were they belligerent? Could they and would they communicate? What was their purpose, intellectual curiosity or the total annihilation of anything that they may come across? Kristen had familiarized herself with various forms of obsequious mannerisms. However, would the aliens interpret the crew's actions as fawning or threat? Well, it was too late to worry now. There was no turning back. Indeed, there was no turning back from the time when the training began and they had left Earth some two and a half years ago. When the hatch opened, a green light lit up in Explorer 1, indicating that it was ready to commence the undocking sequence. At the push of a button, the sequence commenced, preprogrammed and automated in order to take the human element out of the equation. Explorer 1 slowly left the relative safety of the mother ship.

"Clear, we are clear," came the excited response from Explorer 1 as soon as they had cleared the slowly rotating spacecraft. Almost immediately the four crew members felt the artificial gravity dissipate and weightlessness enveloped them; also, darkness enveloped them, except for the onboard instrument panel in Explorer 1 and the soft light of the distant sun. Ken was doing his best to hide his fears.

John said, "Roger that, closing hatch, and again good luck," then he added jokingly to alleviate the extreme tension, "Say hi to them from us. Did you remember to take the bottle of wine and some flowers with you?"

That, at least temporarily, relieved the pressure, but it was very temporary. He could see in the faces of the crew remaining on the mother ship that they were very tense. *It must be that much worse on Explorer 1*, he thought to himself. All joking aside, no matter how trivial, it was time to focus and concentrate on the job at hand. Baz was already busy monitoring the progress of Explorer 1 as it inched toward alien spacecraft Eight. If the crew became incapacitated in Explorer 1 he could take over the controls remotely from the mother ship and navigate it back. However, after the initial hesitation of trying to figure how much thrust to apply and when to apply it, it appeared that Greg was getting increasingly comfortable with navigating the rover.

The explorer rovers were specifically built for this import-ant task. It was designed to carry four, much as a subcompact car. Indeed, it was about as big. However, the top and the bottom parts were made of reinforced clear Plexiglas that provided a panoramic view all around. Looking down from the seated position in the explorer, one got the feeling of floating, which indeed the rover would be doing when it was out in space. The part in front of the rover (where the hood would be on a car) and the back (where the trunk would be located) had batteries, locomotion mechanisms, and a backup cylinder of oxygen, instruments, and computers. Although they were designed for easy egress and ingress, it was airtight when the lid was closed, much like an airliner that could be pressurized for high-altitude travel. To Kristen, it felt as if she were in a deep-sea submersible, only that the explorer rover had a more panoramic vis-ibility. To Ken, it was very uncomfortable. Although strapped to the seat, the fact that he was in zero gravity and this small vehicle was slowly floating away from the safety of the dSE was disconcerting. He was just short of a full-blown panic, suppressing the primal urge to start screaming.

The weapon systems they had loaded into the explorer included highly explosive munitions and close-range items such as an assort-ment of pistols, guns, and grenades. Other than the weapons, Ken and Kristen had with them laptops with various items of informa-tion, both for their use as well as for the aliens, in case they had to communicate. The laptop could potentially make communication easier by rendering drawings that could be shown to the aliens. This EVA activity, code-named EVA 1, was not meant to establish con-tact with any beings that may be present in any one of the pyramids comprising the MG. The purpose of this excursion was to take a closer look at the alien vehicles from the outside. However, unex-pected events occur from time to time, and the secret of success is to expect the unexpected and be prepared at all times. That was the central mantra of the mission, right from the time of its inception.

In addition, the crew was continually made aware of the say-ing that failure was not an option. To this end, Ken and Kristen had their notes and other information on the laptop. Ken had all known forms of verbal as well as written and sign communication that was ever used on Earth. It was possible that all the information on his laptop was useless. Maybe the aliens had a different system of writing or communication that was not close to anything on Earth, past or present. At the very least it would serve the purpose of letting the beings know that Ken was making an attempt to communicate. If nothing else at least he hoped the aliens would interpret his overtures with the laptop as nonthreatening. Kristen had information on various creatures on Earth, including human beings, apes, marine life-forms, as well as bacteria and viruses, both beneficial and non-beneficial. This may be useful information, for the aliens, in case they did not have immunity to the tiny critters, some of which have been around long before humans knew of their existence and have been the bane of humankind. In addition, she had applications that would help her categorize the aliens in the classification scheme currently used by scientists in the various biological sciences, although she was fairly certain that the aliens would need a new branch. The plan was to use the laptop camera and take high-definition pictures and videos. This would be done by launching the zoological application on the laptop which, under normal circumstances on Earth, would analyze the pictures taken from the built-in camera, look for unique characteristics of the subject, and place it in a category and branch of the evolution tree. This was not foolproof; however, it did narrow down the exhaustive search from months to mere seconds. Moreover, the laptop/application would enable the capture of the aliens' image, in case there would be no other opportunity to take any pictures. When the laptop is brought back to the dSE, it could be docked on to the docking station and all new information radio transmitted back to Earth.

It had been a half hour already, one and a half hours for oxygen to run out. Except for the pilot and the navigator, the two other occupants, Ken and Kristen, were looking around and taking in the views. However, Ken was still very agitated, although less so than before. Kristen was completely relaxed and was enjoying the views from the weightless environment and keeping an eye on the pyramids, especially Pyramid Eight. There had been no sign of activity.

The plan was to circumnavigate Pyramid Eight. They were close, about thirty-five meters from it. Noticing the panicked look in Ken's eyes, Kristen said, "Try and relax. Close your eyes and imagine tranquility—shut everything off in your mind, detach it from your body. Imagine that you are looking at yourself. This is a meditation technique that helps."

"Feeling a little claustrophobic," announced Ken, who was not used to being in such cramped quarters. "Close your eyes and imagine your brain is a separate entity looking at the rest of you—as if someone else is looking at you. Believe me, it helps." Kristen attempted to keep Ken calm and stop him using up more oxygen than necessary. After a short time, Ken responded, "I am feeling a bit better now—getting used to it, I think. That technique you told me really helps. Figuratively speaking you have to get the brain out of your body."

Kristen agreed, "Yes, that is a practice I have used frequently in the decompression unit when coming up from a deep dive—"

Explorer 1 was about twenty-five meters away. Manny's panicked words interrupted Kristen. "We have gravity."

"Back off, back off," John's panicked voice came from the mother ship.

Greg took immediate evasive action and fired the thrusters in reverse, to take Explorer 1 away from Pyramid Eight. As he was preparing to fire the thruster a second time, at about thirty meters away from Pyramid Eight, "We are weightless again," announced Manny. Greg hesitated and did not fire the thruster again.

"I think we should approach the pyramid again," said Greg who wanted to try the approach again.

By this time, Ken and Kristen were both clearly panic-stricken and were hyperventilating—more so for Ken.

"Okay, breathe in deep and slow. I don't think we are in any danger," Manny announced, attempting to calm them down. They were clearly not used to this type of pressure situations.

"Repeat, making another approach," announced Greg.

"Wait! Are you being pulled towards the pyramid?" inquired John.

"Negative, we are not being pulled now, nor were we being pulled when we had gravity any more than an object pulls another object in space," announced Greg.

"That is peculiar. I would have expected that the gravity would have pulled you toward the pyramid. Okay, attempt another approach, but be careful and if we, here in the command module, notice anything I will ask you to return. Better take this slow and easy," John suggested.

"Copy that," came the reply from Explorer 1.

Greg fired the thruster again, this time moving close to Pyramid Eight. As soon as they crossed the twenty-five-meter mark, "We have gravity again," came Manny's voice from Explorer 1. He continued, "Looks like, for whatever reason, at about twenty-five meters' proximity there is a gravitational field, possibly being generated by the alien spacecraft."

"Do you have full control of your vehicle?"

"Yes, we do. Controls are not affected in any way, just gravity at this distance."

"Can you tell how much gravity you are experiencing?" John inquired. There were no instruments to detect gravitational field built in to Explorer 1, as none of the designers of the rovers expected there to be any measurable gravity that would be experienced by the rovers. "I think it is comparable to about one g, although it is difficult to tell from a seated position," came the response. "When I pick up my sack of goodies that I brought with me, it feels about the same weight as it does in the TE," mentioned Ken who was considerably calmer than a few seconds ago when they had first experienced the unexpected. They all knew that Ken had brought with him a small bag with items he would need, in case they encountered an alien. John knew that this information was going back to Earth. It would take some time for them to analyze the data and respond back. John instructed, "Proceed with extreme caution and do your routine as planned." Earth was monitoring every communication, so they would hear his instructions to Explorer 1 as well. They had to take some risks, and this risk seemed manageable. Without any risk, they would not be able to accomplish anything.

"Roger that," came the response.

The mission of Explorer 1 proceeded under artificial gravity in space.

"I can confirm that Pyramid Eight is definitely a tetrahedron," informed Kristen. She was videotaping the pyramid as the rover was making its way around Pyramid Eight. "The outside seems to be made of a fluffy material, dark in color, possibly black." She continued, "We are rounding the apex and descending on the far side of the pyramid. The entire surface is coated with the same material, does not look solid to the naked eye, perhaps a nonreflective material. It is as if someone threw a blanket of soft foam over this giant structure. There is no light that we can see coming from the inside. The only thing we feel is gravity that rapidly dissipates beyond about twenty-five meters. We have now descended to the base of the far side and will be going under the structure." Then a second or two later she continued her discourse, "Wow, the size truly becomes apparent when you are underneath. The square base seems massive, perhaps two hundred to three hundred meters on each side. I cannot measure it exactly due to the foam material which also covers the base."

The once-over took forty-five minutes. Greg managed the final part with more dexterity than the initial part, as he had become accustomed to moving the vehicle in vacuum and the varying degrees of gravity close to the MG. "John, we went around the starboard, port, vertex, and base. Nothing is visible except the foam that seems to be covering the alien spacecraft. We have more than enough power and oxygen to go around another circle, but this time we can go aft and stern. Requesting permission to do another round."

"What is your power and thruster level?" John wanted to be extra safe. There was no need to jeopardize anything and launch a rescue mission to retrieve Explorer 1 by sending out Explorer 2.

"We are at 75 percent power and 70 percent left in the thruster. We also have about fifty-five minutes' worth of oxygen and thirty minutes in the reserve tank." This was an average number after a quick scan at the gauges. If Ken's level was accurately checked they would have noticed that it was lowest at forty-five minutes plus the reserve. He had used up more oxygen when he was feeling the anxiety of zero gravity. However, he was getting used to being in this position and was much calmer now. The existence of gravity also helped.

"Okay, go ahead, Explorer 1, but don't take too much time. If resources are down to 40 percent, break off the search and return to the TE. Do you still have gravity?"

"Roger that, proceeding with second pass by. Yes, we have gravity, felt a little weightless as we passed the apex, but other than that, there has been no change, pretty constant all around." By this time Greg was adept enough to speak and navigate at the same time. *Muscle memory comes back fast from all the intense training done on Earth*, he thought to himself.

The second pass through began on the other two of the four angular sides of the Pyramid Eight craft, and Kristen, still videotaping, continued, "This side is also similar to the other two sides, foam-covered material enveloping the structure. Same color as the other sides, looks jet-black, but difficult to tell in the darkness of space." She thought to herself that it would be nice to have a searchlight, as in a submersible, to illuminate the target, but this was not built into the Explorers. So they would have to do with whatever ambient light that was present. To improve contrast and save battery, the instrument panel in the rover was dimmed and Greg and Manny shielded the few lights with their gloved hands. Greg could only use the one hand since he was using the other to maneuver the rover. Next time, Kristen thought, she would bring a cloth or something to shield the instruments, if there were to be a next time. This mission was not over yet. The monotony of the blackness of the pyramids continued. "Rounding the apex, brief lowering of gravity, only an instant, and coming down the reverse side of Pyramid Eight. Proceeding past the base, perpendicular to the first pass through and rounding the base to go back to the point where we started. The length from apex to the center of the base appears to be between 150 to 200 meters tall."

"Permission to return, this run was the same as the previous run. This craft looks exactly the same from all angles." Then Greg added jokingly, "These guys have absolutely no architectural sense, wouldn't want to be an architect on their planet."

"Okay, Explorer 1, return to Mama, what is your status?" John replied, everyone clearly relieved that the first mission had proceeded without incident, thus far.

"We have plenty of energy and thruster left. This time around was just thirty minutes. I am getting good at driving this thing. Last time it took us about forty-five minutes. We have about twenty-five minutes oxygen left on average. Ken is lowest at fifteen minutes, but we should be back in about twenty."

Then it suddenly hit them that Ken would have to go to reserve before they got back. It would take about twenty minutes, all going well, to return. John did not like cutting it this close. Ken would be left with zero and would have used up about five minutes of his thirty in the reserve. John said, 'Ken, you have reserve, when you see the oxygen low indicator, switch to reserve. You have the training, and you have done it a thousand times. Main thing is not to worry. You will all be fine, do you copy"?

Ken responded, surprisingly his concern not evident in his voice, "Yes, I copy, don't worry, I am okay now." Even Ken was astounded how calm he sounded. The last thing anyone wanted was for him to hyperventilate again, and unnecessarily deplete more oxygen, especially since this first mission was proceeding so well. Relatively speaking it was a success. They had not been attacked in any way, and nothing detrimental had happened. True that they had not made contact with the aliens, but on reflection, that was not to be expected on the very first outing. Perhaps the aliens were as circumspect as the humans. John wondered, if they were monitoring the human craft, they should know by now that this spaceship, which was now speeding alongside the alien spaceships, had occupants who were also tentative and, more than anything else, peaceful. Hopefully, John wondered, that is the message that was being conveyed to the aliens.

"C'mon back, I will begin the process to open the hatch," he repeated.

As a true scientist and years of training had taught her, detail is the key to success, Kristen signed off her videotape session with details a researcher would not miss. She continued to record. "Returning to ship. This concludes mission 1 to explore alien spacecraft Pyramid Eight on…" Suddenly she realized that she did not know the date or time. It was all relative in space, and even though the circadian rhythms had returned to the crew, after about two and a half years of HySleep, no one had spoken about which day it was at present. No one communicating from Earth had mentioned it either, presumably purposely. She took a quick peek at the bottom right corner of the laptop where the date and time are displayed and continued, "On June 27th, 2037, at 0355 hours." Then thinking about it for a second, she added, "If the date on my laptop is correct."

Like the undocking sequence, the explorers had a self-docking program, which Greg activated. Pretty simple, it adjusted the speed and rotational velocity based on a marker in the mother ship and navigated itself to auto dock. Greg activated it once he was close enough to the mother ship and saw that the hatch was open, and the self-docking indicator light became green. Twenty minutes later, they had docked and the hatch closed. The four proceeded to get out of their space suits, put them in their docking wardrobe so that everything could be recharged for the next EVA. They walked back through the cylinders connecting the outer units, which housed the explorers as well as the space suit wardrobe, and came into the command center.

"Congratulations! And hopefully, every subsequent EVA goes this well," announced John.

Baz, unable to contain his excitement, announced, "Congratulations to one and all. Did you notice anything of significance? We were all listening to Kristen and her excellent and detailed description."

Kristen responded. "Thanks. And I apologize," she said smiling, "there are only so many ways I can make describing black interesting. No, there is nothing there except for this foam-covered pyramid. It is all black, and it is not smooth. It is as if someone sprayed foam and let it coagulate. It is"—she was looking for the best way to describe it—"like waves on an ocean. If you take a still picture of it from above, you see the up and down indentations of the waves. There is no pattern to the indentations. I could not tell you how thick it is. It could be millimeters thick or it could be a few meters. The onboard instruments could not penetrate it."

As she was describing this, she was also docking the laptop to the docking station and had begun to upload the data to the main computer on board which would in turn send it to Mission Control on Earth via the baseball-size balls left at strategic intervals to boost the radio signals along the way.

Nicole had Ken on the examining table in the galley, normally used as a dining table. She began examining him for any ill effects of the EVA. No one wanted to repeat the scenario of what happened to Deep during the last mission. "You seem fine. Do you feel anything that you want to mention?"

Ken replied, "I feel fine now. I was very nervous at first, but I calmed down during the course of the mission. I think I got used to the feeling of being out there. And I am certain that relaxation method also contributed."

Nicole wanted to make her point and continued, "You came back with your main tank empty and about twenty minutes in the reserve tank. I realize you had ample left in the auxiliary tank, but comparatively the others did not even have to switch to the reserve supplies. You had used up a lot more than the others, and being the linguist, you will be going on possibly all missions. You will need to relax and not use up as much oxygen."

Ken responded defensively, "I realize that. I will be calmer on the next one. This was my first excursion, and I was nervous. I panicked when the gravity suddenly went to zero and then when it suddenly came on when we got close to the pyramid."

Nicole, realizing that Ken got the point, said, "Okay, a suggestion, half hour before the next one, do the relaxation and meditation exercises that you learnt during training as well as what Kristen taught you. Whatever works is fine with me."

Ken responded, "Sure, I will be fine for the next one. There is nothing like the experience of the first EVA. Now that I know what to expect, I will not panic." Ken was getting a little exasperated, but realized that the eight on board were a team and had more than a passing interest in one another's well-being and the overall success of the mission. He said again, a little calmer this time, "Nicole, I will be fine, and I will do the relaxation meditation before we go again."

Nicole did not say it, but thought to herself, *What will happen when things don't turn out as expected?*

PATIENCE

The cyborg was eagerly anticipating the humans to detect the small indentation under the covering and come through the unlocked portal. She was a little disappointed that they had returned. She had to be patient. The humans were being cautious as anyone would under these circumstances, or they had completely missed the indentation. Although disheartened, she would continue with her plans—she had nothing to lose, and the humans had everything to gain. Everything she would do was for the greater good.

EVA MISSION 2

The data from Kristen's laptop was received on Earth.

Due to the delay in receiving the broadcast at either end, multiple sentences had to be spoken at once, whether it was coming from central command or from the TE. The female voice in the speaker came on. "Hi, this is Sarah. We have received the data. Experts are analyzing it. Kristen, you did a great job of recording and describing what you saw. It will take some hours for us to go through it in detail. We are analyzing it in visible as well as non-visible spectrum of light. We also have telemetry and other types of data from the sensors built into Explorer 1. The data it gathered was also downloaded to our main computers. We will apprise you of future activities as soon as the data is fully analyzed and we have the next steps for you. In the meantime, we all want to say excellent job for the crew of Explorer 1 EVA. Please stand by for further instructions. Also, continue to monitor the MG visually as well as by radio. Encouraged by our excursion to their ships, it is possible that they may send an EVA mission of their own. If that happens, do not react. Let them conduct their fact-finding mission and return. Any other action may be mistakenly interpreted as threatening. Like us, they may have weapons that they may deploy. Over to you."

That was unexpected. No one on board had thought of the possibility of the aliens sending out an EVA. When under stress, the human brain will think of the next move to alleviate the stressor, not beyond. These eight humans were under constant stress, no matter how relaxed anyone looked or no matter how much one joked. Indeed, for some, joking in a stressful situation was a way to find mental stress relief. *Wow*, John thought. It would be very difficult to seem natural and not be stressed out if they saw an exploratory vehicle from one of their numerous windows. The pyramids did not have any windows, at least none that the occupants of EVA 1 saw from the outside. If an EVA were to be conducted by the aliens, they would be able to view everything aboard the dSE, due to the numerous windows and portholes purposely built into the main cabin of the dSE cluster.

John, always trying to lighten the tension, responded with, "Copy that. We will make every effort not to flip the finger at them." Everyone aboard laughed, even though they knew that the finger would not mean anything to the aliens. It was important to relieve the monotony as much as possible at any given time, and this was well-known to John. The aliens would probably think of this as a form of greeting. It was indeed a form of communication between individuals on Earth, only that it was not a form that would engender mutual understanding and cooperation between any two humans. Nevertheless, the remark was a stress relief, and everyone had a hearty laugh. "So, if we see them, what do you expect us to do, carry on with our normal task? Over."

By this time each crew member on board was used to the staccato style of conversation with Earth. In case someone had forgotten the question to which the answer had just arrived they looked at the monitor where the question was displayed—having been typed by the crew asking the question. There was also the facility to rewind and replay the answer—the round trip took too long and to ask for the answer to be repeated would be impractical. Sometime later came the reply to John's question, "Negative, we suggest you all form a line standing and showing yourselves, in full view. Keep your hands by your sides, in a natural relaxed standing pose. Raising your hands could be construed as a threat. Our experts here think you should all show yourselves, so that you are all seen clearly, standing next to each other, with the shoulders not touching, so that they know there are eight individuals on board the TE. Over."

John thought that it was interesting that Mission Control was still referring to the mission as TE—Titan Explorer. Nevertheless, it was not something to ask at this point as communication was so difficult. He made a mental note to refer to this mission as TE and simply replied, "Roger that, over and out."

A number of hours went by. No one was keeping track of time. Each individual was engaged in his or her activity. Eating, sleeping, exercising, taking turns to monitor the MG, checking the instruments for external signs of life, using the computer to listen to music or play games or to read up on something new. Not that it was monotonous, the presence of the alien spacecraft barely half a kilometer to the right kept everyone on their toes. Pluto could be seen on the aft side of the ship, now receding from view as the spacecraft sped back toward Earth. The distant Neptune and its thirteen moons were now coming into view from the fore window. Greg, who was looking out of one of the portals at the beautiful silhouette of Neptune, spoke, "Did you know that Neptune has an internal heat source? It gives out more than twice the heat than it takes in from the sun." To which Thor asked, "Fascinating, and how do you know that?" "I studied it. Before this mission, I had graduated in astrophysics, had to learn all that stuff. Now it is categorized in the 'useless information' section of my brain." They all had a good chuckle at that remark. As the rest of the crew seemed to be vaguely interested in what Greg was saying, possibly, if nothing else, to divert their attention from their immediate neighbors, he continued, "The internal heat source is not unique. Saturn and Jupiter also exhibit this phenomenon. Like all gas giants, it does have a rocky core. One of its moons, Triton, is as large as the Earth's moon. The other twelve are pretty much the size of large asteroids. Neptune, too, has rings, but they are not as emphasized as Saturn's. The planet looks blue because it has a lot of hydrogen and methane in its atmosphere. The absorption of red by the methane gas causes it to reflect blue light. When we get closer, you will see a beautiful blue hue reflecting off the surface, much the same as Earth…" He let that thought trail off. The brief interlude had served its purpose. One of the reasons for fatigue is when the human mind is focused on a topic and does not get a chance to think about anything else. This little lecture was a gateway for each crew to think of other things, let their minds drift, wander into a daydream, think about anything else to relieve the stress, perhaps even have a little snooze.

If they were fortunate enough for the journey to continue, the next planet they would encounter would be Uranus, the gas giant, followed by two other gas giants, Saturn with its distinctive rings, then Jupiter, with its enigmatic giant red spot. After Jupiter, there were the aptly named rocky planets, also known as the inner planets. For now, the rocky planets were too distant to see, about two and a half years of journey time at the current speed. Although oxygen and the fusion fuel would last for that duration, water and food would not. The crew would have to go into HySleep at some time before reaching Earth. For now, though, there was no concern about food and water. There was work to be done, preferably peaceful work. The ultimate option, the one that no one wanted to think about, was the nuclear option, quite literally to set off one or more nuclear bombs that were loaded into the spacecraft prior to departure from Earth. This would possibly mean the destruction of not only the MG but also the TE, since no one was certain as to exactly how far they needed to retreat, in space, to be safe. The problem was if it was decided to deploy the nuclear bombs, they would have to eject the bombs from the TE, then retreat to a safe distance. There was really no way of doing that since it took so long for the TE to change direction or speed. By the time it took the TE to change speed, the alien crafts could easily have changed speed or direction, rendering the bombs ineffective. Therefore, they would need to set off the bombs while they were inside the TE, which meant sacrificing themselves. The ultimate goal of this mission was to safeguard humankind. The safety of the crew was secondary. Anything else, any knowledge gleaned, any new technology learned from the aliens would be considered as a bonus. The crew understood this. There were four so-called engineers, in addition to the scientists, who made up the crew. On Earth, they would be known as soldiers, highly accomplished soldiers, the special kind that get recruited into units that are so secretive that only a handful of people know of their existence. They were all prepared for the ultimate sacrifice, if necessary.

Each crew member was in a different place, mentally. They had just had something to eat, and the last spoken word was that Neptune has a blue color just like Earth and Greg had left it at that. One astronaut had drifted off in the direction of Earth, visualizing how Earth would look compared with Neptune. Another had drifted off thinking about other habitable worlds that humans could colonize. The third was thinking about the gas giants and how their collective and immense gravities had kept the smaller inner planets, specifically Earth, safe from asteroids. The rest were napping or blankly staring out of the starboard window, visually monitoring for any signs of activity. During this post-prandial torpor, the speaker came on. "Titan Explorer crew, we have new instructions for you. We have analyzed the data in detail, and the team here indicates that another EVA is required. Although the entire pyramid is covered with this material and is fairly even, at one location at the front of the pyramid, just below the point where the vertices meet, there is a slight indentation. It is as if something large had struck the pyramid and dented it. This indentation is very slight, more like a fender bender, not a full-scale accident. One cannot really see it, unless observed very closely. The same crew as before should go and take a closer look. This time, however, exit Explorer 1 and touch the material that is covering the pyramids. Of course, you will be wearing gloves. However, you may still be able to determine if it is hard or soft. You can get a tactile feel of the material even through the gloves. In addition, take a flashlight and visually examine the material closely. Use your knife to cut a small piece. Make sure it is small. We do not want the aliens to interpret our actions as nefarious or an attempt at sabotage. Do this activity on the pyramid that is closest to the TE craft. Also, be careful not to do anything threatening or sudden. We do not want them to initiate an attack. Gently does it should be the motto. The reason for this is—there may be an entrance, an air lock or something behind the dent. As a first step, we want to find out if this material comes off. In a subsequent EVA, depending on what we find, we can try to take off the cover. Over."

Obviously, due to the limitations of communication, the instructions were prepared in advance and delivered in simple sentences, with time to register and digest the information. If anything special was being communicated that the crew was required to note down it was done so that the crew aboard had time to get the items ready to take notes on their laptop and the same instruction was repeated. The message could also be rewound and replayed. This time, however, the instructions were simple and easy to remember—go out again and try to cut a tiny piece off, and see what it is made of—simple.

"We read you, Mission Control, will start right away, over and out." John did not need to say anymore. The instruction was clear, the purpose was clear, and no one on board had any other ideas or questions when he looked around before acknowledging the instructions. Moreover, this was expected. The first EVA mission was a success. However, more information was needed. Moreover, they were keen to start right away. At the moment they had too much time on their hands.

Although it was not much, the work on the TE was around the clock. Some kind of sleep/wake rhythm had come back to each crew member. It was obvious that they were expected to work 24-7. Therefore, eating and frequent naps had become part of the routine. Not everyone, however, slept or napped at the same time. It was essential that at least two were on guard duty at all times. Guard duty was monotonous. The two responsible for the task had to keep a watchful eye on the pyramids and monitor them electronically. However, the alien EVA had not yet materialized. If the human EVA encountered the alien EVA, the humans did not have a script to follow. John had instructed the crew to improvise. There were weapons on board the Explorer as well as on the TE. One of the support crew left behind would suit up and deploy munitions against the aliens, if that eventuality arose. John had also asked Baz to abandon his support role and be ready to jump into action on his command, if this situation were to present itself.

The same crew readied themselves for the second EVA. It was agreed that Greg, fresh with the new experience of navigating the rover, would be at the controls. Manny would step out from the vehicle and perform the manual tasks requested by Mission Control on

Earth. Ken and Kristen would be seated in the back seats, as before, and support the operation. Kristen would be responsible for taking the visual images as she had done earlier. Ken's main duty was to be available where assistance was needed, as the free hand on the rover looking out for the safety of all, especially Manny. Ken was required to perform each EVA activity, since he was the linguist and communications expert. For his own good and the success of the mission he had to get over his fear of zero gravity and the uncomfortable feeling of floating in space. No one had any clue as to how that communication would take place and what the level of success would be achieved at transferring information between the two species alien to each other. The two rover vehicles used for the EVA activity were identical; John asked that Explorer 2 be deployed for this mission to make sure that all systems on this vehicle worked. Explorer 1 had already been verified as functioning satisfactorily in the first outing.

"Ready to undock," announced Manny, when all four were seated in the rover.

"Copy that, opening the hatch," came the response from the command module, and they went through the familiar sequence of undocking and moving away from the rotating TE.

"Clear, you can close the hatch."

"Roger that. Remember, discretion is the better part of valor. Be careful out there." This time they were going to touch the alien craft. What would the reaction be? The tension among the crew left on the command module was higher. However, the crew on Explorer 2 seemed as calm as before. Especially Ken, he was not hyperventilating, and when Kristen looked over, she noticed that he had his eyes closed, possibly thinking of something pleasant and using the techniques of self-suggestion, hypnosis, or perhaps meditation in order to remain calm. He knew that the weakest link in the chain is the level of oxygen, and if he was down to twenty minutes in the main tank, it was time to abandon whatever they were doing and return. John had revised the minimum threshold upon the urging of Greg that ten minutes plus thirty minutes was acceptable since he had become so familiar with maneuvering the rovers that he could be back within twenty minutes, which would still leave twenty minutes in reserve. John, after some consideration and discussion with Baz, agreed to the compromise of twenty minutes, which would be reviewed and revised down if things keep going as well as the first EVA mission. Besides, this mission was going to the nearest pyramid, the one labeled Pyramid Eight by Mission Control on Earth. If they were going farther there would need to be a bigger margin for error.

Greg surprised himself as to how good he had become. He had the feel of the rover. They made it to the pyramid in less than twenty minutes, eighteen, to be exact. Due to the limited air they carried, the more time they saved traveling, the more time they could spend investigating. They were in front of the indentation. The crew in the explorer located it, and it was a slight depression in the material—exactly as Mission Control on Earth had indicated. "Ready to open the lid," announced Greg. The rovers had a panoramic Plexiglas top hinged on one side so it could be opened like a lid.

"Proceed with caution," came the response from John in the command module.

Ken had just opened his eyes as the cover was pushed back on its hinge. The effect of being faced with wide-open space literally took his breath away. Everything was new to him, and time limitations had curtailed his training program. Whereas before he was comfortable with the knowledge that he was comfortably ensconced with a roof above his head, now he looked up and saw nothing—all the way to infinity. His reaction was palpable. Kristen could see the jolt as his arms and legs quivered. Realizing what had happened, in a flash Kristen held his arms and comforted him. "Ken, you are safe. You still have the seat belt tying you down to the rover. Just think of yourself as being on a roller coaster."

Manny had unbuckled in preparation to reach out over the side of the rover to grab a piece of the material to dissect from the pyramid. He turned around 180 degrees, and while kneeling on the seat he, too, grabbed Ken's shoulder. "Ken, you are safe here. We will not unbuckle you if that makes you feel uncomfortable."

Hearing this commotion in the dSE Nicole chimed in, "Ken, do the relaxation exercises."

There was no answer. Ken's eyes were closed, and no one could tell whether he had lost consciousness. Finally, as John was about to speak, Ken opened his eyes and mentioned, "I hate roller coasters."

A few seconds later he continued, "Sorry about that. I feel fine now. I did not expect what the feeling would be like when the top opened—I panicked. But I am okay now."

After a moment when everyone breathed a sigh of relief, Kristen spoke, "Ken, you stay here and I will help Manny. But we will have to switch places."

Ken insisted, "I am okay, and I will perform my tasks. Don't worry—I will be fine."

John, who did not want a lengthy discussion, cut in, "Ken, what if Manny needs help and you hesitate?"

Ken insisted, "I will be fine. We are wasting time arguing about this. Let's start the process." He was firm and determined and more than anything did not want the ignominy of being replaced by another crew member.

John made the commander's decision. "Okay, but if you feel the panic coming on again, for the safety of everyone, say something. We don't want to lose anyone."

Ken acquiesced to that statement. "Sure, no problem." But he insisted, "I will be fine—it was just a momentary thing."

While the last conversation was occurring, Kristen was continuing to work the camera on the laptop. She had remembered to bring some material to cover the controls in Explorer 2 so that the lights on the instrument panel would not interfere with the laptop camera and the pyramid could be observed in better contrast. Greg was expertly nudging the rover as close to the pyramid as he could. Manny was double-checking that the tether attaching him to Explorer 2 was secure—especially critical after the recent episode.

The rover was about five meters away. Manny was tethered to the rover. He gingerly stood up and put his foot on the side of the rover. He gently pushed off, and Greg had to nudge the rover to hold the position because the free-floating rover reacted to the push by going the other way. The push that Manny took was not as gentle as he had hoped. He was trying to compensate for the artificial gravity of the pyramids, and he crashed into the pyramid. To his surprise it felt soft, as if he had bumped into a foam mattress. If the material on the pyramid was hard, he thought to himself, the force of the impact could have cracked the visor on his space suit helmet, killing him instantly. No one else in the rover realized the force of the impact as sound does not carry in a vacuum and the material on the pyramid absorbed the impact with a soft thud that only he felt and heard.

"Damn...pushed off too strong!" he exclaimed. Gently, with his arms he lifted himself from the pyramid, as if doing a push-up. "This material reminds me of foam." His words were being heard by the other three as well as the four in the TE and also were being recorded in Kristen's laptop. "I feel like I am being pulled gently towards the vertex. That in part caused me to miscalculate my jump."

Greg said, "I know, I am compensating by applying reverse thrust. If you look back at the tether you will notice that it is fully taut."

Ken added, "The tether is at full stretch. You have taken up all the slack, you cannot go any further," as he was holding on to it and helping Manny by pulling him closer to the indentation.

Manny gently pushed at the material in the reverse direction to the gentle tug he was feeling, as if trying to pull the pyramid closer to the rover. The foam gathered a little under the pressure of his hands, but there was no other effect. "Definitely some kind of foam, cannot think of its purpose. When I release the pressure, the foam reverts back to being flat. The gather and wrinkles go away." As he said that, he took out the knife that he had in a sheath, a weapon for close-range combat for all intents and purposes, and tried to scratch the surface of the foam.

Ken became alarmed at what he was seeing. "Manny, Mission Control said to take the material from the corner of the pyramid, what are you doing?"

"I know, I am not taking anything from here, just checking to see what this is made of. And you know what, I cannot scratch or cut it. I am applying full force, but this does not want to be cut. It is like soft foam but resistant to cutting. Very interesting." As he announced that, he took out his sidearm and took aim.

"Manny, wait. Don't shoot—" It was too late. Ken realized what would happen, but he did not see it in time. Manny had already discharged his weapon. There was a flash, but no sound due to the vacuum. The gun recoiled along with Manny, and the top half of his body was pushed in the opposite direction to the projectile and his body somersaulted about his waist.

Ken continued, "Shouldn't have done it, Manny, you may send the wrong message to the aliens."

With the help of Ken working the tether, Manny righted himself. When the projectile hit the foam, the latter seemed to buckle and absorb the impact and returned to its original shape.

"What happened?" The concerned voice of John in the command module was heard in the earpieces of the four performing this EVA activity.

"All okay, a gun was fired and nothing happened. Will provide a full report when we return," Ken informed John in as calming a voice as he could muster, given the circumstances.

Greg indicated incredulously, "Did you see that? When the bullet hit, the foam absorbed the impact and stopped the bullet dead in its track. The point of impact is not damaged at all. In fact you cannot even make out where it hit."

Ken responded, "Yes, and the bullet has rolled up with gravity being exerted by the pyramid and is now about fifty meters further away than the point of impact. It has rolled up in the direction of the pull we are experiencing. I can see that it is now about halfway up the pyramid. Manny, it is time for you to come back into the rover."

"Okay, coming back." Ken helped by pulling on the tether and brought Manny back to the rover.

In order to save time Greg announced, "No need to close the lid. We will be taking an open-air space trip to the edge to see if Manny can cut a piece off. Ken, will you be okay with that?"

Ken, having assisted Manny back into the rover, indicated, "I am fine now. Like I said, it was the initial shock that made me panic." As Manny was back inside and secured, Ken announced, "We are secured. You can take us there when you are ready."

Once they reached the edge of the pyramid, Manny performed another similar activity, this time with a flashlight. "I cannot describe it as anything else but foam. There does not appear to be any place where I can cut a piece off. It seems like it is hewn from one piece of material. It has no joins, even at the edges. Trying to cut…"

Ken noticed Manny's hand moving back and forth in an effort to cut the material. "My knife is getting blunt, but this thing is not coming off. It is so soft, yet resistant to cutting or sawing. I cannot make a dent in this foam."

All this had taken over an hour, and Baz was aware of the elapsed time. "Time to return," he announced succinctly. "You have been out for about an hour and sixteen minutes. I am sure Ken has used up more."

Ken, too, was aware of the time and informed Manny that he was pulling him in as soon as he had sheathed the knife. No point taking any risk of losing pressure. It was certain death if the knife inadvertently punctured the pressure suit. "Ready," Manny announced, and Ken tugged on the cord securing Manny. About three minutes later, Manny was in the rover and Ken had closed the Plexiglas dome and locked the latch. About a minute after that, they were on their way back. After going through the usual process of John opening the hatch on the TE and Greg activating the auto docking process, the four returned to the command module. The explorer docked and started the charging process automatically, readying itself for the next trip. After disrobing from their space suits, they entered the main module where the rest of the crew was awaiting them. All seemed excited and elated, Manny more so than the others. This EVA had also gone mostly according to plan. The only concern was whether Manny was also developing a tendency, similar to Thor, to do things without first considering the consequences. But he, like the others, was too much of a professional. He would notice any unusual tendencies and take corrective action before anyone had a chance to mention it.

After a quick debriefing session on board, it seemed that Ken had learned to control his tendency to hyperventilate. Greg had become very adept at navigating the rovers. Kristen was her usual calm efficient self—going about her routine of docking the laptop and sending the gathered data to Mission Control. It would be some time before they received the information. Various teams analyzed it in every which way and communicated the findings and the next steps to the crew on TE.

However, Manny was still jumpy, with the adrenaline still flowing. Nicole asked him to perform routine exercises to help dissipate the adrenaline. Manny complied. John was slightly concerned about the gung ho behavior Manny had exhibited, but in order to keep team spirits high decided not say anything either to him or discuss it with anyone else. Besides, by design there was no privacy on board the TE. John was commander of the mission not only because of his leadership abilities, but also his knack of realizing when to speak and when to let things slide. He was a keen judge of character. With all the waiting that the crew was subjected to, it would not be prudent to speak about this. The indiscretion could be overlooked as something enthusiastic that a crew member did. Possibly others had wanted to do something similar. If nothing else, it was a tension breaker.

After some reconstituted food and water, the crew on TE was relaxing, doing what they were, by now, accustomed to doing—music, movies, games, exercises, or napping. Other than the two guards, Baz and Thor, who were currently detailed to watch the pyramids, the rest of the crew were engaged in one of these activities which were meant to take the mind off the monotony of space travel. After Manny's antics of shooting a projectile, there was now a much-increased chance that they would launch an attack, although it was unknown what form it would take. The guards responsible for keeping an eye on the MG were watching with heightened intensity, looking for any sign of activity or unusual movement. Self-preservation, no matter how much this mission could be construed as a suicide mission, was still strong and very difficult to extricate from a human being. Only religious fervor or territorial integrity could motivate a human to deliberately take risks to their own life, but even then, the individual had to be trained almost into a trance. Hypnosis is the word some psychologists would use, and only the weak-minded embarked on these kinds of suicide missions. The crew of the TE was anything but weak. They were picked for being strong in mind and body. However, no one could account for a rush of blood, a human tendency no matter how much training one had received. Even the strong make bad decisions, especially in stressful situations. Maybe Manny's indiscretion would be put down to a learning experience and he would not repeat it.

The speaker came on. Mission Control on Earth had analyzed the data and was about to communicate new instructions.

"Hi all, this is Tracey," came the voice with a slight southern drawl. "We have analyzed the data. Good job, everyone. Nice camera work again. Great driving! Overall everyone did a fantastic job. Needless to say, we are as baffled with the composition of the foam material, as you are. The scientists have not seen nor have any knowledge of anything similar to it on Earth. It appears to be soft and yet resistant to cutting and immune to sharp instruments. The best minds here think that it is possibly used as a protective material. During their long journey, they may come across many tiny fragments of rock, ice, and dust floating around in space. The large pieces they can detect and avoid. However, the small pieces may not be detectable or avoidable, and at the speeds they are traveling, if they hit even the smallest ice fragment, the damage would be catastrophic." The speaker had prepared the speech and was obviously reading off some material. Due to communication difficulties, it could not be a smooth dialogue. It had to be a series of monologues, a soliloquy.

Tracey continued with the southern drawl, "When the projectile was fired, the material deformed, as if to absorb the impact, then it came back to its original form." In an effort to keep team spirits high and the attitude as positive as possible, the experts at Mission Control had obviously not wanted to show up Manny and his unintended indiscretion. They were going to sidestep the whole issue with the following innocuous sentence, "We have to be very careful about how our actions are perceived. Henceforth, we have to proceed very deliberately and carefully." She continued, putting a positive spin on the event, "One benefit of the accidental discharge of the weapon was that the projectile rolled up towards the vertex but stopped halfway up the side of the pyramid. You went exactly where we had instructed you to go in the last communication. You were by the slight depres-sion on the pyramid just above the base of the pyramid. That tells us that the gravity that is being artificially generated is stronger near the point where the projectile stopped. As if a magnet had attracted a piece of metal and moved it closer to where the magnetic field is strongest. That also explains the gentle tug that Manny had felt when he was out of the rover. So here is what we want you to do next."

She took a breath before continuing. "We have a theory that since they have not done it yet, they will most likely not launch an attack. So unload the larger weapon in the rover and use the space to load the blowtorch. You will use it to attempt to burn through the material, just a small area for now, as an experiment to check if the foam will burn off. Do not unload all the weapons, just in case something is needed. We do not want you all to be target practice for them. Unload the nuke, which will provide ample room to load the pressurized canister for the blowtorch. Go to the depression and cut out a piece that is about the size of the palm of a hand, about ten cen-timeters by ten centimeters square, no more. We think the depres-sion could be an entryway, a hatch or air lock of some kind located under the foam. The recommendation is to burn off the small piece from approximately close to the center of the depression, not the corner or any other part of the pyramid. This time, however, we are asking that Baz be at the control of the rover and Thor use the blow-torch. John, unfortunately you will have to wait. It is not prudent for both you and Baz to be away from the TE at the same time. Kristen, you, too, stay back for this one. We may not make contact with the aliens this time 'round either. So, to summarize, Baz and Thor will replace Greg and Kristen. Ken and Manny will make the third and fourth members. We thought it is important that we give everyone the opportunity to get used to going out, but we need to balance that with other criteria such as who is staying back in the TE, how many excursions has each individual taken, and other items of that nature. Ken is as he is a master of languages and he needs the training. Each excursion is making him better, and his enthusiasm to get better is noticed and appreciated."

John knew that grounding Manny for EVA number 3 would not send the right message, and Mission Control had also realized that. As for Ken, it was true that he was being a trooper and was determined to get over his anxiety—which was ultimately good for the mission. The instructions were unambiguous. As usual John replied, "Copy that, Mission Control, will comply per instructions," and even before the message was received on Earth, preparations were already underway for EVA number 3.

KEEPING TABS

The cyborg was keeping a close watch and analyzing every step that the humans were taking outside the pyramid. She realized that the visitors were being very tentative—that was to be expected. With no obvious threat, the humans would gradually get bolder and slowly work their way into the pyramid. That was their nature, and she knew it. It was time to invite them in—so to speak. She would make small a nonthreatening gesture and let the curiosity get the better of them. They would have no option but to walk into her trap.

The hatch already unlocked, she had hoped that they would be able to cut through the material—the fact that they could not articulated to her the primitive state of their technology. If she pulled back the cover, that gesture would pique their inquisitiveness. In addition, it would expose the hatch. She had to retract the cover, but she had to time it right. It was a calculated risk as the cover was used to protect the craft from damaging debris. But this stretch of space was relatively free of any small objects. The large planets had taken care of cleaning up the surroundings. However, there was another risk—the cover also made the pyramids invisible to detection by radio waves. This made the craft very difficult to see from Earth, but she did not care about that. The bigger risk and the only reason for using the cloaking mechanism was the potential of exposing the pyramids to the other pursuers—the ones they have been trying to avoid long before the craft from Earth appeared. She was playing a dangerous game, but in her mind, it was worth it. Having thought about it carefully, she waited to make her move.

EVA MISSION 3

It was a small thermonuclear device, but it was hard work unclasping it from the rover and securing it in the hold. The two rovers occupied a lot of space in the dSE, but the four engineers were able to perform the task. More hands would be better, but the already cramped space prevented free movement, and adding more bodies would be a hindrance than help. Loading the canister, full of fuel, to power the blowtorch was much easier. Manny would help Thor when he left the rover for the cutting mission, Ken would use his laptop to record the events, and Baz would navigate.

By now this routine was becoming second nature, even to Baz and Thor, who had not yet been out on an EVA mission. Everyone got to their seats in Explorer 1, and Baz announced, "John, ready for EVA 3."

"Righty ho, copy that, look up and you will see the hatch opening."

In keeping with old sailor talk, "Aye, aye, Captain," came the response from Baz. Moments later the light came on to undock, and Baz hit the switch. Moments later, he said, "We are clear. Close the hatch."

John acknowledged in an even deeper pirate talk, "Shiver me timbers. Ya will 'ave yer wish, lad."

Clearly this had gone as far as it could. Time to get serious.

Greg became the de facto second-in-command when Baz was out, and took over the functions that Baz had performed for each of the previous two EVA missions. From the TE starboard window he saw the rover inch closer to Pyramid Eight. Baz seemed to have the grasp of the controls pretty quick, he thought. From the distance, he saw that the rover had stopped near the depression on the pyra-

141

mid. A quick check of time indicated that Baz had done pretty well. Whereas he had taken almost thirty minutes to get to the pyramid for EVA 1 and almost cut the time by half for EVA 2, Baz had taken twenty-one minutes for his first time out. He had obviously watched and learned. He noticed Ken open the lid and stand up in order to rotate it fully on its hinge and out of the way. Clearly Ken was adapting to this very fast. Then he saw Thor get out of the rover with the blowtorch in hand. When he jumped off he did exactly what Manny had done, crashed into the foam.

Thor immediately exclaimed, "Damn it...It is very difficult to figure out how much force to apply. I barely jumped off the rover. This thing must have pulled me with its artificial gravity."

The other seven humans in the vicinity heard the comment.

"Going to light the flame now," came the voice over the wireless. Greg continued to monitor from the TE. Thor had perched himself as best he could on the face of the giant pyramid. A flame came on and became sharper like a welding gun. He slowly moved it toward the foam so that the hottest part would touch the surface and hopefully cut it. As the flame touched the surface, Thor sensed something moving but could not figure it out. "Something is not right, ahh!"

Greg could see that Thor had moved up the pyramid till the slack on his tether was completely taken up. As he reached the end of the slack he was suddenly jerked back and was turned upside down. This violent action freed the lit blowtorch from his hand, and it started floating in space, pointing in any and every direction at random, with the flame still lit. Manny, who was already holding the pipe feeding the blowtorch from the canister, thinking quickly, pulled the pipe and got control of the nozzle and extinguished the flame. The blowtorch could have burned through a space suit or damaged the rover, if it had come in contact with either of them. The flame was hot enough to melt metal. Thor was floating, being gently tugged upward with the artificial gravity. Baz had instinctively compensated by hitting the reverse thruster. After the flame was out, Manny pulled Thor and straightened him to point the right way up relative all the other occupants of the rover. All this took place instinctively, without a word being spoken. The soldiers were a breed apart, and an almost certain disaster was averted.

Thor finally spoke, a little shaken, even for one as experienced as him, "I don't know what happened. I had just started cutting and had made an incision when the foam started moving. I mean, I had cut the foam. It was starting to melt away." The foam on which Thor was standing had started moving. No one had realized that since each was focused on their activity and it was difficult to see. Thor had felt it because he was standing on the foam. But before he realized it, he was violently jerked back, there being no more slack available on the tether.

Manny had noticed that the foam covering was being with-drawn and informed, "It is moving…Look." He shone the flashlight at the foam and panned it as far as the light would carry. "The foam is moving up, as if it is being retracted." It was difficult to see the dark foam moving. Manny had to look closely and strain his eyes to notice the tiny patterns on this vast expanse of foam.

They watched this spectacle unfold before their eyes. About two or three minutes later, Manny confirmed, "Confirm that, the foam is definitely being retracted." He said this as the end of the foam came into view and journeyed upward. By this time everyone was aboard the rover, the lid closed and ready to make the dash to the safety of the mother ship.

Baz reacted quickly and, as he did so, announced to everyone so they were aware of what he was attempting, "Checking to see where the foam is going." This was not part of the protocol that they were asked to perform for this EVA mission, so he had to keep everyone apprised of every move that he made. With that he moved the rover, with its passengers, up the face of the pyramid. He moved to the very top, where there was a temporary absence of gravity. Looking down from the vertex, "The foam is being retracted into the pyramid through a small opening at the top," he announced.

Greg, playing it safe, issued the order to return. "You should return now. They may start something, now that they are not covered with the material anymore."

Baz and everyone in the relatively defenseless rover agreed, "Roger that, coming back."

Their way back was exactly the reverse—they had to come down the face of the pyramid then across empty space to the TE.

As they were descending the face of the pyramid Ken mentioned, "The color of the pyramid seemed to be only slightly less black than the foam, possibly because it is metallic and reflects more light than the foam. This structure is perfect, I mean, no imperfections. I cannot see any place where there may be screws, rivets, or any other form of joins. This is perfectly smooth. Except, wait"—they passed the point where they had tried to cut—"there seems to be a hatch that can be opened. The depression seems to be a doorway of some kind, an entry into the structure." They had not noticed it initially in the panic. Their eyes were following the path of the foam.

Baz did not wait to study it anymore. There would be more opportunities later, if the aliens did not launch an attack. It was now a good time to get back as soon as possible, without making any mistakes that may delay the return. They did not even have the large weapon. It was unloaded to make space for the welding tool. Besides, Ken had taped the whole event as well as the now naked pyramid. It was already known that the other three faces did not have a similar doorway, as no indentation was found from the earlier EVA missions. The other three sides were perfectly smooth, as if cast from a single piece of metal from a giant furnace and shaped using a giant lathe. The return was uneventful and super quick. Baz made it back in record time, not that anyone was competing, but it was good to know that the return journey could be performed in about sixteen minutes.

After the docking and disrobing, the first item on Ken's agenda was to dock the laptop and send the information back to Mission Control as soon as possible. Time to rest and think about the events that would come later, while the analysis was taking place on Earth. And so, they waited for the next set of instructions. The unspoken but mutually agreed upon routine after an EVA was for the EVA crew to have the first priority to nap. Once refreshed, they could change duties with another person. It had also become common practice by now not to eat alone. These small social etiquettes all helped keep the morale up. Of course, after the incidents with the pyramid earlier, everyone was on edge, in case an attack materialized. Manny had more than redeemed himself, by being alert and taking instant action to control the flame from the blowtorch and thus avoiding a potential disaster and perhaps death. The crew on the TE also noticed that all the other pyramids had also retracted the foam. Earlier they were like dark asteroids speeding toward Earth. Now they looked like sinister objects, with the dark metal periodically reflecting the little light available at this distance from the sun. The crew had no idea of the elapsed time from the time they were woken from HySleep. Neptune, however, first seen from the port window, was now visible from the starboard window, beyond the MG. That provided confirmation that the TE had turned 180 degrees and now was heading in the opposite direction. Everyone, the TE spacecraft as well as the alien ships, was speeding toward Earth. In the far distance was coming into view what everyone guessed was the planet Uranus. They were still too far away to see any of her moons.

"Hi, Sarah here!" the speaker came on suddenly, jolting everyone from their daydream. She continued, "Excellent job on EVA 3. Needless to say, everyone here was very excited at the events that took place. Looks like there is life on board the pyramids. We are, however, as confused as you are, why they are not attempting to make any contact. We feel that they know of your presence, but may be afraid. It does not stand to reason that if they came to explore new worlds, they should initiate or respond by trying some form of communication. Maybe they do not have any explorer rover vehicles as we do, but they could try radio or light transmissions. They have got to have some mechanism to communicate. However, they have not tried anything. One team here in Mission Control feels that they want to lull you into a false sense of security before launching an attack, in whatever form it may be. Another team thinks they have no weapons. A third team believes that every alien is in hibernation and the reactions that you witnessed are purely defensive and automatic. Notice that when Thor tried to cut, the foam retracted not just from this pyramid, but also the others. So the retractions may have been a preprogrammed event, or it may be a reaction to prevent damage. If it is the latter, then we have to assume that Pyramid Eight, where the cut was attempted, sent some kind of signal to the other pyramids. As you can tell, there is no consensus between any team. We just do not know yet. There are still too many questions and not enough answers."

After a brief pause, presumably for the audience to digest the analysis, Sarah continued, "We analyzed the video, and looked at various images of the door lock that you all noticed. There does not seem to be any other way to breach the pyramid. Metal this size will have to be very thick in order to support itself and the internal structure. Otherwise, it will buckle into itself. So the blowtorch will not work. You will run out of fuel long before a hole to breach into the structure can be made. So the only option is to try the door. We looked at the door, and it seems like a simple mechanism. There is a latch which can be turned. It should open inward, into the pyramid, as it may be too heavy to open outward. Also, we think that their craft is pressurized, just like ours. We cannot assume that the air is breathable by us. Nevertheless the pressure indicates that the door could be designed to open by swinging into the pyramid. However, factor in the possibility that the hatch door may violently swing open outward, due to the pressure inside. While unlocking, step aside. We don't want to have anybody slammed by a door. Since there has been no contact and you are getting closer to Earth each passing minute, you have to push on to force an encounter with the occupants, but with extreme caution. It is one thing investigating the outside of the pyramid. It is totally different to breach into their space. They may take extreme offence to that. Another EVA is needed, with the same crew as EVA 3, but this time, replace Manny with Kristen so that if you come in contact with biological life-forms, both Ken and Kristen are available. Baz will navigate. Thor will be the support. If you are successful in opening the hatch, do not enter, look inside from the entrance, close and lock the hatch, and return. This action will hopefully tell them that we are not looking to be the aggressors. Based on the experience with this EVA, a future EVA may require you to go in. However, this should be short. Travel there, open the hatch, and if it opens, close it and return. Simple. If it does not open, come back. Do not try anything adventurous."

Another pause. "Finally we now know that whatever the foam material did, for one thing, it shielded the pyramids from radio waves. Other nations who have radio telescopes have discovered the pyramids and have trained them in your direction. They cannot see much yet as you are so far away. However, many nations are monitoring the pyramids. People are speculating. The internet is abuzz. Social media networking sites are rife with speculation. I will leave it to your imagination. We have had to announce the true nature of our mission to the world, and all the nations send their best wishes to you. It is the interest of humankind that you are representing. We are cooperating with everyone to discuss defensive measures that can be deployed closer to Earth, in case their reasons for paying us a visit are nefarious. That is all for now… Over."

Again, the message was well-thought-out and well delivered. There was no cause for any questions. The message was clear. They knew exactly what the next step would be.

John responded, "Copy, will do exactly as informed."

RISK

By withdrawing the foam cover the cyborg knew that she was taking a risk; the enemy that they had previously pursued into the outer reaches of this solar system could now be pursuing them and could detect the pyramids more easily. But to capture these humans was of paramount importance to her. It was worth the risk because the early withdrawal of the material will only be noticed if and only if the service engineers analyzed the data upon their return to their home planet. Even if they noticed it, she would be long gone. So she would have nobody or nothing to answer to—no realignment of the mind or no retraining and certainly no early termination to endure.

EVA MISSION 4

This next EVA would be a short one. The instructions were clear, open the door, close the door, and come back. Baz had already left his seat to prepare for the EVA. Greg would take up the task of watching and monitoring the fourth mission from the dSE. John, as usual, was at the controls of the dSE. Manny and Nicole were in support of both Greg and John, should they need it.

The increasingly common routine of getting into the space suit, getting into the explorer, and going through the undocking procedure went by without incident. Within fifteen minutes of undocking they were at Pyramid Eight. This was now the fastest they were able to traverse from one craft to another. This time, however, two of the explorer crew would get off the rover and attempt to open the door. The two were Thor and Ken. Kristen would stay on the rover working the laptop camera, and Baz would stay at the controls of the rover, ready to leave in a hurry. Greg, who was monitoring them from the TE, could see that they had arrived and were ready after Ken had opened the overhead lid of the rover.

"Ready to ring the doorbell." Thor was ready to try to unlatch the portal.

"Roger that, be careful and don't let the door hit you," responded Greg with a smile on his face. He hoped that the smile would carry through the wireless, which it did in the lilt in his voice. Thor and Ken looked at each other acknowledging the joke, albeit trivial. Kristen had decoupled the tiny specially fitted wireless camera on the laptop and handed it to Thor who clipped it onto his space suit, like a lapel pin. The detachable camera came with a small power source and was able to relay the images within a short distance of the laptop. It also had circuitry to enhance images in conditions where light was not sufficient and was capable of displaying images to the tiny screen built into the visor of each helmet.

Looking directly at Ken, Thor said, "I will jump first, and then you can jump once I have positioned myself on the face of the pyramid." He wanted to exude confidence as Ken was still not completely at ease with zero gravity. Then he added, "Remember to apply only the slightest of force to push off. The gravity from the pyramid pulls you in." With that he jumped, with the tether dangling behind. Once in position, he beckoned to Ken to follow him, which he did. The gravity was deceptive, and even though he applied what he considered very light pressure to jump, he hit the face of the pyramid. However, no damage was done since Kristen, anticipating this, had held on to the tether and was feeding the slack slowly. Baz compensated for the shift in momentum to the rover caused by the jump with the application of thrusters.

"Nice job, Kristen," Baz acknowledged. Ken was faring surprisingly well. Thor showed no concern at all that he would have to support Ken.

Ken and Thor positioned themselves on the side of what appeared to be the latch, assuming that the hinge for the door was on the opposite end. It would be illogical to have the latch and the hinge on the same side of the door. Then, as planned they unhooked themselves from the tether that had secured them to the rover and hooked themselves to each other.

"Ding-dong," Thor said jokingly as he turned the latch. The undoing of the latch resulted in some air to leak out of the pyramid. The moisture in the air as it escaped made an ephemeral white cloud before dissipating into the vast emptiness of space. Noticing the white cloud, Thor commented, "I think there is some kind of air inside. Not sure if it is breathable." As he spoke those words he put his hand on the door in order to push it open. The door immediately gave way—there was no resistance that one would expect while pushing such a heavy-looking door. The next sound from Thor was "Ahhh!" as he fell in. Since they were precariously perched on the angular face of the pyramid and there were no handholds or for that matter any other support, the artificial gravity from within caused him to lose balance and fall in through the doorway. The momentum of the fall caused him to roll all the way down to the next door, not a great distance but further than the length of the tether. Seeing that Thor was being dragged in, Ken tried to brace himself and hold on to the corner of the doorway. However, due to lack of friction on the smooth metal, he was unable to hold on and was dragged in with Thor.

This was visible from the rover as well as the TE. Baz spoke, "Thor, Ken, are you guys okay?"

"Yeah, okay… Coming out… Slipped and lost my footing… Door opened too easily," was embarrassingly muttered by Thor.

It was dark inside, and they seemed to be falling down toward the base of the pyramid. The distance they fell was very short. The time during which they were dropping was about a second. Instinctively, Thor took out the flashlight and turned it on. They were in a narrow tunnel, a stairway with another door behind them. They shone the light at the door which had a similar latch to the first one. Thor shone the light from the direction from which he had fallen and saw that the door was still open and a set of stairs leading up to the door. They had indeed fallen toward the base of the pyramid. However, the distance of the fall was less than ten meters. Fortunately, they were somewhat cushioned by the EVA suits.

Thor stood up and, while helping Ken to his feet, mentioned, "No damage done except to our pride." Ken knew he was referring to the embarrassment of not anticipating the ease with which the door opened. Ken nodded with a wry smile. Without speaking any further, they made their way to the door, deliberately climbing up step by step to avoid any further awkwardness. Once they were through it Thor closed the latch behind him, locked it to its original position, and the two returned to the rover. Baz looked at Thor and asked, "What took you so long?"

Surprised, Thor detected alarm in his voice. When he looked around to Baz he noticed a tense expression. Surprised, Thor asked, "What do you mean? We fell about ten meters into the pyramid, fifteen tops. We stood up and came out. It had to have taken about ten seconds, if that."

"No, you were gone for about two or maybe three minutes." Baz was speaking as he was navigating back to the TE.

Ken interjected into the conversation, "That is impossible. It could not have been more than ten seconds."

Greg from the TE had a potential solution to the conundrum. "Check the reading on the oxygen tanks and compare them."

Kristen checked and responded, "Okay, Baz has a reading of one hour and thirty-three minutes left. I have about the same. That is the baseline. Looking at Thor's he has one hour and thirty-seven left and one hour and thirty-six for Ken. There is a difference of three or four minutes, but it is not conclusive."

Ken responded, "Well, climbing up the stairs seemed to be more effort than I remember, but I put it down to being a little nervous—hyperventilating. But I am getting better at handling this…"

Someone started saying, "Yes, Ken, you are doing great—"

Kristen suddenly interjected, all excited, "Did you say you ascended some stairs? Do you realize what that means? Whoever these aliens are, they may be bipedal. Or at least their form of natural locomotion could be similar to ours."

Ken also came to this realization. "True, agreed, but we cannot assume that. It could be just a coincidence."

As they were discussing, the rover automatically docked into the TE. A few minutes later they were back on board. John, thinking the time lag could be of some significance, decided to record some of the debriefing information to send back to Earth.

During the debriefing, it became apparent that the door was not at all heavy to open or close—presumably due to some mechanical assistance built into the hinges. Also, there was air inside the pyramid, although its composition could not be verified. The fall was caused by the unexpectedly easy opening of the doorway and the gravity pulling them in. At the bottom of the tunnel into which they had fallen, there was another similar doorway with a similar opening mechanism. They had fallen down in the direction of the base of the pyramid, although the fall was only about ten meters. They would have to fall a lot further to reach the base. However, that could not happen since the door at the base was closed by a similar latch.

They came back to the outside door which they had just opened by ascending the stairs. And lastly, and possibly most astoundingly, there was an unexplained and perceived time difference between the humans outside and the two who had fallen. The proof of this was the increased oxygen consumption by the crew who had remained on the rover as compared to the two who had fallen. However, this was inconclusive at this time, as there may have been many factors which could have caused the different reading on the oxygen tanks.

The images captured on Thor's camera as well as John's debriefed information were sent back to Mission Control. This time, however, the wait for further instructions seemed to take longer. There was puzzling data in the information sent, and presumably the teams of analysts took longer to analyze it. Maybe they could not come to a consensus. They had to think of the safety of the dSE and its crew, as well as its main objective of not letting the pyramids crash into Earth. A crash would be catastrophic for Earth. If necessary, in order to blast them off collision course with Earth, the thermonuclear devices would need to be deployed. But this needed to happen as far out in space as possible so that the smaller fragments of the pyramids, if they were to break apart, would not rain down on Earth. Having many small pieces rain down was as bad as fewer giant pieces or the whole pyramid crashing. This was only if no communication could be established with the aliens or if their purpose was determined to be nefarious. The capabilities of the aliens were unknown, and the actions of the humans, now attempting to make contact, should not be misconstrued by them as offending, in case they launched a pre-emptive strike on the dSE or the Earth. There was no precedent to this situation. One of the main problems facing the crew was how to deal with aliens. In some form and to some extent nearly all humans in history have thought of this scenario. Now that this impending event was close at hand, figuring out what actions to take was becoming impossibly difficult, especially with this seemingly lack of interest shown thus far by the aliens. Judging from lack of contact with the aliens, each passing moment increased the possibility that these pyramids were devoid of any life-forms. Although this was unlikely, it was still a possibility.

Every passing moment the eight pyramids and the dSE were speeding toward Earth. Previously Neptune was visible from the forward window. Now it was seen through the aft window, with its distinctive methane-infused blue hue. The next gas giant, counting from the planets farthest away from the sun, was Uranus. This planet was coming into view from the front window. The largest of the twenty-two moons was also visible. Although the trajectory of the spacecraft did not take them close to the planets, the size of the gas giants made them visible even from this distance. From space, where there is no atmospheric interference to obstruct the view, they could be seen dimly reflecting the weak rays of the sun. Everyone seemed to be focused on Uranus when Greg broke the monotony. "Uranus! That is the planet we will pass next. It has twenty-two moons. Its atmosphere is mostly hydrogen mixed with helium and methane. It is the methane that gives it the blue-green color." Everyone may have heard what Greg had said, but continued to stare out, all lost in their own thoughts. There was nothing much to do till the next set of instructions arrived, or an attack was launched by the aliens. None of the crew expected this level of monotony when they had signed up for this trip. The patience of even the best of the best was getting tested.

"Do you think we should preemptively blast them out of space?" inquired Manny, more out of the need to start a debate than actually meaning what he said.

"What if we awaken a sleeping giant and really piss them off?" retorted Baz. He continued, "I mean, we do not know their purpose. Maybe they are not heading to Earth at all. Maybe they are going somewhere else, and that destination is taking them through the vicinity of our planet. They may be unaware that our planet is inhabited."

"We could try something small to get their attention, a grenade or something like that. We do not have to start with the nuclear option," Thor chimed in.

John, trying to make a joke of this, threw his two cents' worth. "If they did not know Earth was inhabited, they do now. They have a veritable entourage following them."

Ken interjected, "But we do not know what their pain threshold is. Thus far, they have not noticed or seemed to have minded our overtures to contact them. Maybe they do not see our activities as attempts to contact them. Maybe they are just waiting to see how far we go or what we do. They could be just as unsure or just as scared as us. Or maybe they are waiting for instructions from their Mission Control before they respond. I cannot believe, at this juncture, they are unaware of our presence! Whatever it is, they have not launched an attack on us."

That comment had its impact of starting a lively conversation which helped to pass the time—at least until this extremely hypothetical debate ended. They may have gone over the same arguments and discussions several times. No one attempted to keep watch over time. If they did they would realize how slowly the seconds and minutes were moving. The conversation, as all discussions in the past, was reaching its inevitable absurd conclusion. Fortunately, they did not have a new topic to conjure up as the speaker activated.

"Hi, this is Tracey," came the slightly southern drawl. Everyone's attention on the TE perked up. There would be more tasks to perform. Anything was better than just waiting. "Listen up, I have a lot of information and analysis data. First of all, great job with the EVA 4. It was successful, and we have more information than we expected to get from EVA 4. There are still a number of unanswered questions. Firstly, there seems to be a gap of about three minutes, where the camera was not able to communicate with the base unit. That information, along with the fact that Baz and Greg thought you were in the pyramid longer, indicates to us that there is some type of time field that is being crossed when you step past the threshold of the pyramid. We have the recording until Thor fell in, then blank for about three minutes, then the recording starts as Thor walks out. So, based on the approximate numbers since no one was keeping track of time, we figure that the ten seconds or so that you were in the pyramid and the three minutes of elapsed time experienced outside, time is slowed down by a factor of about eighteen. Now these numbers are not reliable. Next time we will have to get a more accurate measurement. This is the gist of the agonizing debate that we have had since the last report was received. We are not sure of what to make of the data." She paused for the information to be assimilated.

"An attack was not launched, or no defensive measures were taken by the aliens. This tells us that they are unaware of our activities or unsure of how to react or want us to initiate contact and do not mind it as long as we do not damage their vehicles. Now, looking at each of these three factors, firstly, they cannot be oblivious to your presence unless they are all in some kind of suspended animation or hibernation. If that were the case, it would be fairly safe to proceed to the next hatch and try to open it. We do not have a choice—we cannot do nothing. We have to take the game to them. At the speed you are traveling, time is running short. Secondly, if they are unsure of how to react, whatever their reasons may be, it would again be fairly safe to proceed to the next step. Third and finally, if they do not mind our attempts to enter their spaceship then it stands to reason that it would be fairly safe to proceed. We are pretty certain they are aware of our presence and also aware of our attempt at entering their craft. We could assume that they are shy, but we may also have come across to them as being tentative, because we are not doing anything threatening or attempting to destroy them. So let's continue to gradually make inroads into their craft, but in small increments. This is what the experts here believe to be the safest course of progress. Notice that we think it is fairly safe. I want to emphasize to never let your guard down. One final option I have not mentioned yet is that they are setting a trap for us. Notice that they may have slowed down. Your speed is now the same as the speed of the MG. Whether they want to ambush us or not, there is no way for us to determine that. We have to forge ahead, carefully, but nevertheless continue onward." Another pause.

"So the same team as before will go out on EVA 5. Thor and Ken will enter the first doorway. Close it behind you in case the second one opens into a pressurized cabin. Then proceed to the second hatch and open it. We cannot tell you what to do after this. You may see things unfamiliar because they are constructed by aliens. This time, Ken will carry the laptop, and Thor, as before, will have the camera attached to the space suit. This will ensure that we see what you see when you send the information back. If you encounter any aliens, we cannot prepare you how to behave, since we cannot anticipate their actions. The only thing we can recommend is that you have to carry your weapons and be somewhat fawning or even submissive. Do not fire the first shot. In addition, you will only have two or three minutes there, because the time elapsed outside of the pyramid for the two waiting on the rover will be about forty-five minutes, give or take a few. We came up with forty-five based on the rough estimate of a factor of eighteen. Remember, this is approximate. If Thor and Ken are delayed or we have not figured the time difference accurately, the rover will wait till the reserve oxygen is down to about thirty minutes, and then return. The second crew will prepare to go out to retrieve Thor and Ken. If you come out of the pyramid and not find the rover in position, radio the TE and wait. If you only plan to spend two or three minutes inside, the crew outside should have ample oxygen. Do you have any questions? Over."

John looked around to see if anyone had any questions. Everyone nodded. The instructions were clear. The back and forth from the pyramid was becoming second nature. "Copy that, no questions. Stand by for further information," John acknowledged. Even before these words could reach Earth, the EVA 5 crew would have gone and come back. But the exercise would only be a temporary relief to the endless monotony.

EVA MISSION 5

"Opening the first doorway," Thor indicated. Another fleeting condensation event, as noticed earlier by Thor, confirmed to him that there was indeed air in the pyramid that was humid. Presence of humidity increased the possibility that there was some kind of living creature inside. Everyone knew that whatever Thor and Ken spoke while they were inside would not be heard outside. Their only hope was that they come out of the pyramid in three minutes, approximately forty-five minutes for the ones left outside. From the dSE, Greg could see Thor and Ken. They looked tiny, like space suited action figures moving around. He was looking through binoculars and could see Thor enter, followed by Ken, who hesitated by the doorway for a second and appeared to turn around to look at something behind him. Then there was complete silence on the radio communicator. Greg wondered if that brief glance was a sign of Ken's phobia coming back. As Ken was doing so well recently Greg decided not to panic anyone. Besides, both Ken and Thor were out of radio communication. Nothing could be done at this time except to wait and see—and hope for the best.

As soon as Ken entered, Thor closed the door and secured it from the inside. Then, he turned on the flashlight and moved over to the second door, closely followed by Ken.

"The locking mechanism is the same," Thor said, and Ken nodded, his laptop recording the conversation. This time the laptop was brought so that there would be no loss of data, as had occurred in the last EVA mission. The reverse was true in that the conversation taking place between the two of them inside the pyramid was not audible outside.

Ken responded, "At least the communicator works inside," to which Thor agreed.

The second door opened, initially with a hiss, as the pressure equalized. Now there was no doubt that an atmosphere existed. Whether it was breathable by the humans was yet to be determined. The door had opened onto a large room. The lighting was dim, and only silhouettes of the objects in the room were visible. The origin of this eerie lighting was not immediately clear. It was as if the walls were dimly glowing. Thor asked Ken to turn off the flashlight as he turned off his. "In case we become easy targets." The inside of the pyramid seemed to be the same color as the outside, dark brown or black. It was difficult to tell which with the light being so dim. The room was square shaped, about thirty meters by thirty meters. There were boxes laid out in a neat geometrical pattern through the entire room, all the way up to the walls. In the dim light, they looked sinister, as if they were robots ready to come to life at the slightest disturbance. They were spaced about one meter from each other, enough for a person to comfortably walk through. Each of these boxes was about one and a quarter meters tall, and the square base was about one meter by one meter. A quick scan around the room Thor figured that there were more than two hundred present. He said in a whisper, "Don't touch them till I inspect them."

Ken nodded, not needing further clarification.

"Going further in to take a closer look," Thor said, so that the images of his actions were recorded with voice on the laptop. Ken had to follow because he was tethered to Thor on a fairly short leash. As they approached the first object in the chamber, their eyes were getting used to the dim lighting. Ken stopped by the object as Thor reached out to touch it. "Hard, possibly made of metal," he announced. He tried to push it gently at first and then with greater force. "Cannot move it," he announced. He felt around the object to see if it had a lid. "Cannot find an opening. It is definitely a container but does not appear to open on any side." Then he walked over to the middle of the chamber, with Ken in close proximity, to inspect a few more of these boxlike things. "Cannot open any of these."

Ken, who was keeping track of time, said, "We have been here for about a minute—give or take. We have maybe another minute before we head back—assuming it will take us the same amount of time to go back as it took for us to get in."

Thor, surprised that time had elapsed this quickly, responded, "Okay, thanks. We better hurry to maximize our time here and get more than we have thus far…which is nothing useful."

Then he moved toward the boxes lining the sides of the chamber and tried to open them, with the same result.

Ken noticed and said, "This chamber, this close to the base, does not seem large enough."

Thor did not understand that last statement and inquired, "What do you mean?"

Ken explained, "Well, the pyramid, at its base is about two hundred meters by two hundred meters. The outside door is about fifty meters up, from the base. We came down some steps and entered the second door. Say we came down about ten meters. At this height, and bearing in mind that the pyramidal shape is larger at the base than the apex, we should have space for a room much larger than what I am seeing. I think there may be another door to this chamber leading to another room."

Just as he finished the sentence Thor spotted another door. This time it was not the heavy-duty kind that they had entered previously. He walked toward the door and opened it.

Similar to the previous instance this chamber, too, was dimly lit and had a number of the same kind of boxes. Now that their eyes had adjusted to the dim lights, clearly visible in the distance was a set of stairs leading up. Thor looked at Ken who knew what Thor was thinking. "We do not have time. We have to get back. They will be getting concerned about us as well, and their level of oxygen will be getting into the red zone shortly." Thor had anticipated the answer. However he had a quick peek at the nearest object in the second chamber to make sure that it, too, did not budge or open. Then suddenly at the other end of the room, where they had spotted the stairs, they noticed a movement. Instinctively Thor ducked behind the box that was next to him, his soldier's training in situations like these becoming evident. He noticed Ken standing in full view staring in awe. He yanked his hand hard, which made Ken almost fall to the floor. Nothing needed to be said, but Ken felt the sharp stare of Thor burn into his neck. Ken understood that he should have ducked down sooner. Then slowly Thor peered from behind the box and saw, in the dim light, a form that was standing by a similar container behind which they were hiding. The top was already open. It had not noticed the humans hidden in the far end of same room. This was the first time anyone had laid eyes on a being from another planet. It was exhilarating and terrifying, all at once—but no time to think about that. The form which they could only see in silhouette seemed to be busy shifting things in the container, looking for something. It retrieved an object and just as suddenly as it had appeared, it pivoted around 180 degrees with surprising alacrity and disappeared. Thor stood up and hurried over to the container whose lid was beginning to shut. By the time Thor got to it, the lid had almost shut. Although for Thor, discretion had never been the better part of valor, he decided not to prevent the lid from shutting, in case his hand got caught. If his hands were caught in the lid as it shut or some alarm went off and they were detained, he would be jeopardizing everyone on this EVA activity. He was there just in time to notice that in the container there were metallic tubes about a foot long and four or five inches in diameter. Each one had a unique marking, but the lid closed before he realized what they were. Ken, who was still tethered to Thor, motioned with his hand in the direction of the door. Thor knew it was time to go. They were lucky not to be spotted, since they were not prepared to spend time in the pyramid on this EVA trip. They exited the second chamber, shut the door, and exited the pyramid.

As they were making their way out, Thor started discussing what he saw with Ken while the details were still fresh in their minds. This was purposely done not only to recap but also primarily to record the events for the benefit of the analysts on Earth and provide them with as much nuanced details as possible.

Thor exclaimed, "Did you notice that the alien was about the same size as a human being?"

Ken, still somewhat in shock, answered, "Yes, and we could not see its feet, but it seemed to glide across the metal floor."

Thor continued, "It seemed to have at least two appendages for hands and was approximately the same dimensions as a human being of a similar height. In the dim light were you able to make out what it was wearing?"

Ken, who was getting his composure back, responded, "No, but whatever it was it looked like it was wearing either a skintight fabric or nothing at all. All I could see was the outline, the silhouette. I could not see the eyes, although there appeared to be a head on the shoulders. There could have been a nose, ears, mouth. I didn't see them."

"Nor did I. We could not see the feet either. It appeared to glide, yet it had what looked like two feet." As they were discussing the apparition that had suddenly appeared and just as suddenly disappeared, they reached the rover. It was waiting for them, and when they started heading back Baz said, "You were gone for just about thirty minutes." Ken checked the laptop and announced, "Oh! My laptop indicates about two minutes and fifty-five seconds."

In the rover, Ken said, "Thor, while we were hiding I noticed some symbols on the box. I would need time to make any sense of it, but at first glance, it was mostly meaningless. I mention it because it did remind me of symbols that I have seen on Earth."

Thor, who was neither a linguist nor an expert in symbols, brushed off the comment. "Probably some alien writing, not worth worrying over at this point. The important thing is the alien that we saw."

Ken nodded; he could not argue the point that the big news was the alien, not some writing.

After they arrived back at the TE, all reviewed the information as it was being downloaded to Mission Control. The recording was also dim. Although the camera was of very high definition and capable of high contrast, it was less clear than the eyes of the humans in the pyramid had perceived. The details were very sketchy in the limited light.

Nicole asked, "So what does it feel like to be the first humans ever to set eyes on an alien?"

Thor responded, "At the time I did not feel like we were viewing an alien. It just felt like we were hiding from an enemy, as if we were on Earth in a clandestine battle situation."

Nicole continued, "I guess I know what you mean. You were playing hide-and-seek with an alien. Only difference is that it could have been anyone."

Ken, recounting the events, added, "Funnily enough, I have never been in the military, but I felt exactly the same as you. It has not dawned on me yet that we just saw an alien. It was as if we were hiding from some mischief, hiding behind a desk from a schoolteacher or something like that. But now I am beginning to realize that we will be recognized by mankind as the first humans to have seen an alien. Still, it is funny. We were not able to make out much detail in the limited light, and it might as well have been a human standing there. We were lucky, I guess, not to have been spotted." Then he suddenly remembered that Thor may have noticed what was contained in the box. "Did you see what the alien was doing?"

Thor answered, "Yes, I almost forgot. I got to the box before the lid completely shut. In the available light, I saw some metallic-looking things, about a foot to foot and a half in length and about four to five inches in diameter. I cannot even begin to guess what they may be, but the box was filled to the brim with them. They were all identical except for what looked like a colored band that went around the diameter. Then it was time to leave, and we left in a hurry."

Ken agreed, "You could say that. Our primary concern was not to be found out that we were there and to get back before the oxygen ran out."

Nicole nodded.

No one was aware of how much time had passed. It was all relative. With no clock and no reference point of day/night, it was only the internal mechanism that is built into each human being that each crew member could estimate roughly how much time had passed from one event to the next. However, after a while even this became distorted, since the natural rhythm of wake/sleep is nonexistent in space. All they could see, at varying distances from the window of the TE, was the passing of the larger planets. Each one they passed indicated to them that they were getting closer to Earth. That was a gratifying feeling, immediately mollified by the fact that these aliens could be belligerent. That pleasing feeling was short-lived. At some point as events unfolded and information was disseminated, Mission Control would announce the next steps that needed to be taken. The astronauts would comply as instructed. Until then they wait. The nature of and future action was unknown. It was positively confirmed, by EVA 5, that the pyramids were not devoid of life. A being of some kind was observed. Next step was to make contact, but how? What would happen if contact was made and the human beings would not be able to communicate? Were they superior to humans or inferior? At least one thing was certain. These creatures, at least the one that was seen, was not some kind of a monster commonly created in artists' imaginations for movies or comic books.

Until now, their focus of attention was Pyramid Eight. John, needing to start a fresh debate, asked, "I wonder what is in the other pyramids?"

Baz offered up his theory. "I hazard a guess that each of the eight pyramids is self-contained. There is no communication between them that we can determine and no transportation that we can see. I think they are all the same, and each one contains exactly the same items as the other. Also, there is redundancy built in, in case they lose one or more in transit."

Kristen agreed, "I agree with Baz. You need redundant systems. There is at least one maybe more identical to the one we have seen. I am pretty certain that we do not have eight distinct types of pyramids, maybe four unique types at a maximum, which will account for the eight, four times two."

Ken, playing devil's advocate, said, "But we have two types only. Our TE consists of six craft and this command module that we are in."

Baz countered, "Yes, but our purpose is different to theirs. We are here to intercept them, and the six dSEs are here to provide acceleration and space to carry our weapons systems as well as rations for the crew."

Thor interjected in this conversation, "I wonder if we will be asked to check out the other pyramids. I would like to make sure that they are all the same. The one we saw firsthand seemed innocuous enough. I would like to know that the others do not have some sort of a weapon of mass destruction."

Talking was good. At least it diverted their minds and prevented them from going stir-crazy. It passed the time that hung so heavy. Conversation killers were not welcome, but reality had to be faced regardless of what it did to the flow of the discussion. This comment though brought about a sudden stop. Each crew member started pondering about their own mortality as well as the fragility of Earth. What if they make no progress and are forced to go back into hibernation? They would travel all the way back to Earth, wake up from HySleep, and find only fragments of rock where the Earth used to be because the aliens had arrived there earlier? What if they were unable to recognize a weapon because of technological differences between the humans and the aliens? They did not have too long to dwell on this morbid thought process. As if Mission Control sensed the plight of the astronauts, this time the analyst from Earth seemed to come to a decision on the next set of activities quicker than the past. Or was it that they were closer to Earth so the time it took for the message to travel was shorter?

EVA MISSION 6

"Hello, everyone, hope you all are well. This is Sarah with the new set of instructions. This time we have something more ambitious." "About time", was the collective thought process aboard the dSE. "More ambitious" directly translated into more dangerous. Some excitement at last—anything to break this monotony. Sarah continued, "We have analyzed the data and do not see anything alarming. That said, please continue to be careful. The last set of data y'all sent was a short transmission anyway due to the brief stay in the pyramid. The lighting was too dim to see anything clearly, even though we used image enhancers. The analysts are not sure what to make of the containers that are laid out in neat rows. Our best guess is that they contain supplies and are opened remotely, possibly from a central console. Similar in concept to our cabinets around the outer walls of the dSE. However, we have designed ours to provide room for movement. The pyramids are much larger so they may not be constricted for space. Therefore, they can spread them across the rooms like they have done. We saw the alien and, as you, were not able to tell much from the dark images. By the way, congratulations to Thor and Ken for not only being the first to set eyes on an alien life-form but also to record it for posterity! Hopefully we will be able to get better images in subsequent missions. We were not able to tell why the alien did not see you. Maybe you were too quick to hide, or the room was too dim for the alien also. Maybe it was not expecting anyone else to be present. At this time there is no point speculating on that matter. It is what it is."

Sarah continued, "We would like Manny, Ken, and Baz to form one excursion team. This way, you have at least one member that can navigate the rover and one who has been inside the pyramid. The second team will comprise of Thor, Kristen, and Greg. Again, one who can navigate the rover and one who has been inside the pyramid. Sorry, John, you will have to stay back with Nicole on the TE and run things from there. The two teams will go out at the same time. Team One on Explorer 1 will go to three pyramids and do a quick survey, and Team Two will go on Explorer 2 to the remaining four and do the same. Each team will go to their assigned pyramid and follow the procedure as before of opening and closing. This is assuming that each pyramid is identical to the first one. If not, use your judgment—if it is not immediately obvious how the hatch works, leave it and move on. Remember that time is of the essence. We can always come back. Remember that the pyramids may be pressurized so be very cautious. Each pyramid should take no more than a minute whether you can open the portal or not. With difference in time elapsed outside compared to inside the pyramid, the person remaining on the rover will be using up more oxygen than the ones stepping into the pyramids." All this was known, but Mission Control had to make sure that everyone was safe, so they always enumerated the obvious especially when it came to safety. "Team One will go to the bottom row of four pyramids, starting from the one farthest away, that is Pyramid Five, and working your way to the one closest to the TE, that is Pyramid Seven. We have already seen Pyramid Eight, so no need to visit it again. Team Two will start at the top, which is Pyramid One, and work your way down to Two and then Three and finally Pyramid Four. If Team One is done quicker than Team Two, take your time returning so that if Team Two needs assistance, you are in the vicinity to provide it. Any questions? Over."

Again, the instructions from Mission Control were carefully constructed, structured, and to the point. There was no ambiguity.

John responded, "Copy that—Over."

Even before the transmission from John reached Mission Control, the two EVAs were out of their docking position and well into their latest mini mission.

John was at the control panel, as usual. However, since everyone else was out, Nicole was performing the task of lookout and communications with the two rovers. She had seen enough during the previous excursions to know what to do. Besides, this was a relief from the monotony since her main task was the well-being of the crew. There had been no danger till now, and no crew member needed any medical or physical help, perhaps some psychological help at times. However, the overall disposition of the crew was very positive. After all the selection process was very rigorous and each had undergone intensive training. On the rare occasions where she felt that an individual may have needed help, it turned out to be either lighthearted banter or some teasing to relieve the monotony or a genuine mistake such as the one that happened to Manny, to which every human being is prone. Most of the adrenaline was worked off by vigorous exercise on the treadmill or the punch bag. This had the added benefit of keeping each crew member fit and strong. It had become routine that each member took turns on the exercise equipment at regular intervals.

The distance from the dSE to pyramids One and Five was approximately the same as the human craft was adjacent and near the center of the alien cluster. The response came back from Explorer Two first—perhaps there was more urgency with this team as they had four to visit, or perhaps because Thor knew exactly what to do and was trained by the military to be superefficient when necessary. "Pyramid One is the same as the other one. I would say they are identical," came the response from Thor as he exited Pyramid One. About a minute later, Baz's voice came across, "From what I have seen of the images on the laptop, it appears that Pyramid Five is similar to Pyramid Eight." Nicole wondered whether Ken had to show the ropes to Baz since this was the first time that he had attempted to open the hatch and go inside. Soon thereafter Thor reported that Pyramid Two was the same also and that he was proceeding to Pyramid Three, the one in the middle of the second row. About a minute later Baz reported that Pyramid Six was identical and that he was proceeding to Pyramid Seven. Just one left to inspect for Baz and Team One. Thor and his team had two to inspect, pyramids Three and Four. However, Thor would be in and out of Pyramid Three before Baz, as Thor was working at a brisk pace and had a slightly shorter distance to cover between pyramids. As things stood now they should be back at about the same time.

Thor announced, "This is proceeding smoothly. At this rate of progress we will be done with our assignment at almost the same time as the other team."

Nicole looked over to John, nodded, and said, "Copy that." Thor had already announced that they were going to Pyramid Three. A few seconds later they were opening the outer hatch of Pyramid Three. As in the other instances, the outer hatch opened without hesitation and they closed it behind them. They then went to the inner hatch and opened it. What greeted them was surprising and completely unexpected.

Pyramid Three had nothing inside. It was a cavernous shell with no floor, except the small balcony-like structure on which Kristen and Thor were standing, and no partitions to divide the area into rooms. This area encompassed in here was bigger than any structure that either of them had seen before on Earth. It seemed larger than the combined area of three or four outdoor sports stadiums and higher than the largest stadium on Earth. They just stood there in utter shock for a few seconds gazing at the enormity of what was before them. The lighting was just as dim as in the other pyramids, and vaguely they could make out the farthest walls. It appeared like it would take a ten-minute brisk walk to get to the other end—whether it was an optical illusion due to the dim lights they could not tell. Thor pointed the flashlight in the direction of the farthest wall. It was too weak for the light to reach that far. They felt like tiny ants in this enormous cavern—what was the purpose of this craft?

As in the other pyramids, the outer hatch was located a few meters above the base, and the inner hatch was a few meters below the outer hatch. However, the inner hatch was also not at the base of the pyramid. Therefore, they were on a balcony, some meters above the base. What was down below?

Kristen noticed something. "Thor, I think this is a trapdoor here. Do we open it?"

Instantly, Thor directed the flashlight to where Kristen was pointing and saw a trapdoor.

Thor, acting quickly, started to open the door and said, "Sure, just a quick peek. It will hopefully not take long. Besides, we can save a future trip to this one."

The door opened, and both peered in. There was a stairway leading down. They went down halfway and stopped to get a bird's-eye view of the single large area that made up the entire base area of the pyramid. There were no partitions, so the area was as large as the base of the pyramid, which was about two hundred meters by two hundred meters. Kristen had estimated the dimensions from the outside during EVA 1. This viewpoint confirmed that the initial estimate was fairly accurate. This chamber was about five meters tall, and contained a number of items spread out neatly over the entire chamber. These could only be guessed as machinery. Like the other pyramids, there was a walkable gap between each row. However, some of the containers were taller than the others. When their eyes had become a little more accustomed to the dim light, they noticed that the taller containers were nearer to them, and the standard-size containers that they had seen in the other pyramids were at the other end. So, it appeared that this space was shared between machines and storage. There were pipes and wires neatly going from one clump of metal containers to another. Thor guessed, "This is probably the propulsion and life-support systems. We did not notice it in the others because we did not go there, but I am pretty certain all the other pyramids have the same mechanism in their respective basements. But there are no signs of life, unless they are hiding somewhere. And I don't see where they could be hiding."

Kristen agreed. There was no noise or vibration of any kind. They were running silently. To her surprise Thor went the rest of the way down the stairs and touched the nearest machine and exclaimed that there was a slight hint of vibration. "We should go now. We have spent more time here than we had planned."

Thor nodded, acknowledging her remark, and added, "We took longer here than the others we checked. The other team will be done quicker than us because we took time to inspect this one. But I think this was time well spent. We will hopefully not need to come back to investigate this one." Kristen acknowledged, "Agreed, if we can avoid any unnecessary trips, it will save time. Time is something we do not have."

As they were exiting Thor noticed two unusual things, that there was what appeared to be an unoccupied console in the middle, and in the corner a walled-off area which appeared to be a room of about twenty meters by twenty meters. He did not wait to study it any further since time was running out. He was wondering what could be in that room. It was feasible that the console was unoccupied—the pyramid could be running on autopilot. But the walled-off area was something he could not shake from his mind.

As Thor and his team were entering Pyramid Three, Baz had announced that they were done with Pyramid Seven and that they had completed their assignment. Baz and his team had exited Pyramid Seven and waited for further instructions. Since Thor and Kristen had not reported yet John decided to let them investigate Pyramid Four, the one that Thor and his team were assigned to check.

John radioed, "Baz, the other team is detained at Pyramid Three for whatever reason. Can you cover Pyramid Four?"

Baz responded, "Roger that, proceeding to Four."

When Thor and Kristen came out of Pyramid Three, they noticed that the other rover was by Pyramid Four. They would not have to investigate that one.

John, relieved upon seeing Thor and Kristen exiting the pyramid, asked as soon as they were in the rover, "What happened? We were worried. You can come head straight back. The other team took care of Pyramid Four."

Thor explained, "Roger that, will explain when we get back. No need to be concerned about anything."

Just as Thor and Kristen got into the rover, they heard Baz announce that Pyramid Four also was identical to Pyramid Eight and that they would return since they saw the other rover already making its way back to the TE.

On the way back Ken mentioned, "It may not strike as particularly interesting that each pyramid has its entrance facing in the same direction. However, what is more than a coincidence is that at the entrance to each of the pyramids we visited, the stairway is aligned with the same constellation. I stopped at the entrance to take a quick peek before entering each one. And, it is the same one to which the pyramids in Giza are aligned—Orion. No one knows why the pyramids on Earth, not just the one in Egypt, are all aligned with the same constellation." After a moment's pause, he continued, "I don't want to alarm anyone, but in Greek mythology, Orion means 'the hunter.'"

Although Ken's comments were heard by all no one had any opinions to offer. Ken was an expert in Egyptian as well as other ancient cultures. Besides, only Ken, due to his expertise, had noticed the alignments of the pyramids with other constellations.

Within minutes of each other both teams arrived and docked into the TE, disrobed from the space suits, and proceed to the command module. It was Thor's turn to explain what he saw, and everyone listened with incredulity. Even as he was explaining, the recorded data was already on its way to Mission Control. Thor also explained about the walled-off area and wondered whether each of the other seven pyramids had a similar construction.

The latest data was sent, and the crew did not know how long the wait would be for the response. There was a twist to the theory that all pyramids were alike. Pyramid Three, the middle pyramid, was different in that other than the machinery it was empty. Why would they take the trouble to journey such vast distances with an empty pyramid? Was it that it contained supplies that over the course of time was exhausted? Or was it that they were going to load something into the pyramid to take it back to wherever they came from? The latter was the more likely scenario since if there were supplies in the pyramid, there would be labeled containers to hold them in an organized fashion so things could be easily found. Unless they jettisoned the containers on their way to this point, for which there was no evidence.

Awaiting the next set of instructions, each crew member went to their favorite vantage point and stared at the glory of space, the visibility unobstructed by atmospheric interference of Earth. These views would possibly never again be comprehended by the eight in the dSE during their lifetimes. The light from the millions of suns in the Milky Way galaxy was dazzlingly beautiful. It formed a tight band and was visible from their rear window. The ancients had divided this band of stars into groups called constellations of the zodiac. In addition to that, the view of billions of galaxies spread out in every direction was breathtaking. Baz said absentmindedly, "To consider that all this started from a single point of singularity, how can this be? Were energy and matter in different forms when they were created? If we had telescopes we could easily see young galaxies where new planets are being formed, the birthplace of stars and planets. In the center of each galaxy, there is a black hole where gravity is so strong that even light cannot escape its deathly grip. If anything were to approach a black hole, it would be torn to shreds as it got sucked into its center. This is the birth and death of stars. What a stark contrast in the primordial tug-of-war. Could these aliens be from a planet similar to Earth, with its own sun and its own planets, one of which was habitable for evolution to take place?" Then in a serious tone which got everyone's attention and indignation, he continued, "They have the mastery of gravity. Can they use this against us as a weapon? I don't want to be negative but we don't even know how to react to this kind of threat. We have nothing to counteract gravity. What if they can use it to deflect our weapons back towards us? We need to keep this in mind in case it comes to a battle for survival and we launch something at them."

He then quickly continued on his original thought, before anyone had a chance to voice their opinions, as if to counteract his negative comment, "The Earth, about 4.7 billion years old, is considered young when compared to the age of the universe, which is about 13.7 billion years old. The human evolution, in this time scale, does not even warrant an honorable mention. If Earth's most significant past were to be documented, the age of the dinosaur was longer. Humans, or more specifically *Homo sapiens,* have been in existence for some hundred thousand years. Did the aliens evolve on their own planet before humans even existed? If so, they would be far superior to humans, although no one on dSE or even on Earth admitted to that possibility. The very fact that they had journeyed a vast distance, more than humans could, proves that they have better technology than humans and had possibly evolved earlier than *Homo Sapiens*."

As the crew viewed through the window, they could now see Uranus in the port window, and in the distance from the starboard window the distinctive Saturn with its pronounced rings were coming into view. The name of this mission, Titan Explorer, was eponymously named after one of Saturn's moons. Greg had taken it upon himself to describe each of the planets as they came into view, possibly as something to discuss or to count down the planets as they hurtled back to Earth. "Although Titan is a moon of Saturn, it is larger than planet Mercury and larger than all other dwarf planets. It has a mostly nitrogen atmosphere mixed in with trace amounts of hydrocarbons. These combine to give Titan its distinctive orange hue. If life were to form anywhere else in the solar system, this is the place where it is most likely to have occurred. The hydrocarbons are the building blocks of amino acids, which is the basis for the formation of life. By the way, Saturn is one of the lightest planets. If we were to be able to put it in a giant tub of water, it would float." It was as if Greg were speaking in the other crew members' dreams. Everyone was now getting used to this infrequent soliloquy. No one said anything, there was nothing to say, but all heard the musings. There was nothing else to do till the next set of instructions came.

Baz continued, "Well, after this one, we have one more gas giant, Jupiter. Then we get to the rocky planets, the first of which is Mars. Then Earth. We are getting closer. All this investigating is taking too much time. Hope Mission Control comes up with something more concrete for us to make contact. All this sneaking around has not accomplished much, although I see why they want to be circumspect."

As if it was timed to coincide with Baz finishing this thought the voice of Tracey came on from Mission Control. "Hi, Tracey here, we have analyzed the data and have not reached a conclusion. We also took note of Ken's observation about the alignment of the pyramids. We can confirm that the ones in Giza are in alignment with Orion galaxy, so if the ones closest to you are in the same orientation, it is more than a coincidence. Our team is analyzing for potential leads on this information, but at this time there is nothing conclusive. The analysts are racking their brains on some old theories that claim that the orientation of the Giza pyramids was to aid communication over vast distances. We will let you know when we figure out something.

"We do not understand why Pyramid Three is mostly empty. They may be coming to Earth for something, but hopefully it is something we can afford to give. If that is the case, then the other pyramids have numerous aliens who may be in hibernation. We think what you saw were just some workers with the task of supporting the mission during their long journey. Now that the latest information has taken a slightly sinister turn, henceforth we want to send just one rover at a time. Also, each mission will comprise of four individuals, safety in numbers. Baz, Thor, Ken, and Kristen will go on EVA 7 and explore Pyramid Eight. We think you will be able to make contact with an alien in any of the seven pyramids. We are not sure if any aliens are present in Pyramid Three. The sole purpose of this EVA is to make contact with them, and therefore, all four of you will go inside. This way, the discrepancy of oxygen consumption will be mitigated since all of you will pass through the time barrier existing between the outside and inside of the pyramids. Once you make contact, we cannot tell you how to react, only that you have to react to your surrounding environment and situation. Be polite, try to communicate, and find out their purpose. Be safe and good luck. The Earth is depending on you. Over."

John responded, now things were getting serious—to actually seek contact with the alien race, "Roger that, over and out."

PROCEEDING ACCORDING TO PLAN

The cyborg was satisfied that things were proceeding according to plan even though she had ordered extra vigilance to watch for enemies coming from another direction. She allowed herself a smile. If anyone were to see her they would ask why she was smiling, but her moving parts did not allow for the smile to be visible externally.

One thing of minor concern was the weapons that the humans were carrying—but it was only a minor concern. Her crew could easily neutralize the primitive weapons that fired solid projectiles. She needed to capture all the individuals. As to how many there were she was not sure. She had counted six—but there could be more that had not shown themselves. She would need to capture them peacefully, to show that not everyone on this craft harbored ill will. Moreover, that is the only way she could try to communicate with them. She would instruct the menial robots to do that work—they obeyed her as if they were obeying the masters.

It was getting close to the time of their arrival. She would soon instruct the menial robots to initiate preparations to wake the masters from hibernation. She was instructed to arrive at a specific time, and she had to make sure that the crafts arrived at that time. She, however, would use her discretion to widen the field and include the human crafts when she made the adjustments. No one would know unless she told anyone. This way she would make sure that they all arrive at Earth at the same time.

EVA Mission 7

To John's surprise, the four identified for EVA 7 were already eagerly on their way to the rover. The mission may be getting serious, but that is why they were here. They may be walking into danger, but it was better than all the waiting around that they were forced to do. Besides, all were acutely aware that with every passing moment, they were getting closer to Earth. A few minutes later, after all the obligatory protocol and procedures, the four left on the TE were viewing the rover slowly inch its way to Pyramid Eight. It stopped as usual, and John radioed, "Keep a close watch on your air tanks." He saw that the message was received as Baz gave him a thumbs-up signal as he was stepping in.

The inside of the pyramids had as yet unexplainable time difference from their immediate surroundings. At last estimation, the time difference was about 18 to 1, so for every minute elapsed inside, 18 minutes would tick by outside. But in this case, that did not matter because a differential in the speed of time did not alter the rate of consumption of oxygen; no one was waiting in the rover. All 4 on this EVA went into the pyramid, so the rate of depletion of the tank would be as calculated earlier for each of them. John started his stopwatch; the clock started ticking—literally. Regardless of the time difference between the pyramid and the outside all 4 needed to come out in 120 minutes per John's stopwatch. Not counting the 30 minutes of reserve, the oxygen tanks supplied about 2 hours of oxygen after every recharge. These were at best approximate calculations. Everyone was acutely aware of these conditions. Hopefully the 4 making this trip would improvise and be able to make the necessary adjustments if the circumstances called for it and get out within

120 minutes of entering. The consequences of not doing so were too painful to imagine.

Thor, Baz, Ken, and Kristen stepped inside the second air lock hatch and through to the first room. Kristen voiced, "We are on our own now. No communication between the dSE and us." No one needed to answer. As before, there was nothing movable present in this room, just the array of containers that could not yet be opened by a human. They all went through the door that had earlier led Thor and Ken to spot the first alien. They were not taking any precautions because they wanted to be detected. When they went into that chamber, it was as before, almost dark, except that this time it was devoid of any alien. Baz and Thor had weapons, pistols as well as rifles slung across their backs. Baz said, "Thor, have your gun ready. We will try to find someone here or keep looking till we find someone." Thor pulled out his weapon and unlocked the safety switch.

Baz, who had seen the images captured by the previous mission to this chamber, indicated, "I am moving toward the far wall. There seems to be an opening there."

Thor acknowledged, "Right behind you." The other two followed nervously.

Baz stopped by the wall, directly behind which was the opening through which the alien had emerged and later disappeared. Baz slowly rounded the corner, his weapon outstretched in his arms, when suddenly something bumped his arm. The thing that bumped him stopped, as a shot was accidentally discharged from Baz's gun. The bump and the recoil of the bullet made the gun jump out of his hand and fall to the floor with a metallic clang. Thor was behind Baz and did not see what had happened, but like the others present he heard the gunfire. Ken and Kristen were behind Thor, and their bodies visibly stiffened with fear when they heard the shot. The thing that had bumped Baz immediately spun around and sped away and down the steps, which was at the far corner of what appeared to be a landing. By this time Thor stepped around the corner where Baz was standing in a trance just in time to see the alien disappear down the steps. The first words out of his mouth were, "If this does not get us noticed I don't know what will."

Baz was too shaken to comment.

Eventually as the alien disappeared down the stairs Thor asked, "What happened?"

Baz picked up his gun and simultaneously responded, "I don't know, I was rounding the corner, and this alien bumped into me. I had my finger on the trigger and the bump caused the gun to go off. The bullet hit the alien's arm, his bicep, I think."

Thor continued, "Did you see blood…or something?"

By this time, Ken and Kristen had also rounded the corner, and all were walking across the landing toward the stairs, in the direction where the alien had disappeared. Baz indicated, "No, nothing, not even a sound of pain. I mean, it happened so fast that I didn't see the face clearly."

As they approached the stairs, Ken asked, "It went this way… down the stairs?"

Baz answered, "Yes, and I have news for you. I don't think it was an alien."

Ken asked, "What do you mean?"

Baz, who was about to continue before Ken had interjected with the question, explained, "I mean, I don't think it was an alien being. It was some kind of a robot."

Thor, who wanted to be sure what they were dealing with and try to assess their capabilities as much as possible before another encounter, asked, "What makes you say that?"

In an attempt to explain what he saw, Baz tried to describe. "Didn't you see? I mean, it had wheels…I mean, it had feet, that it used to walk down the stairs, but it also had wheels. That is why it was able to turn so quickly." He was not making too much sense.

Thor and the other two were thoroughly confused. "What do you mean? Are you saying that it had wheels as well as feet?"

The initial surprise was wearing off, and Baz had time to process the information in his head. Trying to clarify Baz continued, "I saw wheels, no question. Its feet were on the wheels. When it came to the stairs, it somehow locked the wheel and took steps to walk down. It appeared to be like those things on Earth that some police use, or sometimes used in large factories to move from place to place quickly. You've seen them. It has two wheels and a handle that you can hold on to. You step on the platform between the wheels and slightly lean it forward and it moves in that direction."

Thor nodded. They had all seen the electric scooters on Earth. By now they were at the head of the stairs.

Baz continued, "Now imagine that this robot has the left wheel attached by an axle to the base of its foot. The right wheel is similarly configured on its right foot." As Baz was speaking, they started descending the stairs. The lighting conditions did not change. It was as dim as the room they were leaving.

"When you want to move forward on a smooth surface, you use the wheels. When the surface is soft, bumpy, or loose like sand, you lock the wheels and walk, as we are doing now."

Kristen commented as they were descending the steps, "Ingenious, a multipurpose robot."

Baz, still unsure, speculated. "Well, I think it is a robot. Maybe the aliens have shoes that have wheels built in?"

As the conversation was occurring, the entire chamber came into view, and from their vantage point of about halfway down the stairs they could see the expanse of the room. The lighting was dim, but all human pulses quickened because there was some activity taking place in the far corner. There were at least three of these aliens or robots present. One was standing with its back to the humans, and was doing something to the other alien's arm. The third was directly facing the one whose arm was presumably being medically checked. The chamber itself seemed to be some kind of workshop or treatment facility. Not that there were any spare parts strewn untidily. On the contrary, everything was neat and tidy. The only sign that this may be a workshop was the fact that there were three tables in the middle of the room, with enough space between them to easily walk by. The shape of each table was an equilateral triangle, and if one drew imaginary lines around the perimeter of all the tables, it would form a triangle. Noticing this Baz exclaimed, "Boy! These guys do everything in triangles." All around the room were containers similar to the first two rooms that the humans had seen before, the only difference being that they were of different sizes.

The aim of the boarding party was to communicate with the aliens. So they slowly inched down the stairs so as not to raise alarm and walked toward the activity. Suddenly, one of the aliens turned around and moved directly toward the humans. The four froze in place, the front two ready with gun in hand. Although the lighting was dim, they could clearly see that Baz was correct. The movement was smooth—they were moving on wheels. Due to the excitement or terror or both, the four humans had stopped breathing. The alien coming toward them was about eight feet tall—too big for hand-to-hand combat even if the two men tag teamed. Their muscles tensed while they waited for the alien to make the first move. Fortunately for them as it neared the humans it turned slightly and negotiated a path around them and went toward the stairs. As it went by at barely the distance of an arm's length, they clearly could make out that it was a robot. This particular robot, for some reason, was taller than the rest—maybe a robot for a different function. Nevertheless, in the dim light and dark complexion, it appeared menacing. Reflexively, they exhaled as their muscles relaxed. Thor said, "That was the longest two seconds of my life." No one made any comment. It was the same for all of them.

They turned around in time to see the alien stop at the base of the stairs and walk up, as a human would do, except that the wheels were touching the stairs, not the feet. It was difficult to tell whether or not the alien had feet. As the robot disappeared, all four turned around just in time to see that the alien with the bullet wound had his arm yanked out of the socket. They strained to see in the darkness and so moved closer, being careful not to make any sudden moves. They could not see any liquid oozing out. The aliens' interest in them did not change. They continued to ignore the humans. A few more steps, and they were the closest they had ever been to the aliens, and the first thing that became apparent was that these robots had at least one facial feature—they had eyes or sensors, where the eyes would be expected. They were robots, meant for domestic duties.

Baz guessed, "I think the robot that went up the stairs replaced the one which could not carry out its duties."

Thor nodded. All four stood in utter bewilderment and watched the robot that was repairing the one with the bullet wound bring another arm from one of the containers and replace the arm. Then the robot with the new arm went the same way as the previous one and disappeared up the stairs, presumably to carry on its functions or take over the first robot's function. Kristen thought that is probably what they were doing when they were standing in front of each other, exchanging duties. The robot that replaced the arm went to a corner and stood there, presumably waiting for the next task.

With time running out Thor said nervously, "I will approach that robot and see what happens. Thus far, these machines have taken no notice of us." With that Thor moved closer, maybe five meters away, and stopped. No reaction. Evidence indicated that it may not even be switched on. Maybe, Thor wondered, it had switched itself off to conserve energy. He moved to within touching distance. Still nothing. Baz was holding the gun aimed straight at the dormant robot's head, just in case. Thor noticed more details. These robots had other features similar to human beings, two arms, two feet, albeit with wheels, which, as evidenced earlier, could be used to walk up and down stairs. They also had a torso to which the arms and legs were connected. There appeared to be a head on what could best be described as shoulders. The head had some receptors, presumably eyes. There were no ears, nose, or mouth, at least not visible externally. What sort of aliens were these? Thor said aloud, "They have features like humans, arms, legs, a body, and a head. These robots could have been manufactured on Earth, if we had the technology." He gingerly touched the shoulder of the robot. Immediately some LED type of lights came on in the head and neck region, giving a visceral jolt not only to Thor but also to the other three. Baz somehow managed to not fire off another round into the robot. Just as suddenly the lights had some on, they switched off. That was enough of a scare for Thor to shakily say, "Maybe we should look elsewhere. I don't think we will get any reaction from these guys."

Ken asked, "Do you want me to try and talk to it?"

Baz, getting a little frustrated at the complete disregard shown by the hosts, responded a little louder than usual, "We have not exactly been quiet. They all would have heard our conversations. None of them even appeared to notice us. I don't think they are programmed to deal with interactions with nonrobots or even verbal forms of communication. I don't think these robots will react to our overtures." In a slightly lower tone he continued, "What scares me is if there are other robots with the job of protecting the pyramids, and they are built in a similar way to the ones we have encountered, how would we negotiate with them? These robots appear to have eyes only, no ears. And they do not appear to be programmed to deal with any intruders. Yes, they are peaceful for now, but it would be difficult to negotiate with them. If they start attacking, how do we reason with them? How do we try to convince them not to kill us?"

Normally this statement would have a chilling impact. However, in this potentially hostile situation and with so much adrenaline flowing, this statement was received as a matter-of-fact comment. Ken asked, "So what do we do now?"

Baz offered a new idea. "We should go up, see what the other two robots are up to."

This time, they hurried up the stairs, hoping to be able to communicate with something or somebody. When they reached the top of the stairs from where they had descended not ten minutes earlier, they noticed that everything was as before, no sign of life. Baz noticed that there was another set of stairs directly above the one they had just ascended. He suggested, "We can go up this stairway, unless anyone else has other ideas." Visibility was consistently dim wherever they went, and no one could see anything much even though, by this time, their eyes had acclimated to the darkness. The other three nodded in agreement. Going up was as good a guess as anything else at this juncture. Baz was the nearest and was leading the way, rather nonchalantly, since they wanted to be detected by someone so that they could establish some type of rapport. As he reached the top stair, he stopped dead. Thor, who was behind him, did not expect this and collided into his back. Undeterred Baz exclaimed, "Jackpot!"

Kristen and Ken reached Baz's vantage point and noticed what he had just seen. The stairway had opened up into the middle of a circular room filled with many approximately one-meter-tall containers. These containers were arranged around the room in such a way that, looking from above, they would appear to form the spokes of a bicycle wheel. There was walking space around each container. These containers looked exactly like ancient Egyptian coffins—"Hibernation units!" Baz exclaimed. The head of the approximately two-meter-long unit was against the wall of the circular room. The foot was away from the wall closer to the center of the room. "Wow! Here is where they are—at least some of them. There must be at least fifty of these here." He went to one of the containers and tried to see if there was a lid that could be opened. As Baz touched the container, he felt a faint vibration and suddenly a feeling of elation, a sudden jolt of energy. He quickly withdrew his hand and again exclaimed, "Wow! That was weird!"

Kristen, too, placed her hand on the hibernation unit, and quickly withdrew it as if she had received a mild electric shock and immediately exclaimed, "That is indeed weird. I felt a sudden surge of energy, happiness combined with a sense of elation. Touching these units seems to trigger something in the brain." Then she seemed to ponder for a moment and continued, "The closest I can describe it is what you feel after meditation." Kristen had learned meditation to help focus in confined situations in which she sometimes found herself, in the deepwater submersibles or during the long periods of decompression. She had realized that the best way to remain calm, not get claustrophobic, and not feel that time was hanging heavy was to meditate. Indeed, on occasion, she had looked forward to spending some time in the decompression chamber so she could get time to meditate. "Let's not touch it for too long. Although it feels good, we cannot be sure what it is doing to us." They did not need to be told again.

"I cannot find a way to open it," Baz continued, trying to examine the unit more closely with a flashlight.

As the flashlight came on, one of the robots, presumably from downstairs, suddenly came into view. Having discharged its duties, the four assumed that it was on its way down for the next set of instructions, wherever the instructions may be coming from. However, it came straight at Baz who instinctively shut off the light. From the corner of his eyes Thor could see that two other robots, which were not detected when they first came upstairs, had also closed the gap between themselves and the human beings. They were within an arm's length of the humans. However, since their arms were longer, they could reach the human targets. They formed a semicircle and waited.

Back at the dSE, more time had elapsed than what was experienced by the crew of EVA 7. After what seemed like close to two hours, Greg shouted, "The rover is moving!"

John asked, "What? They are coming back already?"

The response from Greg was confusing and frightening. "No, it is moving by itself. There is no one at the controls."

John, running to the window where Greg had noticed the craft moving by itself, said, "Something is going on, and none of us understands it. Did you see a collision between the rover and the pyramid?" In space, even the slightest bump would have a significant reaction especially between a large object as the pyramid and a relatively tiny one such as the rover.

"No, the rover looks intact. Besides, it is not moving away from the pyramid. It is moving toward and underneath the pyramid."

The concern evident in his voice, John asked, "What do we do? There is no time to bounce ideas with Mission Control. We need to do something *now*!"

Trying to think of something fast, Greg offered, "Manny and I will go and try to get it back."

John responded immediately, "No, it could be dangerous. The situation has suddenly changed."

Manny and Nicole had also run over to the window to see what was happening. Everyone was working and thinking fast for a quick course of action. It was merely a matter of minutes before the rover would be captured. Manny asked, "So what do we do? We have to try and stop the rover from drifting away or being captured."

John said, "Wait! Let me think." And then literally a second later, he said, "Okay, let's all go. Mission Control had indicated that henceforth we should go as a team of four."

Greg interjected, "But that will mean there is no one on board TE!"

John looked at Greg and spoke as fast as possible, "If you and Manny go, that will leave Nicole and me here. What do you think we can do without your help and without the rovers? At least this way, we will all be together. Couple of us can rescue the rover and the other two can go to the pyramid entrance and radio for the four inside to come back." Checking his stopwatch he continued, "There is still time in their oxygen tank for us to rescue them and the rover. If we can get to the rover all of us can come back, and if we don't rescue it then we will be in the same place, together. Besides, the dSE can be remotely controlled from Earth." There was logic to what John was saying. At least two engineers would have to go to rescue the rover since one was needed to drive it back. That would leave an engineer and Nicole on the TE. No large weapon systems could be deployed without at least two engineers and a rover. There were lots of small weapons systems on board the TE, but all those were already discounted by everyone as being pathetically ineffective. From previous EVA missions, it was established that the pyramids were made of solid metal so large and strong that no weapons conceived on Earth, except perhaps the largest ones, had any hope of having an impact on them. Besides the largest of the weapons, the ones with the most destructive power were on the rovers. They had unloaded one for EVA 3, and that rover was on the dSE, which meant that the rover that was drifting by itself had one of the other large weapons systems. If captured, it could be used against the dSE and its crew or even against Earth. The destructive power of the device was several hundred megatons, approaching gigatons, enough to blow a significant-size hole in the Earth's crust. The choices were to either abandon the four in the pyramid or enable their return with the rescue of the rover and the weapon on board. Ultimately, there was only one choice. If the roles were reversed, the humans in the pyramid would not hesitate to attempt a rescue, and they would never abandon their kin.

John quickly started moving and addressing Nicole at the same time. "Nicole, it is your choice. Do you want to stay here while we go and rescue the drifting rover?"

Nicole, who did not have to think twice, responded immediately, "Are you kidding? I am not staying here alone."

John had expected that answer. He ran over to the command module and hurriedly left one final message for Mission Control before the rescue. Still out of breath he looked up at one of the cameras and spoke, "The rover used for EVA 7 has started to drift. Cannot determine what is causing this to happen. There is no one piloting it. One unconfirmed theory is that the rover bumped into the pyramid and is recoiling, although we do not know how this could have happened. The team which used the drifting rover is still inside Pyramid Eight. We have to launch a rescue mission to retrieve the rover, or the team has no way to return. It has the large-tonnage weapon still on board. I realize we are breaking protocol by leaving the dSE unattended. However, this is a decision I"—and he emphasized the *I* as he pointed to himself—"have made under these circumstances. There is no time to wait for your response. The doctor has a choice and has chosen to accompany us. You will hear from us when we return. I will leave the exit hatch open for our quick ingress when we return. Over."

With that done, he ran over to where the others were already suiting up for the unscheduled EVA. Once suited, he opened the hatch from a small control panel on the dSE. The hatch door would have to remain open till they returned or closed from Earth. They all made it out in record time, even then the drifting rover had already drifted to midway below the square base of Pyramid Eight. With the use of the navigational thrusters John navigated as fast as possible to catch up with the unmanned rover.

Greg glanced up at the base of the pyramid and immediately commented, "Look! A door is opening on the base of the pyramid. I think that is where the walled-off area is located which Thor mentioned earlier."

Everyone's eyes shifted from watching what seemed to be the aimlessly drifting rover to where Greg was pointing. A small hatch had opened at the base of the pyramid, near one of the corners.

John looked up from the controls of the rover and acknowledged, "I see it. There seems to be some sort of gate opening."

Nicole, noticing the trajectory of the drifting rover, said, "The rover is going towards the opening. They are capturing the rover!" As she uttered those words, the rest glanced down and noticed the rover had changed course and was heading straight toward the opening. Within seconds it had completely entered the opening and the sliding hatch door closed behind it.

Manny commented, "I wonder if they know what is on board," referring to the gigaton explosive device.

John was still navigating to where the hatch had opened. "There is no evidence of an opening here. This door is a perfect fit. No wonder no one noticed it before."

Nicole asked, "I wonder how many doorways are built into the pyramids." It was an excellent question, which no one could answer.

Greg suggested, "John, I don't think we have a choice. We have to go in through the front air locks and try to retrieve the rover."

John responded, "I was just thinking that. You are right that we have to go in to rescue the team and the rover. We also do not have enough firepower without the equipment on the rover that we have just lost." Looking at Nicole, he said, "Nicole, if you like we will go back to the TE to drop you—"

She interrupted, as if expecting the question, "No way am I staying there alone. We all go!"

That response was expected. John navigated the rover to the front where they could enter the air locks. They disembarked the rover and went through the first air lock and then through the second one. As they were carefully walking through the dim chambers inside the pyramid, the rover which was left outside was slowly drifting away and in the same direction, much like the one that preceded it. They, like the four before them, did not know it but were marooned on the pyramid at least till the oxygen that they were carrying with them ran out in about two hours.

MESSAGE RECEIVED

John's counterpart at Mission Control, a woman named Chandrika Gupta, was awakened from her sleep. It was 2:30 a.m. However, she had given explicit instructions to call her anytime, day or night, if it was necessary.

"Hello, Chand, this is Dave calling from Mission Control." Chand, as she was affectionately known to her colleagues, had just put her head down at 10:15 p.m., hoping to get some sleep. Her heritage was Indian. However, her grandparents had immigrated to the USA. She was born an American citizen. She, like the others, had put in late hours day after day supporting this critical mission. She was elevated to lead this group of experts based on her leadership, respect she garnered among the colleagues, her intelligence, and dedication. Fortunately, this night she had decided to sleep at Mission Control where there were many cots available in tiny rooms—for those who needed to work late. Working long hours to support the mission was anticipated, and for that purpose many cots were brought in for use by the support personnel. Chand did not tell anyone that she would not be going home tonight because if the others in the team knew, they would continually bother her for the most mundane of issues.

Clearing her mind, she answered the ringing cell phone, "Hello, Chandrika here."

He repeated, obviously feeling sorry for waking her from deep sleep, "Hi, Chand, this is Dave. Sorry to disturb you, we have a situation here."

The tiny room, closer to the size of a closet than a room, had a cot and a table on which there was a lamp. Ideal to walk in, push the occupied / not occupied slider to show "occupied," lock the door, and go to sleep. When the door closed, the room became pitch-dark, and being in the quiet section of the building, it was an ideal place to get some good sleep. As she turned on the lamp on the table, she began to comprehend where she was. "Oh! Yes, Dave, that is okay. What is the problem?"

"We have a message from dSE that the second unit has had to do an unscheduled EVA."

The message took a while to sink in. Dave did not say anything else so as not to confuse her with too much information in her state of semi sleep. He let her grasp the enormity of what he had just said. This was a major development. "Okay, I am local tonight. I will be there in one minute. Please assemble the team in the war room."

"Most of them are there already, the rest are on their way. A strong pot of coffee is ready." As was the habit with most of the team, whenever they could get a chance to sleep in the Quiet Area, as it was known, they would grasp the opportunity with both hands. For most of them, the last few weeks had been very stressful and extremely draining. Certainly, for the unattached among the team, this had become a second home, although the sleeping room was hardly large enough to call a room.

Chand walked past her office and straight into the boardroom, now labeled as the war room, since almost all decisions were made here. There she found three of the team leads present, with the fourth one, as Dave had mentioned, on his way. Sarah, the communication lead and one of the two voices to the dSE, was also present. Dave walked in with two cups of coffee. "I am glad you were here tonight," he said, handing over one of the cups to Chand. "We received a message from John. Let me play it for you." He typed on the keypad, and the message from John repeated. Dave, one of the lead analysts assigned to monitoring any and all radio signals related to this mission, was the only one of two people till now who had seen and heard the message. The other being the junior lead who was on duty at the time and had picked up the message as it arrived, and notified Dave. As the message ended, everyone in the room looked at one another, assimilating the impact of the message from John. It seemed that John's decision was the correct one. However, it put the mission in great jeopardy. It appeared from the message that there was no dissention in the dSE team. In fact, the idea for them to go and rescue the drifting rover had come from Greg.

It was a while before anyone spoke. Dave said, "I think the decision to go was correct, but we have no way to communicate with them. I am sure John was aware of that when they left the dSE." The discussions started, but it was mostly a futile effort. Everyone at Mission Control was helpless until someone returned to the dSE. The small transmitters lacked power to broadcast more than a few hundred feet. As the remaining options were being discussed the fourth team lead arrived. He had heard the message through teleconferencing, but since he was driving, he had not seen the video. In this case, viewing video was not necessary.

Chand cut in, "I don't think we have a choice at this stage. They are already out and attempting a rescue. They had no time to wait for a confirmation from us, and clearly, they did not wait. All we can do is monitor the images, and see if"—she stopped and cleared her throat and corrected herself—"and see when they come back. I don't think we need to make a big deal out of this when they return, John and the others are experienced astronauts, and they made a spontaneous decision based on their observations and current situation. They were given that amount of latitude, and they acted in the best interest of Earth as well as the four who they felt were stranded in the pyramid."

She paused to enable the others in the room to digest the remark. "I suggest we keep monitoring and periodically send verbal messages, in case there is some kind of receiving device on the pyramid that they can use to tune to our frequency. It should be about two hours for them to get back if they have not had to step into the pyramid, and at least ten hours, if they had to enter the pyramid. Let's hope they have not had any need to go into the pyramid." She was right. No amount of discussion would take them back in time and prevent the departure of John and team on the rescue mission. They all dispersed to their offices and work areas and waited, none of them able to discharge their duties. Chand went to her office and replayed the message over and over, hoping to hear something that could give her a clue, any information that could be a positive sign, something that could be used to rescue them, even from this distance. There was none. She hoped these were not the last words from John that she would hear.

As agreed earlier, after two hours they all convened in the war room. The monitor in the room was already displaying the empty image from the camera on the dSE. There was no sign of any human activity on board. There was also nothing to discuss. The wait would go on. "The visual communication team is monitoring the situation. They will notify us when the crew returns. There is no need to sit here. Let's go and do some work," Chand explained, hoping that no one had picked up on the fact that she had a lump in her throat. Everyone dispersed again to their separate areas. The message being broadcast to the dSE was now on an endless loop, going out automatically every fifteen minutes asking the crew to send a transmission as soon as they could. The messages were traversing the vast distance but not being received by the humans in the pyramid.

Ten hours passed on Earth, and then it became fifteen hours. The meeting had convened again, and Dave spoke, his voice visibly shaking, "They do not have enough oxygen in their cylinders. I don't think they…" He could not finish the sentence. Over the months of training, the ground analysts had built up a rapport with the astronauts. Some had become close friends, others part of a close-knit team, like a family. Some of the ground-based team were alternates, in case one or more of the eight originally picked for the journey for whatever reason could not go. Now, with other ground-based staff, they were assigned duties to support the eight who had made the journey. Although the astronauts were many miles away, their safety for the outward journey as well as the journey back to Earth depended on the team on Earth. The survival of Earth depended on the success of the mission.

Summoning courage, Chand said, "Let's keep sending the messages as we are doing now. We cannot lose hope. Maybe some of our calculations are wrong and the time difference is greater than we thought. Or maybe there is breathable air in the pyramids. We do not know for certain. The dSE will be here, and till we visually verify or get some other evidence to the contrary we have to assume that the team is okay." As she said that, there was a tear that she had to wipe away. There was not a dry eye in the room.

DEFEATED

The four who had come in first were only about half an hour ahead of the four who had just arrived, at least in terms of oxygen consumption. However, due to the unexplained time difference between the outside and inside of the pyramid, a lot had transpired for the team that had arrived first.

The second team had arrived at the same spot where the gun had accidentally discharged. John, who was leading the way, stopped and noticed a set of stairs going down as well as a set going up. The first team had followed the robot down, then had retraced their steps back to this point and then had ascended the stairs up to where they were seemingly cornered. To the left of those stairs there were more stairs, leading both up and down. Farther to the left of the stairs, there appeared to be a long corridor, forking in various directions. The dim lighting conditions made it difficult to be sure of anything, but this area appeared to be a main junction to various parts of the pyramid. John said, pointing to the stairs on the left, "We will go up and check for signs of life." No one had any objection and going in one direction was just as good as going in another direction.

When they arrived at the summit of this stairway, they found a room which looked like the flight deck. It had a central console with what appeared to be knobs and switches. However, like the other rooms, everything was bathed in very dim light. They moved to the console, and John turned on the flashlight. They noticed some markings below and above the knobs and switches and recognized this as the alien language. As soon as the flashlight came on, the robot that was hidden dormant in the recesses of the chamber woke up and on its wheels moved toward the source of the light. John and Greg noticed the movement in their peripheral vision, and instinctively John turned the flashlight toward the movement. The robot was already within an arm's length of John by the time he turned to face it. It extended both its arms and in one quick movement jolted him with a mild current. The temporary paralysis induced by the jolt loosened his grip on the flashlight. It quickly took the flashlight from his grasp and just as quickly held him, to prevent him from falling to the ground. The robot gently let the collapsing body reach the ground and placed him there. Greg, who had his weapon drawn but had his arm by his side, made a movement to aim it at the robot. Even before he could get his arm up halfway to aim the weapon at the robot a second robot that was behind him gave Greg a similar jolt and took the weapon away from behind him. As he was collapsing to the ground the robot cradled him and placed him gently to the ground. Manny, who did not have his weapon drawn, made a move to remove the gun from its holster. He did not even get time to reach the gun. In an instant he, too, collapsed. He also did not fall to the floor. The third robot placed him gently to the ground. Nicole, who saw all this happen in a matter of a second or two, was horrified and fell to her knees by John, expecting the worst. Fortunately, John's eyes were open. "Are you okay, John?"

John said groggily, "Yes, I seemed to be jolted with a current, but I did not fall. The alien placed me down, gently."

The second team was not aware that the aliens that they encountered were in fact robots. A bemused Nicole responded, "I don't think they are aliens. They appear to be some kind of electro-mechanical robots!"

John looked around and carefully stood up, partly to make sure that his balance was back and partly not to be the recipient of another jolt. "Yes, you are right. They seem to have wheels."

Greg and Manny, too, stood up gradually, realizing that they were defeated in less than two seconds. When they stood up, the robot that had snatched the flashlight, which was now turned off, offered it back to John. The other robot offered the gun back to Greg. They carefully accepted it, realizing that neither could be used or they would get another jolt, possibly stronger and longer lasting.

They were in the company of three robots which were positioned in a semicircle.

The first team, in an adjacent room but at the same level, was also cornered. They waited for a few seconds, then Baz tried to step in between the robots. The robot rotated its wheels ninety degrees and moved sideways and blocked his way. Thor tried the same, and he, too, was blocked. Then Thor, who was holding his weapon, tried to raise it in order to point it at the robot. He was not able to lift it halfway when he received a jolt and was relieved of his weapon. The others observed that the robot held him and helped him on his way to the floor, gently placing him there. "*Don't move!*" Kristen shouted, which was fortunate since Baz was instinctively about to raise his weapon. When Thor was able, he gingerly stood up, and the robot offered his weapon back. Thor took it and put it in its holster. There would be no use to attempt to overpower these robots. They seemed to be a step ahead of the humans. Their only hope was to try to outsmart them. Little did they know that even outsmarting the robots was not possible.

The only path that was available to them was toward the stairs that they had come up only minutes earlier. Baz turned to the steps and started walking. One of the robots quickly wheeled around and led the way, and the other one followed the humans. The third robot did not move. It would not accompany them, wherever they were being taken. They were in a single file, robot one leading the way, then Baz, followed by Thor, Kristen, Ken, and finally robot two. When Baz was halfway down the stairs he, on an impulse, decided to test the robot and reached for his weapon which was in its holster. No sooner than he had decided to reach for his gun the robot in front, in one lightning swift motion, lifted its arms backward and had delivered the shock to Baz, which rendered him limp and harmless. In that same unnatural pose, it stopped Baz from falling down the stairs and carefully helped him to a seated position on the step.

"What did you do that for?" Thor exclaimed.

A few seconds later Baz regained enough composure to say, "Just wanted to test. Looks like they have eyes in the back of their heads and their arms are not restricted in motion."

Thor agreed, "Yeah! I saw that. Its arms can swivel a full 360 degrees at the shoulder. If it were a boxer, it could deliver a jab in front and deliver an identical jab behind."

Baz continued, "Although I cannot be sure if they are just very, very fast or if they are picking up on something else."

Thor needed an explanation. "What do you mean?"

Baz explained, "I was testing it. It was so fast that I did not even get as far as touching the gun. What if I were trying to reach for something else on my suit? I have a suspicion that they are picking up on our brain wave patterns. I mean…why else would they give back our weapons?"

Trying to find a more likely explanation, Thor said, "It is possible that they are not taking any chances, no matter what sudden movement you make. They will jolt you into submission. I mean, now that they have guessed that thing by your side is a weapon and that it could hurt them. I am willing to take a bet that henceforth we will have at least one robot within arm's length of us."

As they reached one level down, in the dim light, Thor thought he saw someone ascending the steps in the distance. The clothing seemed to be identical to what they were wearing. But before he could say anything, that suit went out of view. It was indeed the second team that had come to rescue them. But the first team was unaware that they were stranded without the rover and that the second team had launched a rescue mission. Indeed, the second team also was unaware that they were stranded. The rover that had been left outside the pyramid by the second team also had been pulled away. Just like the first one, the hatch door at the base of the pyramid had opened, and the rover had been swallowed up into the pyramid.

As the robot in the lead turned to head down the second stairway, they realized that they were being taken to the medical facility where they had seen the first robot being repaired. Suddenly it occurred to Kristen that no one had recently checked their level of oxygen.

"Damn! I think I am down to the last ten minutes or so of reserve in my oxygen tank. We have been here more than two Earth hours."

Everyone checked their levels, and Ken's was the lowest at seven minutes remaining. Baz had eleven minutes and thirty seconds. Thor had ten minutes and forty-five. Nobody said another word. They did not have a choice. They descended the second set of stairs and moved to the middle of what was identified during their first trip to the chamber, as a set of three operating tables. The humans moved to the center, flanked by the operating tables, and the robots positioned themselves on the other side of the tables. The humans were looking at the two robots that had escorted them, looking for signs for the next course of action. While their attention was on the two robots, the third robot, which was in the room, came forward. "Watch out!" shouted Thor who had noticed it come forward behind Baz. Too late. It had unlocked Baz's airtight helmet/visor and lifted it off his head. Baz did not have time to react. In an instant he was out of his sterile environment and exposed to the alien atmosphere. He stopped breathing, voluntarily, in order to prevent the alien air going into his lungs. The other three stared in shock and horror, unable to move. Even if they tried to move, it would be useless. They would never be able to make it back in time to the outside air lock through which they had entered the pyramid. They did not have sufficient oxygen. Little did they know that their rover was not where they had left it.

The third robot placed the helmet on the table. Everyone looked on and realized that Baz was holding his breath. He reached for his helmet, but the robot was faster and it moved the helmet away. The three looked on, and Baz's gaze turned to his human teammates. He could not speak since he was holding his breath. No one said anything, unable to speak. Very soon, they expected him to fall to the floor and start convulsing and coughing, gasping for oxygen. Then about two minutes of agony would ensue, and finally he would die. Soon thereafter, the others would follow the same fate. Kristen moved forward and gave him a hug. The others also stepped forward and gave him a last pat on the back. Farthest from their minds was what fate would befall Earth.

The second team, too, was defeated. Greg holstered his weapon, and John put away the flashlight. The robots were positioned in such a way that their only option was to go down the stairs. They, too, started going in single file, a robot leading followed by John, Greg, and Manny with Nicole as the last human in the line, with another robot forming the last unit in the line. As they moved toward the stairs and started descending, the third robot turned around and moved toward one of the hibernation units along the wall and pressed something. Nicole turned around to see as the lid opened. She was already taking the first steps to descend, but she got a momentary glimpse of its contents. "My word, what is that!" she exclaimed as she was ushered down the stairs and out of view by the robot behind her.

Back on Earth, Chand convened another meeting, one she expected to be the last. A few days had passed on Earth since the emotional meeting where they had decided to hold out hope for the mission crew.

"I think it is time to face facts," she started saying, staying strong despite the multitude of emotions she was feeling. She, too, had grown close to the dSE crew, with the possibility of a special relationship with John when he returned. She continued, "It has been a few days, and there has been no evidence of anyone returning to dSE. I will run this up the chain of command. A few days ago, when the message from John arrived, I had already apprised them of the situation. I will let them know that there is no possibility of any survivors. I know some of you, indeed all of you, had varying degrees of friendship with the heroes who embarked on this journey." Some of the attendees unable to control themselves started tearing up, and Chand had to take a few seconds and swallow hard. She needed to at least appear strong in the presence of her team. "We have to make alternate plans to defend Earth, which is out of our realm of responsibility," she continued. "However, since whatever we humans devise, it will involve space, I am sure some or all of you and I will have a part to play in the execution of those new plans. I am going to recommend the dissolution of this team, but be aware that you may be called up to become part of other teams. A small core of individuals will remain to monitor the dSE and send messages periodically as we have been doing for the last few days. Needless to say, I will keep the memories of the heroes and this team in my heart, whatever the future holds for us." With the last ounce of effort, she said, "I am proud of the work each and every one of you has performed thus far, and good luck to you all." Just as she finished, tears welled up and streamed down her face. She was not the only one who had to reach for tissues.

Reunited

The first team had finished their hugs and handshakes with Baz. Time was running out. Baz could not hold his breath any longer. It was already a minute and a half since he had taken his last breath. Baz decided to sit down on the floor. The space suits were designed in such a way that the oxygen was fed directly into the helmet. Therefore no one else could unhook their air supply and share it with Baz. The rest of Team One gathered around Baz and looked at him with an expression of inevitability. Their minds were racing to find a solution to the problem. Thor tried to reach for the helmet that the robot had placed on the table, and before he could reach it the robot had given him a jolt and was helping him to the ground. It was useless. They could not save Baz, nor could they save themselves. Baz would be the first to go.

The final moment had arrived. Baz could not hold his breath any longer. He took one last look at his teammates and let out the air trapped in his lungs. The breath came out warm and moist, heated by its extended stay in the lungs. When the lung expels its contents, the reflex action is to reverse the motion and breathe in. This is exactly what Baz did, expecting there to be insufficient life-sustaining oxygen in the gases present in the pyramid. To his and everyone else's surprise, he did not start choking. Slowly with a grin on his face and an immeasurable amount of relief Baz said, "I think this is breathable. There is enough oxygen here to breathe!"

Thor, who was on the floor, got to a sitting position and exclaimed, "That's a relief. At least we will not suffocate to death." Then he added, "It makes sense. They could have killed us before but did not. Something or someone does not want us dead!" While speaking he, too, took off his helmet and placed it on the table.

When the other two saw that Baz and Thor, now both on their feet, were breathing normally, they did the same.

The robots formed a semicircle, which indicated to the human visitors that they had to start moving. One robot, which was already in the room, stayed back as they formed a single file and marched like before, a robot leading and one at the back. A door at the other end of the room opened, and they went through. They would not be going back in the direction from which they came. They had no idea of how to open the internal doors in the pyramid. Beyond the door, they took a circular stairway leading down. They arrived at a large room full of cabinets similar to what Thor and Kristen had seen in Pyramid Three. "This must be the basement!" exclaimed Thor. The lighting was still low. It appeared that the circular staircase was not close to the outside walls of the pyramid. It was somewhere in the middle. The lead robot led the way to one corner, which seemed to have a partition wall and a room behind it. A door automatically opened as they approached the room, and there was a sudden gush of air, as if the room had been in a vacuum. The lead robot stood to one side, a clear indication that this is where they were to be confined. Baz and the team entered the room and stopped dead in their tracks, horrified at what was in front of them.

The second team was coming down the stairs when Nicole caught a glimpse of what was in the alien hibernation chamber. Instinctively she had exclaimed something which made John stop and look back. However, she was ushered on by the robot to keep moving down the stairs which prevented her from taking a longer look at the contents of the hibernation chamber. "What did you see?" John inquired.

The astonishment evident, Nicole responded, "I thought I saw a human being!"

It took a second or two for that information to sink in. John asked, "Who was it?"

Nicole responded calmly, "Oh! Not anyone I recognized, I don't think it was one of us, I mean, from the first team."

Greg interjected, "Then who could it be?"

They had reached the bottom of the stairs and were now walking toward the other stairway that the first team had descended about twenty minutes before. "I just had a glimpse of the open hibernation chamber, perhaps a second or less. It appeared that there was something there that had the features of a human. I mean, it looked like a human being—sleeping."

They were now descending the second stairway to go to the room with the tables. As this information was being digested, Nicole continued, "It had a head, hair on the head, its arms were on its side, and it had feet. It was about five feet tall, maybe five feet two. I mean, if someone flashed a photo of a sleeping human being for a second and a photo of what I saw, I would say both were humans. Only..." She stopped.

Greg asked, "Only what?"

"Only that the complexion—the skin tone. It was reddish brown."

Manny, who was unusually quiet till now, jumped into the conversation, "Are you sure?"

Nicole confirmed, "There is no mistaking that fact. There was back light in the hibernation unit, and I could see that part of the feature clearly. I may not have counted its toes or fingers, but I saw the distinctive features, a head, torso, limbs, just like us. And of course, the reddish-brown skin tone."

John, who was not too convinced, suggested, "Could your mind be playing tricks. We have all been under considerable stress."

Nicole was sure of what she saw and affirmed, "I saw what I saw. I don't think it is stress related."

They arrived at the table and due to the dim light, slowly realized what they were seeing. On top of the table were four helmets, and as they got closer they could read the names written on the front of the helmet to identify to whom it belonged. The labels read "Thor," "Kristen," "Baz," and "Ken."

Greg said rather somberly, "They are helmets. This could mean that they are dead."

John was examining one of them to make sure when the third robot came out of the darkness and twisted off Greg's helmet. Greg, too, instinctively held his breath when John said, "I don't think they are dead. There is no sign of struggle, no dents, or scratches on any of the helmets. I think they took it off voluntarily. At least some of them took it off voluntarily. Greg, try to breathe." A few seconds later, there were eight helmets on the table.

Again, the robots formed a semicircle and gradually began to close in, leaving no doubt that the four humans were to proceed in a particular direction. Greg attempted to pick up his helmet from the table but was prevented by a robot which blocked his way. The four humans had no choice but to follow the footsteps of the previous four without their helmets. Soon the four found themselves in the basement of the pyramid. Upon reaching the room at the end of the pyramid, the door opened. Teams One and Two were reunited. After the perfunctory greetings and hugs Baz said, "I knew you were here."

John, astonished at that statement, asked, "How?"

Similar to a curtain opening in a theater, Baz and the rest of Team One stepped out of the way. Behind them John could see the two rovers, intact but secure in the hold where they were confined. "How long have you been here?"

With all the excitement, no one was sure of how much time had elapsed, and Baz suggested, "Difficult to tell, maybe fifteen minutes."

John, smiling and clearly relieved that everyone was okay thus far, quipped, "So you have not formed an escape committee yet?"

Baz continued, "Where can we go? Even if we can open the hatch and drive the rovers out, we do not have our helmets. I wonder if that is why they took them, or maybe they knew that if we had our helmets on, we would die when we ran out of oxygen, without realizing that there was breathable air in the pyramids."

John responded, "Greg tried to get his helmet, but was prevented from doing so. I get the feeling they want to keep us alive but in captivity. I wonder if they know we need more than just oxygen to stay alive. Besides, there is probably no way of getting out of here."

Baz confirmed, "True, we checked. There are no visible ways of escape that we can see."

Speaking speculatively Manny offered, "We have the rovers. At least one of them has the large weapon."

Although it was a speculative suggestion, John stopped that thought process. "I don't think we can deploy anything at this point. It may be useless. There are eight pyramids, and we may end up damaging just one. Besides, they want to keep us alive, and I don't know why. They had enough opportunities to kill us, many times over. They could have destroyed the rovers, but they decided not to do so. I think the robots have secured the pyramids, as per their programming, and are awaiting further instructions from their masters when they wake up from hibernation. Based on what Nicole saw, that may be imminent."

Baz added, "And I am certain they are monitoring us, not necessarily through cameras. Did you see how quickly they reacted to counter our every offensive move? They may be telepathic robots! I am fairly certain, if we even think of arming our large weapon, one of those things will come in and neutralize us. I don't want to take that chance. I agree with John. They are keeping us alive for some purpose. We may yet have the option of negotiating with the aliens when they wake up. I don't think violence will work. They have us outgunned in the most elegant way possible. We are in their domain."

Nicole, eager to share the news of the aliens, said, "I briefly saw one of the aliens which were hibernating, just as I was descending the steps. One of the robots had opened the lid, presumably to wake them up. They have a lot of the features of humans. It was only a brief moment, but I could make out that they are more like humans than the grotesque monsters that we may imagine." She paused for a moment as if to reflect on what she had said before proceeding with her thoughts. "One thing that has been puzzling me was how the robots could jolt us with exactly the right amount of energy to knock us out temporarily. I mean, too much energy in that jolt could kill us or incapacitate us for longer, and too little would have no effect. They knew how much to use. Perhaps we have a similar disposition to the aliens that are hibernating."

Kristen added, "I have this strange feeling in my head. It is almost like someone is trying to tell me something. I cannot explain it—only that it is strange. Every time I try to use my meditative technique to calm down I have this interference. It is weird—maybe it is something to do with this pyramid. This shape is supposed to have weird properties."

Ken offered his opinion. "That is what I have read in several books. Pyramids are supposed to channel energy. Perhaps it is affecting you more than others."

Everyone was silent. There was nothing else to do. The room was bare except for the two rovers. They spread out in the room, some sitting on the floor, some in the rover which was the only thing with seats, and others lay down on the hard floor to take a much-needed nap. In the dim light, it was easy to fall asleep. They were forced to wait till such time as the door opened and they would be escorted upstairs to meet the aliens, or the floor opened and they would get jettisoned into space. If they had a window to the outside, they would have noticed that the pyramids had already started slowing down, having passed the orbit of Mars.

Executed to Near Perfection

Every step she had planned had happened exactly as designed, except the last and the most critical one. In the room when the first team and then the second team were encircled, she had tried to communicate with the humans. It did not work—although she had a similar brain, she had been trained for special communication. The human brain was designed to be trained—that is why it is so flexible, but prone to problems. That is when she had the idea to show a hibernating being to the human so as to make them curious. She has to send them back to their craft, knowing fully well that at least one team would come back in an attempt to communicate with an organic life-form. She has to make sure that when the humans came back to meet the commander of the mission she would be unreachable. The commander and the others would soon be waking up from hibernation. She did not want to answer any questions that would potentially give away her intentions. Her plan was only partially completed. She would instruct the menial robots to let the prisoners go. When the hibernating life-forms awoke, which was imminent, she would busy herself in an area of the pyramid that would be hard to reach performing some unnecessary service to a critical component. She would tell no one of her location and would spend as much time as possible doing this work so she could avoid answering questions. Now for the final adjustment in time and they would be at Earth shortly.

HOME

The equivalent time on Earth that elapsed was close to one year since the incarceration of the human astronauts. Mission Control was proceeding with the assumption that the crew of eight had perished in the execution of their duties. On Earth coordinated preparations were made for the reception of the alien spacecrafts, almost all of which involved some kind of explosive device being deployed in space. This was the one instance where space-based weapons were officially sanctioned by all nations. These weapons trained at the approaching pyramids had a secondary purpose. Due to their advanced technological prowess, the fact that there were weapons trained at them had not gone unnoticed by the alien robots. However, the best weapons that Earth could muster were no match to the capability of the aliens and therefore were being ignored as the source of possible danger.

The human intruders incarcerated for a short while in the pyramid, although unharmed, were confined to a small room at the base of Pyramid Eight. In the same room were the two rovers that they had used to arrive at the pyramid. Although the prisoners had all their weapons at their disposal, they didn't dare to attempt deploying any since there was a strong suspicion that they were being telepathically monitored. They had waited in the confines of the prison chamber for many hours, but no one could be certain of the duration. Morbid thoughts were creeping in, as it happens to every human after an extended confinement. Even to these trained astronauts, their mind started to wander about extended duration without food and water. The only solace was that this was not solitary confinement; they had one another's support.

Sitting around with no external stimulus, any physical need becomes more pronounced. Manny expressed his need for sustenance with the comment, "I feel hungry. We have not had anything to eat or drink for a while. I am ready to start banging on the door and get some attention."

Ken responded, "I am not sure if any of us can explain that we need food and water."

Manny, who was clearly the most under duress, responded, "We can try improvised sign language, by pointing to our open mouths. We have got to do something before it is too late."

As he was saying that, two robots came in bearing the helmets which they placed on the floor. Baz glanced at John as if to confirm that Manny's thought was telepathically picked up by one or many robots, which is why they came in with the helmets. John shrugged his shoulders. He was not yet convinced, and all the evidence could be a series of coincidences. To John, Baz's theory, albeit sound in logic, was still circumstantial. The robots stood there as the crew gently picked up their helmets, lest they were subject to another electrical jolt. However, this time it appeared that the robots wanted them to put on the helmets. Baz had assistance from Manny to reattach the oxygen supply that had earlier been disconnected by a robot. There was very little left. However, if they were allowed to go back immediately, they could use the emergency oxygen in the rover and make it back on time into the dSE. Unaware that they had stopped in a stationary orbit around the Earth, they made their way into the rovers. As they closed the overhead lid of the rovers, they noticed that the robots had exited the room and shut the door behind them. Then, as if by magic, both the rovers lifted off the floor. The door beneath them opened, and the rovers moved toward the open hatch and exited. The two pilots took control of the rovers and started navigating toward the TE, Nicole suddenly exclaimed, "Look! Where are we?"

Everyone turned their heads to look in the direction where Nicole was pointing and clearly saw a blue planet beneath them, with familiar outlines of continents. No one spoke for several seconds as they gazed at the round bluish object in the distance at which Nicole was pointing, wondering if they were dreaming or if it was a cruel trick played by the aliens. From their position in the rovers, no one could tell for certain. Moreover, being in space, they could not tell if they were still moving or had stopped. They were tracing the outlines of major landmasses to make sure that their eyes were not playing tricks, after that extended confinement.

Then Greg said incredulously, "Looks like Earth!"

The rest of the short journey to the dSE was done in near silence, each one trying to control their elation at seeing what could possibly be Earth, but wanting to first confirm before celebrating. The only words spoken were whether or not the object in the distance was Earth. How was it possible that they arrived at Earth so quickly? It had taken them approximately two years or more to get to the rendezvous point near Pluto, but they had come back in a fraction of the time. At this range, if the blue planet below was indeed Earth, communication would be much easier. There would be almost no delay in the radio transmissions. Their hunger gone with the mounting elation, they nervously waited as the automatic docking feature was engaged and the rovers started the docking procedure.

Due to the much shorter distance of the rovers to Earth, this conversation was faintly picked up by Mission Control on Earth. It was with increasing alarm that Mission Control had been monitoring the approaching pyramids and dSE throughout the entire journey. The rate of approach of the pyramids appeared to be fluctuating. However, they could not figure out why the speed of the dSE was also varying in lockstep with the pyramids. It was as if the Earth-based instruments were constantly malfunctioning. Mission Control had them recalibrated several times. At this speed, they had no way to stop or slow the dSE. If it continued at this velocity it would crash into or overshoot Earth and keep going, depending on its trajectory. Much to their relief, however, when the pyramids as well as the dSE were close enough to be in orbit they had both decelerated dramatically and placed themselves in a geostationary position above Earth. The person on duty was suddenly startled to attention; there had been no radio signal until now, just a background hiss. Then suddenly human voices were picked up. Due to changes in personnel, she was new and had not heard any of the astronauts' voices before now. She contacted Dave who was still in charge of this team, a team that was composed of mostly new members. He contacted Chand while on his way to check out the recording of the human voices.

Dave arrived at the desk of the person who had alerted him earlier. "Okay, so you said you heard something?"

"Yes, it was a distinctive female voice followed by a male voice. The transmission was not directed at us. Here, listen to this." And with that she replayed the recording.

The voice was faint because the weak signals from the rover were not intended to traverse space. It was meant to be for local communication only. There was a lot of hiss and other radio disturbance, but the voice was clear and intelligible and in English. Dave was confused, unable to make out the speaker of the words through all the interference.

Dave wondered if there were any attempts to communicate with the source of the voice. "Did you try to contact them on the same frequency?"

"No, not yet, I wanted you to hear it first. They are not asking us for anything. They are conversing amongst themselves as if they are completely oblivious of us. What if we say something and they stop talking? I am not even sure if it is the astronauts. It could be the aliens mimicking human voices."

"You are right, good thinking. Chand is on her way. We will discuss this and figure out an appropriate course of action."

Just then Chand arrived at a run and, still out of breath, asked what was going on. The message was replayed for her.

Dave asked, "What do you think—could it be…"

Chand interrupted him before he could complete the sentence, "Let's investigate more before we draw any conclusions."

She was right. Dave went to the assistant and started to explain what needed to be done to identify the source of the voices. As he was explaining to her they were interrupted.

"Mission Control, this is Commander John Cook. Respond if you copy." This time the voice in the speaker was clear, the signal stronger and devoid of any interference. They had entered the dSE, and the transmissions from there was much stronger. On Earth, however, if anyone was monitoring the video images from the cameras on the dSE, they would have noticed all eight come into view. However, this was discontinued after a few days of checking the video images since there was no trace of the humans and it was assumed that the astronauts were lost for good.

Chand immediately said, "Follow me," and they ran over to the war room.

As Dave turned on the speaker and monitor, the unmistakable voice of John came through again, "Mission Control, this is Commander John Cook. Are you there?"

The three in the war room could now see the crew staring with trepidation into the camera and monitor on dSE. As the camera in the war room fired up, the image and sound were relayed to the dSE, and the images appeared. The eight saw that the images that came up on the monitor were anxious faces of Chand, Dave, and the assistant.

Chand spoke first, "This is incredible. You are all safe!" Her voice was wobbly. She could not speak anymore. That lump in her throat that was choking her gave way, and the emotions welling up from her heart resulted in a fountain of tears. She took a deep breath as she wiped her face and heard John for the first time in in a long while.

John's voice softened when he heard Chand. He knew from the way she sounded that she had an emotional episode. "We cannot believe that we are so close to Earth." He managed to keep it at a professional level.

Tears of joy all around were soon replaced by more serious conversation. Communication was easier, and the dialogue was in real time, no long pauses anymore.

While the famished crew on the dSE ate their ready-to-eat packaged meals, John and the rest of the crew relayed their experience to Mission Control.

Chand, composing herself, continued after several minutes. "Since you are back it looks like I have work to do. But this work will be far more enjoyable than the previous few months. I will need to assemble another team. There is a lot to be done. You…I mean, we humans have not met the aliens yet. That has to be arranged. Whatever reason the aliens had on embarking on this journey, they are here now and I think they meant to come here. We also have to figure out who stays on the dSE a little while longer and who comes back immediately to terra firma. We don't know anything about communicating with our new guests or with the robotic life-forms on the pyramids. While you were incommunicado we had been doing some research, both in terms of deploying defensive procedures as well as analyzing data that you all sent before the err…incarceration," she said with a smile, "the details of which will become obvious in due course. We are glad you are back and safe. The word has already spread like wildfire over this facility, and there are literally hundreds of people by the door of this room. I will have to address them all in a conference and make the good news official, then later a press conference for the news media. I would much rather have these problems than having to explain your disappearance." Chand was gushing, jubilant, and joyous all at the same time. Words were coming out thick and fast. She had to actively compose herself and stop from talking anymore, and give the crew in space a chance to respond.

John corrected Chand. "We have not met the aliens either. Since our last communication we have only been dealing with what we think are robots. There has been no meaningful communication between us and the robots. Although, Nicole thinks she momentarily saw an alien. We suspect the alien was being awakened from hibernation."

Chand responded, "Copy that. We will be back with further instructions shortly. By the way, do you know why or how you all got back so quickly? I mean, the return journey was a fraction of your outward journey."

With the jubilation of being so close to Earth, no one had thought of why or how they were able to get back faster. John responded, "Frankly, we do not know. Nor do I believe any of us have had time to think about it—we are all so ecstatic at being back. My best guess is that we were probably being towed by the pyramids. It appears that the aliens are capable of projecting tremendous power. We cannot match them in the slightest."

Chand replied, "Well, that is another item that I have to add to the list. I will alert the proper authorities to be prepared for any eventuality. We do not know what their intentions are. Stand by for further instructions. Now that you are here, I can tell you that we were very concerned at the speed of the dSE and the pyramids. At the velocity you were traveling, at least according to instruments on Earth, we did not think there would be any possibility of stopping. We had remotely turned off the propulsion mechanism in the hopes of slowing the spacecraft, but that did not work. We were bracing ourselves for an impact, if we could not deflect the spacecraft and the pyramids or to see you whiz by like a comet. Over and out."

The conversation with Mission Control was over for now. Baz was thinking about what Chand had said about the speed and after the meal said, "If we were really traveling at a high speed, we would have had to start deceleration possibly just after we passed Jupiter. Apparently, we came all the way to a few hundred miles of Earth before we stopped. If that were the case, if we were in the dSE, we would have been crushed due to the g-forces. With hindsight, it was a good thing we were in the pyramid."

Thor was confused and asked, "Don't you think if the dSE were subject to such g-forces that, too, would break apart?"

Baz answered, "The dSE is bolted together with metal screws and welds which can withstand many more g's than a human body. A well-trained human cannot go beyond ten g's." Then pointing to some small items that no one had noticed earlier, he continued, "You see all the things we had left on the table, they have all fallen and have slid to the front of the ship because some strong force was being applied to the dSE in order to decelerate it. If we were here when the force was applied, we would have been crushed like grapes."

That made everyone wince. He did have a point. They were extremely lucky that they were not here during the deceleration.

A few hours later and after a much-needed nap, the familiar voice came on the speaker, "Hi, y'all. This is Tracey. Welcome home from all of us here." Although they were not quite home yet, it still gave them a warm feeling to be this close. Earth was now only a short trip away. "We have been trying to communicate with the pyramids, but they maintain radio silence. The Mission Control commander has managed to get most of her locally based team back together.

As to the others who are farther away, they are being brought back urgently. The rovers and the space suits will be ready by now. We want four of you, John, Kristen, Nicole, and Ken to go on another EVA mission—mission 8. We are not sure if they have locked their external hatch. If you have access as before—go to the chamber where Nicole saw the no-robotic alien. From your description, that chamber appears to contain the controls and where you will find the nonmechanical aliens. You can try to communicate with them as best you can. We don't know what language they speak, so you have to improvise. If they are human in appearance there may be some hope of finding some common ground to communicate. Clearly, they mean no harm, but be careful."

Kristen wondered about the protocol. "Do we take our helmets off after we close the second air lock?"

This was a much better situation. Two-way dialogue in real time was possible. Things could be discussed that was not possible in the past. Moreover, items could be relayed back to Mission Control much faster. The wait time would be minimal. If emergency escape was needed, it could be accomplished more easily. Indeed, the crew that put the dSE together was already on its way to dismantle four of the six individual crafts that made up the dSE and send each one back individually. They would leave just two crafts as well as the main module where the astronauts spent most of their time in space orbiting Earth. They would also bring fresh supplies for the eight crew members. Out of the two crafts that were left, one was the dSE that contained the weapons, and the other was the dSE that was used to dock and undock the rovers. The food supplies were in cabinets in the main command module which was literally and figuratively the hub of all crew activity. Taking four of the six dSEs back would mean that if any future space activity were needed with regard to the aliens, there was more than one available. Four dSEs were being brought back so that they would be available on Earth. No one knew what would transpire with the aliens.

After a moment's pause, presumably while she was checking with the others in the room, she said, "Yes, show as much of yourselves as possible, but with the space suit anything more than your faces is difficult, so yes, take your helmets off."

John, who had seen the other rooms, asked, "What about the other chambers in the pyramid? They appear to be labyrinthine structures with a number of stairways, passageways, and chambers."

After another pause, she said, "If you do not find anything in the control chamber and if you are unopposed, then you can investigate the other chambers. Remember not to split up. All four of you must be together at all times."

After another brief pause, she announced, "And there is one more thing. There is an asteroid that is in direct collision course with Earth. It is very large in size. We have prepared countermeasures. As to how effective they will be no one can be certain. If it hits, there will be almost complete devastation."

John couldn't hold back the irony. "Great, we first get a visitation from aliens, then almost immediately Earth gets destroyed." After thinking for a moment, he said, "Maybe they came to witness the fireworks. Could this be a coincidence?"

Tracey continued trying to allay any concerns. "No need to worry about the asteroid at this point. Because an asteroid impact, no matter where it happens, has global implications, we have another team cooperating with space agencies around the world to figure out ways to neutralize it. The international team is operating in various countries under the banner of Defense Shield. We will update you with the progress on the asteroid when we get more information. We wanted to communicate this to you since one of the most likely countermeasures is to try and blow it up in space. If communication with the aliens is established you may need to explain to them that we are not attacking them."

Sent to Pyramid One

The cyborg sent commands to the other menial robots to force the humans to make sure that the rover is towed to Pyramid One, should they attempt to return. She was certain that the rover and its occupants would return, and she wanted to make sure that the occupants would meet with the mission commander. This is what the commander would want and would not question this decision. She would then disappear to some corner and begin servicing some component so that she could not be easily contacted.

CONTACT, AT LAST

The four identified for the new mission were John, Kristen, Nicole, and Ken. If they were to make contact, there should be a person of authority and experience. That was John. Nicole, by virtue of being the first human to lay eyes on an alien, albeit in hibernation, automatically became the choice to accompany them. Ken, being the linguist, had to be part of the team since he had vast experience in languages. Although all of them were Earth languages, he could identify any patterns, symbols, or anything that could give the humans some idea to help decipher the language. Kristen would accompany them not only to make up the numbers but also as an expert in biological life-forms, in case that expertise was required. There was no need to send any weapons or combat experts since clearly the humans were no match for the aliens in this department.

After the extended period of inactivity accompanied by several naps during their incarceration in the pyramid as well as more inactivity and consumption of food after arriving back at the dSE, the crew was ready to go as soon as the instructions came. They were already on their way within twenty minutes of receiving the instructions. By inference, they were heading to Pyramid Eight as this is where Nicole had seen the alien. However, as they were heading for the pyramid, the rover and its crew became aware that the gravitational effect they had previously encountered in the near vicinity of the pyramid was now affecting them at a greater distance. They were more than four hundred meters away, and yet they felt the gravitational effect in the rover. They had a strange sensation of being dragged away from their destination.

Kristen, not knowing that John was trying his best to navigate, mentioned, "You need to apply the down thrusters. We will miss our mark at this trajectory."

A little irritated that the rover was not behaving in a predictable manner, John responded, "I realize that. I am trying to change course, but this thing is not responding."

Kristen, undaunted by John's struggle with the rover, asked, "Are you at maximum thrust?"

John's response was not comforting. "Yes, but the rover is not changing direction. It is not responding to my input although I am at full power. It seems to be moving all by itself. It appears to be heading to Pyramid Three. I am going to stop struggling trying to maneuver this vehicle—It is futile. I am turning this off. Clearly, they want us to go to a different pyramid." With that he let go of the controls and let the rover drift to wherever it was being pulled.

Nicole offered the obvious. "But that one is empty. Why is it heading there?"

John, after a moment's pause as they passed the entrance to Pyramid Three, said, "No, we are not heading to Pyramid Three. We are heading higher, looks like Pyramid One. I wonder if the top brass is in that one. I wonder if the pyramids are arranged in some sort of hierarchy."

As they approached Pyramid One, the rover slowed down and they could see the hatch at the base open, as it had done in the past when the empty rovers were captured. Once inside, the hatch door closed, and with a whoosh of air replacing the vacuum created when the hatch door opened, the door at the other end opened. At the door were four robots expecting their arrival—waiting to escort them to their destination. The humans disembarked, took off their helmets, and left them in the rover.

John mentioned the obvious, "No sense arguing with them. They obviously wanted us to come here. Maybe we will have better luck meeting and greeting aliens in this pyramid." No sooner than he said that, one robot moved to the back of John and held him firmly by his arms so he could not lift them. The second robot approached him from the front and with one arm clasped his jaw so his mouth would open and took a swab culture of the inside his mouth. This happened so quickly that no one had time to react. Before John could say anything, the first robot released him and moved to Kristen who was standing next to him. Her hands were also firmly but gently pinned against her body so she could not move them. The second robot took a second swab from her mouth and placed it in a container.

By the time John had regained enough composure to speak, the pair of robots had moved on to Nicole. John quickly said, "They are taking swabs from our mouth. Let them, it does not hurt."

No sooner than John had completed his sentence, the robots had already completed taking the sample from Ken. John's assurances were almost redundant since they had no choice and everything happened so quickly. Nicole wondered aloud, "I cannot understand what they plan to do with the swabs?" Of course, no one had an answer for that—but they would find out soon.

They all silently and apprehensively started walking, following the robots, nervous as to what they may encounter. The inside was still as dimly lit as before. As they stepped through the door, the robot in front started leading them toward the stairway leading up. They all understood that they had to follow it. The second robot followed them, last in line. The first robot led them across the basement which was identical to the other pyramids; at the far end of the basement was a circular staircase, similar to the one which they had descended in the other pyramid when they were apprehended. This led them to the area where the shooting incident had taken place in the other pyramid. In front of them was a long corridor. As far as John could see in the darkness, it appeared to be circular. Presumably, John thought, if one were to walk along this corridor, one would come back to the same spot, if it indeed was circular. John was correct in this assumption. Just as he was walking and this thought was going through his mind, the robot stopped and turned right to go up another set of stairs, a stairway not previously used by any human. They were being led to a new area of the pyramid. John imagined this would be an adjacent room to the one Nicole had momentarily spotted the alien being aroused from hibernation. At the top of the stairs, they all stopped in their tracks. What met their eyes was beyond belief!

Back on Earth, preparations were already in advanced stages for the arrival and the welcome of the aliens, should they avail themselves of human hospitality. Little did they know that the aliens had no intention of leaving the pyramids—unless it was absolutely necessary. In addition, space-based weapons were already deployed, but it was becoming increasingly obvious that none of the bombs, nuclear or conventional, high-intensity lasers, or any other top secret weapons would be of any use against these solidly built pyramids and its defense mechanisms. Maybe none of these would be necessary. It may become a moot point if the aliens had come to expand their horizons and make contact with Earthlings, just like Earth has been attempting to contact aliens.

Part of the arsenal that was deployed in space, with the agreement of all nations through the auspices of the UN, was aimed at a new threat to humankind, an asteroid named Apophis. The previous analysts had predicted during the years leading up to 2010 that Apophis would collide in 2035. However, in 2030, better studies in the trajectory of Apophis had indicated that the 2035 encounter would not take place. It would merely be a near miss. However, the subsequent encounter would result in a direct impact. The size of this asteroid was so large that the aftermath of the collision was classified as total devastation, which meant a 90 percent or greater loss of life. No human would be left alive; the only life remaining would be the size of bacteria or smaller. The well-known and fundamental problem of blasting an asteroid with an explosive, in order to deviate it from its course, is that the one large asteroid could break up into many smaller chunks and still rain down on Earth. Many small asteroids would have the cumulative impact that would be worse as compared to one large asteroid, thereby rendering the exercise useless. However, humankind had no other choice. There was no better alternative. They had to try this option and hope for the best. It was better than doing nothing at all.

A portion of the original team was redeployed to work on the imminent asteroid impact problem. A number of weapons contributed by various nuclear powers were already situated in orbit around Earth. Various space agencies were waiting for the right time to deploy these weapons. It would be a nuclear fission and fusion display, the likes of which had never been seen before, and very likely would never be seen again. Since the entire planned arsenal was already in space, the rest of the eight remaining on board the dSE needed to be brought back to Earth to prevent them from becoming casualties in case an explosion occurred in their vicinity while they were still on board. On Earth, they could function as support to the four who were now in Pyramid One.

One of the things that the dSE team on Earth had discovered, before being disbanded, was that each pyramid was almost the same dimension as the great pyramid of Giza, in the Valley of Kings in Egypt, built more than two thousand years ago. The height of the entrance from the base of the Giza pyramid almost exactly matched the location of the entrance to the alien pyramids. The path, just beyond the entrance, was almost identical, leading down first, then across the pyramid. Then from that first chamber, there were other corridors, stairs, etc. It was possible that there were other similarities. However, not enough was known of the alien pyramids. The dimensions of the alien pyramids were calculated from extrapolations based on the images sent by the human astronauts. The support team at Mission Control had started to look into the orientation of the Giza pyramids to see what stars they were aligned with and if it was possible that the alien pyramids could have originated from those locations. The support team consisted of scientists, historians, as well as archeologists, and they were attempting to investigate the similarities between the alien pyramids and the ones on Earth in the hopes of getting some useful information. It was well-known that the three major pyramids in Giza as well as the three pyramids in Teotihuacan, just north of Mexico City, Mexico, were of the same orientation as the Orion's Belt in the constellation Orion. In fact, one of the long-standing conundrums was why were these pyramids in Giza and Teotihuacan of such similar dimensions? The base dimension of the two pyramids is exactly the same. The Giza pyramid is exactly twice the height of the Teotihuacan pyramid. These pyramids were built thousands of years ago on different continents. A basic question the team was attempting to answer was how could they be so similar and what relation could they have with the alien structures? Could the known similarities of the pyramids built on Earth and alien spacecraft pyramids be coincidental, or was there something else that the humans did not know yet? Most importantly, could they learn anything from the pyramids on Earth that could relate directly to the ones that were currently and menacingly in orbit?

There are numerous other pyramids on this planet. Thousands of years ago when the pyramids were built on Earth, the locations of these pyramids would be too far for humans to travel. People during those times did not travel far. The best means of transportation was by foot, and a select few, mainly soldiers, had horses. There were some ships, but those were mainly for fishing in the immediate proximity of the coast. Why were these structures in the shapes of tetrahedrons independently constructed, in different continents, all those years ago? Was it true that an object, such as a fruit, placed at the vertex, experienced some special energy or force that made the item last longer than if it were placed somewhere else? These questions were being pondered by the team at Mission Control when the astronauts were in the midst of the EVA activities. When the humans became incarcerated in the pyramid, this team as well as most other teams was disbanded. Only a skeleton crew was left in place to monitor the approaching TE and the pyramids.

Although Nicole had only briefly caught a glimpse of the hibernating alien, what greeted their eyes during this latest EVA to Pyramid One was astonishing. John, Kristen, Nicole, and Ken stopped in their tracks as they reached the summit of the stairs and viewed the spectacle in front of them in utter disbelief. The room was well lit, but the source of the light, at first glance, was unclear. In what appeared to be the control center or some sort of a hub, there were many more of the robots doing various tasks, and interspersed with them were the aliens, now up and about from their hibernation. They were all of varying heights, but by Earth standards, they would be considered below average as compared to a western male. At first guess their height varied from five feet and one inch to five feet and five inches. All appeared to be male, had long shoulder-length black hair, and their skin color was reddish brown. Although it was difficult to see under the hair, their head seemed slightly more elongated at the back. The crown of the head seemed longer than usual as compared to a human. They reminded Ken of the depictions of ancient Egyptian pharaohs in paintings as well as sculptures. Maybe the ancient Earth artists were more accurate in their depictions than the modern humans gave them credit. First the pyramids, now aliens that looked like the artwork on those pyramids—was this another coincidence?

They could easily be human beings, if not for the skin pigmentation. The elongated skull could be considered as individual variations in any given population, although to have more than a few in the same location would be considered as unusual. They were each wearing an elaborate headdress. Presumably the more elaborate, the higher the rank or authority. Their limbs were identical to human limbs, although one got the feeling that the arms were slightly longer than a human's of similar stature. The hair was straight, black, and shoulder length. The eyes were large. Their bodies were covered with some kind of thin loose-fitting material, definitely alien material. The closest equivalent on Earth would be silk. Some had the full-length Middle Eastern-style djellaba, and others had a loose-fitting top and a knee-length kilt or shorts. It was difficult to tell which since they were so loose fitting. The neck, wrists, and ankles were decked with bangles and bracelets of varying kinds; it was possible that they were not just ornaments. Some of the neck ornaments were very elaborate, coming down to their navel, assuming they had a navel. Ken was thinking that some of these garments were similar to the ones represented in the paintings found in and around pyramids on Earth. Now it became clear to the humans why there was breathable air in the pyramids. These aliens needed it just the same as human beings.

Nicole mentioned to no one in particular, "This explains the presence of oxygen here. These aliens seem to be carbon-based lifeforms." Through the corner of her eyes she could see the rest of the group nod in agreement.

Then Ken made an interesting but factual observation. "These aliens are not big by human standards. They are about the same height as the people were, on average, about four or five thousand years ago. But they must be extremely intelligent and more advanced compared to modern-day humans. They may have had several thousands of years of evolution more than the human race has experienced. I wonder if the early humans would have physically resembled these aliens more than we do now." This comment would prove to be more prophetic than anyone realized at the time.

As the humans were transfixed with this sight, one of the aliens made eye contact and beckoned them in by a wave of his hand. Ken, noticing a peculiar phenomenon with what they were witnessing, mentioned quietly, "None of the aliens seem to be speaking!" In fact, for such a hive of activity that they were witnessing, everything was whisper quiet. As they stepped into the control room they noticed something else that took their breath away.

Simultaneously, on Earth, preparations were being made to blast the asteroid. It was still some distance away, but it was better to try to neutralize it farther out in space. This way, if it were to break up as predicted by some scientists, Earth would have more time to deal with the fragments. The countdown to launch the first of the defensive measures to attempt to deviate the course of the asteroid had begun; it would be launched in two hours, T minus two hours. The European space agency was taking the lead on this, with Mission Control in the United States focusing on the aliens and the pyramids.

Mission Control, which was monitoring the cluster of pyramids as well as the approaching asteroid, noticed one of the pyramids break off from formation and move in the direction of the asteroid.

Mission Control decided to alert Defense Shield. "One of the pyramids is approaching the asteroid. Abort the launch."

"This is Defense Shield. If we abort now, it may be too late, and we will not be able to deploy secondary measures."

Mission Control pointed out the obvious. "We realize that, but we do not want to explode a nuclear device in the proximity of the pyramid. Maybe they have more effective measures to deal with the asteroid."

Unconvinced, Defense Shield responded, "You don't know that for a fact. Maybe they are just investigating it. Have you been able to make contact with them?"

Mission Control had to alert them of the presence of humans. "We have sent a team of people to the pyramid cluster. We are still unsure if they were able to make contact with the aliens yet. They were supposed to go to Pyramid Eight. However, they are now in Pyramid One. We don't know if it was by choice or if they were forced there."

"Did you notice which pyramid is approaching the asteroid?"

"We believe it is Pyramid One, the pyramid that contains the humans sent to make contact!"

"Sorry to hear that. Maybe we have to make that sacrifice to save our planet!"

Deep down everyone at Mission Control knew that the humans aboard the pyramid would need to be sacrificed, if necessary. In order to save an entire planet with billions of people, the needs of the majority must be placed before the needs of the few. Everyone also knew that every second of delay in launching the countermeasure meant time lost to save Earth. A decision would have to be made soon, a decision not based on emotion relating to the occupants of Pyramid One.

Inside Pyramid One, John, Kristen, Nicole, and Ken, having been summoned by what looked like a high-ranking alien, had just stepped inside the cavernous room that appeared to be the control center. What they saw defied imagination. This room was about 20 meters from the apex of the pyramid, possibly the highest room in the pyramid. From the ceiling to floor there was a 360-degree panoramic view of space. It appeared that the metal outer layer had slid away from all around this part of the pyramid and revealed a transparent window through which observers could look outside. And although there was bustling activity in this room, everything was very quiet, except for an occasional click from the control panel and the whir-ring of the robotic wheels as they went about their tasks. Even the controls, or what they assumed to be controls, were not numerous. A few buttons accompanied by some unrecognizable characters formed the main control panel. It was simplicity to the extreme; perhaps the alien equivalent of computers controlled every function of the craft. But, even then, there were too few instruments of the type found in Earth-based crafts. In front was a monitor which was displaying data, none of which was legible to the humans.

Then the data on the monitor faded away, and four images of babies were displayed in four equal sections of the monitor. The babies became infants, toddlers, then young children. The humans were mesmerized at the images. They each recognized one image since it was them. The toddlers became young teens, then older teens, young adults, and then fully mature adults of about the same age as they were now. It was slightly embarrassing since the images did not have any clothes. But it was unmistakable. It was as if someone had taken a photograph and put it up on the monitor. After the initial embarrassment, slightly tempered by the fact that the humans knew they were not looking at pictures of themselves, Nicole could not hide her astonishment. "This is incredible. This explains the swabs that were taken earlier. Their technology is incredible—how do they know to decode our DNA? How do they know to stop at approximately the same age as we are now? Is there something in our DNA that tells them how old we are?"

Obviously, no one could answer that question. The images on the monitor shifted back to data. Although no one knew what the data meant, they all suspected that it was some sort of analysis of their DNA. Since they could not fathom the meaning of the information on the monitor their gaze shifted to the window and the incredible views of Earth and the surrounding space. As they were taking in this unique perspective John whispered, "Look, we seem to be moving. We are not in formation with the rest of the pyramids."

Kristen whispered back, "Or they are moving away, we cannot tell which." She was, of course, correct that it was difficult to determine without the aid of instruments. They could see the seven pyramids out of one side and Earth on the adjacent side, but a little more time would have to elapse before they could discern if it was they or the other seven that were moving.

The humans looked at the alien who had beckoned them in; they noticed that his attention was diverted at something out of the opposite window. John and the others turned around to see what the alien was looking at; for the moment, nothing was visible in the foreground. The background was full of bright stars, just as it was in all directions. A couple of minutes passed, their gaze shifting from the alien to the direction in which he was looking. Intermittently they looked around the room to see the robots busy working away and the other aliens either looking in the same direction or working on what appeared to be the control panel. Then suddenly Nicole whispered, "Look, there is something out there."

The rest of the humans were already looking in that direction, but now they started squinting their eyes in an effort to see what Nicole had noticed. "I see it," Ken whispered back. A few seconds later, everyone could see it, a tiny speck, which was gradually and steadily growing larger.

John whispered, "I am willing to bet that this is Apophis, the asteroid that is supposed to be on collision course with Earth!"

They looked out of the other window and saw Earth, and sure enough the asteroid and Earth were approximately in the same line. Even if the asteroid were slightly off course, the gravity of Earth, as it got closer, would pull it toward Earth. John continued, "I wonder what they want to do?"

"Mission Control, this is Defense Shield in Europe. We want to let you know that it is impossible to abort the launch. We communicated with the Mission Control manager who ran it up the flagpole. I am told that it ultimately got to the secretary general of the UN. We don't know how or what went into their decision-making process—Our orders are to proceed as scheduled. We see that one of the pyramids is approaching the asteroid, but our analysts say it will be too late if we wait. We are proceeding as planned."

This situation was not envisioned when the plans were made to blast the asteroid, and therefore there was no protocol to abort the launch of the Defense Shield-controlled weapons. There was no consistency among the two main space agencies involved with regard to aborting the launch. It made perfect sense that delaying any further would put Earth in jeopardy, so the safety of Earth and the masses that live on it took precedence.

"Defense Shield, this is Mission Control, copy that and proceed as planned," came the reluctant response.

As John was drawing the imaginary line from the asteroid to Earth he noticed, at the corner of his eye, a momentary bright flash. He whispered, "Earth has launched its defense against the asteroid. Hope we do not get caught in its blast."

The other humans turned to where John was looking but saw nothing, but they instinctively knew what he meant. The asteroid progressively kept getting larger. The pyramid and the asteroid were narrowing the gap. There was still silence around them except for some clicking on the control panel and some whirring of the robot wheels. The pyramid and the bomb were approaching the asteroid. John wondered if the aliens knew what was about to happen. If he were to alert the aliens to the bomb, they could neutralize it and put Earth in danger. If he did not, the pyramid could get blown up and the occupants of the other pyramids could attack Earth and destroy it. Maybe the aliens recognized that the asteroid posed a great danger to Earth and that is why Pyramid One was on its way to the asteroid, he was not sure. He had to decide one way or the other, and ultimately decided to warn them.

He waved his hands, and when the alien looked at him he mouthed the word "bomb" and performed a gesture with his hands to indicate what is commonly recognized as an explosion. Ken joined in this pantomime, although being the linguist he still did not know that they would understand. The alien looked puzzled, so finally John pointed in the opposite direction, the direction of the approaching bomb. The alien looked in the direction they were pointing but did not initially seem to understand. Then he looked back at John and nodded, then he again fixed his gaze in the direction of the asteroid. How could the humans know what the aliens understood or what they did not. Their gestures and mannerisms would certainly be different. They are even different in various parts of Earth. At least he appeared to acknowledge the presence of the quickly approaching rockets loaded with massive bombs.

"I hope they know what is in store for them in the very near future," John whispered.

"I cannot think of any other way to alert them. I have not heard a word of speech from them. They may be communicating telepathically with each other," Ken whispered back.

Little did they know that their minds were being monitored, not just by the aliens.

EXPLOSION

The pyramid was above the asteroid at a distance of about half a kilometer. The asteroid was so huge that the occupants of the pyramid could see the front as well as the back of the asteroid from opposite windows of the pyramid. They could also see the sides of the asteroid. Due to the erratic rotation, the view of the asteroid from each window kept changing. The pyramid and the asteroid were now traveling in the same direction, toward Earth, and the explosive device launched from space was on its way to meet them. From the window, the humans and the others could clearly see the direction of motion of the asteroid. This trajectory would result in a direct hit to Earth. In the distance, there was a tiny speck heading toward them. They could not see it clearly at first, but progressively this speck was getting larger.

John, who was getting slightly impatient, said, "I wonder if they have a plan, and what it is, we just seem to be hovering over the asteroid. Are they examining it? They have to do something and get us out of here, or there will be an almighty explosion shortly, at close proximity."

Suddenly Nicole said, "Look, we seemed to have moved a fraction to the left." They were all looking from the window that had the view of Earth and trying to mentally draw a picture of their direction of motion.

"Yes, but look at the bomb. It is very close and getting closer. It could detonate at any time."

The detonation time was preprogrammed into the onboard electronic systems in the missile. It was decided that automation of this event was better and more accurate than to do it manually, as a manual remote trigger would increase the chance of malfunction, not to mention the politics of who gets to decide when to set it off. Worse still, if the detonation were mistimed, then the impact would be minimal at best or have a negative impact of speeding up the asteroid. Therefore, simple programming and a proximity sensor would ensure that the explosion would occur at exactly the optimal time.

Sure enough, slowly, the pyramid seemed to be dragging the massive asteroid out of harm's way. "I wonder how they do that. They have got to be using gravity," John commented, the relief clear in his voice. However, the tiny speck that was the warhead altered course and was still heading their way. Another few minutes passed, and the pyramid had dragged the asteroid far enough to neutralize its threat to Earth. However, the homing mechanism in the warhead made slight corrections to keep it pointed directly at the asteroid.

"Now we have to get out of here," he continued. However, the aliens did not seem to be in any hurry to get out of the vicinity. John looked again at the alien whom he had tried to communicate with earlier and repeated, "We have to get out of here now!" He started animatedly gesturing and pointing, hoping the alien would understand that he meant for them to get out of their proximity to the asteroid. However, the alien glanced at John and, unperturbed, resumed his original activity. It appeared he did not want to move out of the way.

Looking at his colleagues John said, "I hope they can read our minds! If they cannot, let me wish you all"—he held out his hand and looked at each one of the humans standing there—"the very best of luck in the afterlife. I cannot see how we can survive a nuclear explosion."

The others grimly nodded in agreement and shook one another's hands.

As they were quietly pondering their final moments, they were witnessing a long, sleek, and sinister-looking metallic object approaching them at great speed. Although the thrusters had burned out, the frictionless environment meant that the missile had not lost speed. From an initial sense of foreboding the humans had transitioned to a feeling of inner peace. A strange calm had descended over them. Each human knew that their final moments had arrived and death would be instantaneous and painless. There was nothing they could do, captive as they were and not able to either communicate or use the machinery to move out of the way. It was too late now. The missile was too close, and even if they started to take defensive measures, they could not avoid the full impact of a nuclear blast. It was only a matter of a few seconds. The anticipation was growing to the point that they wished the agony of waiting would not last any longer. Then it happened—the nuclear device detonated. The humans turned away, reflexively tightening every muscle fiber in their bodies.

There was never a time and probably never will be a time when any human would purposely be this close to a nuclear explosion. The asteroid broke up into smaller pieces, just as predicted by the scientists on Earth. They had also hoped that the fragments would disperse, but the pieces of the asteroid did not scatter. This would be a major disappointment when the scientists would find out in a few moments.

All this was being monitored on Earth as well as the remaining crew on the TE.

"Defense Shield, this is Mission Control. We confirm the breakup of Apophis into several fragments. We do not know the status of the pyramid."

"This is Defense Shield, we confirm your findings. For future reference, this way of mitigating a threat from an asteroid is not appropriate. We should not try this again. We see that several fragments of Apophis are continuing in the same direction as before the explosion. Since Apophis was already moved by the pyramid by the time of the impact, we are relieved to state that none of the fragments are projected to impact Earth. Due to the debris clouding our radar imaging we cannot locate the pyramid. We will contact you when we have a positive ID. Hopefully they survived the explosion."

This exchange was being heard on the speaker on the TE. However, even from their vantage point, the crew also was not able to see the pyramid or any large pieces of the pyramid. The cloud of debris was too large and was obscuring their view.

"Mission Control, this is Baz on TE, we, too, are unable to locate the pyramid," came the very concerned voice that was heard at Mission Control. "Standing by to launch a rescue mission, if required."

UNAFFECTED

In Pyramid One, John and the other humans witnessed a nuclear blast from less than a kilometer away. On Earth, a blast at this distance, even with the smallest nuclear device, would have vaporized everything in its vicinity. Fractions of a second seemed like hours as the dumbfounded humans continued to anticipate their demise. In the immediate aftermath of the explosion, the pyramid went dark for a brief moment and shook due to the shock wave of the blast. Everyone was violently shaken, and some, who were not able to grasp on to something stable, fell to the floor. Even some robots fell, and those that did not fall remained standing with considerable effort. Immediately thereafter, as the asteroid broke up, the pieces crashed against the pyramid. Initially it was the smaller pieces that impacted the pyramid, causing loud crunching sounds inside, similar to a blender if it were turned on with rocks inside. This caused more chaos and confusion among the humans and robots. Then the larger chunks of the asteroid hit the pyramid. These had more momentum and shook the pyramid even more violently. Both the robots which had somehow stayed standing as well as the robots which had fallen and were attempting to get back to their feet fell to the ground again. Under other circumstances it would be comical to witness such an event. In the chaotic situation, the humans had not noticed that the pyramid had suddenly become dark inside, save for the dim background lighting. The humans continued to observe this melee, wondering why they had not perished yet.

As everyone regained their balance, the humans noticed that the darkness was caused by the protective shield that was instantly deployed to cover the windows. The shield was being pulled back now, and they could see that they were in a cloud of dust and debris of what used to be Apophis. Although they were not out of danger, none of the boulders were impacting the pyramid anymore. With the chaos somewhat abating, Kristen finally spoke, "They must have activated the defense mechanism. That is why it suddenly went dark inside. All the windows are covered with that foamy stuff we saw earlier on our first EVA mission. I guess this partially explains its purpose." Only a few seconds had passed since they felt the full impact of the blast, but she like the others had forgotten that they were supposed to be dead. John realized that they were still there and said, "We appear to be alive! How is that possible?"

A few seconds later, the realization gradually dawning on each human that this was not the end, John exclaimed, "Well, I don't know about the rest of you, but I do not want to go through the last ten seconds again as long as I live."

The others nodded in agreement, too awestruck to say anything.

Slowly the dust appeared to be clearing. Looking from the outside it was the pyramid that was moving out of the chaos. Observing all these events the humans on board the pyramid concluded that using the gravitational engines, the aliens were pulling the asteroid away from its collision course with Earth. When the bomb had exploded it had caused the dust and debris to collide with the pyramid due to the attractive gravitational field around it. That is why the debris did not scatter away from the pyramid. Instead it started clumping around the pyramid. The supposition by the humans was that aliens must have been performing this task manually, since they saw some activity on what appeared to be the control panel. In the aftermath of the explosion the computers on board must have detected the fragments impacting the pyramid and must have instantly taken control and evasive action at the same time and instantly reversed the gravitational field to repel everything from a boulder to the myriads of tiny dust particles to reduce damage. That is when the crashing and banging of the boulders against the outside of the pyramid had stopped. All this took no more than five to ten seconds.

"Mission Control, this is Baz, we see the pyramid. It appears to be in one piece," he euphorically shouted into his microphone.

"We have just picked it up on our instruments. How did it survive that explosion?"

"No idea, but one thing is certain, our Earth-based weapons are useless against them."

Apophis was safely dragged by the pyramid out of the way of colliding with Earth. Then Defense Shield's nuclear explosion had fragmented it. Now the bits and pieces would continue on a new trajectory that would completely miss colliding with Earth. This would happen till its course intersected with some other planet. Laws of physics meant that over time, the gravity of the larger pieces would attract the smaller pieces and a new Apophis would be formed, possibly in many thousands of years. For now, Earth was rendered safe by the aliens. Had it not been for them, the explosion would not have been much help since the fragments, some the size of a building and others the size of a bus, would have rained down on Earth causing as much or more devastation than a single piece. The pyramid made its way back to the others and took its place at the top, the same location that it had left.

ALIEN TALK

The humans and the alien life-forms had regained their composure. Some aliens had left the bridge, presumably their work done for now, or maybe for a break. Some of the robots had also left the bridge. The activity level was much subdued compared to the time when the humans set eyes in the room just prior to the asteroid encounter. One of the aliens still present was stationed at what appeared to be a captain's chair. This was the one who had beckoned them in when they had first arrived.

Again, he looked at John and motioned him to sit on a chair that a robot had just brought into the bridge. This appeared to be an ordinary chair. However, there was an attachment on the backrest which supported a hollow pyramidal-shaped piece that could be lowered on to the head, rather like the hair dryer at a salon.

Ken whispered, "I think he wants you to be seated there," pointing at the chair.

"Yeah, I got that too," he replied, the reluctance to sit down in that strange chair obvious in his voice. There was an amount of trepidation to comply with this request. None of the humans knew what the tetrahedron-shaped device would do to the brain, especially after they had analyzed the human DNA in a matter of minutes. Nevertheless, there was no choice, so he walked toward the chair, with the robot standing behind it, and sat down. When he became comfortable, the robot lowered the pyramidal device. When lowered, it extended down to his mouth. John lifted his hands to feel the hat, and it felt metallic. Needless to say, it was opaque; he could not see through it. The only vision was of his legs and the floor when he glanced down. The pyramid was anchored at the back, and it fit snugly around the brim of his head, so that any lateral movement

236

was not possible. In fact, his head could not be moved at all, in any direction. He tested to see if he was tied down. To his relief he could slide down on the chair and move away. To him, it was of immense comfort and relief that he was not tied down or restricted in any way, only that when he was seated comfortably, he could not move his head. It felt as though there was some kind of electronics in the hat or the alien version of it, he could not be sure.

As he sat there, with almost no visual stimulus, he began to wonder why the aliens preferred triangles and tetrahedron shapes. His mind began to wander, the other humans looking at what was about to unfold.

As he was thinking about pyramids, his thought process was interrupted, almost as if it was not him that was interrupting it. A thought came to his mind as if it were saying, *We are from far.*

He thought he was drifting away in the first of a wave of daydreaming scenarios. He had to stop and focus, so he checked himself mentally and determined that he would not let his mind wander. He could not see anything of consequence, so there was no visual stimulus. It was difficult not to think of anything, and so his mind began to wander again. Before he knew it, he was feeling with his hands the arm of the chair and thinking that this was made of some alien material, metallic but not constructed from ferrous material like the park benches on Earth. As he started to drift off into another wave of daydreaming, his thought was involuntarily interrupted again. *We come to visit.* Again, he stopped himself, thinking he had to focus. But focus on what? Usually a visual stimulus is needed, and the mind follows from that stimulus. John was not able to see anything, and he was increasingly getting the disconcerting feeling that he was not entirely in control of his thought process. Was it some kind of brainwashing that the aliens were attempting to perform on him?

After a few more minutes of him sitting and not letting his mind wander, the robot lifted the pyramid-shaped hat. John noticed that nothing had changed around him, and mostly to his relief the other three humans were still standing nearby, looking incredulously at him. He gingerly stood up, in case the robot had other ideas, and walked over to the others.

"It was a strange feeling. My mind began to wander, and every time it did, I thought I was daydreaming that I was speaking with the aliens. It was a strange feeling! It was as if I did not have control of my own thoughts!"

"I think I know what they are up to. Let me try," Kristen said and walked over to the chair and sat down. The alien looked surprised initially, but a second later the robot lowered the pyramid hat onto Kristen's head. Kristen, having spent many hours in confined spaces in deep-sea submersibles and countless hours in decompression chambers after surfacing from various dives into the depths of the ocean, the one thing that she had learned over time was to be calm and relaxed and let the mind rest. She also took lessons in meditation where sometimes the technique is to let the mind go blank, not think of anything. One is even supposed to not think of the process of not thinking of anything, a very difficult thing to do especially since every mind is geared to think of something all the time. Even in sleep the mind is somewhat active at times, when it resorts to dreaming.

Kristen let her mind go blank, as if in meditation, and immediately she sensed that there was something interrupting her, forcing her to come to terms with a voice in her mind, a voice that was not her own. It was as if there was a distant voice giving her instructions, as if she was having a particularly vivid dream. The voice was saying, *We have traveled a long distance to come here. This is not the first time that we have visited this area. We come to take with us what we need.*

That was a shocking statement. She was not sure that she had heard it correctly. Was it her own thought, or was she picking up the aliens' communication? One thing about which she was correct, it was indeed telepathy that the aliens were using to communicate. She decided to ignore the last sentence and asked through her thought process, *Where do you come from?* She repeated the thought a few times so that her inquiry would get through. She was not sure how to think since this was the first time she had encountered such a situation. Besides, in what language does one think? Sometimes thinking is not in a language at all. It is just a process of actions. Active thinking such as encounters or conversations that one may have had is in the native language of the person. Passive thinking such as admiring a flower or a painting is language independent. Some say that most dream sequences are language independent, although the exception to that is that some vivid dreams that take on physical manifestations, such as verbalizing, may involve a language. However, one does not think in entire sentences. Instead one thinks of things that needs to be performed or a process that needs to be followed, such as directions to a location. Even humans with multilingual ability do not necessarily think in a language. If one had to verbalize thoughts, speaking would be a long and tedious process.

Some people on Earth have telepathic abilities, and others can develop it through practice. Some telepathic abilities are present in animals as exemplified by their premonition of impending disasters, such as earthquakes etc., where the creatures flee from the sight of trouble before the calamitous event takes place. In addition, pets such as dogs have the ability to sense when its master is ill and behave differently. In humans, twins are supposed to have some telepathic abilities, and the same is the case with a mother-child bond. Unfortunately, these abilities are not nurtured and are lost over time as the child grows. But the innate ability is retained which can be cultivated at any time. Some people however, train for a lifetime. They being the religious leaders in our society. They spend a significant part of their lives in deep meditation; whether it is called meditation or prayers, it amounts to the same. In fact, scientists have measured the power of prayers and have found significant changes in the brain immediately after the prayers as well as the electrical activity outside the body. The findings are as yet not fully understood. The deliberate ability to change of the ability of the brain to have this capability is achieved through training. The training process first involves making the mind quiescent and then trying to read the thoughts. Kristen had taken classes in meditation that enabled her to calm her thoughts; she had needed to relax and not let the long periods of solitude in the decompression chamber get the better of her. People who are not able to do this internally take medications to help them. An anxiety attack in the decompression chamber when the decompression is not complete could be fatal since the individual stricken by the attack is liable to do irrational things such as opening the chamber to get out.

Apparently, in the current situation, clearing the mind of other thoughts enables the human mind to acquire the ability to pick up the alien thought projections. The thoughts did not come in the form of a language; instead it was more like when you wake up from a dream. You know that you had a dream, but you do not know in what language the dream occurred. Kristen found the experience disconcerting at first. It was as if there was something in the back of her mind that she was trying to recall and the only way she could remember it was when it jumped into her active consciousness. She likened it to going to a store with a mental shopping list and forgetting one item. In order to remember what it was one would walk the aisles almost aimlessly glancing at all the items on the shelf. It is only upon spotting what was forgotten that the item suddenly jumps into active memory. Similarly, this process was composed of picking up signals and moving it to active consciousness so that the information could be processed and assimilated. She wondered if the aliens processed it the same way and if their processing was more efficient than what she was doing. Anyway, this method was working for her, and it was better than not being able to communicate at all.

The question was sidestepped with the response, *You do not have to repeat. We can read your thoughts, and the device over your head enhances our thought for you to understand. This is how we train your kind.* The alien could not help thinking that he had communicated with her before, but that was impossible. Not only did these creatures not communicate like his kind, but also this was possibly the first time that she had communicated via the thought language—the special pictorial language. He quickly put it out of his mind.

During this time, the three humans standing there noticed that the alien was deep in concentration. They did not know what was taking place, whether Kristen was successfully communicating with the alien and if so how was she doing it. More concerning was if Kristen was all right or whether that device over her head was adversely affecting her. All around them the activity of the robots and other aliens was continuing. They were performing their assigned tasks, albeit at a reduced pace now.

The alien continued, *We want to meet your king.*

Kristen did not know how to answer that comment. *The commander of our mission is John. He was on this chair before me.*

He is the leader of your planet? Kristen thought she detected a surprised tone to the question.

Kristen had to explain further. *No, there is no leader of the planet. He is commander of the mission. Like you, he commands our spacecraft.*

The surprised thought came in stronger that before. *What do you mean there is no leader of the planet? When we came here before we made a king.* He uttered a word verbally that sounded like "Khunmkfeu" that no one understood and then continued with this thought communication, *And put him in control of the civilization!*

Kristen thought that name sounded like an ancient Egyptian king, but she could not be sure—Ken was the expert. She, however, wanted to simplify things till she was ready to address his inquiry. *When did you come here before?*

We have come here several times. When the people were not like you. They were different and not advanced in technology. They lived in caves and huts and hunted animals to eat. We changed them. When we came back again we made some more changes and made one of them king. What happened to his descendants?

Kristen had to discuss this with her team and Mission Control. *I have to take a break. This way of communicating is very exhausting.*

With that she lifted the thought intensifier hat and stepped out toward her human companions.

"They can read our thoughts," she remarked to the other three. "That pyramidal hat is a thought intensifier, for those of us who do not know how to communicate telepathically."

John, clearly relieved, said, "That is reassuring. We were not sure what that device was doing to you. So what did they say?"

"Well, the one I was communicating with said that they have come here to take something, not sure what it is, but that was before I started getting comfortable with the communication process. He, I mean, the alien, wanted to see the leader of our planet. I told him that there is no leader of Earth. He seemed surprised and maybe a little disappointed by that. He also mentioned that they have been here several times in the past. My impression is that they were here a few times thousands of years ago. He said something about changing the people, I don't know what he meant by that. He also mentioned that they put a king in place. Presumably he wanted to see the king's descendants. We have a lot of communication to do, but it is exhausting. Now that we know what is needed, I propose we take a break, eat something, and come back in a few hours and do this over again."

John read between the lines. Kristen wanted to discuss this with Mission Control and come back prepared with answers.

Kristen and the rest looked at the alien. He was already looking at them trying to read their thoughts. No sooner than Kristen could figure out how to inform him of their intention, the escort robot came into view. The alien gestured with his hand for the humans to leave, and they followed the robot to the rover waiting in the basement area of the pyramid.

Return to Pyramid One

On their way back, the crew in the rover noticed that two of the six dSEs were already undocked from the cluster and the crew was making preparations to send it back to Earth. Once that was complete, they would undock two more and send those back, leaving just two and the command module in place from which to carry on the activities. There would still be ample power available for the crew in the two remaining dSEs with their engines actively running on hydrogen fusion power. Once back at the TE control center, Kristen spoke, "I have a feeling they cannot read us when we are out of their view. I think we have to be in their line of sight for the telepathy to take place." Then she added, "Thankfully." She continued, "I was not tired really. I wanted to know how to handle them. I did not know how to answer the questions they were asking. It was difficult not to let them suspect that I needed a break to collect my thoughts. I was picturing a wall clock and visualizing the ticking of the seconds. I think that did the trick for now."

The others on the TE agreed, and these comments were heard at the Mission Control on Earth. As if in response the speaker from Mission Control came on. It was Tracey, and she said, "Hi, y'all, hope your visit was successful. I know that we are all relieved to see the destruction of the asteroid. We are not sure what happened, but we are sure glad that all four of you are fine. We monitored your return to TE from the pyramid through our instruments. It is your turn to speak and give us an update—we are all gathered here to listen and take notes." The last sentence was said with a detectable smile in her voice.

In the TE they all looked at Kristen for her to start providing the update, firsthand. Kristen finished swallowing the food that she was chewing on at the time and began to speak, providing the whole experience from the human perspective of the destruction of the asteroid to the telepathic communication that took place. She mentioned the fascinating episode with the swabs and the DNA sequencing, the image projected on the monitors of when they were babies to present time.

A few seconds later the answer came back. "The same four of you have to go back again. You have to find out exactly what they want. Please explain to them the situation on Earth. We do not have a planetary leader. Instead there are many nations and many democracies. There is no king, other than it being purely symbolic in some countries. Explain as best as you can and explain truthfully. However, we have to know what they want, why they were here before, and what they mean when they said they made a king and put him in control of the civilization. We feel they may not be here to hurt us. They just saved us from near complete destruction by moving the asteroid out of collision course. By the way, take your time, finish eating, rest if it is needed. Although they may be more powerful than us, time is on our side." Then she added, "So to speak, since they have the secret of manipulating gravity and possibly time itself. Also, we want each of you to take the portable radio communicators with you. This may save some time in case you need to communicate with us and you are not in the TE. At least it will save some trips back to the TE. Make sure your earpieces are in so the communications from us to you are not audible to the aliens. In case they do voice pattern matching to figure out our language. Lastly, we do not have any information on why they did the swab and how or why they were able to project images of you on their monitors. Our best guess is that they are trying to figure out the human behavior. We were surprised that they allowed you to see those images—we think it is on purpose that they showed you what capacity they have."

All eight continued with their meal, not hurrying in the least. When they were done, they silently went about preparing to go back to Pyramid One. The procedure to go out of the dSE had become second nature by now. Not only had they memorized the process during training, but they also had executed the procedures many times during the trip. The safety checklist was ingrained with the muscle memory reinforcing their actual memory, and the four went about the tasks, to return to the pyramids, almost subconsciously. This time they set a course for Pyramid One, and as they approached it the gravitational force from the pyramid took over. John was somewhat relieved because otherwise he would have had trouble navigating the rover through the opening at the base of the pyramid and parking it inside.

This time the welcoming party was a pair of robots. Since they did not speak, at least no human had heard them utter anything, and the humans knew the protocol, they were in the main area of the pyramid in next to no time. Kristen had already taken the hot seat, and the robot obligingly lowered the thought intensifier. Kristen took just a few seconds to clear her thoughts and got ready for the telepathic communication.

Welcome back! We have many questions. are you ready? The alien jumped straight to the point. Kristen suppressed the thought that was about to pop into her mind, wondering if dispensing with pleasantries was their culture, in case that thought was picked up by the alien and misconstrued as offensive. Clearly, until now, the aliens were behaving as though they were superior to the humans.

Kristen also dispensed with the pleasantries and came straight to the point. *I will do my best.* Then she instinctively thought she would take the initiative, instead of passively answering questions like a scared child, and fired off the first question, *Is this how you always communicate, or do you also speak with your mouth?*

There it was again. Every time she spoke, he had this feeling that he had communicated with her before. But that was impossible—they had never met. The alien, a little startled, answered the question, *We can speak with our mouths, but we find that this way of communication is more efficient. Besides, you will not understand what we say just as we do not understand what you say.*

It was gratifying to know, whether true or false, they were unable to understand the language that the humans spoke. Nevertheless, this was turning into mind games, both literally and figuratively. The alien did not complete the answer by stating that they could read the human minds. So she kept the initiative by firing the second question, *How far can this type of communication reach?* The answer to which was *We have to be looking at the person or persons with whom we are communicating.*

Kristen continued, *What is your name and rank, and what is your role?*

My name is Atra-has. He projected proudly, wondering if the human would know the relevance of the name. It was more than a coincidence that the name was very similar to his uncle's Atra-hasis, who happened to be the commander of the very first mission to Earth. In addition, he, among others, stayed back in order to ensure that the mission was successful, therefore almost surely sacrificing himself for the cause. Quickly Atra-has came back to reality. *And my rank is commander of this mission. My role is to achieve the mission objective. We have been sent by the leader of our planet to get some things from your planet that belong to us.*

The name Atra-has was verbalized. This was the second time any human had heard the alien speak, and it sounded very like a human voice. The human onlookers wondered why he spoke. They would find out later from Kristen, during the debriefing, that this was his name. Kristen, becoming more confident of this method of communication, decided to interrupt before Atra-has could finish with a question.

Where do you come from?

He answered by shifting his eyes to the monitor. The humans followed his gaze. The monitor gradually zoomed in from a top view of a spiral galaxy, which looked like the Milky Way. Then to a region of stars along one of the outer spiral arms of the galaxy—much like the position of Earth. It kept zooming in till a star and a few planets were visible. Then a red dot appeared on a planet, signifying their planet. Kristen and the other humans were convinced that the galaxy was the Milky Way. There was another highlighted planet on the monitor, and everyone knew it was Earth—due to the other planets in the vicinity of the nearby sun. Visually no one could tell the distance between the two planets, but just noticing the number of stars between them, it was obvious that the humans had no hope of traversing the distance with the current technology.

Kristen persevered without giving Atra-has a chance. *How do your pyramids, these vehicles that you are traveling in, work? What makes them move? Do you have some type of gravity engine?*

Yes, we have mastery over gravity. We also see that your race does not. We use gravity to travel vast distances and also use this principle to control time, although there are limitations. The pyramidal shape of our vessels and some other important objects has special powers that can harness the use of gravity and other forces.

Kristen wanted to make sure. *Was this used to move the asteroid away from impacting Earth?*

Atra-has answered, *Yes, and we also knew that the explosion would take place so we had to move the asteroid farther than we had planned. That is why we were so close to the asteroid at the time of the explosion, as we were still moving the object. At first, we were pulling the object towards us. Later when it was broken down to pieces, we had to push it away. The machines in the craft can do that by themselves.*

Kristen decided to make a statement to inform Atra-has that Earth was prepared to destroy the asteroid. She said, *We sent the weapons to destroy the object. It was not intended to harm your crafts.*

Atra-has, to her surprise, responded, *I know. Those weapons cannot harm us. They are too weak. The object was intended to collide with the planet on which you live. That is why we came here at this time.*

Kristen was surprised and somewhat confused with this answer. She also sensed that Atra-has was getting frustrated with her statements and questions. Nevertheless, she decided to persist. *Are the robots also capable of reading thoughts?*

Yes, some are. They cannot speak at all since there is no need for them to communicate with us by speaking! This last comment came in a little stronger than usual, possibly his frustration coming to the surface. She also felt like she had almost picked up on something that the alien did not want to communicate, something that was not very pleasant. Unperturbed, Kristen continued, *How do you tell which robot—*

Enough! I will ask some questions now! Atra-has could not hold back any longer. Possibly no one on the pyramid or even on his planet treated a high-ranking official this way. The humans watching could see the veins popping by the side of his head and wondered if it was the normal coursing of blood through his body or if he was getting visibly agitated.

Kristen decided to back down and let the alien ask the questions. After a second, presumably to compose himself after that outburst, he asked, *You said before that you do not have a leader. How do you—*

Let me explain. She knew she was tempting fate by interrupting, but she wanted the aliens to know that although not as technologically advanced, the human race was not timid. Whatever the aliens had experienced during their previous visits to Earth centuries ago, the human race had changed and was vastly different now. *There is not one leader for the planet. We are divided into many territories, and each unit has a temporary leader who is selected by the people. There are a few exceptions, but generally this is the case.*

How many territories are there?

Close to two hundred. She knew that Atra-has would not understand that number. This was one of the drawbacks of communicating this way. Numbers could not be communicated since the numbering scheme was developed on Earth, and was almost definitely different than that of the aliens. The human-alien communication was limited to expressing high-level ideas only, unless either one of them got more familiar with the language of the other. The alien was saying, *What...*, when she, realizing that Atra-has was looking at her since he was communicating with her, lifted both her hands and balled it into a fist and opened them twenty times. She had noticed that the aliens also had five digits per hand. Atra-has stopped in mid sentence and counted. Presumably he understood since he went on to the next question. *How many individuals per territory?*

It varies.

How many individuals in total?

About ten billion on the planet. And then realizing he would not understand the number and there was no way to represent that big a number with her hands she came up with the best approximation that she could. *Less than the number of stars in this galaxy.* Of course, there are many more stars in the Milky Way than people on Earth, but under these circumstances this was the best approximation that she could muster.

There was silence for a while. She could not see what was happening since her eyes were covered by the thought intensifier, then she heard a command being given to one of the other aliens or robots, she could not tell which. *Send message back with information that our task is difficult since there is no planetary leader. Instead we have to approach many smaller units to take what we want with force. There are [some garbled words] individuals on the planet now. And get [garbled words] here immediately.*

Kristen guessed that the garbled words were probably their approximate representation of the ten billion individuals on the planet. Also, she was not sure if it was a warning or if she was not meant to pick up on the communication from Atra-has to whomever he instructed. Either way Kristen now knew that they meant business. They would not come all this way to go back without completing their mission. No matter how prosperous a planet was, this task would have taken a lot of resources to be put together and it would not be a trivial expedition.

Kristen decided to wrest the initiative again, and although she could not see the alien, she asked, *Will you accompany us to meet with our people on earth? We have a number of questions and want to understand a lot of things about you.*

After a brief pause the answer was *We will land our craft when the time is right. First, we must plan.*

That seemed fair enough. They were not trusting of the humans. If the situation were reversed, Kristen thought, and the humans had traveled to another planet the answer would be the same.

You mentioned that you were here before. Did you study us in your previous visits?

That question seemed to confuse the alien since he took a long time to answer. *Yes, we have studied you. We made changes to the people. We made one of us your king and left him here. We left instructions to gather items we need. Do you have shapes that look like this craft?*

There it was again. They have come for something, but they are not revealing what it is that they need. What kinds of changes did they make? Was it manipulation of the DNA to which he was referring but was unable to communicate effectively? Was Ken right when he had previously observed that there was a resemblance between the aliens and humans? More to the point, they left one of their own here on Earth as a king. That did not make any sense at all. There would not have been a concept of a king in very ancient times when the prehistoric humans were still migrating and occupying uninhabited lands. Kristen had these fleeting thoughts and hoped that the alien had not picked up on the thoughts. She decided to ignore the question and ask, *What kinds of changes have you made, and what is it that you need?*

This time it was the alien's turn to ignore the question and repeat his previous one, *Do you have shapes that look like this craft?*

Yes, we have some on Earth, but they are very old. We do not build these kinds of shapes and of this size anymore. What kinds of changes did you make to the humans? She repeated the question. All the while the communication process was through images. Although this was a faster way to communicate, it was still taxing for someone not used to it. Besides, Kristen had to interpret the images and convert them to a form she could understand. It was almost as if she were trying to read hieroglyphics.

I cannot explain in ways you can understand. The best way to explain it is we changed them before they were born. You are the same as us.

That was a revelation. Could he mean the aliens had manipulated the DNA of the ancient humans. How far back in history did they change the human DNA or the precursors to the human DNA? Many more questions came up in the marine biologist's mind. Kristen was intimately familiar with the process of evolution, and she had to suppress the thought of whether the human evolution was speeded up by the alien intervention. Every organism on Earth has DNA, and some of the larger animals, certainly the mammals, match the human DNA by over 95 percent. The great apes have a 99 percent match with the human DNA. At what point did the intervention occur?

Did they create the ancient humans, including the Neanderthals, and then fine-tuned the process to make the present-day humans? No one knows why the Neanderthals did not succeed in the battle of evolution. Did the aliens have something to do with it? Did the DNA-tweaked Neanderthal outsmart the non-DNA-altered Neanderthal, or did the aliens create an entirely new species which killed off the Neanderthals? Besides, what did he mean, "You are the same as us"? Do they have blood flowing through their veins? Do they have the double helix and twenty-three pairs of chromosomes? These were the fleeting thoughts going through Kristen's mind. She was not concerned of being read by Atra-has because even if some of her thoughts leaked out the alien would not be able to comprehend the Earth-based scientific terminology. Nevertheless, she still tried to suppress the thoughts. The alien continued, *We changed the people so they could think like us.*

Kristen tried assimilating this information. Humans, or at least the ancient versions of the humans, were thought to have evolved in what is present-day Africa. They were supposed to have migrated northward to the present-day Middle East and Europe and then further east and west to occupy lands that were uninhabited at that time. The aliens must have intervened during the northward migration and changed the genetic code so that the migration and evolution continued with the modified DNA sequence encoded in every subsequent generation. So, they must have come here much before humans were in their present-day form. Perhaps Atra-has could not provide, in a meaningful way, the number of ancient humans used in their DNA experiments or the time period of when this occurred. He had no way of being specific with numbers in a way that the human, with whom he was communicating, could understand.

All this revelation was making Kristen think, and she was taking a long time to process the information that was being supplied; nevertheless the alien continued. She was still unsure whether Atra-has was able to pick up on her attempt to analyze the data.

We made a structure like the shape of this craft. We left a king to collect material we need and to guard the structure till we came back. We have to go to this structure and collect the material stored in it.

It was slowly beginning to make some sense now. Whenever the aliens had come to Earth in the past, they had certainly come here during the time of the pharaohs, since Atra-has mentioned that they built a pyramid and left a king to guard it and fill it with whatever they needed. Now the question was "What did they need?"

Again, there was silence for a while when Kristen did not know what was happening. If Atra-has was thinking, he had it down to a fine art since she was not picking up on his thoughts. He had much more experience to be able to think without transmitting his thoughts. Then she heard him communicating to someone else, just like before. *Make plans to go to the [garbled location or coordinates] soon. We have to see for ourselves what the Earth beings are describing. We may not be able to get [garbled words], but we can get the [more garbled words].*

When there was a little gap, Kristen decided to probe a little further since there were so many questions—*Why did you choose this planet?*

After a brief pause, presumably to collect his thoughts, Atra-has decided to provide a brief history. Either that he thought that Kristen had many questions or he must have sensed her frustration in the short answers he was providing thus far, or that they had decided to land on Earth and consequently reveal a little more information. Whatever the reason, Kristen was not expecting what was about to be disclosed. *We have traveled and searched many planets. This and a few others are very similar to ours. Like the others we had to make some changes to it. When we first came here, there were very large animals. It was too dangerous for us. We changed your planet by creating a large explosion. We came back later, and all the large animals were gone. We came back again when it was safe and left smaller animals among the animals already here.* The mental image he was projecting was of ancient pre-humanoid-like creatures that existed way back in the evolutionary tree of the human race. This creature, the Australopithecus afarensis, which later became Homo erectus, was thought to be somehow linked to the human race. He continued, *This is what we wanted. We then created people like us from one of the apelike animals. Because the new creature had more abilities than the native animals, they survived. This is also what we wanted. We again came back and made more changes. The last change we made created even more superior beings, more like us. We had hoped that these superior beings would dominate your race and eventually take over, just like the previous time. But our enemy arrived, and we had to fight a war here. We defeated them and then had to clean up everything before we left. These were our orders.*

He paused, since he was distracted by something showing up on one of the monitors. Then satisfied that it did not need immediate attention, he carried on from where he had left off. *We left some of our own to be leaders. These are the ones we seek now. We told them not to mix with the others. After the war, we left more of our own to rule and collect what we want. But it looks like none of our own has survived. Maybe our enemy came back after we left. It does not matter as long as we get what we came here to collect. Last time we came we took some of the items we need and also some of the earth people, but now we need more.*

He stopped at that point, and Kristen did not know if it was on purpose or if he had revealed more than he had intended. Whatever the reason, the last sentence was a shocking revelation. They had taken some human beings in the past, and now he wanted more. But for what purpose? They had taken some of the items they needed. What could those items be? Kristen had not taken long to ponder these questions when Atra-has communicated again. *We have decided to land on your planet and see for ourselves. We will go to the location where we had gone in the past. We also need to collect our lost crafts that we lost in the war with our enemy.* Questions were slowly being answered, but more questions were cropping up. Where were these crafts to which Atra-has was alluding? Anything as big as these pyramids would have been found long ago, just the same way as the Egyptian pyramids were discovered. Could it be covered in the snow and ice of the Antarctic?

Kristen's questions and thoughts were coming in thick and fast. Among all the questions she had, Kristen ventured to ask an easy one to get the ball rolling, *When did you come here last?*

Atra-has responded, *In this trip!*

That stopped her in her tracks.

SUMMONS

The cyborg was asked to report to Pyramid One—it must have taken quite an effort for the menial robot to find her to deliver this information. She could not dwell on how or how long it took for the menial robot to locate her whereabouts; she had to figure out why she was being summoned. This may not bode well for her especially if her master found out her true intentions. She had to go there with some other thought process going through her mind. Otherwise, that would be the end of everything. It would be the end of her, her plans, and her attempt to end a horrible fate reserved for the humans captured from this planet. She would get into the small pod and travel the short distance to Pyramid One.

Alien Landing

Kristen stood up to stretch her legs, having been seated on the hard bench-like chair for a considerable amount of time while she was communicating with Atra-has. She noticed a new robot appear. She thought this robot looked strangely familiar. All of them were almost identical, and she could not tell them apart, but why did this one stand out. No sooner than the robot appeared, it turned around and marched out in the same direction from which it came. She refocused and announced to the rest of the humans that the pyramids would land on Earth. Immediately after Kristen finished, Nicole said, "Look! We are moving. I think we are heading towards Earth. Shouldn't we be sitting or be strapped to something?"

John responded, "Yes, ideally we do, but no one here, including the aliens, seems to be concerned with that. I wonder if there will be the usual reentry buffeting that we experience in our spacecrafts."

John decided to take out his portable radio communicator and transmit the plan as he understood it to Mission Control. He spoke into the communicator, not knowing whether his radio signals would reach their destination, "This is John, alerting you that the aliens with us on board are preparing to land on Earth." He was surprised to get a response into his earpiece. "Copy that, Commander, all eight crafts are approaching Earth and are entering the atmosphere at different locations. Do you have any other news for us?"

The humans followed Kristen as she walked toward them. When she reached them, she provided a quick synopsis of what had transpired, only highlighting the important items, all the time keeping the communicator on to transmit so the ground staff also heard the narrative. She said that the aliens were responsible for the demise of the dinosaurs, were responsible for creating the human race, and that they wanted to take some humans as well as some other items. Those items were as yet unknown either because it was not revealed yet or due to the language barrier. She also mentioned that the aliens were aware of the Apophis asteroid and that the timing of the aliens arriving here was not completely coincidental. The best she kept for last, stating, "Atra-has said that they did all this during their current mission. I am pretty sure I did not misunderstand him. But I guess that is not the primary concern right now."

Just as she finished, the message came back from Mission Control, saying, "We are sending a welcoming party as soon as we can determine where they intend on landing. We are trying to work out the logistics through the UN channels. The UN agrees that we should be present at the landing location of the aliens, and they are representing us to enable us to be present at all the landing sites. We are confident that no nation will reject this request."

As those words were being spoken, the imaging equipment and cameras started to display life on Earth in great detail. As they kept zooming in, individuals on Earth going about their businesses, completely oblivious to the spacecrafts, were displayed as if it were some kind of a documentary. The humans on board could not recognize the place, but it seemed to be some kind of a bazaar or a flea market. Kristen and Nicole noticed that the aliens were intently watching the life as usual that was unfolding before them, and wondered what they were thinking. The aliens were deep in concentration watching the people walk, stop to speak, or buy something or just haggle about the price of some item. Remarkably, sounds were also being picked up, presumably through some supersensitive microphone, but the language made no sense to the humans or the aliens on board the alien craft. Ken, being a linguist, mentioned, "This seems to be some sort of Arabic language, but I cannot pinpoint from which region. Either the sensitive microphones or the electronic gain is causing too much distortion to make out the language. I can only pick up a random word or two, but they are meaningless to me."

Then the monitor cycled again, starting from a wide-angle view and progressively zooming to a more and more detailed view. At the broadest and least detailed view, they noticed that there were some areas highlighted with yellow flashing dots. There were many yellow-colored dots on the monitor and one of green color. The humans wondered what these flashing dots were meant to represent, but clearly, they were not going toward any of the yellow dots. The trajectory of the pyramid was superimposed on the monitor, and it appeared that the pyramid was heading toward the green dot.

The portable communicator came on again, and it announced, "This is confirmation that they are not all going to the same place. It appears that they are all going to different locations, eight crafts to eight different locations!"

They did not have long to wait to arrive at the upper reaches of Earth's atmosphere. There was no buffeting as the humans were expecting. When a craft enters the atmosphere from orbit, the angular velocity of spacecraft coming in contact with the increasingly thick air creates tremendous heat, lots of vibration, and turbulence around the craft. The early Apollo reentry vehicles had what is called an ablative material to protect the occupants. As technology progressed, the shuttles had a silicone-based tile structure that dissipated the heat and protected the reusable craft. Earlier inspection of the pyramids by the TE crew revealed no material of either kind. However, the pyramids were not hurtling toward Earth. They were entering in a much more controlled fashion.

John announced, to no one in particular, "No one seems the least perturbed by the reentry. It appears that they are using gravitational power from their engines to control the rate of descent. I think we can call them engines. None of us has seen where they are located or what they look like. I don't expect to feel any vibrations or buffeting during this phase of the journey."

Then the excited voice came on the communicator, "One is going towards India, one to Egypt, one in the general direction of the Atlantic Ocean, one to the Yucatan Peninsula, one to the Chile-Peru region, one to the Siberian part of Russia, one to Australia, and one to southern Japan. We are trying to figure out if there is any significance with these destinations. However they are too high in the atmosphere to pinpoint the exact landing location."

Then John suddenly remembered that there were four other astronauts left on the dSE. He was still responsible for them as their leader and commander. He spoke into the communicator, "What about the rest of the crew on the dSE?"

The response came back almost instantaneously, "We will bring them back to Earth by the conventional means. They are in no danger. They have ample supplies of food and water and other necessities."

Ken mentioned to the humans in his vicinity, "I definitely believe the sounds we are hearing are in Arabic. I believe we are going to a location somewhere in the Middle East." Just as he said that, one of the larger and ancient man-made objects came into view, albeit it was distant and faint. He continued, "And I believe we are headed toward Egypt—I see the great pyramid of Giza. There is no mistaking it—even from this altitude. I wonder if the aliens had a hand in its construction. It has always been disputed as to the technique and method of construction."

The communicator came on again, and this time the speaker proclaimed that they knew where the spacecrafts were going. "We believe we have figured it out—Your craft is going to the great pyramids in Egypt. The second one is going to the Bahamas, to the region of the Bermuda Triangle, we believe. The third one is going to the anomalous region in Mexico called Zona del Silencio, or the Zone of Silence. The fourth one is going to the region of Chile/Peru called Cuzco where the Nazca lines and other ancient relics are present. The fifth one is going to a region in southern Japan known as the Devil's Triangle where equivalent conditions as the Bermuda Triangle exist, and the sixth one is going to Western India where there was a mythical kingdom called Dwaraka, now under the ocean. The other two we are not so sure. We think they are going to eastern Siberia where some unexplained phenomenon exists and the one to Australia to a region called Black Rock. Black Rock also has some weird things going on. All these are locations where we humans have not been able to adequately explain the strange conditions that exist. The exception is Dwaraka, which does not have any anomalous conditions. It is the mythical place where the Hindu god Krishna is supposed to have ruled and had epic aerial battles against forces of evil. They will not find anything there since the location of the mythological city is now underwater. We are investigating to see if there is any circumstantial evidence linking Dwaraka or the god to these aliens. Various teams are monitoring and checking to see what evidence exists to link these locations to past visitations and if we can associate these aliens to these locations."

John was not sure how they came to this conclusion. "How do you know where all the pyramids are going?"

The voice in the communicator announced, "By the way they are spreading out and the trajectory they are taking, extrapolation, and some deductive reasoning by the team here, we can say with a fair degree of confidence that the locations are pretty accurate. It is conjecture at this point. They could alter course dramatically once they are closer to the Earth's surface. But, the amateur archeologists among us think that these are the places of interest. The team here thinks that they are going to the anomalous regions on Earth. They must know or have something there that we have not yet figured out. All except Dwaraka, we don't know what they hope to find there or even if they are heading to that location."

The announcer continued, "The president has been notified. The order from the president is where possible, to get the US or NATO military personnel with bases closest to the potential landing sites to get to the site. Of course, we do not know if the pyramids will actually land on Earth."

John felt it was quite a stretch by Mission Control to guess where the alien pyramids may be going. He was certain that the aliens had not understood a word that was spoken, so the conversation would not influence the aliens' decision-making process. They may be able to read the human mind, but they had not yet mastered the Earth languages.

John noticed that they were at approximately eighty thousand to ninety thousand feet above the Earth's surface. He had flown into space and orbited Earth enough times to be able to guess the altitude with a fair degree of accuracy. "We have entered the upper reaches of the atmosphere. There will not be any reentry concerns," he said into his communicator but meant more for his concerned team in the pyramid. As he uttered those words, he saw a visible sigh of relief from the other three. The immediate response from Mission Control was "Roger that, we have you at seventy-five thousand feet and descending at about a thousand feet per minute."

A quick mental calculation by the humans in the pyramid revealed that at this rate of descent, they should be on terra firma in about seventy-five minutes. Normally, coming back to Earth from any space travel, let alone one of this duration, would cause any astronaut to feel a sense of jubilation, anticipation, and euphoria. None of the Earth-based space farers had thought about it much less anticipated reaching Earth anytime soon, let alone in the alien space-craft. None had the exultant feeling of coming back home. Although none had thought about the possibility of an untimely demise, there was no evidence that this eventuality was imminent or likely. Now that they were this close, there was a feeling of guarded optimism about the positive outcome. They were close to Earth. In the worst-case scenario, they could at least make a run for it. If they knew the layout of the pyramid, they could find the exit—or could they? On land, they would be among their own. The aliens would be outnumbered. But would they be allowed to go outside once the pyramid had landed? Would the pyramid even touch down on land or hover at a safe altitude? Each astronaut was absentmindedly looking out of the window, immersed in their thoughts.

No one knew exactly how much time had passed, but a gentle pressure on their body, which made their knees buckle slightly, making them hold out their hands and take a small step to regain their balance, announced their touchdown on Earth. They had finally *arrived!* They did not know exactly how much time they had spent in space. It was however a long, long time. Still the feeling of euphoria had not enveloped them. They all looked at Atra-has, and he motioned Kristen to get into the chair—he wanted to communicate with them. Kristen obliged and sat down in the chair.

Atra-has spoke, *We have arrived at the location where we instructed the building of structures similar to our craft. I will go in and fetch the items we came here to get. You and the others will wait here for my return.*

Kristen thought this was the best chance to ask for permission to go out—based on the response she could determine if they were prisoners or guests of the aliens on their own planet. She thought transmitted, *We have not stepped outside in a long time. We would like to go outside.* To her surprise Atra-has agreed without hesitation. Perhaps they were guests after all, but their hopes would soon be dashed when it came time to step out.

Kristen relayed to John and the others this news, and a slight feeling of optimism and relief descended on all of them.

Unfortunately, this team was comprised of individuals who were not trained in the art of warfare or to fight out of a situation such as this. The experts in warfare and fighting were, due to unavoidable circumstances, left behind on the TE. In case Kristen, Nicole, Ken, and John had to make a run for it, they would have to improvise and do the best they could. If fighting ensued, they would have to figure it out on the move, but a person running for their life would get the inner strength to succeed. That was their only hope. But no one was thinking of this lest the aliens picked up on the thought. All they were thinking of was setting foot on grass, mud, sand, or whatever it was on which the craft had landed.

ELATION

Once in Pyramid One, the cyborg reported directly to the bridge where she saw the four humans she had seen before—she may have stared at one female a second too long. She received instructions from her leader and servilely responded that she understood and would comply and then turned around and marched out. When she realized that they would be landing on Earth she could hardly control her joy. The leader had initially instructed her that she would stand guard of the humans while he went out to investigate after their craft had landed on Earth. She obeyed and dared not think of the relief of not being summoned to be questioned about the humans. She continued to focus on the fact that they were close to the planet—her planet. Then she was told that she and other guards would escort the humans out of the pyramid, but on no account were they to be released. Her elation was so intense that had this fact been communicated to her face-to-face by her master, her plans would have been easily deciphered. Luckily for her this message was sent via a menial robot—she could have sworn even the robot gave her a second glance since it was not able to understand her excitement. Now she had to think, and think hard and quick. There was no time to waste.

THE RETRIEVAL

The president was notified of the events taking place in space and all over the world. She had expected this event was coming—she had access to the presidential files and knew the history of all the secret programs that were put in place by the presidents that came before her. Of all the secret programs this one was special. According to the presidential files this program was started in the late 1950s. The space race was a cover to develop technology to meet the aliens in space. Somehow with over seventy years of development, the technology appeared to be nothing compared to what the aliens had.

The president gave orders to send a crew to each location where it was certain that the pyramids would land. Crews were to go from the nearest military bases which were established in friendly countries. The orders were to not initiate violence or even contact, if possible. They were to only observe and defend, if necessary. Egypt was the newest member of NATO after the democratic uprising that occurred some years prior. There was a base with US, European, Egyptian, and other personnel located in the outskirts of Cairo. International members from this base were sent to the location where the pyramid had landed. Upon arrival, the military staff saw that a small crowd had already gathered around the new pyramid. The strength of the crowd was growing, but anticipating this, the military had brought barricades and started setting them up at what appeared to be a safe distance from the pyramid. At first sight, the new pyramid was at least as tall as the ancient monument, but provided a stark contrast to the monument. Its black facade in a light sandy environment was dramatically different from the Earth-based structure. It was late afternoon, and this being close to the equator, the sun would set in a couple of hours. Military personnel were setting up audiovisual equipment in various vantage points on land as well as on planes and helicopters hovering around the potential conflagration. The images from the audiovisual equipment were beamed to the command center in the United States via high-bandwidth satellite links. In addition, TV crews started to gather, adding to the steadily increasing chaos.

The personnel gathered around the central command was also growing. Everyone who had authorization to enter the room was there. Others who had clearance were trying to assign themselves tasks that would enable them to get into that room. All the vantage points were occupied; the viewing gallery that was reserved for high-ranking personnel was also filled to capacity. The three monitors, each the size of a cinema screen, were all glowing brightly with more and more images occupying the area. These monitors were arranged in a semi-circular configuration around the very large auditorium. The controllers could enlarge or shrink each image on to the central or side monitors, depending on the level of interest or activity. Otherwise, the image would be one of a myriad on the side monitors, still large enough for everyone in the room to see. Currently, the image of the large alien pyramid occupied the monitors, and silhouetted in the background in stark contrast against the setting sun was the ancient pyramid built with stones.

When the potential landing location of the pyramid heading to the Bermuda Triangle was determined, a squadron of six US high-speed Marine helicopters and a plane, which had been prepared earlier and in standby mode at the Air Force base in Jacksonville, Florida, was instructed to intercept and watch the pyramid from a distance. These choppers and plane were equipped with cameras which also were capable of transmitting images to the command center. In addition, they had various weaponry including missiles, high-caliber machine guns, and smart bombs. Although there was some amount of nervousness to send the choppers and planes to an area which in the past had accounted for the disappearance of numerous planes, boats, and ships, it was determined that it would be worth the risk. Moreover, most of the disappearances were of solitary crafts. Hopefully a squadron would be able to help and support one another and prevent any mysterious adverse outcome. In any event, this operation was classified as a necessary risk. They could not let a spaceship from another planet roam about on Earth without being watched. The aliens would know and indeed anticipate such an escort.

As the squadron set a course to rendezvous with the pyramid, it noticed that the spacecraft was gradually losing altitude and was slowly approaching the ocean surface. The rendezvous point was due east and not very far off the coast of Jacksonville. The time to get there was minimal. As the pyramid descended and its proximity to the choppers increased it was unbelievable to see a large structure hovering in the air unsupported. The pyramid was floating about three hundred meters from the surface of the ocean and not being held up by anything. The cameras were turned on, and the images beamed straight to the command center in the Pentagon. This image initially occupied a monitor on the side, until the controller moved it to the central monitor. The image of the pyramid in Egypt moved to the side monitor. There was no activity taking place there at this time. The pilot in one of the choppers announced, "This is incredible. The structure has no business to be floating or flying—I mean, look at it. It doesn't even look like an object that can fly." One of the other pilots said, "Look below, I see ripples in the water." At that very moment, the instruments started to misbehave. "Command central, I have a malfunction in a number of my instruments, switching to manual flight."

Another chopper pilot also made the same announcement. "Instrument malfunction, switching to manual and line of sight." All the choppers announced the same problem of instruments not functioning. The squadron leader announced, "Team, switch to manual and keep your eyes on the pyramid. That will tell you which way is *up*." The support airplane pilot, who according to the plan was circling above these dramatic events, announced, "My instruments are fine, sending telemetry data if it will help navigate or to prevent uncontrolled loss of altitude."

One of the chopper pilots shouted into the radio, "Look down at the ocean, I think something is coming up!"

The crew pointed the camera at the ocean surface, and sure enough, an outline of something dark could be seen slowly rising through the clear waters. A minute later, a dark object started breaking through the surface of the ocean. About a minute later it was clear of the ocean and floating about fifty meters below the pyramid. The whole scene was breathtaking, the plane circling around the central point, the choppers around a pyramid three hundred meters in the air, and this large object just below with water still dripping from its crevasses.

THE ESCAPE

When it was time to step out, three new robots appeared with orders to escort the humans out. Kristen, noticing the familiar robot, said, "I guess we will not be left alone," to which John wondered aloud, "Wonder why Atra-has agreed to let us out as easily as he did? Was it to show everyone that he has some hostages?"

He continued, "They are carrying something—looks like weapons. Hope we are not being held hostage or sacrificed as a show of strength. Thus far I have not had a good feeling about the aliens. We should be ready to make a run for it. If we do, we do it together. No one gets left behind." Then immediately all the human beings looked around to see if anyone had picked up on the comment. Atra-has had left the bridge earlier, and everyone else, including the robots, at least outwardly seemed to be either preoccupied or busy.

Then Atra-has arrived at where the humans and the robot guards were standing. Upon his arrival one of the guard robots motioned the humans to follow them. As usual, there was one leading and this time there were two following. It appeared that the robot leading was of a higher rank, although outwardly all robots looked identical. The entire entourage followed Atra-has down the steps to the main hall that ran around the inside of the craft. If they kept going they would reach the inner portal which led to the outer portal. The anticipation with the humans was rising. Soon they would be outside. As they walked through the pyramid two more aliens and four more robots joined Atra-has. The whole group stopped because Atra-has had stopped, presumably to give them some instructions. Thankfully, this was only a brief interlude. Atra-has finished and started walking again. The newly arrived aliens went in a different direction. The newly arrived robots were each carrying what appeared to be weapons, similar to the ones being carried by those guarding the humans. When the entire group came to the main portal to the pyramid, one of the robots moved ahead and opened it. As soon as the door opened, a mild breeze wafted in, fragranced by *Earth*. This was not the sterile, purified, odor-free air that they were breathing all this time when they were ensconced in the TE or the alien craft. This was the true, original, genuine air produced on Earth. The humans could not see the reaction of the gentle waft of breeze on the olfactory senses of the aliens. The humans all reacted the same way—they took several deep breaths and savored every inhalation.

No one realized that one robot—a cyborg—was relishing the air in a similar manner to the humans. Her elation was so similar to the humans' that the leader was not able to distinguish the thoughts running through the prisoners' minds or the cyborg's mind.

In a single file, each one started descending the steps of the alien craft. The portal was so narrow that it was only wide enough for one person or robot to pass at a time, similar to the great pyramids constructed on Earth. Among the humans, Kristen was first to the door, then came Nicole, Ken, then last in line was John. There was a robot leading the entourage and more robots following them. As Kristen reached the door she noticed that she was quite high up, about a third of the way up from the base of the pyramid. Coincidentally, the entrance to the great pyramid of Giza as well as the other pyramids was about the same distance from their respective bases. This was easy to estimate by sight due to the proximity of the alien pyramid to the stone structure constructed on Earth. Kristen wondered if the construction of the Giza pyramid was from the same blueprint as the spacecraft then realized that this was probably true. As if to confirm, she heard Ken mention, "Now that I am seeing this under different circumstances, I believe the pyramids built on Earth have the same type of structure as this one." Almost unconsciously she followed the robot in front of her to the exit portal. She stopped at the mouth of the portal to take a moment to admire the view from this vantage point. The robot was descending the steps. She followed it down two or three steps then suddenly stopped in amazement. Looking down at her feet, she realized that she was descending some steps to the ground. What was previously a smooth outer surface of the pyramid had now morphed into steps. She did not give it too much thought because she, like the others, was too excited to be able to place her feet on terra firma.

Upon reaching the ground and the initial excitement abating, Kristen said, "What is that?"

The others in the team looked around to what Kristen was staring at, and Ken mentioned, "Looks like some kind of palanquin or litter and four more robots." Then after a brief pause he said, "In the ancient as well as medieval times, kings, high-ranking officials, and other wealthy individuals used this mode of transportation for short distances. Slaves or soldiers would carry the platform on their shoulders and walk or jog to get from one place to another." Then after a longer pause he asked the obvious, "There are no supporting beams. How could this be carried by anyone?" Soon their collective curiosities were answered.

Atra-has stepped on to the palanquin, and the other nonrobotic aliens turned and returned to the pyramid. A few seconds later, the palanquin rose about a meter. No one was lifting or holding it up. John said, "This is a vehicle, not powered by manual means. They must have miniaturized the gravity drive that powers the spacecrafts."

As he completed his sentence, eight robots in formation, two at each corner of the rectangular palanquin, started to move forward with the self-propelled palanquin in the center. They increased speed at every step until they were running. The robots, although wheeled, were not using that for locomotion. Instead they were moving like humans on foot. Wheels on this surface would be a hindrance, getting stuck in ruts or getting clogged with sand. John estimated that they were all moving in formation at about twenty miles per hour, almost a full sprint for a human. They were heading toward the great pyramid of Giza.

John continued, "There is just one alien and eight robots—Wonder where they are going. They could not be going to meet the leader. Surely, there is a need for more than one individual alien for a meeting or conference."

K. PAUL GOMEL

To that Ken replied, "I have a feeling he is not going for meet-ings. Like he told Kristen earlier, I think he wants to investigate the Giza pyramid built by Pharaoh Khufu."

Kristen looked shocked and asked, "Pharaoh who?"

Ken responded defensively, fearing he may have said something wrong, "This pyramid, the largest of the bunch in Egypt, was built by Khufu."

Kristen responded, "That is what I thought you said. When I was communicating with Atra-has, he used that name, but I did not follow since he pronounced it differently. He said 'Khunm-kfeu' or something close to it. Now the penny drops. He was looking for Khufu. I wonder how he died."

Ken responded, "The body was mummified perfectly, but the cause of death is unknown. But why is Atra-has looking for him now? How can he expect Khufu to be alive?"

No one could answer that question.

The prisoners were standing by the base of the alien pyramid, its dark color a sharp contrast to the surroundings. However, that fact did not register since they were all observing the spectacle of the palanquin and the sprinting robots. Within one minute the palan-quin and robots approached their target, the great pyramid of Giza. They noticed that there were four guards with weapons blocking the entryway. John said, "I hope, for their sake, they have not been ordered to stop the aliens."

Just as he said that, the four humans guarding the pyramid made a move to point their weapons at the approaching aliens. No sooner than they could move their weapons, the front two robots still at full gallop rotated what they were holding in their hands, and within milliseconds, all four guards fell to the ground, a large hole through their torsos, a pool of blood by their feet, and dead before they hit the ground. This was a devastating display of firepower. It confirmed that what the robots were holding were indeed weapons. Moreover, the weapons did not make any sound, nor was there any noticeable flash or recoil, and yet it was lethal. The human guards did not have a chance. As the cliché goes, they did not know what hit them. For that matter, no human knew what hit them. At this point, the gathering crowd started backing away.

Nicole's natural medical instinct was to move toward the stricken guards. Not knowing if they were dead or still alive, she wanted to go and help them. One of the robots, quick as only a machine can be, swung around and blocked her way. It was only now that the realization came to the humans that they were indeed prisoners.

John said, "If that is how they perform close-quarter combat, flesh and bones do not have a chance. This is why these robots are wearing the heavy protection. That show of strength was as much for us as it was for everyone else gathered here. That was to tell the crowd not to interfere and to warn us not to even think of escaping. See the weapons that the robots guarding us are holding. They are identical to the ones just used. If we even think of making a move, we are toast!" Then he added, "It is sad about those soldiers."

By this time, the palanquin and the entourage had arrived at the base of the stone pyramid and Atra-has had stepped off. He was looking around at the crowd and assessing the danger. He motioned two of the robots to stay at the base and started climbing up the steps with the other six.

Kristen said, "What was the last thing you said?"

John repeated, "If we even think of making a move, we are toast."

Kristen said, "Wait!" and closed her eyes.

Atra-has had made his way up the steps and had ascended to the pyramid entrance located approximately one third of the way up from the base. There he motioned two more robots to stand guard at the entryway and proceeded inside the pyramid. John thought he would be out soon. Whatever chance they have of escape must be executed now, or they may be the "guests" of the aliens for a very long time, maybe even forever.

He looked at Kristen, as if to say something, and immediately stopped. Kristen had closed her eyes and was in deep concentration.

As if a bolt of lightning had hit her, the nearby cyborg spun around to respond to the thought waves coming through to her. Initially she had feared that the master, Atra-has, had returned, but a quick glance revealed only the humans and the guards in the proximity. Where were the thoughts coming from? It had to be close, yet the thought pattern was unfamiliar. Then the cyborg noticed Kristen, deep in thought.

The humans, except Kristen who had her eyes closed, were watching the cyborg slowly turn around, and around again, as if it were looking for something. To the extent a robot can display an expression of surprise, this robot was displaying it. There was something happening. Maybe Kristen was able to establish communications with the robot. Whatever she was doing, she had to do it quickly. Atra-has would be out any moment, and he would not be happy, finding nothing inside but some hieroglyphs.

Kristen was saying telepathically, *Do you communicate with thought?*

The robot answered, *Yes, how did you know—*

Kristen interrupted, *This is how I communicated with Atra-Has earlier, did you not see?*

The robot answered, *My duties are as a soldier to interpret and communicate thoughts from the leader and pass on the message to the other lower-order robots. I was not in the same room as you were.* This was the standard answer that she would give anyone. Suddenly she realized this was not just anyone. It was a human—like her. She immediately changed her tone, to the extent that it can be done in telepathy, and said, *I have been trying to think of a way to communicate with you. You had not responded before when I tried.*

It took a fraction of a second for Kristen to realize that the cyborg was referring to the time when they were first captured. Kristen responded, *We did not know that this is how we had to speak.*

Then Kristen continued, *So you are the only one of the three guarding us who is capable of communicating like this?*

The cyborg responded succinctly, *Yes!*

Kristen opened her eyes and relayed this to John and the others. Appreciating the situation, John decided to directly ask for help. Not realizing that the gender of the cyborg was female John quickly responded to Kristen, "Ask if he will help us. There is not much time.

The scout party will be on their way back from the other pyramid soon. You have to make this short and sweet."

Surprisingly, as John was completing the instructions to Kristen, the other two robots started walking away, one toward the pyramid and up the stairs and the other toward the other side of the pyramid in a slow march.

Now that telepathic communication was established Kristen did not need to close her eyes. She had to only focus on the cyborg and think the thoughts that she wanted to communicate. Wondering how she could appeal to the empathy of a machine, she asked, *Can you help us? We are held prisoner here, and we want to go and see our families.*

Surprisingly the robot answered, *Yes, I anticipated this request, and moreover I wanted to help you anyway! I could not think of a way of telling you this since I cannot speak, but now that we have found a way to communicate, it makes the task easier. I have sent the other two robots, one to replace my weapon and one to scout around the back. They will be back shortly, so we must run. Now!*

Kristen said, *Thank you!* not sure whether this term of gratitude meant anything to the alien robot.

The four of them started running toward the crowd and where they could clearly see military personnel. It was about a kilometer they had to traverse before they would be lost among the crowd and military personnel. To their surprise the robot also was running with them just behind Kristen who was the last one. Kristen tried to communicate with the robot, not sure if she would be able to run and do telepathy.

Why are you coming with us?

I will be terminated because I allowed you all to escape.

Why are you allowing us to escape?

Because I, too, am a prisoner, and I do not like what they do to prisoners from this planet. I want to try and stop them from taking any more prisoners from here.

The magnitude of that information made Kristen almost trip and fall. She had to stop running to avoid taking an inadvertent roll in the dirt and to regain her balance. This robot was a prisoner?

Surely the robot was delusional, if that were possible for a nonorganic thing. Or maybe there was a short circuit in the electronics. Kristen continued the inquiries. They still had some running to do.

Can you tell me why you think you are a prisoner?

John, who was leading the group to safety, glanced back and saw Atra-has emerging from the pyramid of Giza. He saw Atra-has furiously gesticulating to one of the robots, as if he were giving them some instructions. Atra-has had not realized that the prisoners were escaping. As if by instinct, the other humans turned their heads to see what was going on behind them. The escaping robot also looked back, strange instinct for a robot. They were still about 250 meters to safety.

The robot responded, *My name is Lela, or it was before I was made into this. I look like I do because the lords put my brain in this body. I was like you before they did this to me and some of my people. My body is already dead, and my brain will die if I stay with them or if I come with you. I want to help you so they do not subject any more people to this kind of existence.*

Kristen said, *You mean you were a female person like me?*

They had made progress undetected; they were a mere one hundred meters from safety but quickly getting fatigued. Lela was capable of greater speed but, on purpose, was last in line with Kristen. Although completely out of breath, Kristen could communicate because she was not using her vocal chords. The soldiers and the crowd could be heard louder now, cheering them on and to run faster. John quickly glanced around and saw that Atra-has had finally noticed that they were escaping. John tried to warn the others by shouting as loud as he could, but he could not muster enough energy to overcome the noise of the crowd and his need to gulp air. The noise of the crowd was now at fever pitch.

The robot answered, *Yes, just like you.*

At this point Kristen was not analyzing the information, just asking questions and getting more data.

Still at a full run, the first of them was almost to the barricade where the crowd had gathered. Another glance around and John noticed that one of the robots had aimed the weapon. John reached the barricade where the military and the crowd had parted slightly to let the astronauts to safety. The rest were very close behind.

Kristen continued, *What do they do to put you in this body?*

Nicole was next to reach the safety of the crowd followed by Ken. Kristen and Lela were just a few steps behind. John turned to see that the robot, which was taking aim, was ready to fire. He was horrified to see that Kristen was still about twenty meters away—she would not make it. He tried to summon all his strength to scream for Kristen to zigzag. Just then Lela turned around and saw that the weapon was about to be fired and noticed that Kristen was in direct firing line. Lela moved to block the line of sight, and as she did so, the lower part of her body and legs disintegrated, small pieces of metal strewn all over, shot by the alien weapon. That selfless act saved Kristen. Since they had reached the crowd, all they had to do was to mingle and they would become relatively inconspicuous—except for the astronaut clothing. But the crowd was dense. As he reached the safety of the crowd, the commotion behind him caused Ken to turn around. He saw Lela lying in a heap, her lower extremities nonexistent. Kristen shouted, "Ken, help me drag the robot." The second shot was about to be fired, but fearing a riot from this animated crowd Atra-has asked for the robot to stand down and the weapon to be lowered. He was still at the stone pyramid, and a riot would leave him stranded there. It is not that he was afraid or in any way doubtful of the power of his weapons. He was under instructions to keep things as calm as possible. With Ken's help Kristen dragged Lela to safety, using her arms to pull her. The crowd reformed around them, and Atra-has or his robots could not distinguish them as individuals.

John said, "Keep running," not realizing that Atra-has had decided to let them go—for now.

Kristen and Ken continued to drag Lela, but the robot, even with everything below the waist missing, was very heavy. Extreme exhaustion slowed them to walking pace. Shortly thereafter they had to stop to catch their breath. Kristen saw a red liquid, possibly lubricant, oozing from below the shattered torso of Lela.

Kristen said, *Lela, what can we do to help you?*

Lela responded, *It has been a long time since anyone has called me by name. It makes me very happy.*

The signal from Lela was weak; Kristen was having trouble picking up on Lela's thoughts. Lela continued, *I thought I could show you what they do, but I cannot. Open me up and you will see...*

Kristen was confused, *Lela, are you there?*

Lela, her thought signal very weak, tried to respond. *Open me, and you will see...*

With that there was no more communication.

A military truck arrived, and with the help of the soldiers, all the astronauts and Lela were loaded and taken to the local NATO base. Atra-has, realizing that if he were to start shooting indiscriminately, he may not be able to get back to the safety of his own pyramid; he decided to let them go. There were too many people around, and although he had the capacity to neutralize most of them, he did not want to take that chance for the sake of four individuals. Besides, the robot had been mostly destroyed. It would be easy to destroy the rest of it. However, he could not shake the feeling that he had lost another valuable resource.

LANDING

For an onlooker, the scene was magnificent. Helicopters were hovering around the alien pyramid about three hundred meters above the ocean surface and with its reflection below it. The aliens had retrieved a sunken pyramid, and it was also floating above the ocean surface about fifty meters below the pyramid that salvaged it. The only difference was that the pyramid that had just been brought up from the ocean floor was upside down, so it looked like a large flat mirror was placed along the horizontal plane. Looking from the side, they looked like mirror images of each another. Back at headquarters, everyone was transfixed to the monitors, the middle monitor now showing the fantastic image. The squadron leader in one of the choppers announced, "The recently arrived pyramid must have somehow brought the lower one up, from the ocean floor. How and when did the first one sink? By the way, my instruments are functioning correctly. I guess this answers the Bermuda Triangle riddle. Hopefully we will not have to worry about that anymore."

One by one the rest of the chopper pilots reported that their instruments were now functioning normally. In addition, one of the pilots reported, "There appears to be a large hole on this side of the pyramid they just brought up. Looks like some weapon blew a hole in it. The metal is bent inward as if a missile punctured the outer wall." The monitor in command HQ switched to the camera in that chopper, and all could see to what that pilot was referring. Then the squadron leader announced, "Okay! We are moving." The choppers got out of the way, and the leader continued, "We are heading west, so we will be in US waters in minutes." The pyramid configuration moved slowly, as if one of them was carrying a heavy weight—which it was, albeit with gravity power and not tethers. The speed slowly increased, although it was still within the capability of the choppers which were following. As the procession moved toward Florida, the pyramid that was being towed slowly rotated and within a matter of a few minutes was positioned the correct way, with the apex pointing up.

When they came to a flat open area just outside Jacksonville in Florida, the disabled pyramid was gently set down, and the other pyramid also landed next to it. The choppers, cameras, and the airplane were there to witness all the events and were hovering for the next event to take place. The leader radioed, "Do we also set down or remain airborne?" The response was "Maintain your position and do not approach the alien crafts."

They did not want the choppers to be threatening to the aliens in any way. The choppers had taken the familiar position of encircling the pyramids at a height of about five hundred meters from the ground and about the same distance from the pyramids. The cameras were trained on the pyramids, and the monitors at command central were showing images of the pyramids from various angles. Only a few minutes had elapsed when a small portal opened on the side of the functioning pyramid. A small object came out of the opening, and as soon as it cleared the portal, it closed. The object was the size of a compact vehicle, possibly even smaller. It was an aerial vehicle moving around just like the pyramids. The cameras zoomed in on the object, and it was clear that it was a vehicle of some type. There were transparent windows through which could be seen a humanoid form. But at the cameras' extreme zoom setting the vibration of the choppers prevented the details to be closely observed. If it were to be construed as a flying saucer, it did not fit the typical description of one. This one was almost cube-like in appearance. In fact if wheels were placed at all four corners, it would look like a very clunky automobile. However, this did not have wheels, and was more of a flying machine as opposed to ground-based transport.

It slowly rose up in the air to match the altitude of the choppers and started to approach one of them.

The pilot, trying to hold back a slight level of panic, radioed, "What should I do?"

The squadron leader, not having been trained in diplomacy or dealing with aliens, deferred to the command HQ.

The radioed instruction was "Hold your position. They probably want to inspect. They are probably just as curious about us as we are of them."

When the craft got to about fifty meters from the chopper, it appeared to start spinning. On closer inspection, the craft was not rotating or revolving. There was a light, appearing to be plasma or something similar, emanating from its midsection, which appeared as if it were going around the craft, much like the rotors of the chopper. The spinning light made it look like the craft itself was spinning. When it was ten meters away, the pilot, now visibly nervous, radioed, "They are very close, I can almost tou—"

Just as he was radioing, the light spilled out toward the front of the craft and on the chopper. It made contact with the rotor blades and sheared them off. It was as if the proverbial hot knife had sliced through butter. There was no impact on the alien craft. The chopper and the pilot, who had his finger on the trigger, lurched as the blades broke off. The violent lurching inadvertently fired a couple of missiles, which were armed and ready. The pilot, as he was trained to do, instinctively moved his thumb to the high-caliber machine cannon and fired off a few rounds into the alien craft as his craft plummeted toward the ground. There was no hope for him to eject at this low altitude. Sadly, upon contact with the ground, it exploded into bright orange flames which briefly shot up about fifty meters into the air. Both the laser-guided missiles found their target. Surprisingly, the alien craft which was in close proximity to the chopper also fell.

The reason for the crash of the alien craft was not immediately obvious. As the rotor blades sheared off the airworthiness of the craft was instantly compromised. It began falling, but due to the angular momentum of the remaining spinning rotors and the weight distribution, the craft started falling backward. That meant that the weapons, which normally fired parallel to the ground, were pointing directly up. For the pilot, under severe duress, the training instinctively took over. He, as was taught to him, moved his thumb to the machine gun trigger and fired as the chopper fell backward. This had resulted in the bullets hitting the underside of the alien craft and had damaged its machinery. So it, too, fell like a stone on top of the burning wreckage of the chopper.

LELA

The drive to the NATO base took less than ten minutes. The road going away from the pyramid was almost empty. The road going the other way was packed with traffic—everyone going to catch a glimpse of the new pyramid and possibly an alien or two.

While they were in the truck, Kristen relayed the discussion she had with Lela to the others. Nicole, the consummate physician that she was, was already examining the remains of the robot with the hope of helping. She touched the still oozing red liquid that was coming out of the robot and proclaimed that it was blood. Nicole opened the now loose flap on Lela's back, the robot was lying face-down on the truck floor. "Look!" she said, "There is a brain of some kind in the abdominal cavity." Then pointing to the side, she continued, "It looks like these tubes are carrying blood. And on the other side are tubes with some other liquid, possibly for hydraulics. If this is true then these robots possess tremendous power. There is still some blood left and the pumping mechanism is still functioning. Help me to hold these tubes shut." That temporarily staunched the flow. Nicole and Ken held two tubes shut till they reached the base. As soon as they got to the base John asked the driver to take them straight to the infirmary. Once there Nicole asked for a gurney and wheeled Lela to a ward.

Nicole said to one of the nurses, "Quick! Get a blood type."

The nurse was looking quizzically at Nicole who, realizing that there was no time to waste, repeated, "Nurse, get a blood type of this," pointing to the small amount of blood that had oozed on to her fingers and hands.

The nurse obeyed and jumped into action and within seconds came back with, "Doctor, this is type A."

Nicole, being the resident physician for the mission on dSE, knew the blood types of all the other astronauts. She said immediately, "Ken, this is your type, do you—"

Even before she had completed the sentence Ken jumped in and, rolling his sleeve up, said, "Where do I lie down? Take as much as you need."

Within moments, a bag was filling with Ken's blood. In the meantime, Nicole had cauterized the leaking pipes and reattached where she thought the broken pipes needed to be attached. As soon as sufficient quantity had filled, the transfusion to Lela began. As she was working away she mumbled, "I am clueless with this. I hope my guesswork is good enough."

Kristen, who with John was watching the proceedings in fascination, moved closer to the bed and started the telepathic communication with Lela. *Lela, are you still there?* and *Lela, wake up, we need to talk.*

After two or three minutes the robot seemed to stir a little. Their excitement could not be contained. Nicole mentioned, "Kristen, continue, it seems to be having an effect on Lela."

After a few more minutes of coaxing, Lela finally responded, *Lela [garble, garble, garble] ready for duty.*

Kristen said, *Lela, it's okay, you are safe now. No need to report for duty."*

The power to some of the interfaces was restored now, and Lela moved her head to look around and finally at Kristen. *Where am I?*

Kristen said, *Lela, thank you for saving me. If you had not blocked the...* Kristen could not continue since she did not know what she was saved from. She only knew that if Lela had not done what she did, then Kristen would be without the lower extremities of the body and quite possibly dead.

Lela responded, *I know. I do not have much time left. I do not know how or why you brought me back. Even if I were to survive, I would not last long because my food energy and power energy are low. The pain is very...* Her thoughts drifted.

Ken suddenly remembered what Baz had speculated earlier about being fortunate that they were in the pyramid when the deceleration had started and asked, "Kristen, do you think you can ask Lela why we were in the pyramid and not the dSE just before stopping?"

Kristen looked at him and said, "That is a good question, but I am not sure if I can. I just don't know how. Let me try…"

Kristen tried two or three ways of asking the same question so Lela could understand, and finally Lela responded. Kristen looked at the group and said, "Yes, it was by design. Lela was aware that we would be crushed to death by the g-forces. But that was not the only reason we were in the pyramids. She said that it was her intention that we start communicating with Atra-has before we landed here. She had hoped that they could turn around and go back before reaching Earth. She said some other stuff that I did not understand, but essentially she confirmed that one of her objectives was to protect us."

Since this was in much friendlier surroundings, Kristen was able to relay the information in real time. John had his communicator turned on so the information was also getting to central command.

John said, "Pain, how can there be pain?"

Almost in anticipation, Lela said, *To prevent us harming ourselves, they have wired up our brain to some parts of our body. The pain keeps us from harming ourselves, just like you.*

Lela continued, *Listen to me. They have come to get people from here. I was just like you, but was born in Aten-Heru. They put me in this metal body.* The name of the planet did not make any sense to the humans. Even if this planet could be seen with the array of Earth and space-based telescopes, there was not even the remotest chance of identifying the planet to which Lela was referring. Lela continued, the signal fading slightly, *They plan to come here from time to time to get people. They breed us and train us to speak through thoughts when we are young. Then when we are older, they put us in robots.*

Kristen was astonished and could only ask, *Why?*

Because they could not get robots to be good enough to satisfy their needs. Communicating was becoming an effort. Lela continued feebly, *They are always fighting with the planet near to Aten-Heru.* She had to stop. Realizing time was short she made a tremendous effort to continue. *They call it Garg-Ar…In their language it means "the enemy"…*

The more robots they can have that are like me…the stronger they get… The other robots are not like me…Most do not have a human brain… They cannot think! So they are easily defeated in battle…Sometimes they had battles here…on this planet…because the enemies…also come here to…prevent them…from being able…to build robots like me. Lela had to take a break. The signals were weak and coming in staccato style.

Kristen mentioned out loud that Lela was getting weaker. Only Kristen could tell that since she was communicating with Lela. Nicole turned to the nurse who was standing bewildered, wondering what was going on, and said, "Nurse, is there anyone else here with type A blood?"

When there was no response, Nicole said again and louder, "Nurse?"

"Yes, Doctor, I will go check."

Nicole said, "Hurry, we may be losing the patient."

The short break helped. Lela continued, *They were here in the past…I know because I saw the records they kept during the journey… They keep careful records because they travel in time as well as distance… When they were asleep, I read the records. That is what I was doing when you first came to the pyramid…I am the one who fixed the damaged robot when your weapon fired. They do not know I read. I shared it with some other robots who are like me…If you find one like me…they will help you…No robot like me wants to live like this. We cannot open the latch to our brain to self-destroy…I know that the masters did not expect this level of technology here. They were certainly surprised.*

Then she paused momentarily, to recuperate a little, then continued, *They want people such as you…And they want the shiny metal… They have run out on Aten-Heru. They also want to get a craft…that fell long ago…when they were having a battle here…with their enemy Garg-Ar. That craft has a lot of shiny metal.* Her energy level as well as the blood supply were critically low. Nevertheless, she mustered enough strength to continue, albeit faltering. *There are no other planets…where this can be collected…because they cannot land there. Atrahas had gone to the pyramid looking for the metal. According to their records…they had put one of their kind in charge here to collect as much metal as they could.*

Kristen said, *Don't worry, he will not find any there, because it has been moved.* She purposely held back the fact that most of the ancient pyramids of Earth had been looted long ago and what was remaining was in museums. The rest in secure government vaults around the world.

Lela did not seem to care about that. She was getting very tired now. With the final bit of strength, she marshaled enough strength for a final thought. *You must leave me...and go far away. I am dead anyway...because my power source is almost all gone. I helped you because I...or robots like me, do not want to live this way. I want to die...and am happy that it has been for a good cause. They have put a device... in me that tells them where I am...This is how we cannot escape. They will come...and destroy everything...in my vicinity...Leave me and go! Now!"*

The nurse came back with some information about the type A blood donor, but Nicole beckoned her to be quiet and told her, "It does not matter now. I don't think we can save the robot." The nurse was as confused as ever wondering why they were trying to save a robot with type A blood.

Kristen started to say, *Thank you—*

Lela interrupted, *Go! Now!*

That was the final thought that Lela could muster. Kristen was repeating everything verbally as it was taking place. There was no way for Nicole to check for a pulse. However she did see that the blood had stopped flowing through the tubes. Power had run out. Nicole could see that the pumping and breathing devices had stopped. The diagnostic lights inside the body cavity dimmed and went blank. Lela was dead.

John spoke, "Let's evacuate this whole base. If Lela was right, then the interplanetary visitors will be visiting this base with bad intentions." Looking at the nurse, he said, "Evacuate the base, sound the alarm, do what you have to do but get everyone out of here *now*! We may be in imminent danger of an attack." The nurse was again dumbfounded. John went to the fire alarm, broke the glass, and set it off. Then he looked at the nurse again and said calmly, "You need to sound the alarm now and get everyone out of this entire base. *Now!*

Hurry!" This time the urgency sank in, and she scurried off to raise the alarm.

Nicole said, "Just a second, I am curious to see how this works." Kristen was already one step ahead removing the protective cover from the abdominal cavity. There, as if nature had gone horribly wrong, in the chest cavity, was a human brain. Nicole was thinking, *I bet you looked beautiful when you were a complete person...*

All the internal systems had completely stopped. Nicole said, "Look at these foot-and-a-half-long cylindrical objects." This is what Thor had seen the first time he and Ken encountered the alien inside the pyramid. "It appears that the items in the container were power and sustenance. Look here," she said pointing at one of the containers, "this one has a blue-colored band, and this other one has a green-colored band. These are color coded since it matches the colors of the receptacles where the cylinders fit. I guess these have to be replaced periodically to keep these robots powered up."

True to her profession, Nicole felt the transparent container holding the brain. Immediately she exclaimed, "Wow! This part is cool to the touch. That is possibly to keep the brain functioning optimally. The brain is very sensitive, and it cannot get too hot. The power systems must have components to support this optimal temperature. I wish I had more time. I could learn a lot from how this is constructed and help save human lives."

Kristen unplugged something from the side, and it looked like a power source. At the same time, Nicole did the same from the other side. What Nicole took out was just over a foot long and had electrical terminals. After examining it for a second Nicole said, "This appears to be a battery or some kind of power source." Kristen, who was holding a similar but slightly larger cylinder, responded, "If what you have is the power source, then what I have must be sustenance for the organic portion of the cyborg." Everyone looked at her quizzically, so she continued speaking while still examining Lela. "The organic part has to get energy from somewhere. We get our energy by eating. What about this thing? It does not have a mouth or any other visible means to eat. They must have these replaceable, reusable capsules to provide energy. Otherwise, the organics would not last long. Ah! Here it is. This is definitely food source since the tube carrying the blood comes to this chamber where I just pulled out this capsule. They must have some kind of food source that is easily err… digestible. This, I am willing to bet, also has the necessary hormones to keep the brain alive. This capsule possibly also doubles as collector of waste material."

In the background, a loud claxon came on with an announcement to evacuate the base.

Nicole continued, "This is why I want to check. There has to be lungs of some kind as well as some type of pump to keep the blood flowing and oxygenated. Not to mention something to make new red blood cells. This has got to be transplant surgery in the extreme. We are not capable of doing even a fraction of this."

"Ah! Here it is. Just following the tubes, here is what looks like a portion of the lungs." Pointing to an area where the belly button would be, she pulled out another capsule that had many perforations. "These are the lungs."

It was becoming difficult to concentrate with the gradual increasing of the decibel level and frequency of the blaring claxon.

"Well, this is all one needs to keep a brain alive, simplicity to the extreme, but frighteningly advanced technology. I know we cannot do this here on Earth, but we probably will not want to. To think that human beings were bred to satisfy the needs of an advanced technology, they must have designed us to be simple. No one purposely designs anything that is too complex to maintain."

Ken, who had been quiet all this time, remarked, "It won't be long before we can do this."

Even with the loud alarm system making it difficult for any verbal communication, everyone heard this and turned to him wondering what he had meant.

Ken clearly needed to clarify, and responded at a very high volume so he could be heard and avoid the possibility of having to repeat, "We already do something similar with HySleep. We keep the brain alive and unconscious with all the other organs functioning just by the use of chemicals. We humans are close to the point of taking the brain out of the skull and keeping it alive indefinitely."

Due to the crushing noise the collective grimace could not be heard, but was palpable. Now was not the time to discuss this. The racket was beginning to interfere with the ability to concentrate.

After further examination, she incredulously announced, "Look at the way they have hooked up the brain to the various sensors, eyes, ears… These interfaces are so advanced, and the parts exposed to the liquid are made of gold. I am certain gold is a key ingredient to making a cyborg like this."

Ken, who had been looking at the innards of the cyborg with fascination, observed, "I wonder how long these cyborgs are meant to live? I also wonder how the nutrition cylinders were first tested on humans, I mean, humans who still had their brains in their skulls? They may have taken groups of people to various controlled locations, fed them varying diets, and then devised the best formula for sustenance depending on how they coped. If I have to relate what we are observing now to ancient literature, I can identify numerous stories in various parts of the world where groups of people disappear for a number of years and then they come back, none the worse for wear. I guess we never hear of the ones who do not come back. I wonder if this is what some people refer to as manna. I think these ancient stories had large elements of truth to them but were either misinterpreted or written with the limited vocabulary present at the time. Due to the original misinterpretation, lack of language, and the passage of time we are unable to ascribe the true meaning to them. But you have to admit, the connection exists."

That last sentence or two had to be shouted. The "evacuate" siren was blaring at full blast now. They could not stay, even if they had wanted to, for fear of permanent damage to the eardrums.

Undaunted Nicole continued her detailed examination. She pulled out another tube which squirted some red liquid, fortunately missing everyone as it fell to the floor. "Ah!" exclaimed Nicole. "Here we have the unit that produces the red cells. It looks like it is artificially produced. I bet you that all the cyborgs have blood type A in order to make it efficient to mass-produce these things in a factory. I would love to examine it."

"What?" was the collective response.

The earsplitting sound had become almost intolerable. John grabbed Nicole by her hand, took the unit she was examining, placed it down, and then said, "We need to leave *now!*" emphasizing "now" as much as he could. Although he was literally a foot away from Nicole, she did not hear a word he said. But she understood and immediately stood up.

John was at a run with the rest following.

A sergeant who was running toward them stopped and said, "Commander, your transport is waiting."

THE ESCALATION

The pilots in the other choppers saw in horror the events that had just taken place. This was not missed by the aliens in the pyramid, from which the downed craft had emerged. The missiles struck the pyramid and exploded, as designed, but there was no visible impact from the outside to the pyramid. To the naked eye, there was not even a dent at the site of impact. Almost immediately, the same door on the pyramid opened, and four other flying crafts flew out. As they came out they went straight up to a height of about two hundred meters, higher than the choppers, and spread out in four opposite directions. The staff in central command, witnessing this, immediately scrambled a squadron of fighter jets. It would be ten minutes approximately before they would arrive at the battle scene. The choppers had to fend off the aliens until then.

The four that had just emerged were flying much faster than the previous one. It appeared at first that they were flying aimlessly. However, it was a show of strength. They wanted to show that they were more maneuverable and faster than the military helicopters. They were flying back and forth to form a giant plus (+) sign over the pyramid.

Central command radioed, "Don't back down, hold your positions. Maybe they are testing us to see if we want to be the aggressors. Just as a precaution, lock your missiles on to the crafts."

A few moments later the airplane pilot radioed back, "They are small and fast. It is not easy to lock on to them."

The alien craft had gone back and forth three times. Then the radio signal from a pilot came, "Locked on to one." As he said that, the alien crafts, in unison, turned on their light which appeared to make them spin. This to the chopper pilots meant that they also had turned on their weapons and were preparing for battle, since this was exactly the precursor to the previous incident.

"Locked on to the second one," a pilot announced.

At that moment, the plasma from one of the crafts spilled out as if it were fluid, just as had happened earlier. Only, this time, it was ejected from the craft as if a bolt of lightning were stemming from the craft. The bolt, as soon as it left the craft, became transparent, so the humans could not see it. However, milliseconds later, it crashed into the tail section of one of the choppers and sheared off the tail. The chopper started spinning violently. The trained military pilot knew exactly what had happened and took protective action. He cut the power and descended rapidly and landed hard. The chopper for now was unusable, but at least everyone was alive though severely shaken.

At that point a pilot radioed again, "Locked on to number three."

The command came, "Fire the missiles at will." At this point the choppers fired, and each missile found its target. The small crafts were not able to sustain such an explosion and crashed and burned.

"Locked on to the fourth" was radioed by a pilot.

At this point the squadron leader radioed, "Permission to engage the pyramid."

Command central said, "You saw what happened. The pyramid is not vulnerable to our missiles."

The squadron leader said, "They may be sending more of the crafts. I have an idea to take them out if they intend on sending more."

"Permission granted."

At that point, the door opened, but it was not to deploy more, but to return the one remaining alien craft.

The squadron leader had to act fast. The door would not be open for very long, as was evidenced in the previous occasions. As the door opened and the craft entered the pyramid, two more missiles were fired straight at the entering craft. Both the missiles found their target, which was the small alien craft, just as it entered the pyramid and the door closed.

RETURN TO GIZA

By this time Atra-has was back in his pyramid. However, a few minutes later, he returned to the Giza pyramid with equipment, some of which were carried by the robots and the rest on the palanquin. He left four to guard the outside and took the other four with him. He knew the layout of the Giza pyramid as well as he knew his spacecraft. It was as if the blueprint for the Giza pyramid came from his architects who built the spacecrafts—which was true. The entrance was a similar height from the ground. The passageway at the entrance was sloping down. At the end of the passageway it opened into a large chamber. However, the spaceship was much more elaborate with many storage areas and space for machinery. Once he entered, he stopped midway down the main passageway, checked some faded but still visible hieroglyphs, and instructed his robots to cut a hole in the wall at a specific location. He obviously knew something that no one else on Earth did.

The equipment that was hauled from the spaceship was assembled, which, due to the narrow passages and cramped space in which to work, took longer than Atra-has anticipated. The robots, although only slightly larger than an average human, were relatively large to work comfortably in the narrow passageway. However, the cutting process was short. The equipment they used cut through the huge block of stone as if it were as soft as a giant block of Styrofoam. The side where the incision was made was perfectly smooth, and the edge was sharp as a knife. As the stone was being cut by the robot Atra-has wondered if the other places where his peers had used similar tools to build stone structures had survived the ages. This particular structure appeared fine on the inside; the outside was showing the signs of neglect and disrepair. One of the robots pushed the stone so it fell inward, revealing a new chamber. No human had knowledge of this chamber.

A light was brought in by a robot. It revealed another sarcophagus. Humans would need to do carbon dating to determine the exact date of the mummy in the sarcophagus. However, it may have been a relative of ancient royalty or the main architect of the pyramid, assuming the architect was human. Until now, the architect of the pyramids was unknown as was the location of his burial. Atra-has ignored the remains of the dead being. It had a slightly bulging skull, much the same as his race of people. Regardless, Atra-has ignored the mummy in favor of what he had come here to retrieve. He found some valuables that were placed there in the burial chamber all those years ago. Since this chamber was not discovered by the humans, all the things were exactly as they were originally placed. The items were placed exactly as he had expected, since it was his race that had taught the humans to do these rituals. The other chambers he had visited earlier, to his dismay, were all empty. Atra-has instructed the robots to collect, in a container that one of the robots had brought, only the items of interest to him. The amount of gold would fit in a medium-sized bucket. He would take it to their spacecraft. They carefully only took the items that were made of gold and left the other ornaments and decorations behind. He had no use for them, and he had not journeyed this vast distance for those items. He was clearly displeased with the few items that were present; he did not come all this way to take a bucket full of gold—not after what was collected in the past. He could not understand why there was no gold left even though they had left behind not one but many of their own—with specific instructions to accumulate as much gold as possible. They even made sure to make one of their own kind a king before leaving. Now they would have to rely on other sources on Earth and maybe even other planets. They could not invest this much time, expenses, and resources again. His superiors would not be happy. This was a time of war, and much gold was needed. But where were the descendants of his people that had been left behind? How could he find them on a planet with so many of the Earth people? After all, he and his people did not look very different from the locals, at least not visually. He did not know about the locals' intellectual capacity, although it was vastly underestimated as compared to the records. He would have to update the records for any future missions.

REEVALUATE STRATEGY

Atra-has brought the loot back to his pyramid and was still in shock and disbelief that there was not more to be found. He was wondering how these genetically engineered apes could without help get into a structure, such as the one constructed here by his people, and empty its contents. Perhaps the aliens who were left here to control and maintain these creatures provided help—for reasons unknown? But why would they? He needed to contact the other vehicles that had flown to various parts of this planet to see if they had been more successful at finding the metal. But before that, he would have to take care of Lela. He could not let the robot fall into the enemies' hands. The last thing he wanted was for the enemy, the ones whom they had chased and in turn may be chasing them now, to find Lela and get a strategic advantage by reverse engineering a technology. They had invested so many resources to develop the technology—he could not take the chance of leaving it, nor could he go and retrieve it. He had to destroy it beyond recognition. Moreover, desertion, lately one of the myriad of problems afflicting the cyborgs on Aten-Heru, was punishable by death. At the very least, it would be a lesson to the remaining cyborgs.

Atra-has had a little time while the tracking system located Lela's exact location. He had to think and reevaluate his strategy. Apparently, this journey was not going to be as straightforward as originally anticipated. But he was up for the fight. In order to figure out his next course, he took his mind back to when he had started preparing for the trip. He had read that the military commanders had the technology for a robot but needed an organic brain as the control mechanism. They could not harvest the brains of their own species for use in cyborgs, even if that brain came from a soldier. If the population found out, the generals and commanders would be finished—maybe even executed. Yet they needed a malleable brain that was capable of thinking like them. If only they could develop an animal that could take commands and process thoughts, they could harvest it to be fitted into machines.

The answer that they had devised was to do this experimentation on a distant planet and at a time in the future. The thought process when the plans were devised was that on Aten-Heru the population would be clueless since there would be no proof of ethical transgressions—from their perspective the events on a distant planet had not happened yet. The bureaucracy would also be eliminated. For that, they had to find a suitable planet and bring a suitable animal capable of receiving genetic modifications. Then the plan was to engineer it with their own genes so it would be able to take commands, perform tasks, learn, and process information. They had planned to leave the creatures on the planet and let them breed. Whenever they needed a new stock, they would come back and take as many as they wanted. The planet was large enough to sustain many individuals. The plans were to take multitudes of these genetically modified apes as necessary and breed them in captivity. This would reduce the number of times they needed to journey this far and would also keep them in a controlled environment. When these modified apes were sufficiently trained they would be able to remove the brains and put them in the machines and use them to fight their war. It was hoped that war or the constant threat of war would allow them some latitude with keeping and breeding these creatures. Sometimes it was prudent to use any means necessary to win wars—Atra-has being a military person understood that.

Over time the people of Aten-Heru would get used to the idea and eventually forget about it—especially when no civilian was allowed to see the creatures held only at secure military installations. When there was no need for any more of these artificially created beings—at the end of the war—they would simply stop visiting this planet.

Atra-has continued recalling what he had read—the locator was still trying to pinpoint the location of Lela. He had read during his research that in order to put the plan in place to develop a cyborg, his predecessors had traveled great distances in time and undertook meticulous search of many planets to find one that was habitable—and somewhat similar to Aten-Heru. He did know one thing—the length of the day here was almost exactly the same as it was on Aten-Heru. The travel in time was the most arduous part since careful calculations were needed before the mechanism could be engaged. To avoid potential problems every vehicle had to travel a certain safe distance from Aten-Heru before being allowed to shift in time. Prior to arriving back at Aten-Heru every time journey in either direction necessitated a journey back to the time from which they had left plus the time that would have normally elapsed. No one was allowed to gain or lose any time, or age at a different rate to the people they left behind. The sophisticated computers calculated and controlled time shifts.

Having found a suitable planet—they had to make it habitable to their people by destroying the large animals that were present. He had only seen pictures of these animals. They were strange-looking beasts—some of the larger ones had massive legs and tail, and tiny arms. They had eaten the initial contingent of scientists—the scientists had no chance, even with the weapons they had at their disposal. It looked like all the animals here were in early part of their evolution—this being a young planet. These animals posed a huge danger to everyone. All the work they had planned to do could be literally eaten by the monsters. They had no choice but to cleanse the entire planet. After the large animals were killed, by sending a large rock from space to crash into the planet, they had to wait for it to stabilize. They had speeded up the process by carefully traveling in time. Then they started the bioengineering work on the apes that they had brought with them. Finally, they had to select the right kind of life-forms that resulted from this initial work. Then the plan required them to fine-tune their work in order to build in a level of intelligence and capability to learn. All the while they were developing artificial means to keep the organic circuitry alive outside of its host body. They accomplished this by eliminating certain parts of the brain—that is why the creatures did not have an enlarged back of the head. All this expense and time had been worth it; it was an investment in their future existence. Every scientist was surprised to see the final product—it looked almost exactly like a person from Aten-Heru—except the elongated skull. The resources were not unlimited, and time was short—so they decided to go with this final product. The documents he was reading did not contain what part was eliminated from the brain to make it rounder—that information would be available somewhere else. Atra-has's superiors had told him that this was all the information that he was allowed to know—the rest, he was told, was irrelevant to his journey.

Atra-has looked around to see if any of his aides was coming in his direction. The locator was taking time tracking down Lela. No one was approaching him. Maybe she was taken to a bunker—it did not matter. The locator was accurate and always found the signal from the transmitter built into the cyborgs. Atra-has continued to recall the information he was given. In order to maintain a level of secrecy and avoid delays due to bureaucracy they had traveled to an isolated spot of the universe in their future. Each subsequent visit was a little further out in time from the initial visit so that the new creations had time to stabilize and evolve. As is the case with long-term projects, there was never enough time, and the scientists had to cut corners. They were not able to do all the testing that they had planned.

Inadvertently, he wondered, were the engineered creatures given more capabilities than their original calculations had projected—even though a part of the brain was missing? Those capabilities could only come from one place—the Aten-Heru DNA which was used to create them. The Earth woman had told him that there were many territories on this planet and each one had a leader. Was this need to organize an unintended consequence of the design that was implemented? Was there some other need that made all the humans and cyborgs in Aten-Heru to silently revolt by not obeying orders? After all, these creatures could be considered as not-so-distant cousins to his race. Did the people the previous missions had left behind intermingle with the creatures? The scientists had predicted that their progeny would not be viable. Even if an offspring were to be delivered, there would be severe genetic abnormalities. Some of the remains he saw in the stone pyramid indicated that to be the case.

The inception of this special project to create this new race had begun only a short time ago—on Aten-Heru. On this planet, however, several thousand years had passed. The commanders on Aten-Heru, with input from the scientists, had indicated that a fresh batch from this planet would be uncontaminated with these rebellious thoughts. This new batch was many years more evolved than the earlier batch because the military scientists had given him a range of years within which the new sample was to be collected. Atra-has had chosen a time directly in the middle of the range—any soldier would do the same. The first batch that they took back was very adaptable. They showed tremendous capability to learn. However, the bioengineers had carefully built in the need to be subservient to a greater power. But they could not build in longevity like the people of Aten-Heru had. Even with their extended longevity, due to the elapsed time, the original personnel who were left behind to organize the collection of the metal had died. They contained both genders, so their offspring should be on this planet. When the beacon was turned on, while they were still descending to the planet surface, the descendants should have picked up the signals and arrived at Atra-has's vehicle. Unless the descendants had deviated from the prescribed plan and intermingled with the creatures. After all, the creatures did have a resemblance to their creators. Atra-has did have a fleeting thought, when the astronauts were brought to him, that both the women were attractive. If that were the case, there would be no one to respond to the beacon.

Atra-has was still waiting for someone to come and alert him about the exact location of Lela. He let his thoughts go back to Aten-Heru. Ever since he was old enough, he could remember the war. It was a constant presence in the lives of the people there. It was a nuisance for the restive people of Aten-Heru—it had been going on for several millennia. He had joined to help end it—once and for all. The current generation was promised that it would be over soon. This new development, the creation of these creatures, gave the Aten-Heru side a significant advantage. They could outfit a large number of cyborgs—maybe even thousands of them, and send them to the enemy planet. If they got through they could create considerable destruction. In the panic, with the enemy defenses down, they could sneak some more troops and cyborgs and cause pandemonium. If the cyborgs were not able to get through, they could try again—there would be no explaining to do since no Aten-Heru soldier would have lost his life.

At this point in time, no one even knew why the war started or what they were fighting over. There would be periods of lull, but suddenly one side or the other would select a leader who would start the hostilities all over. Generally, in order to cement his position as leader, a war would be initiated under the guise of attempting to acquire more territory. The quiet period between wars was not for very long. In each lifetime an individual would have seen a few skirmishes or full-scale battles. Then the recovery would be long and arduous. The strangest thing of all was that the two sides had not even met face-to-face. The only encounter was in battles. There was no chance of diplomacy since they did not speak the same language; they had developed independently of each other and in some minor respects were biologically dissimilar. Aten-Heruans had a derogatory name for their enemy. Garg-Ar. Presumably the enemy must have had a derogatory name for Aten-Heruans. This did not help matters at all since each side considered the other to be less than worthy of living. The only thing they knew about each other was that both the planets were capable of supporting either life-forms. If the opponents were successful in capturing Aten-Heru, the Garg-Ar people would presumably take over the entire planet, and the fate of Aten-Heru race would be numbered.

It was a quirk of fate that billions of years ago, the two nearby planets had formed similar orbits around their respective hospitable stars. Life had started and evolved independent of each other, or that is what the Aten-Heruans believed. No one on Aten-Heru knew what the enemy believed. Current technology allowed one to traverse the distance between the two planets in a reasonable time—without going into hibernation. Moreover, it was also strange that life had evolved and developed at approximately similar pace and they were at about similar level of technological advancement. If one thought about it critically, one could surmise that someone or something had spread the life from one planet to the other. Either that or they had started the seeds of life on the two planets simultaneously. Maybe they did it to see if life on one planet developed quicker than the other. Whatever their purpose was no one on Aten-Heru was allowed to think of the beings from the other planet as anything but an inferior species. There was so much propaganda that it was an anathema to even discuss Garg-Ar as an equal race. They were vermin and had to be exterminated.

Atra-has continued with his thoughts. During his preparation for this trip he had read that fortuitously the original explorers had found a lot of gold on this planet. It was a completely unexpected find, and they altered their plans and left a contingent of personnel to organize the collection of this metal. This was a commodity that was essential to making those thousands of cyborgs. They did not have to go to other potentially inhospitable planets in search of gold. It was right here—in abundance. Gold has a unique property of not corroding, therefore could be used for circuitry in the machines. Gold did not oxidize, so it could be used in the presence of liquids without having to go through the expensive procedure of periodically replacing the circuits in the cyborgs. It would last the lifetime of the cyborg. It also makes for good circuits. It is very conductive. Therefore, the interface between organic brain containing liquids and machine circuitry could be achieved through gold connections. In addition, gold is an almost perfect reflector of infrared radiation, so it was planned for use on small fighter spacecraft used in deep space battles as well as exploration. These crafts typically had thinner outer skin so needed additional reflective material. There were so many essential uses for this material that it was almost worth it to make this journey only for gold.

Atra-has had read that when his predecessors had realized that there was gold here, they had requested volunteers in Aten-Heru to live on this distant planet and supervise the collection of gold. They had a stock of bioengineered labor force that was freshly created and could be used to extract the metal. The volunteers who were willing to stay would be kings. More than kings they could be gods. They would have the aura of the creator. These creatures would do anything the supreme lord commanded. Both the stock of bioengineered beings as well as the metal to make the circuitry would be brought back from this planet, on an as-needed basis. On Aten-Heru, it was not easy to extract the metal anymore. They had to go through extraordinary lengths to mine for the metal. But accidentally they had found a rich vein on this planet and had already transported huge quantities in previous missions.

What was especially pleasing to the leaders was that there was a stock of bioengineered beings here that could be used to do the hard work of extracting the gold. The same creatures could be transported to Aten-Heru and made to breed in order to farm the brain. All they had to do was to leave a small number of Aten-Heru volunteers here on this planet to collect the gold for a time of need. There was no guarantee that these volunteers would be able to get back, but their descendants would be able to go back to Aten-Heru. The plan was that if the descendants decided to return, some other volunteers would be recruited to continue the effort—until such time as needed.

But the descendants were not responding to the beacon. Somehow all the volunteers seemed to have disappeared. More to the point, where was his brother who had volunteered to stay back to help with the cause? There were a large number of these creatures on this planet. They appeared to be organized and more advanced than Atra-has was led to believe in the reports he had read. Indeed, some had come into space. None of the reports had indicated to him that there was an innate capacity in these creatures to construct a space-faring vehicle. So who is this race? They look similar to the ones transported earlier to Aten-Heru. But were they genetically one and the same? Did the DNA that was put into them evolve and thus led the Aten-Heru volunteers to have relationships with the creatures? This problem would be addressed later. He needed to come up with a strategy to address the immediate problems. The first task was to find the craft that was left behind for the volunteers to use, in case they needed it. That way maybe those who stayed back could be found. The finding part was easy. In fact, the old craft had already been located, and one of the crafts from his battalion was on its way there to extract it.

Unfortunately, during their last trip to this planet, the enemy had also made the same journey. Arriving here sometime after Atra-has's spacecraft had arrived, they had waged a fierce battle all this way from home. Fortunately, the Aten-Heru side won, destroying all the ships except for one. They had chased that one across the outer reaches of this planet's solar system. But it was futile—it had escaped and presumably returned to its home planet for reinforcements.

On his return back to this planet, Atra-has had received orders from the scientists back home to arrive at a certain time, a time in the future of where they were. Prior to going into hibernation, he had instructed the lead cyborg, Lela, to make time-travel adjustments to arrive at the instructed time. If they arrived at this juncture they would have ample time to neutralize the asteroid before impacting Earth. He had also instructed the cyborg to make the final corrections slowly and not to overshoot the mark or to risk collision by jumping too far forward. Their time-travel calculations had projected an asteroid impact with the planet, which they had to prevent. Apparently, the cyborg was planning something during the time he and his staff were hibernating. It was possible that the enemy may have seen the rich resources here and may be sending another contingent of battleships, this time more powerful and better equipped. However, that victory, which was many thousands of years ago by Earth standards, was at the expense of considerable losses on Atra-has's side too. Many of his space crafts were destroyed. At the end of that battle, he was left with just two of them. One of them, which he had managed to load with the metal, had crashed into the ocean, leaving just one to return home. Thinking of those past events, his current armada had no time to waste. In order to avoid another conflict and potentially more losses, they had to quickly collect the supplies and depart immediately. Otherwise, this mission would also be in jeopardy. Moreover, this time it would be more complicated. The locals appeared to possess vastly greater technology than in the past. It could end up being a three-way battle. And if Garg-Ar made contact with the locals first and made an alliance, it would make it that much more difficult. Maybe Aten-Heru should initiate the first contact. But who should they contact? There was no one ruler for the entire planet, as the creature woman who was able to communicate with him had said earlier.

Thinking about the chronological sequence of events and also recalling the information he was given had helped. In his mind, he had formed a strategy. He would collect as many creatures as he could, check a few locations for the presence of the metal, and then go to where the loaded pyramid was recovered. In the course of these tasks, if he were able to contact someone powerful, he would try to initiate contact in order to form an alliance. He did not need the alliance; he did not want the creatures to form an alliance with Garg-Ar. If this planet needed to be destroyed, a last resort, he could accomplish that too.

Atra-has was in such deep thought that he did not notice his lieutenant arrive. After the obligatory salute, the lieutenant communicated with Atra-has. In return Atra-has gave some instructions. Soon thereafter a small craft left Atra-has's pyramid. Within seconds it located Lela's homing device and, with one surgical strike, launched a weapon which cut through several floors as if they did not exist. Lela's brain was already dead. The weapon, however, vaporized the hard exterior shell. The small craft then returned to its dock in the pyramid. There was one more thing that Atra-has had to do, then he would leave the area and head east. He could not wait any longer for the homing signal to be picked up by the descendants of his people. If they had not arrived by now, he had to assume either that they were not going to come or they could not come or they were all dead.

HOMEWARD BOUND

While they were lugubriously running out of the buildings John asked, "What transport?"

The sergeant responded without slowing down, "We were instructed by the Pentagon to have you back stateside ASAP. That is why they sent an SB which is currently waiting on the tarmac with its engines revving."

The SB78B was designed to be fast. It was developed for supersonic transportation of troops anywhere around the globe. Its primary use was to send an advance regiment of soldiers into volatile areas, until larger numbers arrived via traditional means. The SB78B was developed from high-speed drones capable of carrying a huge tonnage of ordnance, both conventional and nuclear. To everyone's relief the troop carrier version of the jet had a pilot at the controls. John immediately recognized the airplane. A version of this with rocket boosters was used to launch the dSEs at an altitude so it could reach orbit more easily than launching from ground level. When the astronauts were boarding they noticed that the aircraft was cavernous and, other than a handful of soldiers, basically empty. The sergeant accompanied them to their seat, which was anywhere in the plane which had such a huge seating capacity. Due to their exhaustion, they unanimously elected to sit in the closest seats to the door.

John said, "Thanks," to the sergeant, and as he was leaving to close the fuselage door John inquired, "Will we be in Florida in about two hours?"

The plane was already moving, so the sergeant, as he was shutting the door, responded, "We will probably do better than that."

By the time they had settled in their seats the plane had already taxied to the takeoff point, and the pilot announced, "Here we go."

A surge of acceleration and within ten seconds they were airborne. The plane was lightly loaded, so there was ample power. Within two minutes they had reached forty thousand feet. They would be cruising at this altitude and breaking the sound barrier by more than a factor of two.

This was the first time in a very long time that John, Nicole, Kristen, and Ken had time to relax and put their guard down. It had been a very hectic few days, and other than brief catnaps, none had any significant sleep during that time. John asked the sergeant who had escorted them on board, "I would like to change out of this space suit. Do you have any clothing lying around? I am sure all of us would like to change into something less stale and more suited to Earth conditions. We have been wearing the same thing for the last few days." The sergeant smiled and said, "We kinda anticipated that request. I can do better. We have some standard-issue clothes and an assortment of food," and within a few seconds came back with both. Given the circumstances, the astronauts gladly accepted the unflattering clothing and started digging into the food. Having some solid food, even out of a paper bag, after eating packaged material for such a long time, was an unexpected luxury. Anticipating their next request, the sergeant also thoughtfully brought a can of cold soda for everyone—it was gleefully accepted. They had consumed only water for the last several months.

Ken, who was pondering the events, mentioned matter-of-factly, "I have lived in various parts of the world during my time and have always wondered why every culture values gold so much. I know gold is fairly rare, but so are some other metals. Why gold?"

Nicole, walking over to the seat after changing into the overalls, offered the invitation to Ken, "Do you think it is something to do with the alien visitors?"

Ken did not need any encouragement. He effusively continued, "I think so. We, as a race of humans, have a predilection to gold. Every society and culture values gold, even though it is very difficult to mine. Added to that the mining process, whether it be large-scale industrial mining or artisans scraping the surface of the Earth, is very toxic both to the environment and the individual engaged in finding it. But people risk their lives because society puts such high value on gold. Many cultures give gold as a gift to a parting bride. Ever wonder where the practice came from? Besides, why did Atra-has go to the Khufu pyramid, and how did he know exactly where to go? Did he read the original hieroglyphs? Was there a symbol indicating which way to go?" Then looking at Kristen for confirmation he continued, "While you were speaking with him, I, too, was trying to read his thoughts. Although I am not nearly as proficient as you, I did pick up certain thoughts. As I had suspected, the thoughts come as symbols, don't they?"

Ken looked at her for confirmation, and Kristen, somewhat surprised, nodded affirmatively as she was too busy savoring the food in her mouth. Ken continued, "See the relationship between the two? The thoughts are symbols. They help in faster communication. Those exact symbols are written as hieroglyphs." Kristen continued to nod, her face now expressing shock with the realization of what Ken had said. The other two also had a similar expression of astonishment. Ken made his point by stating, "That is where the hieroglyphs come from. It is a way to communicate among these aliens, and that is why they write that way too. Khufu also communicated that way. He must have been the alien that Atra-has mentioned earlier."

He had the rapt attention of the three who had by now all changed into the overalls. Kristen was still wondering about the gold. "Fascinating as it is about the hieroglyphs do you think it is in our DNA to have affinity for gold?"

Ken swallowed the food he was chewing and said, "Yes, I think so. Of all the items one can buy, why would wealthy societies in Asia and other continents go out of their way to buy a metal as a wedding gift? I am not necessarily speaking of ornaments or jewelry. I am speaking of gold ingots or gold coins. Even the less wealthy purchase gold ingots or coins to give away. Money would be just as valuable and more flexible. Or maybe some other gifts that would help the newlyweds set up their home. However, the parents of the new couple give as much gold as they possibly can afford. The purpose is to help them in their journey in life, just like we were programmed to give it away to the aliens when they made an appearance to this planet. Today it is customary to give gold, but this practice may have its roots in traditions imposed on humans by the aliens—to further their cause. It could have started as a means to appease the king, who was possibly an alien. The king would store the gold awaiting its pickup. Why did the Incas store so much gold? They apparently did not use it for anything. Some of what was left over was pillaged by the Spanish. Only a fraction of what the Mayans were supposed to have has been found. Where did the rest go? Did you know, if we piled up all the gold in the world in one place, it would fill just two Olympic-sized pools? Today, that is all the gold available on Earth sitting in the vaults of countries and homes of individuals. If the aliens have come here for that precious metal, they may not realize that they have already depleted Earth of gold. What we are extracting now is more difficult to mine, more toxic to clean and less pure, since all the gold that is easy to find was already mined and transported to their world."

John said, "Ken, I think this is a stretch—"

Ken jumped in, "I agree that we do not have any empirical evidence, but it makes one wonder…," letting the sentence hang for a moment.

Everyone was too tired to say much. They were sitting deep in thought mulling over what Ken had just said and enjoying the food from the paper bag. Ken was the only one with his mind racing trying to piece the incomplete puzzle—he had another thought. "Based on what Atra-has told Kristen earlier, I think the asteroid was originally set in motion by the aliens to destroy Earth. The aliens, when they were here last, probably wanted to destroy Earth at some date in the distant future. So they had carefully calculated a proper trajectory for the asteroid and had sent it on its way—knowing fully well that they did not have to be 100 percent accurate. Gravity would do the final targeting. I am beginning to believe that this was meant to be some sort of a natural time bomb. That is how they had depopulated Earth of the dinosaurs, and this is how they could leave no evidence of their intentions—even if they were, for whatever reason, unable to get to Earth to clean up their handiwork. Their arrival here at this time was not a coincidence. They wanted to pick up whatever they came here for before Earth got destroyed by Apophis. If they are successful at finding what it is they came here to get, will they destroy Earth before leaving?"

With that chilling question, which no one wanted to mull over in their current state of exhaustion, thankfully Ken took a break from speaking.

The silence did not last long. However, to everyone's relief, when he continued speaking again, it was on a different topic. "Did you wonder why the alien crafts went to the places they did. They were not going there at random. One went to the Bermuda Triangle. I am pretty sure they have something there that was causing all those anomalies. I cannot be sure what it is, but I am sure we will find out once we land. Another one went to South America where all those interesting lines are present, called the Nazca lines. I am sure a lot of gold was found there. The current conjecture is that some mountains of solid rock were cut down but no one has been able to come up with an acceptable answer of how it was done. Knowing what I know now, I am sure they were mining for gold and must have found a rich vein, maybe even several of them. They decided to cut down the mountains. How else could ancient man who only had tools made of sticks and stones reduce a mountain or two to less than half its size?"

The others were slowly coming around to thinking that Ken may have a point—either that or they were too tired to be analytical. Their bellies were full, and they had not slept in a while. They had all heard of the Bermuda Triangle as well as the Nazca lines in Peru, and no one, until now, had an explanation of how or why they were there.

Ken, appeared to have been energized by the food he was eating, continued, "And another one went to Japan. There we have, according to legend, the tale of Utsuro Bune, which translates to Hollow Ship. A woman is supposed to have emerged from an alien vehicle carrying a box supposedly containing the head of someone she cared for deeply. Now, over time, the legend may have become somewhat fuzzy. But the essential element was the fact that she was carrying the head of a person. What would be the use of carrying a head? Maybe she rescued it from the aliens, or maybe she was an alien herself and was carrying the head for laboratory tests…" Ken let those words hang in the air. Then he continued, "There is also the Dragon's Triangle, just to the south of Japan. Similar conditions exist there as in the Bermuda Triangle. The Japanese government strongly advises everyone to avoid the area—just as the authorities around the Bermuda Triangle recommend the avoidance of certain parts of the Atlantic Ocean. In the Dragon's Triangle, there are massive and ancient relics which are now underwater. These have been the source of much conjecture and intense debate. Why would the aliens go there, other than to find some evidence or results of their previous visits? They could not have built the structures underwater; it must have been dry land at some point in the past. I think Atra-has is looking for something in those areas. Perhaps they are looking for evidence of their previous visits, or maybe they left something there. Maybe these were the hubs where gold mined in various sites in the local region would arrive. It could be collected in those large stone structures which, in the case of the Dragon's Triangle, are now under-water. Maybe the pyramids in Egypt were also one of those local col-lection hubs. They would stay there, safe in the forebodingly massive structures, till the interstellar pyramids arrived. Then they could be easily moved to the pyramids for transportation to the alien world."

The others were intently listening to Ken. They did not have any arguments against his theories. What he was proposing was slowly making sense, especially in light of what they already knew.

As a result of years of teaching experience, Ken had a way of stating the obvious in thought-provoking ways. "Then there is the pyramid that went to the western part of India, to a legendary city of Dwaraka. Dwaraka is submerged now, but in the past, according to mythology, it was a great kingdom. In the ancient Indian scriptures, it was the scene of great battles. That in itself is not surprising. There have been numerous battles in the human history. A number of those have also been documented in classical literature. What makes this one surprising is that some of the battles, according to Hindu mythol-ogy and ancient texts, were fought in the air—they were aerial bat-tles. What earthly power ten thousand or more years ago was capable of flying, let alone aerial combat? Legend has it that bolts of lightning emanated from the crafts flying through the air which destroyed the city with explosions as well as the ensuing fires. Maybe they were the same kinds of bolts that killed the soldiers who were guarding the pyramids. Then there is the legend where the mythological character Hanuman carried a mountain from the Himalayas to the modern-day country of Sri Lanka. Why would ancient humans come up with such an impossible feat? These deeds are clearly impossible, and anyone telling such stories, during that time in our history, would be ridiculed. But it is a serious mythology. Maybe it was a machine that took off and landed. A mountain looks like a pyramid from a distance, an apex and a broad base. Since the eyewitnesses of the time could not interpret what they had seen, they built a story around it, and that has endured and become a mythological legend."

Then he looked around at the others and asked, "Does that sound familiar? If you ask me, it sounds like an air raid and missiles, or something to that effect, being dropped from the flying machines."

Everyone was captivated with what Ken was saying, their fatigue dissipating a little as Ken was narrating his opinions. Similar to a class of students, they collectively gave that distant nod that one does when deep in thought with the thought process stimulated. Ken knew he had captivated his audience and so did not wait for anyone to jump in. "What are they looking for in Dwaraka? It is a city underwater! What are they looking for in the Dragon's Triangle? Are they looking for something that may be stored there in the giant underwater stone structures? In the pyramids…in the Bermuda Triangle…? These are specific places to visit. Why those locations? If it is gold they are looking for, and humans have found precious little on Earth, then we should not allow them to take it. That resource belongs on Earth. It belongs to the people of Earth."

He let the listeners cogitate on that thought for a second while he took another bite, chewed, and swallowed. Then he continued on another theme, "Ever since our encounter with the aliens, I have been wondering what their purpose was to visit us. Surely it cannot be a social call. That much is patently obvious. It appears that they were a little surprised with the level of technology and sophistication we possess. It is as if they are the masters and we are meant to be the subservient race. Atra-has said that his race made us. Maybe it was genetic engineering. Assuming what he said is true, and I don't have any reason to believe otherwise, maybe they programmed us to want to believe in a higher being. Why else do humans want so desperately to believe in an entity for which there is no proof of any kind? Maybe they programmed our DNA to want to dispense with rational thought and believe in something which does not even have anecdotal evidence. I am not the first one to suggest this theory. Ancient texts found in modern-day Iraq talks about this very theory. In fact, these texts are so old that they are written in cuneiform. They were found in an area commonly believed to be the cradle of civilization, known as Sumer in those times. The Annunaki people who lived there were supposed to be aliens, I mean, nonhumans, who were using humans for their benefit. I always wondered why this region became the cradle of civilization. Is it because, with the help of the Annunaki, the humans here had a jump start on the rest of humanity? If you start thinking along these lines, things start to make more sense. Maybe these places where Atra-has sent his crafts were, in the distant past, local storage depots. These depots where precious metals and other items mined in local regions could be safely stored. I suspect gold is what Atra-has was looking for when he went into the Giza pyramid. He sent the other crafts to investigate other such locations. I know that some of these places were ancient centers where a ruler lived. I am beginning to think the king was an alien and was instructed to collect all the necessary items. The aliens would periodically come here, load up their pyramids from these depots with the help of the robots, and return to their home. This could be done quickly and efficiently, perhaps at night. Till a hundred years ago, electricity was not widely available, and three hundred years ago it was unknown. If a freighter craft came at night the locals would be none the wiser. Before electricity people feared the dark and did not venture out at night unless it was absolutely necessary. In case there were any chance eyewitnesses, the individual would not believe their own eyes and would be too embarrassed to mention it to anyone. Even if someone was foolhardy to tell the tale, their sanity would be seriously questioned, and over a year or two their accounts would be forgotten."

Kristen, like the others, was captivated with this discourse, but could not help feeling a little frustrated at the seeming lack of direction. She interjected, "Ken, where are you going with this? Are you saying that there is no God?"

Ken was on a roll, and although he heard the question, he did not address it. Instead, he continued, "To the technologically uninitiated human of the past, the aliens were God. What was it Einstein who said, 'Technology sufficiently advanced is indistinguishable from magic'? To the humans two or three thousand years or more ago, all this was magic. In a way, even to us, it appears like magic, all this antigravity machines, telepathic communication, and the weaponry that we have seen so far. Wonder what other surprises they have in store for us…"

He paused for a moment to let the idea settle and also take a breath and another bite of the food. Then he continued, "All around Earth there has been evidence of alien intervention, in one form or another. We chose not to believe in what we see. Instead we believe in something that is neither material nor physical. We believe in an entity for which there is no proof, and yet we are happy with it because it gives us a sense of peace. It lets us believe that there is a protector for each individual. Why?" He answered his own question, "Because we are programmed that way. It gives us comfort to believe that someone or something is out there looking out for us. This is, of course, not true. Other than some anecdotal evidence, and I use the word 'evidence' very loosely, there has been no individual who has been saved through divine intervention. No evidence that cannot be attributed to luck, and luck has befriended the pious as well as those who do not participate in religious or spiritual activities. If you look at it objectively, religion has caused more grief in the history of Earth than anything else. So if you added the numbers up of how much suffering religion has caused versus how many people have been saved due to divine providence, you can logically come to one conclusion only—that the concept of God is highly questionable. Why people persist in this illogical choice is completely counterintuitive to me. Even today people are needlessly perishing in the name of religion. We highlight differences between each other rather than similarities. Why?" Without a pause for the others to formulate an answer he answered his own question, "I believe it is because we were programmed to be combative. They created us with a certain set of characteristics which is manifesting itself in humanity."

There was a stunned silence, except for the monotonous drone of the aircraft. Like a professor in a classroom Ken stopped to take a breath and a sip of soda and let what he had said sink in for a second, then continued, "Think of it another way. As far as we know there has never been a thinking being of any kind on Earth. Earth has been populated by animals for millions of years. In the past it was dinosaurs. Later it was various other animals. In all those millions of years, we have found no evidence of any creature on Earth capable of thought, using tools or constructing anything. Then suddenly the human evolutionary tree begins. Of course, there are numerous branches in the evolutionary tree, but out of nowhere, a being capable of cognitive reasoning, a sentient being, appears. Think about it. There is no advantage in the evolutionary increase in intelligence to sustain life. As long as the animal can kill and eat, the increase of cognitive growth serves no purpose. Just look at the prehistoric creatures which have survived the mass extinctions and are alive today—crocodiles, alligators, turtles, sharks, and others. They have been present for millions of years without any growth in their brain cavity. As long as you find your niche there is no reason to invest energy in evolving the intellect. Yes, it is true that animals get faster or slower or adopt different colors to camouflage better against the prey. But the development of the brain is not high on that list of evolutionary needs. We are mammals and no different from any other animal on Earth. Unsurprisingly we are no different than humans of even three thousand years ago—when the pyramids and countless other structures were built. Our diets are different as a result of technology. Hence, we are bigger. But essentially, we are the same as the men and women of a few thousand years ago. We will still be the same a few thousand years from now. It takes a special set of circumstances to evolve a brain capable of critical thinking. Earth never developed a creature capable of thought, until *they* introduced it." Ken was pointing in some vague direction, but everyone knew, in his mind, that finger was pointing to the aliens. Without a pause he continued, "If all the living creatures had a seamless progression of evolution since the last mass extinction, it stands to reason that other creatures could have evolved intelligence to a much greater extent than they have. Left to nature, why should it be the sole right of humans to evolve an advanced brain? Did you wonder why we look so much like them? Maybe we are partly them. Maybe *they* are meant to be our gods. Maybe Earth needed a few more millennia before any of the native species could evolve into something capable of processing logical thought. Maybe the aliens have a few hundred thousand years, or more, of head start in terms of evolution compared to Earth. Remember the universe is nearly fifteen billion years old, and the Earth is just less than five billion years old. There could have been many opportunities for life to evolve elsewhere, long before Earth. In fact, entire civilizations could have formed and disappeared before Earth was even formed. Just because we have not found it, it is absurd to think there is no other intelligent life elsewhere in the universe."

Then after a moment he sardonically added with a wide grin on his face, "Maybe the creationists were right after all. We were all created…by the aliens."

Their attention was diverted just in time to hear John say, "Roger that."

John had no problem with the argument that Ken was making. However, he was beginning to feel uncomfortable at the thought of humans being custom-made creatures. He gave a discernible sigh of relief when he had to interrupt this intense discourse and announced, "This is all fascinating. I am sure we will have a chance to find out in the very near future. Just got off with Mission Control. They have been listening too. They think we should shut down for a while and take rest. We all have finished this delicious fast food, and we should rest now. There are likely to be more encounters with Atra-has. I just got word in my communicator that there has been a skirmish with one of the pyramids in Florida. Looks like there will be more action, and we need to be up for it."

Everyone was so intently listening to Ken that no one except John even heard the communicator come on.

John continued, "One of the pyramids has landed there. They did not say any more because they do not know and they don't want to get close enough to investigate. They are waiting for us, specifically Kristen, to arrive, in case we have to communicate with them. They don't want to risk anything. So I suggest we take a nap and try to catch up on some much-needed sleep. I am sure someone will wake us up when we arrive."

With that, the four astronauts settled down for a short nap. They would be arriving at the base soon. Having just eaten a hearty meal and their level of exhaustion sleep came immediately and was deep and dreamless—almost like going into hibernation.

CARNAGE

"Sir!" The voice was distant but unmistakable.

"Sir!" There it was again. What was that? Someone was pulling his arm—should he run? Was someone after them, or was it only a dream?

"Sir!" This time it was closer—too close, almost directly in his ear.

John opened his eyes and saw the sergeant looking directly at him from about two inches away. His hand was gently tugging on John's arm. When the sergeant saw that John had opened his eyes he said, "Sir, we have landed and the transportation is ready for the four of you."

"Wha...what? Already? Tha...thank you," he mumbled. John took a minute to get his bearings. So much had happened, and they had not rested in a while. The rest was too short—he could do with a few more hours of sleep, but it would have to wait. John realized that it was not a dream, no human dreams during deep sleep. He and the rest of the astronauts were in such deep sleep that even the noise and vibration of the airplane landing did not rouse them. Thoughtfully the sergeant had made a large pot of strong coffee and was holding a cup for John, which he thankfully accepted. As John cleared the cobwebs and realized where he was and what would happen next, the sergeant had woken the other three from their slumber. He had a cup of coffee for all, which they gratefully accepted. John got a modicum of comfort in realizing that the other three looked equally tired and were taking their time in shaking the sleep from their heads. They must all have been in deep sleep, which is why they all appeared to be so disoriented—they were woken from almost a state of hibernation.

They disembarked from the airplane and boarded a military transport chopper to be taken to the place where both the pyramids had landed. The anticipation would not last for long. The pilot mentioned that the journey time would be just fifteen minutes—a little more time to let the caffeine kick in. A familiar voice from central command brought them back to reality. "Hope you all had a chance to rest during this short journey. Your vigilance is of paramount importance. What you are about to see is a fantastic sight, two large pyramids parked in the fields with choppers and military personnel around in a circular perimeter. There has been no movement since the missiles exploded inside."

That got their attention immediately. John responded without being able to hide his surprise, "Missiles? How on earth did the missiles penetrate the outer skin of the pyramids?"

The voice from central command answered, "The missiles did not breach the skin. The explosion happened inside the pyramid."

John, even more incredulous, said, "Wait, you set off an explosion inside the pyramid?"

Central command continued, "It was mostly luck. Our pilot was aiming for the small shuttle craft that had come out and had destroyed one of our choppers. We were retaliating. He was given permission from command central to fire at the craft to prevent us losing another of our choppers."

As the speaker was narrating, the four were looking at one another, shaking their heads in complete disbelief. This could trigger hostilities that could end very badly for the people of Earth.

The speaker continued, "The craft was moving towards one of our helicopters when the missiles were deployed. Suddenly it veered off of and headed back to the pyramid. The target-seeking missiles also changed course and followed the craft. The portal on the pyramid opened to let the craft in. As it crossed the threshold into the pyramid, the portal door closed behind it but not before letting the missiles into the pyramid. The portal shut, the missiles found their target, and here we are. There was nothing we could do about it."

As this was being described John, who had covered his face with his hands, was lost for words. After a pause to see if there was any response, the announcer continued, "The explosion was contained within the pyramid. There is no external damage to the pyramid. But we want you to go in and take a look. The only thing we can report is that the entry point which is used to access the pyramid by foot, the one that you all have been using to get in and out, has blown off. We have a fire engine already deployed to the area. You can use the ladder to ingress the pyramid."

John finally said out aloud, "This could be very bad for us. These pissed-off aliens could have laid a trap for us. You still want us to go in to investigate?"

There was no choice. Someone had to investigate the carnage, so the speaker confirmed, "Affirmative, there has been no activity. Maybe we need to rescue or lend a hand, if there are any casualties. Judging from the lack of activity, it may be a recovery mission."

John asked, "Are all of us going in?"

Central command explained, "That is correct. You as the commander, Nicole as the medic, Kristen as the communicator, and Ken as the linguistic expert, in case that expertise is needed. Moreover, since the four of you have already established contact with them, there may be some comfort to the aliens to think that they are dealing with the same individuals. Plus, there is safety in numbers, but we do not want to send too many, in case it is intimidating. Backups are standing by, if that is needed."

John responded, "Copy that," then looking at Kristen he said, "If you see anyone inside, you will have to try and apologize and explain that this was a mistake." Then he took the finger off the button so he was not transmitting and said, "We only just escaped from the clutches of the aliens. Now we are heading back inside. This could turn out to be interesting."

Kristen, looking very concerned, said, "I will try. I don't know how to express remorse." Then after a moment's thought she added, "Or for that matter I cannot even express the word 'mistake.' I have not yet picked up on expressing feelings."

Almost as an afterthought, John said, "We will not carry weapons, just in case it gives them the wrong impression. Even if we did carry weapons, it will be useless against these aliens. They can easily outgun us assuming we even get a chance to use them. We will carry the medical emergency kit only and whatever essential items Nicole thinks necessary."

As John completed the sentence, the site of the conflagration came into view. The visage was indeed fantastic. The pyramids were parked in the middle of a large clearing, and a few military choppers were parked around the pyramids at approximately a distance of two hundred meters. About another hundred meters away were military personnel, and their numbers were such that they almost made a complete circle around both the pyramids about four to five persons deep. They came from the various branches of the military as evidenced by the colors of their clothing. The chopper landed in a gap between the already parked helicopters, and the astronauts disembarked.

They made their way to the pyramid that had experienced the explosion, identified by the fire truck with an already extended ladder parked next to it. Kristen looked around at the other pyramid and exclaimed, "Unbelievable! Look at that hole in the other pyramid. Wonder what caused that?"

That was a question that no one could answer. However, it did seem frightening that something could cause that kind of damage to a structure that was seemingly indestructible. Not even a nuclear explosion followed by fragments of a meteorite striking the pyramid, in space, had caused the merest scratch on the surface.

John announced into his radio communicator, "We are at the fire truck and proceeding to the top."

"Roger that," came the response.

With the help of the personnel, the four started the long climb to the top of the ladder and the entrance to the pyramid. The fire chief helped them with a small helmet-mounted camera powered by a small fuel cell-based battery pack that could, if necessary, last months without recharging. With the camera secure on their helmets they started climbing. Only halfway up it seemed precarious, and anyone with even a hint of vertigo would not make it to the top. Fortunately, none had that condition or was hiding it effectively.

They all had been trained well and knew how to control their basic innate feelings and emotions in situations where they had no control.

John was the first to the top, followed by Nicole, Kristen, and lastly Ken. They all successfully got off the ladder and realized that the outside door, as reported by HQ, was missing. A few steps in and they saw that the inside door was also open, although it was still on its hinges.

In order to keep the command central apprised of what they were about to do, John announced, "Entering the second portal." He knew this was redundant—there were multiple cameras trained on him and the portal. But if this was a trap and the aliens jammed the transmission from the communicator once they were inside, it would be better to know sooner rather than later.

"We see you," came the response.

Although it was bright and sunny outside, due to lack of any illumination, everything beyond the second doorway was dark—like a narrow-mouthed cave. They stepped through the second portal, John leading the way. A few paces in through the door everything was very dark. It would take a moment for the eyes to adjust, walking in from bright sunshine to almost total darkness.

John took three paces from the doorway and stopped dead on his tracks. Nicole looked at him to see why he had stopped so abruptly and then followed his astonished gaze. She remarked, "What the hell happened here?"

Journey East

Atra-has saw his tiny craft come back from its mission to obliterate Lela. He commanded the pyramid to journey east. Lela was a casualty of war, within the acceptable limits of tolerance per the calculations done prior to the journey. There were other cyborgs that he could use to replace Lela. At this time, John and the others were still in the airplane heading west. Atra-has's concern was mainly to collect what he and his race needed and take it back to his world. If he was successful, there would be accolades, promotions, and more importantly a step closer to victory in their continued and everlasting battle. His journey would take him in an easterly direction, mostly over land. They would then arrive at a triangular-shaped peninsula, the north of which were some of the largest mountain ranges. On the way there, he would make two stops, each to pick up certain kinds of people. The individuals he was looking for were the kinds who could communicate telepathically. These were the individuals who spent most of their time training their minds to meditate, to contemplate God. The pyramids' machinery picked up these hot spots and displayed them on the monitor. These hot spots were identified on the monitor as yellow-colored dots.

Atra-has knew that the yellow dots represented major religious centers and the peninsula was called India. He knew this because he had picked up the human thoughts, particularly Kristen's, as they were observing in astonishment during the descent from space.

Certain human individuals were predisposed to introspective thinking. This was by design. Over time through natural selection, this DNA designed by the aliens would become diluted—nothing that could be done about that. However, some individuals showed an enhancement of the trait—very crucial to the aliens' needs. This is what the aliens needed. A great proportion of these individuals with these traits tended to spend most of their lives in the service of God. Due to this attribute, they congregated in specific areas. The fact that they would flock to certain locations was well-known to the aliens. These locations were originally identified by Atra-has's people. This is where the Earth's natural forces, fueled by the natural magnetic fields, are the greatest. Centuries earlier, in order to speed up training, this is where structures designed to enhance these forces were constructed by Atra-has's people. This is also where Atra-has's people, assigned to the Earth project, were leaders of the community and would instruct the creatures in ways of enhancing their mental prowess and civilized living. The aliens wanted their new creation to succeed and thrive, not become extinct due to lack of know-how.

The original goal was identifying the candidates by training the mind, while simultaneously using these creatures for labor. Ultimately, the objective was the transportation of the qualified individuals to Aten-Heru. Although Atra-has did not know these locations personally, he did have illuminated dots on the map generated by the machine to guide him to the magnetic forces. With the help of these forces and structures he expected to find a target-rich area where he could pick up these creatures for use with minimal training. He was not surprised to see so many target-rich areas displaying on the monitor which were spread out over the planet. This strong DNA trait made the creatures who were attracted to these locations ideal candidates to be brought back for breeding. It was the breeding aspect on Aten-Heru that was proving to be difficult—very few viable candidates were being produced. It appeared that genes with this trait were not always being transferred. Looking at the monitor display of the surroundings, he was surprised to see that some of the original old stone structures built all those years ago still appeared to be in fairly good shape. He thought, over time, wind, rain, heat, and cold would have caused at least some of the structures to collapse. At the very least he expected the outer edges of the stone structures, exposed to the elements, to become more rounded.

What Atra-has did not know was that these places he was viewing on the monitor had names such as Palmyra, Baalbek, etc.

Unknown to him, the humans had already found out what caused some individuals to behave in a certain way. This even had a name—the God gene. When this gene was expressed prominently, it predisposes the humans to a life of piety, contemplating and serving God. This is exactly what his people had designed, and he knew exactly how to find them.

The fact that Atra-has could not find any of his own kind was immaterial now. He could not waste time looking for them. He had orders and priorities. He knew how to get the target humans loaded into the pyramids without any trouble. The pyramids were equipped with a device capable to generating telepathic signals which would lure these individuals into the pyramid. People who were capable of receiving the signals are the ones that his planet needed, and they would not be able to resist it. They would just walk in, in almost a trancelike state. The creatures were bioengineered that way. Thinking of this, Atra-has felt all-powerful. He and his race were the overlords. They had designed these beings, and they still had control over them. Although Atra-has was astonished at the magnitude of growth on the planet and the creators never perceived there to be this many people, he was confident that he and his troops were in complete control. Yet he was becoming concerned with what his commanders wanted to do once the target creatures were collected. Did they want him to leave this planet intact, or did they want him to destroy everything? Both options were within his capability. In his mind one option was becoming less palatable.

After a couple of stops en route to the east Atra-has remembered that he had not heard from the other pyramids. He gave the appropriate instructions to his lieutenants, and within minutes it was apparent to him that one of the pyramids, code-named Vima Nan, was not reporting back its status. There was no communication of any sort with this one. He concluded that it had to be some sort of malfunction; he did not think that the local population was capable of destroying one of their warcraft before the lieutenants on board the pyramid were able to send a distress call. In any case he had more work to do. He had to find the shiny metal first and then look for Vima Nan. Hopefully it was something as mundane as a malfunction of the communication equipment. This was the craft they had deployed to retrieve the pyramid that was shot down over the ocean by a Garg-Ar battleship, in a previous battle on Earth all those years ago. The people of Garg-Ar, Aten-Heru's neighboring planet with whom they were waging this never-ending war, had sent their own battleships to Earth. Momentarily Atra-has had a frightening thought. Had the Garg-Ar squadron already arrived? Was there another ambush like the one that had originally damaged and drowned the pyramid into the ocean all those years ago? He would have to retrace his steps and find out what happened. He immediately put that thought out of his mind to focus on the human craft that was tracking them. He could not allow himself to worry about things he could not control. In good time, he will address the craft that had not reported its status.

Diego Garcia, part of the Chagos Archipelago, is a remote atoll in the Indian Ocean, at least a thousand miles from the nearest major landmass. Located on an atoll in Diego Garcia is a military base, primarily used by the United States. The islands in the archipelago can be considered as tropical paradise. However, today they are inhabited by military personnel only. No one is allowed to come near the atoll. The island is governed by the UK government, which had its inhabitants moved to other locations. Located at this remote base are long-range US Air Force bombers. These bombers are now capable of circumnavigating the Earth without refueling. From this base, an airplane took off to rendezvous with the pyramid. Currently the pyramids were over the Indian airspace heading in the southerly direction—toward Diego Garcia. As the airplane approached the pyramid, the pilot and commander on the airplane radioed, "Central command, we have a visual on the alien craft. They are at about 5,000 feet altitude, and we are looking down at them from about 20,000 feet. We have turned around 180 degrees and are following them. Awaiting further instructions."

The answer from HQ was "Observer 1, stay in visual contact with the craft and report on anything they do. Do not approach or engage. What is their heading?"

The pilot responded, "Base, we are presently at about 22 degrees, 14 minutes north, and 68 degrees, 58 minutes east. They are heading in a southerly direction over the Indian landmass. If I had to guess, they just took off from somewhere. We did not get here in time to see where they had landed, but I can guess they were on the ground since they are gaining altitude. They have climbed to 15,000 feet now and holding steady at that altitude."

HQ responded, "Observer 1, by their pattern, they are visiting the ancient and mythological places. The satellite images confirm that they had landed near the city of Dwaraka. Dwaraka, if you did not know, is of mythological significance. They had also landed in at least one other place prior to Dwaraka. Maybe they were looking for something there. For now, just track them and see what they are up to."

The pilot said, "Roger that, they are holding at 15,000 feet and traveling southerly over the landmass at about 1,000 knots."

Atra-has saw on his monitors that the human craft that was following him was harmless. The heat signatures of the craft indicated that it was not capable of great speed. The pyramid could go much faster. He had reduced speed in order to identify landmarks that he had in his archives. When he spotted the correct location, he would land and collect what he needed. Quick analysis from the defensive systems built into the pyramid indicated that the craft's weaponry would not be capable of inflicting even the slightest damage to the pyramid. He saw on the monitor that the craft was of ancient design. Back on his planet these kinds of craft were not even interesting enough to be in museums. This kind of flying craft was merely a stepping-stone which led, several generations later, to what they had today. He could safely ignore it and let the built-in automated systems and other personnel track the craft for any signs of aggressive behavior. If the craft misbehaved or showed belligerence of any kind, he would not hesitate to swat it like a fly. He would only destroy it if it posed a danger or interfered with their ability to accomplish what they had come here to do. He did not want to initiate any aggression—it would be imprudent, and he had orders not to do so. Moreover, he wanted to play it safe since he did not know what had happened to the craft that had not yet reported, before he took any aggressive action. Maybe these creatures had developed a technology of which he was unaware.

An hour or so later, the pilot radioed to the HQ, "Base, we are just passing the southern tip of India and will be passing over Sri Lanka very soon."

HQ responded, "Roger that, keep them in sight."

A few minutes later the pilot radioed, "Passing the southern coast of Sri Lanka. They are losing altitude."

A few seconds later HQ responded, "Maintain your distance." This obviously meant that the airplane piloted by the humans needed to lose altitude.

Atra-has's records indicated that he should be flying over dry land. However, no matter what direction his eyes and the monitors viewed, all he could see was miles and miles of water. No land anywhere in sight. He could not understand why this part was under so much water. He did not realize that during the previous visits Earth was gripped in one ice age after another. Consequently, the seawater was less, mostly held in miles of deep snow and ice starting at the poles and extending hundreds of miles in every direction. Now that the climate had warmed, the water had melted and dramatically increased the levels of the ocean. Moreover, this region was very earthquake prone and over the millennia had subsided enough to be completely submerged.

The pilot radioed, "Base, we are heading in the direction of Diego. Current speed indicates that we should be there in about 75 minutes. Altitude maintaining at 3,000—" The communication stopped abruptly.

HQ, alarmed by this sudden cut in communication, said, "Repeat that. Observer 1, can you repeat. We lost you."

The pilot and the support crew were gawking out of the window. Finally, the pilot spoke, sounding incredulous, "Holy cow! Communication is fine. I was shocked to see this incredible sight in front of us. We have never flown at this altitude and at this location…ever. From this altitude and in bright daylight, we are seeing something never witnessed by a human."

HQ, sounding much relieved, said, "You are seeing a sunken city, right?"

The pilot was as surprised at the comment as he was with what he was seeing. "How…how the hell did you know?" and immediately he added, "Sorry…I mean, how did you know?"

HQ said, "That is okay. We can all relate to your astonishment. We were kind of taken aback also when we learnt of this. We know because we have a group of analysts trying to make sense of what has been going on. We want to get to a point where we can predict what they will do next. But sadly, we are not even close to that point. But while doing some research, these analysts came up with some ancient literature. They supplied the key word to search for Sri Lanka, Indian Ocean, Diego Garcia, and the key phrase 'points of interest' and 'ancient relics' to search the database, and lo and behold, the logic and the AI algorithms came up with some interesting hits. Apparently, there is an ancient Indian literature book called the Sangam literature where there are references to a landmass called Kumari Kandam. We don't know what made this landmass sink. The experts believe it may be a combination of plate tectonics and the melting of ice after the ice ages. When these err…'tourists' came here in the past, it is possible that the landmass was above water. Who knows, it may be something similar to what happened to the mythical place called Atlantis. We are pretty certain that this ancient submerged city is what they were looking for. They may be as surprised as us to see this part covered by the ocean. This region has not been explored because this is not in any of the air or shipping routes. There has, thus far, been no need to travel here because it was always assumed that there was nothing here. This area is as remote as the Easter Islands or the middle of the Pacific Ocean, if not remoter. At least tourists go to the Easter Islands. This is as remote as remote can be on Earth. Wonder what they will do next. Keep tracking them and report back if you see any changes."

As this was being relayed, the pilot and others in the aircraft were in rapt attention of the view unfolding under the ocean. Buildings of various sizes were clearly visible. Presumably they were made of stones, much like the incredible and ancient stone carvings of the

Ajanta temples in India or stone structures of the pyramids in Egypt or Gobekli Tepe in Turkey or even Puma Punku and Tiahuanaco in Bolivia and many others around Earth. Some of these structures were dated to about 15,000 years BCE. All these defy explanation of why, how, and by whom they were built. The conventional belief was that ancient humans built them. However it has been impossible to prove how they could have performed these feats with hand tools. Various colors and shading were discernible that were either the stone or the corals that had attached themselves to the structures. The spaces between these buildings could be interpreted as streets, and they were wide and long. One could imagine trees growing along the streets. The latitude of this landmass, were it above the ocean, would be tropical. So there would be dense foliage, tall trees, and lots of flowers and fruits. There were large gaps where one set of stone structures ended and the next one began. This could be interpreted as locations where various towns and cities were constructed. With the sun overhead, they could see the outlines of structures and major landmarks. However, it was difficult to estimate how deep the land had sunk, or the ocean had risen, or both. If the sun were at a different angle, this place would have gone unnoticed. The timing was fortuitous. After about an hour of travel, they came to the end of the landmass. A rough estimate of the north-south length was about 1,500 kilometers. They could not estimate the width. It was too wide an expanse to even hazard a guess.

Atra-has thought this was a lost cause. There was nothing here that he could salvage. En route to Kumari Kandam, Atra-has had flown over the area that today is called the Persian Gulf. Atra-has's maps indicated that the gulf had been much smaller and the land area much larger during the time when these maps were drawn. What had happened in the years after the maps were made? Cartography was an automatic process, but had no one checked? Why was there so much more water? This is where his people had built the labs and conducted genetic experiments with the human population. This is where the final version of the human form was developed and perfected. This area, unknown to Atra-has, was what the humans referred to as the mythical Garden of Eden. Except for some stone structures his people had cleaned out this place before they left so no traces of experiments could be discovered. The way it appeared, even the stone structures had disappeared, subsumed by water, just like Kumari Kandam.

As Atra-has remembered from the briefing, this was the location where the labs were constructed thousands of years ago. It was a densely wooded and secluded area. There was nothing other than trees and animals for hundreds of miles around. This place was selected because it did not have any population at the time. It was at a favorable geographical zone, and other encampments were set up all around the Earth at approximately this latitude. During the time when they were first setting up camp at this location, the ice caps were higher and consequently the sea levels lower. Now, however, the land where the labs were situated was under the ocean. If one were to draw a line from encampment to encampment, it would be a straight line circumnavigating the Earth. It was designed that way due to the favorable forces present at these locations. In the past, when active work was being carried out, he had visited parts of this imaginary line.

Humans had detected anomalies in these places and had their own names for these regions. This was, of course, unknown to him. These locations today were known to the humans as Valley of the Kings, the Bermuda Triangle, Dwaraka, Garden of Eden, Zona de Silencio in Mexico, the Dragon's Triangle off the coast of Japan where monumental stone pyramids were found under the ocean etc.

He had sent the other pyramids in his fleet to visit these other locations. He had sent a couple from his fleet to locations favored by his enemy to investigate if there was any activity by the Garg-Ar army. Thus far, the report was favorable—there was no enemy activity at these locations. This was the only piece of good news he had received since they arrived on Earth. There was also another similar setup of encampments in the southern hemisphere corresponding to the natural forces generated by Earth. In addition, there were other random camps in other locations which did not correspond to any specific latitude or Earth's magnetic forces—Atra-has did not care about these random camps since they were meant to be temporary way stations. However, the main ones on the same latitude were connected with invisible magnetic forces emanating from Earth. These favorable magnetic forces helped with the communication with their world, which, due to time travel, was in a different time. Communication with their world needed these tremendous forces which could only be generated by large bodies such as planets. Again, unknown to him, humans called these forces ley lines.

Atra-has looked out of the window and then at the monitors. The pyramid was still traveling over the ocean in the area where he expected to see a major landmass. He wondered how the climate here could change so drastically in such a short time that critical landmasses were now submerged. Disappointed as he was, he would have to give up on locating this missing landmass as a source for his loot. He ordered the craft to turn around and head back. He would have to go searching for Vima Nan. This trip was not turning out the way it was planned, at least not in terms of the shiny metal that his civilization needed. They had successfully collected some locals at earlier stops, but they would not be of much use if no more metal was found. Finding the two items was closely intertwined. The locals who were picked up earlier were already being prepared by the menial robots for the long return journey.

The humans were cooperating with the robots because they had no choice. They were wired to feel comfortable with the artificially generated thought sequences which directly affected certain areas of the brain, an area which got its significance from the gene VMAT2—the God gene. These thought sequences were being generated by machines—in effect the human minds were being manipulated telepathically by the machines. This is how they were designed. Complete submission was the only possible response for a human when exposed to the power of the telepathic machines. This same technique was used to get them on board. It was in their DNA, the DNA over which Atra-has and his race had complete control.

Observer 1 radioed, "HQ, this is Observer 1. Our guests have made a 180-degree turn. They are heading back."

The response was "Stay on their tail, Observer 1. We believe they may be disappointed, if they were looking for the landmass. Keep your distance, but don't let them out of your sight."

"Roger that."

Soon the velocity of the pyramid picked up, and it was impossible for the airplane to keep up. The airplane was asked to stop attempting to pursue and return to its base in Diego Garcia. Satellites were then used to follow the trajectory of the alien craft, and very soon it became apparent that it was heading toward the Bermuda Triangle. Some more helicopters from Jacksonville were scrambled to meet the fast-approaching pyramid. The pyramid descended rapidly, and once it was in sight, the cameras in the choppers started beaming images to the central command. The pyramid approached close to the ocean surface, and after stopping briefly, presumably for the instrumentation to check for the presence of the sunken pyramid, started heading west, toward Jacksonville.

It was alarming to the humans monitoring the events that the aliens did not take more than a few seconds to detect the absence of the sunken pyramid. Presumably the location of the sunken pyramid was previously known or the fact that it was already lifted out of its watery grave was transmitted to the rest of the pyramids as the procedure was being undertaken.

What the humans who were watching this failed to realize was that with the right technology, from certain points on Earth the magnetic forces could be used for communication. The pyramids sent earlier to these locations were in the same approximate latitude as one another and could use the natural magnetic forces generated by Earth to communicate with one another in a way that was as yet undetectable by humans. This same means of communication was also used by the aliens to communicate with their home planet. However, the round trip for the messages to reach their home planet took longer. Since the pyramid was not underwater off the coast of the Bahamas anymore, without hesitation Atra-has headed straight to the location in Florida where the two pyramids had landed. It appeared that the plans to resurface the pyramid and get it on land were meticulously drawn up since. Atra-has knew exactly where he had to go.

HQ had to act quickly. Atra-has was only a few seconds from their location, and the four astronauts were still investigating the damage done by the missiles. They needed them out of the pyramid now!

The humans inside the pyramid had stopped abruptly. What they were seeing was complete destruction inside, although from the outside the pyramid looked fine. This macabre sight was slowly registering in their minds when the radio communicator came on.

"HQ to John, you all need to get out of there immediately. Atra-has is coming your way."

"Copy that, HQ, we are exiting now. There is nothing to see here anyway."

They turned around and exited the pyramid, each sliding down the extended ladder, fireman style, onto the fire truck. No sooner than the last person reached the truck, the ladder was retracted, and the truck moved away from the pyramid. They were all looking up in an easterly direction, and soon the approaching pyramid came into view. It came in fast, and at about forty to fifty meters above the ground it slowed down and gradually landed close to the bombed-out pyramid.

John remarked at their technology. "You have to marvel at their technological advancement. The controls are so precise. They can come in to land so fast and slow down at the very last moment. Then when they land, no debris or dust is kicked up as you would expect when a chopper lands."

They were all marveling at the approach and landing when HQ came online.

"John, what did you see in the pyramid?"

John responded, "That is easy to answer. Everything inside is destroyed. It is pretty gruesome. No one could have survived the blast. Whatever the outer walls are made of, the interior is not made of the same material. It is destructible. The entire interior was a huge mess. All the walls and floors were destroyed. It was as if a bomb had gone off inside a concrete shelter—where the outer walls would be intact but everything inside would be mush."

Ken added, "I saw what appeared to be a robot or two, could not tell how many, but they were in pieces. They did not survive the explosion, and if the war robots with metal skin were in that state, then none of the flesh and blood aliens would have a chance of surviving the explosions."

THE ARRIVAL

The president and her entourage had arrived at the location incognito. No one except the "need to know" group knew of her presence near the pyramids. Now there were three pyramids. Surrounding them some distance away was the military personnel, one group of which contained the president in fatigues, so that she would blend in and not become a target for the aliens. This fact was known by some people at the Pentagon. However, it was not mentioned to the astronauts.

The fire truck stopped at the perimeter formed by the military vehicles and a contingent or more of military personnel. The pyramid landed, and almost immediately Atra-has along with a few other aliens and robots exited the pyramid. The humans knew where he was going. Atra-has and his entourage made their way on the litter to the bombed pyramid. The litter approached the pyramid of interest and ascended to the height of the opening. The occupants stepped off the litter which appeared to hover effortlessly. It was still a miraculous sight to John and his crew. The others seeing this for the first time were transfixed at the events taking place in front of them.

It did not take long. Atra-has and his entourage came out of Vima Nan pyramid almost immediately. He had seen what the astronauts had seen only minutes earlier. The inside of the pyramid had been destroyed almost beyond recognition. Its entire crew was dead, and the robot pieces flung in every direction inside the pyramid. It was not capable of flying since its internal machines were also pulverized. It had to be towed, in the same way as the pyramid that was retrieved from the ocean. This was turning out to be more of a disaster than he had planned. Certainly, they had not planned for the loss of an entire craft at the hands of the local population. However, this could be handled; they had enough redundancy built in, in case of eventualities like this one. They came out and onto the hovering litter and returned to the pyramid that they had egressed a few minutes earlier. Atra-has needed to think of his next move. He did not know how the pyramid was destroyed. He was getting more than a little irritated. But he had to keep his composure. From his perspective, it may have been a fluke, or the humans may have something that was powerful enough to destroy the inside of the pyramid. His initial impression of communicating with Kristen and studying the attitude of the others was that the humans were peaceful enough. Did the commander of the destroyed pyramid do something stupid to provoke the humans or was this their way of showing strength? He would have to take some time and think of his next move.

But he could not take too much time, lest the enemies from Garg-Ar arrive with reinforcements and start battles like the last time a few thousand years earlier. He had chased the one remaining Garg-Ar craft to the edge of the solar system, but to no avail—it had managed to escape. Cleverly the craft had not traveled in time—with the equipment they had it would be too easy to pursue. Instead it had used the naturally occurring celestial bodies in the solar system as shields. It traveled in space, hiding behind planets, moons, and asteroids, using up precious time, time that Atra-has did not have. The Garg-Ar craft had used its gravity engines to clump asteroids together. They sent a few of these in different directions, thereby creating diversions. Not knowing which one to pursue Atra-has had been forced to give up the chase. They managed to escape by hiding behind one of these decoys.

Once Atra-has had given up the pursuit, the Garg-Ar craft had gone to a safe location outside the solar system and jump in time to the period from which it came. Atra-has, suspecting that the Garg-Ar captain after escaping would then be ordered to come back with a new entourage of warships, had decided to proceed with his original mission without wasting any more time. Moreover, Atra-has had orders to make minor time adjustments on his travel back to Earth. The intent was to collect fresh supplies of humans and the shiny metal and return to Aten-Heru quickly. When Atra-has originally left Aten-Heru, the idea was to travel a great distance in time—that jump would be several hundreds of thousands of years. It would be a major jump. The adjustments to jump forward in time on the return journey to Earth were minor—just a few thousand years. After this correction, they would still not be at their normal time. It was during this journey to Earth and after the minor jump forward that the humans had tried to intercept them in space. What Atra-has did not know was that the minor adjustments in time were causing the humans to constantly miscalculate when the aliens would arrive on Earth.

John, Kristen, Nicole, and Ken were transfixed at the gravity-defying litter and its movements between the two pyramids. To be able to control gravity is impressive. To build machines using the knowledge is even more impressive. On Earth, the so-called God particle, better known as the Higgs particle or the Higgs boson, had been verified in the CERN facility in Europe just a few years earlier. The postulated particle was finally verified in experimentation at the Large Hadron Collider by smashing particles together and studying the resulting debris. The Higgs boson is what makes things clump together. The current scientific conjecture on Earth is that gravity is like light, both particle and wave at the same time. If more knowledge of the Higgs boson could be used to manipulate gravity, as the aliens appeared to be doing, the advancement on Earth would jump in leaps and bounds. This would be a leap of greater magnitude than the invention of transistors that made computing possible. Earth was far from fully understanding this knowledge, let alone building devices using this knowledge. The aliens had not only used this technology in machines for local travel, but also they had used this knowledge to build interstellar craft. It was frightening to think how old their culture was and how advanced it was. It was anyone's guess what other capabilities they had, both as living organisms and in weapons systems.

"Hi there!"

They looked around to where the voice had emanated and saw, walking toward them, Thor, Baz, Manny, and Greg. After the perfunctory greetings, John asked, "So when did you get here?"

Thor, as is his wont, had initially greeted them with a loud "Hi there," responded, "We landed from orbit only a few hours ago. The chiefs thought it better we come here in case we are needed. Also, we are well rested, unlike you guys who I believe have been on the run ever since we parted company. You guys look shot."

John responded, "That is true, but I cannot say it has not been exciting. We have also learnt a lot with Ken sharing the knowledge of his experiences." There was just a minor touch of sarcasm in his statement.

Thor continued, "We have been given all the information, but there is one question I wanted to ask. Was it Lela who Ken and I saw when we first made eye contact with the aliens?"

That was a good question. None of them had time to ponder who it was that they had seen. John responded, "More than likely it was Lela. She probably lured us in before the aliens had been revived from the hibernation. Why do you ask?"

Thor, while processing what John said, responded, "Then it was a cleverly thought-out trap to keep us there and force us to confront the aliens. I ask because I was wondering if it was the aliens who initiated for us to be captured or if it was the robots, specifically Lela."

John was also putting the puzzle pieces together and stated, "I guess we will never know. I think it was Lela because we were captured when the aliens were still in hibernation. If they were awake when they saw us, we do not know what would have happened. I am sure Atra-has was surprised when it was reported to him that there were prisoners on board. Maybe it was Lela who facilitated some of the events that transpired. The way she led us further and further into the pyramids, the way she orchestrated the removal of our helmets so we could breathe the air in the pyramid and the way she organized our capture. We will not know for sure. Maybe her actions saved our hides. Thinking back, I think she was in complete control of our actions. We did not have a choice but to take the actions that we did. If only we knew before the aliens were aroused from their hibernation that Lela and Kristen could communicate, things could have turned out differently."

Thor concluded that thought process with, "See, that is exactly what I was thinking. I think Lela was behind most of Atra-has's decisions. She very cleverly manipulated him, played them at their own game. She played us too. If she were alive we could have gotten some advice from her. But since she is gone, if we can do the same to him as she did, maybe there is hope for us all." Everyone simultaneously arrived at the same thought, only that Thor verbalized it first.

As John was responding with, "That is easier said than done—" he was interrupted.

"Sir! There is someone who wants to speak with you!"

They turned around. What they saw was a senior officer addressing John. The officer repeated, pointing behind him, "There is someone who wants to see you all." In the background, there was a throng of soldiers. All eight followed the officer, making sure that the fire truck was used as a shield between them and the pyramid. When they arrived at the gathering, the soldiers parted slightly to let the senior officer and the eight to walk into the circle. To their surprise, they were standing in the presence of the president of the United States.

They were lost for words, so dispensing with pleasantries, the president spoke first.

"Good afternoon, ladies and gentlemen. I have been briefed of the events thus far. Needless to say, this is a very momentous occasion for all of us." Pointing to the pyramids, she said, "As we all know by now, these are aliens. There is no protocol dealing with alien diplomacy—as of yet. I know because I checked." That quip made everyone within earshot laugh out loud—especially since it was the president who made a joke. She summarized what she knew. "They told me that the aliens are looking for gold, and I am told they have some humans on board the pyramid." This was news to the four astronauts. They did not know that there were humans on board. Without a pause, she continued, "Rescue of the humans is first and foremost priority. It does not matter from which country they were captured. If they don't want to be on the pyramid I want them back on land. Needless to say, we need to diffuse any hostilities, get the

K. PAUL GOMEL

humans back, and not part with any of our precious metals. I am also told that one of you effectively communicated with an alien."

Kristen spoke up, "That would be me, Madam President." The president responded, "Under the circumstances, let's dispense with formalities for the sake of expediency, call me Amy, AK or just ma'am."

"Why was it that only you were able to communicate with them?" the president asked with the urgency evident in her words.

Kristen was mindful that being curt would seem disrespectful and started explaining, trying to use as few words as possible. "Ma'am, I don't know precisely why I was able to communicate. My only guess is that I have trained myself to meditate, due to the long hours I have had to spend in the decompression chamber after a deep-sea dive. I am a marine biologist and dive frequently. Decompression and therefore meditation is a regular part of my professional duties. Meditation has been shown to change chemistry in the brain. This is similar to praying. It has been scientifically shown that the brain chemistry alters to provide the person praying or meditating a sense of calmness, alertness, and increased sense of energy. Meditating requires practice and requires the calming of the mind. I am guessing that once the human mind is calm, it is receptive to telepathic communication." She allowed herself a little smile at the thought that she was brief and to the point without being impolite.

The president asked, "What do you mean 'scientifically shown'?"

Kristen thought, *Here we go again*, and responded, still trying to be conscious of the urgency, "Scientists have done experiments to see what power meditation and prayers have on people. In these experiments, an electroscope was used to measure the electrical strength in the brain while meditating or praying. Since prayer generates energy in the brain, this was measured. The brain was also monitored in an MRI machine and the activity charted. This activity is always observed in the same part of the brain, no matter who is praying." She stopped only for the briefest moment then added, "There is some belief that these waves that the brain produces are particles and can even be generated artificially—through meditation. This gene that causes this euphoric feeling, although not identified, is sometimes

340

known as the God gene. Some people have this sensation expressed in more pronounced ways than other people. We all try to get this elated feeling, some with more success than others."

The president, looking incredulous, said, "You mean brain waves are particles?"

Ken, who did not have any hesitation to be effusive, jumped in, "Ma'am, I have studied various cultures and religions. This is not news to a lot of practitioners of Eastern religions. Energy, indeed everything, has always been known to be vibrations. We know scientifically that fundamental particles, such as light, are just vibrations. In modern vernacular, these vibrations are called strings. So in this interpretation of physics, a particle is a string and a string is a vibration. Light is both a wave and a particle. Just as light is affected by gravity, if we have sufficiently advanced technology we could do what the aliens are doing with gravity. This, too, is a particle. In current interpretation, all particles are strings. Both light and gravity were never considered as particles a long time ago. I wouldn't be surprised if, after more research, we find that thought waves were particles. If it is a particle, it is a string or a vibration. Our guests on the other side of this fire truck probably already know this. Maybe they even designed us that way. I personally have firm conviction that everything in the universe is made of vibrations or strings, just as the ancient Hindu scriptures proclaim. Maybe the ancient humans got this knowledge from past alien visitations. We just need to understand and tap the potential." Ken said more than he had intended to, bearing in mind the urgency of the situation, but he felt he needed to explain this to the president.

One of the staff sergeants came into the huddle and mentioned to the commanding officer present, "Sir, we have done a preliminary search of the downed chopper and the alien craft. The craft is destroyed. However, other than a seat, we did not find any control mechanisms. We cannot figure out how it could fly without someone controlling it."

This was an opportune time for Ken to press home his point. "This is an indication that all their crafts are controlled telepathically. They have instruments capable of picking up human or alien thoughts and make the craft move accordingly. This can only be done if the instruments can pick up something, and that something are particles of thought. They are generations ahead of us. They use gravity to fly and thoughts to maneuver the craft. We, however, use satellites to fly drones. It is scary to think of what else these aliens can do."

The staff sergeant continued, "We found plasma generators and magnets. We think this is what we saw when the plasma light extended toward our chopper." The staff sergeant was an engineer, so he knew what he was saying. He confirmed the reason for the crash. "Plasma is what destroyed the main rotor on the chopper, which made it crash. If they could release bolts of plasma or whatever it was, like bolts of lightning, we have no defense against it. When we examined the rotor on the downed chopper, it was cleanly sliced off…no jagged edges…like slicing through an apple with a sharp knife."

The aliens were still inside the pyramid, so the discussion and planning could continue for now. The president asked, "I want to hear your opinion firsthand. What is it that they want?"

Kristen was the first to respond. "We…I mean, I believe, and all of us share this opinion, that the aliens want three things. They want to get some gold. For some reason that I have not yet figured out, they believe they are entitled to it. They also want some humans, possibly ones with the prominent God gene. This last point about wanting humans is mostly conjecture on our part based on what Lela said and what we have pieced together. Lastly, they wanted to retrieve their sunken pyramid."

The president was getting better information directly from the astronauts. They had not just traveled a vast distance—clearly, they were figuring things out and piecing facts together. She continued the fact-finding. "Have you found out why they need the humans and the gold?"

Nicole jumped in, speaking rapidly, "I had a chance to examine Lela. She told us that the human brains are harvested to be used as a control mechanism for the robots. The gold is for the circuitry, since it is inert and is a good conductor. That means it will never corrode in water or most liquids."

The president continued asking, "Why do they need humans? Can't they use their own kind?"

It was Ken's turn to cut in. "We believe it may be something to do with ethical issues. We don't consider the use of animals for cosmetic testing very ethical. They, being an older and presumably more mature civilization, may not consider the use of their own species, for this purpose, to be ethical. You would expect that as a civilization gets older it gets more empathetic toward lower forms of life. But they are in the middle of a war, as Lela mentioned earlier, so ethics took a back seat. They had to come up with something new, and breeding an almost new species was their answer."

Ken paused for a second and, noticing the quizzical expression, decided to explain by using an example. "If I am allowed to draw an analogy, we humans have done barbaric things in the past. For instance, far from their home the minions of King Leopold II frequently mutilated humans in what is now known as the Congo region because quotas were not met. There was no one to report the atrocities. Similarly, the Spanish did awful things to the natives in South America. Again, this was far from their homeland and no one to carry the news. There is a myriad of other instances where the 'civilized' people did terrible things far from their home—in every instance the news of these appalling acts were not reported. One of the only reasons it stopped was because either the population being subjected to this violence was defeated, exterminated, or news of the carnage reached the home country of the people committing these atrocities. When the news reached the populace, the people were incensed with what had occurred. That is why the aliens bred humans so far away from their own planet—news cannot get to the population of their planet. Atra-has and his people aboard are the only ones capable of spreading the news on their home planet, and I am willing to wager that they can be controlled by their superiors."

The president, finding it difficult to believe that humans were simply meant to be control mechanisms for cyborgs, asked, "Are you certain of this? Did one of them mention this during your communication?"

Ken, sensing the deepening irritation, responded defensively, "No, ma'am. This is conjecture at this point, just an informed guess based on what little evidence we have collected thus far and the brief encounter with Lela, the cyborg that helped us escape."

The president pondered on this information for a minute, wondering if this is the reason mankind has such a predilection to waging wars. Then, letting the information settle, she said, "Well, we will go with that analysis for now. Other than what the aliens say, have we found any evidence of what they claim about engineering the human DNA?"

This was a question that Ken alone, in that group of people, could answer.

This was not going to be easy to explain. Ken took a deep breath and resumed. "There is plenty of evidence both direct as well as anecdotal to indicate they were here in the past. Of course, the most overwhelming evidence is when their leader, Atra-has, told Kristen that they 'made us.' To back this up, there is other incontrovertible evidence, but we are a skeptical race. We let our minds embrace what we want to believe, not necessarily what our eyes see. However, if we apply the same skepticism to religion or God, we would not believe in either. We chose to ignore things that are in plain sight and chose to believe in something we have never seen or felt." The president knew to what he was referring. Ken paused only briefly to see what effect his statement would have before resuming. "They have been here before, and they have also spent a lot of time here in the past. The evidence is there for everyone to see. No one questions how and why there are so many ancient stories and mythologies referring to aliens. Perhaps not directly, but every religious literature as well as countless nonreligious texts refer to aliens. Then there are ancient constructions all over the world such as the pyramids in Egypt and Mexico, the Nazca lines, the massive stone constructions in South America, Middle, and Far East. Nobody has been able to adequately explain how the stones were cut with such precision, let alone how they were moved into place. Looking at the gravity drives they have and plasma cutters, things begin to make sense. Of course, the direct evidence is the retrieval of the pyramid that we all observed. That pyramid must have crashed here much before our time."

Ken wanted to go on speaking which, as a teacher, he enjoyed. But he did not want to come off as too condescending in the presence of the president. There was also a question of time. The aliens could make a move anytime for which they needed to be ready.

After a brief pause to assimilate the information the president responded, "But that pyramid could have crashed into the ocean as recently as a hundred years ago. Humans had no way to detect flying objects then. We had no radars or satellites to detect them. How do we know that they were here in the distant past, not just a hundred years ago?"

Ken said, "Yes, ma'am, that is true. However, some of the ancient structures that are standing today or those that have been preserved for posterity have been carbon-dated to more than ten thousand years ago. In some cases, they were as old as fifteen thousand years. And these are only the structures that we have found. There are numerous others that are in too much disrepair or too remote to preserve. Please bear in mind that these structures are made of natural materials, so they degrade over time. Despite the natural forces, for so many structures to remain more or less intact, it is a feat of engineering that the ancient human race did not possess. And it is not just a question of impossibly large monolithic stones or caves, such as the Ajanta caves in India, being cut and carved with precision. It is also a question of accurate alignment with specific stars. There are also many structures in Puma Punku and Tiahuanaco in Bolivia. They are massive stone structures cut with the kind of precision that cannot easily be replicated even today with all of our machinery. To think they were made with hands is nothing short of implausible. One cannot get precision like the kinds we see with hand tools alone. Besides, the greatest clue to their being here in the past is that they seem to know where they are going. They obviously could not have figured this out after they got here less than a day ago. They went directly to points for which they had coordinates from previous visits. All these are the places we humans find extremely interesting and many individuals have spent lifetimes investigating the relics. Also, if they were here only a hundred or so years ago, they would not have been surprised at how many people are here on Earth. The alien had asked Kristen during one of their communication sessions, and Atra-has appeared to have been surprised by what Kristen had told him."

The president admitted that there was evidence that they were here more than a hundred years ago. Now she was planning for next steps. "Okay, so you have a point. Let's go with your analysis, for now. What do you think we should do?"

It was John who chimed in, "Thus far, they have seemed to be logical and thoughtful. At least Atra-has is, and he appears to be the leader of this unit. I could not tell if he was making all the decisions or if he was getting orders from his planet. If he was getting orders, then they are using some metaphysical means to communicate. Nothing known to *our* science can accomplish a round trip in a reasonable amount of time. Even as far as the end of our solar system we had to lay down communication relays. I mean, look at the problems we had when we went to investigate. Ma'am President, in answer to your question of what I think *our* next move should be, I think, and I believe my colleagues concur, we should wait and watch. We should let them make the next move. However, we should be ready to respond quickly. Whatever Atra-has is, he did not give me the impression that he is a patient being. On the other hand, for whatever reason, he does not want to use violence."

The president nodded that she agreed that this was the best course of action. In the chess game of diplomacy, it was important to make the correct moves for the best possible outcome. Clearly, not enough was known about the aliens' capabilities to make any move at this juncture. It was going to be a waiting game.

UNDERSTAND MOTIVES

It was a warm night in Florida. The setting sun was casting long shadows of the pyramids as well as all the equipment across the grassy plain where the conflagration was taking place. The Marines had already set up powerful lights and generators in preparation for the night. Soon, the hum of the generators would pervade the quiet expanse of wilderness. Some tents with cots inside were set up, which would be the makeshift command center as well as a resting place for the nonmilitary personnel. The discussions were going on as preparations were being made for nightfall.

The lights came on at dusk and lit up the entire area, as if a sports arena was being lit for an event. The light reflected off all the objects except from the matte black pyramids. Whatever material the outer shell of the pyramid was made from, it did not reflect much light. From a distance, the scenery appeared like a painting, and the area that the pyramid occupied was painted black by an artist. The scene could only be described as surreal. Whatever Atra-has was waiting for, he was taking his time.

The president and some other high-ranking officials as well as the eight astronauts were in one large tent discussing as they were eating some packaged meals. The president asked, "Can we somehow help the humans on board escape the alien pyramid, and also not give them any gold?" Baz responded, "I think I know where you are going with this. However, I don't think we can trick them. They are way too intelligent for any simple tricks. Besides they can read minds. Back in space when we were first captured we performed a simple experiment, but it backfired on us. We tried to raise our weapons but even before we could make the slightest move to do so, we

347

were disarmed. They are always a step ahead of us. They may also possess greater firepower."

"I keep forgetting that they can read minds. With that ability we need alter our way of thinking," the president admitted.

"But why did they come here, to Earth?" she asked after a moment's pause to collect her thoughts. Clearly, the previous answer had not assuaged her.

Ken jumped in, "I think they cultivated Earth." He stopped speaking for a second, collecting his thought. Then, satisfied how he would explain, he resumed, "If you look at the history of Earth, long ago there were dinosaurs. There were many mass extinctions on Earth, but the latest one was by design, their design. It would be simple for them, with their time-traveling capability, to go back sixty-five million years and send a meteorite to wipe out almost all life on Earth. They would only have to revisit Earth a few times to record how Earth was recovering from that devastation and what kinds of life-forms were flourishing."

Ken did not wait for anyone to interrupt. "During the time of dinosaurs there were no humans. Dinosaurs lived on Earth for millions of years and evolved. Comparatively, the bipedal hominid being, which evolved into present-day human, has only lived here for about three hundred thousand years. Homo sapiens have been in existence for even less. My conjecture is that the meteorite or meteorites were sent to Earth by the aliens to make the planet habitable to a smaller and more intelligent species. Now, if or why this actually happened, only they can tell us. Maybe the aliens tried to coexist with the dinosaurs early on when they came here but were stymied by the presence of the large predators. Maybe they were predisposed to some ancient Earth disease with which they could not cope. Whatever the reason, I think they had a hand in making Earth what it is today."

Ken waited to give someone a chance to respond to his statements. Since no one spoke up, he resumed with his hypothesis. "The way they could sterilize Earth was to destroy everything. The simplest way was with asteroids or meteorites. This may be how they knew Earth was doomed had they not prevented Apophis from impacting Earth. They needed more humans, so they moved Apophis away from colliding with Earth."

He paused again to see if anyone would speak. He was introducing a lot of new ideas in his discourse. But everyone was listening and not disagreeing with his theories. No one spoke, so he carried on with completing his thoughts. "Look at it this way. There was nothing intelligent here about sixty-five million years ago when the last large meteorite struck and the last major extinction event occurred. Why would there suddenly appear intelligent life on Earth after so many millions of years of life?" This was rhetorical questioning. He did not expect an answer. "Then when literally and figuratively the dust from the meteorite impact settled maybe hundreds of years later, they brought their Noah's ark. I am beginning to think this reference to Noah's ark is more accurate than the old interpretation of the physical transference of every species of animals onto a boat. They brought DNA samples of all their animals from their world which they wanted to populate here. They possibly have a way to reconstitute the DNA into living animals to accelerate evolution. We humans can do that to a limited extent in the lab today. We grow ears or other appendages for people who lose them in an accident or as a result of a disease. DNA is easy to carry. Just one of those pyramids will comfortably carry multiple copies of every species. If you want to be pedantic, you could ask if they brought the bacteria or viruses also. I don't know the answer to that question, but that is immaterial since the bacteria and viruses adapted and evolved to infect or live symbiotically with the new species now occupying Earth. I am willing to wager that we, humans, are at least a 99 percent match with the aliens. Ma'am, you understand that what I have said is only my theory based on what I have learnt in the past through my school and recently with the alien encounters." He consciously had to stop, in case he began to pontificate too much.

The president nodded, indicating that she understood.

Nicole, who was listening in fascination, like everyone else in the tent, echoed, "I tried to get a sample while we were their guests, maybe hair or a nail clipping that had fallen, but no luck."

To Ken's surprise, the president asked him, "Why do all this work?" She wanted to know more.

He responded, "I want to reiterate that this is my personal theory, based on my prior knowledge and what I have learnt from the aliens thus far. This knowledge continues to evolve as we glean more information with every encounter. To answer your question, I believe they did this initially for one purpose only. That is to develop brains for their war machines. Just as we believe that the mixing of DNA of different species is abhorrent, their advanced culture also did not permit such experimentation on their own planet. They may have tried various combinations of DNA and created many animals here, humans being one of them. I believe that is the reason why 85 to 90 percent of all DNA in all vertebrate species on Earth is similar. They brought with them or created all the animals on Earth today. That is why some of their scientists could experiment with interspecies manipulation, as depicted in some of the ancient Earth-based paintings. One can see humans with the head of an eagle, elephant, or lion. Mythology has horses with wings or horns. I don't want to bore you with mythological names for each of these animals. Essentially, they wanted to produce the best possible and viable species that could reproduce, a species that was far enough removed from their own, but close enough to be able to take telepathic commands."

The president was listening with fascination, as was everyone else in the tent. When Ken stopped, there was dead silence. What he had said was shocking but plausible. Finally, the president asked, "This is a whole lot of expense for just creating war machines?"

Ken responded, "I respectfully disagree. We have such a huge military budget. We go to extraordinary lengths to keep our troops out of harm's way. We have pilotless vehicles of all kinds. In situations where humans are absolutely necessary to go into harm's way, would you rather send a living human being or a surrogate? As the president, you have a better grasp of this than I do, but I would like to think you would send something just as good, but not a human. If we can have an army of robots, drones, unmanned ships, and all that is required for an effective military force and still be able to control them from a safe distance, wouldn't you and the legislative branch pass laws to fund that as a more effective way of waging wars, even if it is more expensive? Indeed, if surrogates could be sent to meet our guests," he said, pointing in the general direction of the pyramids, "would you rather not have sent them, instead of us? If you analyze it this is a logical progression of the art and science of the making of a soldier. In the past, successful empires such as Greece, Rome, or Egypt were dominant during their time because they trained fearless soldiers and invented better ways of neutralizing the enemy. Part of the process was physical training, part was brainwashing. They created a special infantry. Successful leaders created environments where military success was revered in civil society, and the soldiers were willing to fight to the death for the leader and country. Indeed, in most cases in the past, it was an honor to die on the battlefield. Along the same theme, later in our history, we created a class of soldiers who were almost superhuman. We called them Special Forces. Every country has them. These very capable people are picked to join the Special Forces teams. After rigorous training, they are able to achieve more, both mentally and physically, compared to the other soldiers. Therefore, they can be trained to a vastly higher degree than a regular soldier. However, they are still humans. Even though they are capable of more, in the battlefield they can still get hurt just the same as any other human. In an advanced society where the people react negatively to news of casualties of war, the next step would be to create soldiers who are more immune to weapons and more capable than an ordinary mechanical or electronic device." Then Ken added, to make the point, "And it would not matter if they perished. I think the aliens experimented with robots and were not very successful. We saw some robots in the pyramids. But the higher-functioning robots were the ones with organic brains—cyborgs, as they are commonly called. The logical next step for them was to create another species for this purpose. They could not possibly use their own species to do this job—it would be tantamount to torture not deserving of the victim. If this practice were to happen here there would be international and unanimous pressure to ban it. It would be an abhorrent practice."

The president briefly pondered on the words and then nodded in agreement.

After a brief pause for the previous statements to have the desired impact, Ken continued, "Maybe they had too many casualties, maybe their populace got tired of waging constant wars and the resultant casualties, maybe they came up with a technical solution but not an ethical solution, and maybe they had the technology already available to carry this through. If you do not include the development of the technology they used to travel, it could really be not such a big expense. Just the same way as one does not have to bear the expense of inventing an airplane before manufacturing one, or one does not have to bear the expense of inventing a motor car before making a new one. Given that the scientific technology of the gravity mechanisms was known, the space-faring pyramids were already available. The hibernation mechanisms were already known. The only expense for the alien race was to find a suitable planet and cultivate it."

The president understood and nodded. That was a key fact that Ken had stated. If the technology was already in existence, it was relatively straightforward to send a craft to a distant planet whose existence or destruction did not matter in the least. All they had to do was to find a potentially habitable planet. There are billions of suns, and a number of them have at least one planet orbiting them. In the Milky Way alone, there may be many potentially habitable planets.

There was something that was bothering Ken. "What I have learnt about these aliens over the last few days and weeks has an uncannily close corroboration with the texts that I have read in the past. That said, there is still something significant that I cannot explain. I cannot figure out why there are depictions of wars of almost nuclear proportions that have been documented in many ancient texts. Hindu texts such as the Mahabharata, even the Old and New Testaments, and numerous ancient texts have phrases describing flight. All the theories I have just shared, whether right or wrong, can be logically derived. However, I can find no logical explanation for why there were aerial battles in the distant past—aerial battles in ancient times documented in texts that date back centuries, many thousands of years ago. Ancient humans, contemporaries of the Neanderthals, have written and drawn about flight and flying in aircrafts and waging wars in the air. How this is possible is beyond explanation."

Various options were being discussed in earnest and their logical outcomes verbally played out, when one of the staff sergeants came in and announced that other pyramids were zeroing in on their current location and would be arriving soon. The discussion soon turned to why they may be coming to their current location. Perhaps Atra-has was waiting for their arrival and would be ready to start hostilities or if they were coming there because Atra-has had commanded them to come here. Would it be better to try to engage them while they were in the air, or would it be better to bomb them after they had landed?

Soon the discussions were moot since one by one the pyramids began to land. They did not show any hostilities; to the contrary, the doors did not even open. If they were communicating, it was not decipherable. All frequencies were being monitored, and some garbled radio broadcast was being picked up from the locations of the pyramids at a very unusual wavelength. The experts were trying to analyze the data by running them through the high-performance computing network that the organization known as Search for Extraterrestrial Intelligence (SETI) had at its disposal. Finally, SETI had a source of alien communication that it had been searching for all over outer space for so many decades. Ironically it was emanating from their backyard. The common conjecture in the tent was that they may be using telepathy for communication. However, there would have to be assistance from external devices to intensify the thought waves and transmit them, since the astronauts believed that telepathy worked in line of sight only. It was almost eerie with the dark silhouettes of the nine pyramids standing there in the middle of Florida wilderness.

Until now, any information that the humans had regarding the aliens was what they had voluntarily shared. There was nothing that they knew about the aliens with 100 percent certainty which they had acquired by themselves. The speaker in the tent was still broadcasting conversations between HQ and anyone else that they had contacted in order to get even the most basic information from the aliens. HQ was not leaving any stone unturned; they were investigating every avenue that was available to them. The conversation among the astronauts, the president, and other officials had subsided; an uncomfortable silence had descended in the tent. The lull in the conversation forced their attention to be diverted to the speaker. Thankfully someone had turned up the volume of the speaker in the tent. They heard someone from HQ contact SETI and inquire whether SETI was able to make any sense or even detect any transmissions originating from the pyramids.

An overly ebullient scientist from SETI, who was unable to control his zeal, was heard saying, "They may be using quantum entanglement to facilitate communication with their own planet," to which a bemused nonscientist from HQ asked, "What is quantum...What did you say?" The scientist was heard replying, "Quantum entanglement. Not much is known about this at the moment, but basically it postulates that particles can be separated by great distances and still be able to affect each other. The distances can be from one edge of the universe to the other. The distance can be great or small. To my knowledge this science is in its infancy—no one on Earth understands it in too much depth. Those who research in this area believe that this phenomenon can be used to communicate or transfer anything. But this is the only explanation I have. I can see that there is a glow, but that is about the extent of what I have." HQ asked in a surprised tone, "You mean to say that the pyramids are glowing?"

Immediately regretting that he was using jargon not understood outside the scientific community, the SETI researcher hurriedly cut in, "No! No! It is not literally glowing. This is a term we use to signify that there is some sort of transmission—on our instruments I am detecting all kinds of particles coming from all the alien crafts. I cannot figure out why." He paused to take a breath. His enthusiasm unabated, he started again, "We have a lot to understand yet. I don't even know what amount of energy is needed to generate this kind of density of rare particles. I am guessing some part of this particle stream is being used for communication. In the ancient scriptures, it is written that everything is made of energy. We don't know how they came up with that theory. We have kind of verified that to be true with string theory, where tiny packets of energy are supposed to make up the fundamental particles." After a slight pause he decided to elucidate since the SETI scientist did not know who all were listening and some part of them may not fully understand. "Quarks and leptons." Whether or not the audience wanted to hear more, as long as he had the floor he was only too happy to continue talking. "This is not well understood, and there is a lot of research going on to understand these concepts. When we understand this maybe we can understand how these aliens use gravity at will, communicate, or even how they build their weapons. We all know that nuclear fission and fusion release a lot of energy. This is how far we, the human race, have come in using atomic energy. We can split atoms. Atoms are made of fundamental particles. Can you imagine if we can figure out how to use fundamental particles, outside of the lab, for our energy needs? We would not have any energy concerns. These aliens are playing with the fundamental particles. They must seemingly have infinite amounts of energy." He was on a roll and needed to take a breath before continuing when the person from HQ cut in. This was way too much information under the circumstances, and more importantly it was not helping. "Hold it! Hold it! Thanks for the explanation. We will get back to you for further clarification."

After the briefest of pauses, before the scientist had a chance to start talking again, the communication ended with HQ stating, "Okay, we request that you keep looking and let us know as soon as anything meaningful is found," knowing fully well that there would have to be an unlikely event of a paradigm-shifting discovery in the next few minutes for that to be true.

It had become late, and the conversations in the tent did not have much of a chance to get anywhere after that exchange. The president suggested that they go and take as much rest as they could get. The next steps would be discussed in the morning when they were less tired, unless the aliens forced their hand before then. Each retreated into the individual smaller personal tents and was resting or trying to sleep. At about 4:45 a.m., the call came that someone had exited the main pyramid and was standing in the middle of the clearing.

FINAL CONFLICT

The president had retired to an adapted Army mobile command center. This was solidly built from metal alloys—not the fabric-based tents. It also contained communication equipment and other amenities. The president wanted to stay local, so this was the best makeshift structure that could be mustered at short notice. She could not be allowed to stay overnight in a collapsible tent, even though there were multiple hundreds of military personnel for her protection. The others who had dinner with her earlier had retired to their individual fabric tents. Due to the circumstances, no one was able to fall asleep—not even the president. The rest of the military personnel, mostly soldiers, were taking turns on duty. The ones on duty had instructions to look out for any signs of activity emanating from the pyramids. It was about 4:45 a.m., still dark. Dawn was at least two and a half hours away. Everyone was awake, playing through various scenarios in their minds. A military guard noticed the door to Atra-has's pyramid open and someone making their way out on the litter. The guard alerted his next in command who gave the order for the chief of operations in the area to be notified. The chief then gave the orders to have the president and the others alerted. They were all able to arrive at the clearing quickly. John wondered aloud, "I wonder what is going on?" They did not have long to wait for the answer.

It was Atra-has. He was standing there as if expecting someone to approach him. He must have sensed Kristen's presence in the vicinity. He had been ordered to communicate with an authoritative human and try to get as much of the precious metal as possible. If that was unsuccessful, he was asked to return with the human cargo. They would then have to go to a less hospitable planet and expend more energy and precious time to try to get the metal. The orders had come from Aten-Heru. The commanders on his home planet were not happy with the current developments. Their war plans would be delayed until they obtained the metal.

Moreover, they had indicated to him that on no account must the scenario that had unfolded centuries ago happen again. Currently, Garg-Ar warships were closing in. There was potential for another battle—on Earth, which had to be avoided. It had caused havoc in the ancient past, and it should not be repeated now. All evidence of battles that had taken place thousands of years ago had been painstakingly removed by Atra-has's people, and no trace of alien presence was left on Earth—or so they had assumed. This was necessary for the human progress to proceed as designed. Otherwise, the God gene would not be effective.

Aten-Heruans had carefully crafted the humans to have intelligence; any evidence of alien presence would prevent the human beings from blindly believing in a higher power. The aliens needed the God gene to work in the human population. From the aliens' perspective, Earth was a carefully constructed experiment. They wanted the humans to believe in a ubiquitous and eternal entity and not have any skepticism about its existence. They wanted the maximum number of people to be able to develop key areas of their brains—achieved only through self-reflection. The ones who maximized their time doing this were the perfect candidates for cyborg deployment. If people started questioning the existence of this supernatural being, they would not be inclined to pay homage to it through introspection—meditation. In that situation finding the right candidates would be that much harder. Aten-Heruans had thus painstakingly cleaned up the remains of past battles.

However, little did they know that ancient human texts, unsophisticated as they were, still managed to document these battles. In the past when the Garg-Ar battleships had followed them to Earth and had waged a war here, the human civilization was ancient and sparse; the aliens of the past knew that the humans were not sophisticated, and the hope was, over time, they would forget all about the aerial battles. Nevertheless, there were some eyewitnesses who managed to document these battles in ancient texts and drawings.

These exist today as cave paintings and in ancient scriptures such as the Mahabharata and Sumerian scripture.

If there was to be another war with Garg-Ar on Earth and Aten-Heru won this war, Atra-has realized the remains would need to be cleaned up all over again. His orders were to return posthaste. They were not to wage any battles on Earth. They were not to wage battles in space either—they needed to deliver their cargo safely. That is why Atra-has had come out to discuss the options. He had reported back that the population of Earth had evolved and had become much too erudite to be taken for granted. Although not as advanced as themselves, they could possibly have weapons that could potentially inflict some damage. Still the commanders had ordered Atra-has to leave no trace; perhaps they did not realize the full impact of the situation on Earth. He could see that today the humans were much more sophisticated and therefore would have means to document the existence of the foreign race on this planet. When he got a chance, he would explain this to his commanders. But that would not happen until he returned to his planet. Remote communication was lacking that personal touch. Atra-has wondered if this would possibly be his last mission, maybe the last mission ever to this planet. The only other mission to Earth he could foresee was an undertaking to destroy the population of Earth, so that it would not fall into enemy hands. In a way, it would be merciful to put this race out of its misery. Humans were designed to seek something that was unattainable.

The entourage arrived at the clearing and was waiting for the next move when the president, looking at Kristen, said, "I guess you had better go forward and see what he wants."

Kristen stood there as if transfixed for a second, then she said, still looking in the general direction of the pyramids, "He is already communicating with me. He wants me to go forward and speak with him." As she completed the sentence, she turned around to make eye contact with the president. At that moment, the president also seemed distant, as if occupied by some other thought.

The president responded, "For a second I thought I was hearing voices in my head." Then she said, "What did you say..." Recalling the last thing Kristen had said, she responded, "Oh yes, in that case, you had better go ahead. We are all here watching your back."

"That is how he communicates. Maybe he is trying to contact 'the leader'!" Kristen said as she stepped forward with a feeling of trepidation. Everyone else was thinking of the appropriate response in case hostilities broke out. The Earth-based weapons systems seemed to be woefully inadequate.

As Kristen approached, Atra-has did not waste time. Perhaps the perfunctory greetings were not part of their culture. Perhaps he dispensed with them in order to save time. Looking back, almost none of their previous conversations had started with any form of a greeting. In any case, Atra-has started even before Kristen had stopped walking. *We came here to get this thing.* He lifted his hand in which he was holding an ornament made of gold that he had picked up from the pyramid. *We cannot find it in the structures where they should be. Other places are underwater and cannot be reached. When we came here last, there was less water and more land.*

Kristen, who was fitted with a two-way communicator, in case she wanted to confer with someone, decided to also take an authoritative stance and responded. Ignoring what Atra-has had asked she responded with, *It appears you have several of our people in your craft. You must release them.*

Atra-has was not happy with the response. Time was being wasted. The enemy was approaching, and battles could not be fought on this planet—not again. Clearly his superiors had made a mistake in asking him to navigate this far into the future. Originally it was never intended to let these creatures survive for this long. Once their war with Garg-Ar was over the need for this planet would also be over. They would then have two choices, either stay away from this planet during this time period or to wipe out this planet long before the creatures developed this much. Due to calculations unknown to him, he was ordered to come to this time. The decision to eradicate the creatures and wipe this planet clean would be that much more difficult—but at least it would not be his decision. These creatures appeared to have a need to protect their kind—just like the Aten-Heruans. With each interaction, he was learning that there was an increasing number of similarities these creatures had with his kind. This woman in front of him was demanding the release of her people. The more he wondered, the more similarities he could see between his race and the creatures. He forcibly stopped himself from that line of thinking—he could not think that way. The creatures were a means to an end. He could not think of them as sentient beings. He had to neutralize the situation, both in his mind and the one that had presented itself in front of him. He needed to leave quickly. Violence would not help achieve his objective. He decided to take the high road and responded calmly. *We must leave soon. We are looking for this*, he said again, holding his hand up. *Tell me where it is. We will take it and leave without causing you any harm.* That last sentence was not necessarily true. He did not know what his commanders would instruct for him to do. Whatever it was, he would have to carry out his orders and hoped there would be no suffering.

Kristen was thinking that he did not realize that gold was a precious metal on Earth. It could not be handed over. The political and economic structure on Earth would fail with catastrophic consequences without it. Not knowing exactly how long they had traveled to get to Earth, Kristen hazarded a guess. *You traveled for such a long time to get here. Why are you in a hurry to get back?*

Atra-has was beginning to realize that he had to invest some time to explain. It may be quicker and more productive rather than to try to force an answer. He responded, *We are being followed by our enemy. After we land our craft at the correct location we can use the power of this planet to speak with our home planet. They told me that we should not have another battle here. It is better if we battle them somewhere else near our home. We have instructions not to leave anything behind, and if we battle them here there will be a lot of pieces to pick up.*

Kristen noted his conciliatory note and decided to reason with him about the hostages. *When you came here last time we were not as organized or a civilized society. Today things are different. We care for each other. You have our people. We cannot allow you to take them with you. Can you release them?*

The other humans gathered around were observing the two standing there and seemingly looking at each other. No one knew what was transpiring between them, although most of the observers knew that they were communicating. There was occasional nod of the head by Kristen and occasional lifting of Atra-has's hand as if he were communicating about the gold in his hand, but otherwise no movement.

For a brief second, his blood began to boil. What does this creature mean, "We cannot allow you take them with you?" Who does she think she is to allow him to do anything? As soon as the anger appeared, he realized that he had to control his emotions. These creatures were indeed more like Aten-Heruans. The very fact that he got infuriated told him that he was beginning to treat Kristen as an equal. One does not get furious at a pet, not in this fashion. Getting enraged would not help his cause. He calmed down. Fortunately, as a military person, he knew how to hide his emotions while communicating with his superiors. Luckily the woman had not picked up on his anger. Atra-has calmed down and responded. *We came here for some people. We cannot go back without them. If we go back without them, this mission will be a failure. We could not find any of this material here*, he said lifting his hand again. *We cannot go back with nothing.*

Kristen decided to relay verbally over her communicator. Of specific importance was the fact that Atra-has had said they are using the power of Earth to send signals a vast distance. She enumerated by saying that the craft has to land at a specific location—presumably the location of religious edifices if they are constructed at the right place. The transmission was picked up locally as well as at HQ. Analysis of the conversation began immediately, with the analysts trying to figure out what can be relayed back to Kristen so she can persuade the visitor to give up the human cargo.

The communication continued as Kristen went on, *How would your people feel if some foreign invader came to your world and decided to take some people back with them, especially if you knew that the ultimate reason was to use their body parts and internal organs in their machines?*

Atra-has looked confused. Obviously there was a misunderstanding. He explained, *Lela gave you some information, but I don't* *think it was complete. We train the people so they do not miss the parts that are taken away. By the time the training is done, the subjects look forward to the procedure. Besides, there is no pain. Otherwise, we would not do it. But we had trouble with the last group of people we took. I think someone…*There was a slight pause, almost a hesitation. Then without wishing to reveal too much, he finished his thoughts, *Our enemy has done something to you all. We have not been able to figure this out yet, but we will. Remember we created you to accept this procedure.*

How many more surprises did they have? Kristen first relayed this information over her communicator. How could their enemy have tinkered with the humans to make it difficult for Atra-has and his people to make the human subjects into cyborgs? Kristen was reaching a dead end. With her limited telepathic vocabulary, she had no other way of asking for the same thing again. HQ must also be coming up empty. Otherwise, they would have communicated something to her.

With the latest news, discussions were taking place among the senior military personnel, the president, and the human astronauts. Ken mentioned, "I think whatever was introduced into us by the other alien race, it has become an intrinsic part of us. So much so, it is something without which we would not consider ourselves humans."

The president asked, "What could it be that they introduced? We have to find out before we let them go back. But that is a secondary goal. Our primary objective is to keep all of us safe and also to try and get the freedom of all the humans that they have captured. Having said that, do we really want to find out what the other alien race could have done to us?"

Ken responded, "Whatever the second alien race did to us, it makes us who we are. So, to echo your question, do we really want to find out what they did? And, do we want that undone?"

Everyone was looking quizzically at him, so he felt the need to explain. "What makes us *human beings* is a result of what the two groups of aliens did to us. If we take that away, will we still be humans?" Then after a brief pause, as if to mollify his opinion he said, "Admittedly no one yet knows what they did, but I don't think it was anything radical. I mean, Atra-has did not think we were any different when he first met us. So it is not something that is outwardly noticeable. It does not manifest itself physically. I think it was something subtle, and if I had to guess, it is something to do with our brain, something that affects our makeup, how we react to certain stimuli, maybe even the way we think."

He was more right than he knew as regards the subtlety, but he could not have been more wrong as regards the importance of the modification to humans.

Kristen's voice came over the tiny earpiece that each of the senior members was wearing. "He says that time is running out and they have to leave. They have no wish to wage a war with their enemies here. They want the four of us to go with them. He says that he will bring us back."

The president's patience was wearing thin. She had heard the conversations till now as relayed by Kristen. Instinctively and without warning she yelled into her communicator, "No, that is not going to happen. I will not permit any more of us to be captured. First ask him to release—"

That is all that Atra-has needed—for the leader to identify herself. Even though the words were unintelligible to Atra-has, a person who spoke like that and with that much emotional weight and authority had to be higher ranking than anyone else in the vicinity. Due to the presence of numerous people around him, he had not been able to pinpoint the exact source of brain wave patterns his instruments had picked up. After landing he had instructed his subordinates to track the human in charge and capture it when it uniquely identified itself. The situation played itself much better than he had anticipated because this human could not suppress the same anger and frustration he was feeling. It was as if he were tracking one of his own kind. More and more he was beginning to realize that these creatures were very like his race. Maybe prolonged exposure to them would convince him, as it had presumably convinced the people who were left behind, that the similarities were far greater than the differences.

All he had to do now was to peacefully kidnap the leader. The president was not able to finish her sentence. A tractor beam lifted her and started to transport her to the pyramid. There was a surprised look on her face as she was being lifted. She tried to struggle, but struggle against what? This was like magic. She was not restrained in any way. She just started to levitate and move toward the pyramid. No one could shoot. Even if Atra-has were shot, the president could not be saved. Besides, there was no guarantee that Atra-has did not have some sort of defense mechanisms in place, of which the humans had no idea. At that moment, one of the presidential guards, detailed to protect the president or die trying, lifted his weapon in order to fire at Atra-has. Even before he was able to aim a small portal opened on one of the pyramids and a plasma-like weapon fired. The soldier and a few others around him dropped to the ground, dead. Upon closer examination, the wounds of the dead soldiers were cauterized. No blood was flowing, but there was a hole in their chest and abdomen areas. They were dead before they even realized what had hit them.

In this commotion, John screamed, "Don't shoot! Just don't do anything! Do not move a muscle! Or we are all dead. They can read our minds!"

Obviously, the aliens had come prepared. Once again, it was shown that the humans were no match against the mind-reading and seemingly more intelligent aliens, with weapons systems that far exceeded the best technology that Earth could muster. Moreover, it was more proof that the casualties inflicted by the humans were pure luck. The aliens were determined to get what they came for, peacefully if possible.

Atra-has continued, *We cannot wait any longer. We have to go. You and the others can come with us. If we are victorious we will bring you and your leader back here.*

Kristen relayed this information over the communicator.

Kristen, John, Ken, and Nicole did not have a choice. They had to at least make an attempt to rescue the president. But why did Atra-has need the president and the other four? Was it that if he kidnapped the president, the other four would follow?

HQ did not take long to instruct the next set of orders. The instruction came almost immediately that the four should go to attempt a rescue. In fact, they gave the order for the other four astronauts, Baz, Manny, Thor, and Greg, to also accompany the entourage, with their sole objective to get the president back safely. Until then, there would be complete media blackout on Earth. They did not want a panicked populace, nor did they want anarchy. The vice president would be sworn in, in secrecy.

Atra-has's litter took him to the pyramid entrance where he disembarked. The litter returned for the astronauts who had the invitation to go aboard. However, Greg, Manny, Baz, and Thor also boarded the litter—in his haste to depart, Atra-has had not communicated with the rest of the aliens or the robots that only the four would be accompanying them. The litter then entered the pyramid through a separate entrance and docked itself. So, the additional four had managed to slip in, in plain sight. Now, the nine humans were in the aliens' domain, albeit on Earth.

One of the menial robots who was guarding the entryway saw all the humans get into the pyramid. It then proceeded to lock the door in preparation for liftoff. Just as the door was being shut there was a loud and thunderous bang, and the whole pyramid shook, jostling all its occupants. The robot was knocked off its feet, then stood up and ran to the nearest weapons station. Atra-has looked concerned and communicated to his cohorts. Kristen translated as, "The enemy is here and are engaging us."

In this position, Atra-has and his entourage were sitting ducks. He had miscalculated and spent too much time trying to appease the humans. Consequently, the enemy had arrived, and it was too late to take off. Something had to be done. He had to engage the enemy although he had strict orders not to do so. However, he would rather return home with the cargo on board than get annihilated on this planet. There was no time for the massive pyramids to get airborne unscathed. The only logical solution was to deploy the small crafts to draw fire away from the massive structures. This was not an ideal solution, but there was no other choice. So Atra-has made the difficult decision. He gave a command which Kristen interpreted and relayed to everyone else as, "They are deploying the small flying craft to engage the enemy." In the melee, the exit door was not completely locked. The robot responsible for this task had been asked to drop everything and immediately proceed to the dock to help launch the crafts. None of the aliens noticed that the door was not fully secured.

PRESIDENTIAL EXIT

Orders about the VIP prisoner were not broadcast beyond those who already knew. Greg, Manny, Baz, and Thor, who had snuck into the pyramid, had proceeded to make their way through the interstices of the basement of the pyramid. They made a beeline to where they thought the president would be held prisoner. Due to the fact that they had been in the pyramid several times in the past, they were somewhat familiar with the internal layout. So while the other four astronauts went to the bridge, Greg, Manny, Baz, and Thor headed straight to the bowels of the structure in search of the president. That is when the whole pyramid shook. This made all the robots stop whatever they were doing and hustle to perform their emergency routine of manning weapons systems. Information flowed into their circuitry to start defensive action. The movement of the humans in pursuit of the president was not impeded at all. Their presence inside the pyramid was not noticed by Atra-has, and therefore the robots were not instructed to do anything about the intruders. So the four humans went looking for the president among a hive of activity.

Soon they heard whooshing noises. Kristen and company guessed those came from the small fighter craft departing the pyramids to start the war that was about to begin. Baz and Thor split from Greg and Manny to look for the president. They had the communicators so they could keep in contact. They headed, almost running, straight to the basement where they thought the president would be held captive, to approximately the same location where they were held during the journey to Earth. One of the containers that they had come across in the past had its lid open and was being tended to by a robot. As the robot was closing the container, Thor caught a glimpse of a person in hibernation. Thor mentioned, "They have

367

stored the humans in these containers." He did not have to mention that their primary objective was to rescue the president. They were forced by circumstances to take on the duty of presidential protection and rescue. The robot closed the lid and went about executing its orders. Almost without a pause, the humans continued in search of the president. Soon all four arrived, from different directions, at the same door. When they opened the door, which was surprisingly simple from the outside, they found the president pacing in the confined area.

Manny stepped in, while the other three kept guard. He asked, "Ma'am President, are you hurt?"

"No," came the response. He hurriedly instructed, "We have come to get you out. Please follow us."

The president, looking concerned, said, "Do you know which way to go?"

Baz responded almost absentmindedly as he was scanning for any sign of danger, "Yes, ma'am. We have a pretty good idea. We spent some time here on our journey back. We may not know every nook and cranny, but we know in which direction to head to get to the exit." These four had now become bodyguards to the president, as they would have to take a bullet or the alien version of it for her, if necessary. They walked nervously and as quietly as possible, each to the left and right and front and back of the president.

The president asked, "What were the two loud bangs and the shaking I heard earlier?"

The rescue party all had the communicators and had heard what Kristen had announced, so Greg responded, "We believe it is the enemy of the aliens who have started the hostilities. And we believe these aliens are responding by sending their craft to engage them. Perhaps that is why we were able to get in so easily when all the robots and the other aliens were preoccupied with the battle. The enemy may have caught these guys somewhat unprepared. With some luck, we should be able to reach the door. Getting down from this height is another challenge that we will have to figure out, but we will cross that bridge when we come to it."

They walked vigilantly and silently the rest of the way and arrived unimpeded at the exit door. They found the inner door open and the outer door unlocked. They exited the inner door, and automatically, out of habit, Greg closed it shut while Thor announced on his communicator to the personnel on the ground to deliver a rope or a net. They knew instinctively that although jumping from this height was an option, the consequence was certain injury. There was a very good possibility of severely broken bones or even a breakage in the vertebra. The consequence for an older person, like the president, was even worse. However, Thor's communiqué was picked up, and a fire truck sped toward the pyramid. The truck was equipped with an air cannon which could fire rescue equipment into burning buildings to help with the rescue process when speed was of the essence. In this case, they had loaded a rope to fire into the porthole, one end of which was attached to the truck. As if the tension was not already high enough, the fire chief announced to the person responsible for firing, "Take careful aim. We do not have too much time." The rope was fired and caught at the first attempt by Thor who secured it to the door. The president, with surprising alacrity for a person of her age, slid to the ground. No sooner than the president reached the truck, the rope attached to the truck was released, and it backed up at high speed to relative safety.

While the president was descending, the four consummate professionals were planning the next few steps. They looked around to get a good view of what was happening. In the airspace around their vicinity, they could see one of the newly arrived airships. It was impossible to estimate how many more there were on the other three sides because the pyramid they were in blocked their view. But it was almost a certainty that there were more. They were surrounded and sitting ducks. They had to get the humans out and get out of the area. The enemy may have equal or greater firepower. Once the president had safely descended to the ground, Thor said into his communicator, "We are going back to rescue the others." This was not a request for permission, not that anyone at HQ would have disagreed. Almost immediately the affirmative response was, "Roger that, be safe."

LUCKY DIPLOMACY

The four soldiers reached the command center of the pyramid to find a hive of activity. Kristen was trying to concentrate and pick up what was being communicated, but being relatively new to this she was finding it difficult to pick up much with all the cross chatter. It almost seemed like the new arrivals were not noticed at all. Baz went up to John and whispered, "We need to get out of here *now*," emphasizing and enunciating the "now" so that the others heard it also.

John responded, "We know," and pointed to the monitors in front of them which were displaying four large crafts hovering, with some smaller ones approaching. Due to the urgency Thor had not previously given attention to the shape and size of the enemy crafts. Now he, as well as the other three, noticed that the enemy crafts were of different size, shape, and color to the alien pyramids that they were presently occupying. They had a dome, like the dome on a place of worship. The bottom half was cube shaped. It looked like some buildings that exist on Earth. The color was stark white, a direct contrast with the dark, almost black pyramids. The enemy crafts looked like giant white cathedrals.

Thor said, "They are close, very close—almost overhead. We are sitting ducks," to which John responded, "I had suspected that they were in close proximity. There have been some panicked actions here. You don't have to be able to speak the language or know telepathy to notice this fact."

Another thunderous noise and violent shaking of the pyramid and a smaller monitor showed one of the other pyramids being completely obliterated. The method of destruction was surprising—it was as if the weapon of choice was to do damage to the target but leave the surroundings unscathed. The projectile, if it was a solid since no one could see it, penetrated the pyramid and caused it to implode. Once the pyramid was crushed, as if a soda can were being compacted, the whole structure collapsed onto a large heap of fragments, each one being no bigger than a soccer ball. Due to the nature of the weapon, presumably something to do with gravity, the fragments were all curved into odd-shaped spheres. It was accompanied by a sudden gush of wind from all around which appeared to converge on the debris and rise vertically up over the pile of wreckage. The rising vortex was visible since the wreckage was smoldering hot and the wind rising from it was smoky white, as if it were gas rising from a volcano. From inside of the intact pyramid, it was difficult for the humans to tell what effect it had on the ground personnel who had been keeping watch. They hoped that the soldiers and others on the ground, especially the president, had pulled back to a safe distance. Fortunately, the pyramid that was obliterated was one of those that had already been destroyed by the missiles. Of course, the enemy did not know that the vehicle was completely devoid of any living beings as the missiles had already seen to that.

Thor reiterated, "Come on! Let's get out of here. We could be hit any minute!"

Kristen said, "Wait, I have an idea to possibly save all of us." Looking at John, she asked, "John, radio back to HQ to get the choppers airborne. I will try to communicate with Atra-has to get his flying crafts back into the pyramids." In the meantime, the large enemy crafts had engaged the smaller vehicles deployed from the pyramid, and a few of them had already been shot down. The small crafts were zooming back and forth trying to avoid the firing line of the weapons from the white craft and shooting what can only be described as pulses of energy. Each time the small craft was hit, it disappeared in a flash of light and intense heat. There was almost no discernible debris that fell to Earth.

Ken quietly made the observation, "The pulse cannons are shooting something other than material or lasers. We can neither see nor hear them being fired. It appears to be a different kind of weapon than the ones used on the pyramid. I cannot tell if they are firing antimatter?" The other three noticed his observation on

371

the monitor and just shrugged. This question could not be answered now. Something to do with antimatter was the only way one could explain the almost total annihilation of the flying crafts that were hit. Almost no debris fell to the ground. It was almost as if the weapon of choice was to destroy the flying craft and not injure the people on the ground. The witnesses were seeing that as soon as the craft was hit, it exploded into nothing. The smaller crafts were taking heavy casualties. It was only a matter of time when there would be none left.

Damage was being inflicted on the white craft but not enough to bring it down. As far as the new aliens were concerned, this situation could go on till there were nothing of their enemy left. All this was being viewed in the control room of the pyramid as well as at the Pentagon.

John radioed, "Get our choppers airborne and ask the pilots to head towards the new ships. Kristen will try to get the small craft back. We are going to try to prevent this thing from escalating any further."

The response was instant, and the incredulity in the voice obvious. "Why would we send our choppers into harm's way?"

John responded, "Kristen is going to try to convince Atra-has to bring his small crafts back. If it works, we can stop a full-scale battle. If it does not, we can get the choppers to turn tail and return."

"Roger that" was the curt response.

John looked up at Kristen who was already trying to get the attention of Atra-has.

Not now! was the furious response when Kristen tried to get Atra-has's attention. But Kristen persisted. *You are in a difficult situation. Possibly we all will be destroyed. We are trying to save everyone. We are sending our craft. Hopefully they will not destroy us if you get your small craft back.*

It is said that war is the ultimate form of diplomacy. In this case, the diplomacy had to be dialed back. Not an easy task. Atra-has did not have to ponder this for long. He knew it could be a matter of seconds before the new aliens fire another bolt of energy and destroy more pyramids. They had grossly miscalculated the time of arrival of the new visitors to Earth, and were now in a position where they could lose everything. In those intervening seconds, another pyramid got the full fury of the weaponry and was destroyed in an identical fashion to the previous one. This time it was one of the pyramids that was fully functional and manned by the aliens. It seemed like they had developed a special weapon meant just for the destruction of the pyramids. Kristen and everyone else could see the grimace on all the aliens' faces. Then another was hit. Thankfully, this was the pyramid that was retrieved from the ocean.

Atra-has had no choice. One by one his pyramids were being picked off, and he could not do anything about it. He was in an extremely compromised position. He could not win. Anything was better than being target practice for his enemy. This woman, for whom he had much disdain, was offering help. Not that he had anything against her individually. In fact she was competent and also good-looking. How could anyone from this planet help? They were designed to take orders. But there was no choice. There was nothing else he could do to preserve himself. Atra-has gave orders for the small craft to return.

Kristen could pick up some of the chatter, and she interpreted the response as surprise and confusion. Nevertheless, the order was issued. She was able to pick that up as well.

The crafts started to return as the choppers climbed and headed toward the new alien crafts. Everyone was bracing for the ultimate and horrible fate for the human pilots manning them. They waited; John felt perspiration trickling down his face, which he wiped away. He wondered if the others were as tense as him. Although each one of the eight was trained to deal with adversity, when danger is staring you in the face and you are resisting the adrenaline-infused urge to turn tail and run, all the training becomes evident. Among the general population, except in very rare cases, self-preservation overcomes everything. However, no matter how much training one has had, the stress level will be sky-high. John wondered what his pulse and blood pressure would be now, probably off the charts. At least they had the company of one another. They saw the choppers approaching, and through the communication system they could hear the instructions from the Pentagon for one chopper to approach as close as possible to the white enemy craft. With the backdrop of the giant spacecraft hovering a half kilometer aboveground, the chopper looked tiny, as a gnat would be to a human.

They waited with bated breath. They heard the returning of the small craft, which presumably went back to its docking station. The helicopters approached the enemy craft slowly, almost inching their way toward the large craft, suspended in midair. The imperious behemoths could squash the tiny choppers like bugs, if they wanted to do so. Perhaps they were awed by the ancient technology. Perhaps they did not feel threatened by the tiny choppers. Whatever the reason, they allowed the choppers to approach. It appeared that the technology in the enemy craft was similar to the ones in the pyramids, in as much as the drive mechanism was based on the mastery of gravity. One chopper started to inch forward. It seemed that the pilot of the chopper was approaching a window. The window appeared to be tiny from this distance compared to the rest of the craft, but as the chopper approached it, its relative size became obvious. The window was at least as large as the cross section of the chopper. It hovered there for a while, and they heard the pilot radio base, "I am trying to get them to land. I am pointing and motioning in a downward direction. I don't know what else to gesture. Hopefully it will not be misinterpreted."

HQ was heard instructing, "That is good. Now all of you back off slowly and land, in their line of sight."

The choppers slowly backed off as instructed and gradually landed on the ground. Atra-has, seeking confirmation, asked Kristen what was going on. Kristen responded that they were trying to get the craft to land. She interpreted Atra-has's expression as disbelief.

If the atmosphere was not tense before, it was now. Atra-has realized that there was nothing to stop the new aliens to destroy all the pyramids in a matter of seconds. All the small craft had returned to the pyramids, and the choppers from Earth had landed. Atra-has thought to himself, *If it were me, I would take this chance to eliminate the enemy and return home.* The wait continued, the tension increasing with every passing moment. The longer the wait, the greater the chance that the enemy would finish the job of destroying all the pyramids. There was complete silence, everyone's eyes riveted on the monitors.

However, after what appeared to be an interminable wait, the enemy craft moved. They started their slow descent. After it became obvious that they were landing, there was a collective exhalation. The tension diffused rapidly. Even the aliens appeared to be visibly relieved. Their appearance had become softer, as the tension drained from their faces and bodies. Their movements became less rigid and more normal. Only the robots were completely normal throughout the whole ordeal. Presumably they were all the ones without human brains in them. The humans allowed themselves to give one another a handshake or a quick hug. The immediate crisis was averted. A new one just beginning.

The question in everyone's mind was why did the enemy give up its position of strength? All they had to do was fire some weapons and all the pyramids would be destroyed. Did the enemy have compassion, or was it just curiosity? Whatever it was, the humans were thinking how would they be able to communicate with the new aliens. Would they employ the same communication mechanism, or would it be via spoken words?

MORE REVELATIONS

HQ spoke first, "All of you come out of the pyramid. There is a truck waiting for you outside. It will take you to the enemy craft."

As they turned to leave, Atra-has projected a thought to Kristen. She stopped walking.

John asked, "What happened?"

Kristen did not say anything at first, then a few seconds later relayed to John as well as HQ, "Atra-has wants John and me to stay back. We don't have a choice."

HQ responded, "Kristen and John, stay where you are. We will get you out shortly. It looks like no one is going anywhere for a while. The rest of you proceed out of the pyramid and board the truck."

One thing was true. No one was going anywhere. Now it was a question of waiting. At least this time it would not be tension filled, at least not immediately.

As instructed, the others walked out and descended the ladder which was brought to transport them to the enemy spacecraft. This was displayed on the monitors which Atra-has and his people as well as the two humans left on the pyramid were watching. Also watching were the people gathered in the Pentagon.

As the truck approached the enemy craft, it appeared to grow in size. It grew larger and larger as the humans got nearer. When they were finally at its base, it appeared about 50 percent larger, in all dimensions, than the pyramids. When they arrived as close as they could comfortably get, the driver said, "I don't see an opening. Where do I go?" The answer came in the earpiece, "Keep circling till you see an opening."

After going around a few times, a portal opened at a height that was not easy to access. They did not have long to figure out how to get in. The metallurgy was beyond comprehension. As awestruck as they were when they first saw the pyramids, this was a craft from yet another world. The design was such that the metal with which the craft was constructed, warped, and bent, and almost magically steps appeared. This kind of technology was only theorized on Earth. The new aliens had implemented it effectively on their space-traveling vehicles. Of course, some of the other technology was comparable between the two alien races. It had to be for an effective status quo to exist between the two warring nations. As they were entering, Ken was thinking, if only humans knew what powered these vehicles, Earth would be on an equal footing with the interstellar visitors.

Kristen and John, as instructed, remained at the pyramid with Atra-has. They had no choice, but they did have their communicator with their earpieces. Nicole was asked to go with the rest, not because a physician was needed, but to send a message that both genders are represented in the human delegation. With a great deal of trepidation as well as excitement, similar to what they felt when they first entered the pyramids in space, they climbed up the steps. Only this time, the tension was not quite as palpable since they were on Earth. As they walked up, reverberating in Ken's head were the words that he had spoken earlier, "Any technology sufficiently advanced is indistinguishable from magic."

From the outside, the personnel gathered around saw the six climb up the steps and disappear into the craft. They were at some distance from the craft, so only those observers with binoculars could clearly see what was happening. The president had been escorted out of the area, first on land, then by chopper to an undisclosed location. She was not too far away in case she had to return, but she was in a more populated and secure area where there would be safety in numbers.

As they entered the craft, they noticed a large open area which was brightly lit, both from the sunlight that was streaming in from behind them as well as artificial lighting present inside the craft. The height of the room was about three meters. As soon as they took a step inside the craft, the stairs disappeared as magically as they had appeared. Baz looked back and down and noticed that if they had to jump, it would be about thirty meters—doable but with consequences. Inside, no one was visible. The humans wondered if they were being monitored. They walked away from the portal, but other than the entrance behind them, there were no other obvious openings through which they could proceed further into the craft. It appeared as if they were in a large room with only one door that was behind them. Not knowing what else to do they slowly proceeded further toward the wall directly opposite the entrance. Fortunately for them the portal behind them did not close, that gave them a sense of security.

As they approached the wall, a doorway appeared to open; only it did not open. A rectangular space of size three by two meters appeared to melt away in the wall. This was truly extraordinary to the astronauts. On the way in through the magical door, Baz purposely brushed, almost banged, into one end of the opening with his shoulder to check to see if it was solid. It was solid. He grimaced because he hit the wall too hard. The others turned toward him to see what had happened. Baz sheepishly responded, "That's okay. I was testing the strength of this wall." The others knew that Baz was planning an escape route, if they needed to retreat in a hurry. These new aliens had some new technology to tout; only they were not touting it since it was probably second nature to them. What was this material, and how did they do this trick? This was not something that they had time to ponder. They had other pressing things imminently at hand.

As they entered the opening and their eyes adjusted to the bright lights they could see many sarcophagi-like containers all over the wide expanse of the room. The room was about four meters tall. The distance directly in front of them was about thirty meters. It appeared to be longer from side to side at about forty meters. In the middle of the room was a stairway. Panning all around, there were no other obvious entrances or exits. The six looked at one another as if to confirm that they should make a beeline to the stairs.

They started to walk past the sarcophagi-like containers when Ken suddenly stopped in his footsteps with a sharp exclamation. The others stopped and turned to him to see what had happened. He was staring at one of the sarcophagus, eyes wide and mouth agape. "What's wrong?" asked Baz.

"Look at the words on the side of these containers," Ken said excitedly. All the rest of the group could see were some squiggles, to which Nicole responded, "Do you mean you recognize the script?"

"Yes!" Ken was almost shouting with excitement. As a linguist, he had learned the root languages, the ones which had given rise to a number of modern languages. But to see a somewhat familiar language on an alien spacecraft was unbelievable. How could they have learned an ancient language from Earth, unless it was the other way around? He realized he was shouting. He toned it down and continued, "This is almost like the Phoenician script." He took a deep breath and waited a few seconds. No one uttered a word, still shocked at why there would be an ancient and now a defunct language scribbled on the sides of these boxes arranged out neatly all over the room. Excitement unabated, Ken exclaimed, "I think, given time, I could decipher this!"

Nicole asked, "What does this say?"

Ken tried mouthing the words. "Tar…tar tam…tar tan okee. I think it says tar…tam…okee, but I don't know what it means."

Thor chimed in, "Let's open it and see if we can put an item to the name," as he tried to manually lift the lid. Baz and Manny joined in to help. It was so firmly closed that it did not even budge. The boxes outwardly appeared to be made of thin material. But the substance was so strong that three adults straining to open the lid could not move it in the slightest. Thor continued, "Well, there goes that idea. Seemed good at the time. Nothing else to do here. Might as well continue on into the hornet's nest."

They continued walking toward the stairs. When they were about ten meters from the stairs, they heard footsteps descending. Instinctively they stopped, hearts in their mouths. They were in a compromised situation, no weapons in their possession. They stood there rooted as the footsteps got louder. It seemed to be just one alien coming down the steps. They did not know what to expect, maybe a hideous monster where eye contact would be next to impossible. They did not have long to wait.

The footsteps grew louder until two feet became visible. The feet were wearing soft white shoes. The footsteps continued, and gradually the rest of the legs, the torso, and the arms became visible. The alien seemed to be wearing overalls, just like the ones that humans wear, work clothes. The overalls were white in color with assorted items hanging from a belt around the waist. The items could be weapons, a possibility that the humans could not ignore. Imminently, the rest of the person came into view, and surprisingly this alien looked exactly like Atra-has and his race. About the same height, weight, and skin tone. Athletically built as the aliens from the pyramid, its movement was easy—almost a glide, an easy gait that comes from being strong and muscular. Of course, it was difficult to say how strong or muscular due to the, presumably, standard "one size fits all" overalls. This individual was not smiling, nor was there a stern look; the look was neutral, if anything soft and relaxed, almost as if welcoming a guest into their domain.

Without speaking, the alien beckoned to them with his arm to follow him upstairs. They obediently followed him up the stairs to what looked like the bridge. At first glance, all these aliens were identically dressed, white overalls and soft shoes. This room could be mistaken for some sort of laboratory—clean, tidy, white in color, and with everyone dressed in a variety of very light pastel colors going about their business. The humans stood in line shoulder to shoulder looking at the hive of activity. It was as if the color of the outfits determined the duties that the individual performed. Certain colors were clumped together in specific sections of the bridge. Could they be cybernetic organisms, like the ones present on the pyramid? That question would be answered soon. A marked difference between this and the bridge on the pyramid was that this place had some noise, verbal noise. The cacophony of sounds was emanating from the verbal communications of these aliens. As the scenery unfolded, it became obvious that this room could be some sort of nerve center for the craft, maybe the bridge.

Here, too, there were giant monitors, flickering lights, panels, control switches, and all the other paraphernalia associated with the central hub of a spacecraft. The only difference was that some of the scribbles were recognizable by Ken.

Baz turned as if to say something and noticed Ken staring at some lettering on a panel closest to them. He was trying to decipher the words. Baz asked, "Do you understand the writing?" Ken shook his head and said, "I can partially read what is written, but the language is foreign. It is too much of a coincidence that I can read these words that I learned a long time ago. What I learned as ancient and lost language has got to have roots from this race of people. Over time, the script remained, and I think the language evolved. So although I can read, or I think I can read, I cannot make head or tail of this language." Ken's struggle with attempting to read had not gone unnoticed by some of the aliens. The alien who had led them in had disappeared into the crowd. Just as the humans turned around to face the hive of activity, one of the seated individuals got up and approached them.

He was within the limits of the other aliens in height and weight and had an easy gait as the others. He seemed slightly older than the rest of them, and seemed to have a pleasant demeanor. He approached the humans and moved his arms outward with palm facing up, right leg in front and a slight bend at the waist. It seemed to say welcome. Certainly it was nonthreatening. The humans hesitated and bowed a little, which seemed to satisfy the alien. Then he said something which made Ken exclaim. He looked at the other humans and excitedly said, "I understood one word of what he said. I believe he said, 'Welcome.'" All the conversations were being monitored at the base, but they were maintaining radio silence so as not to interfere with the humans. Suddenly, the radio crackled in their ears, "Ken, respond with as much as you can."

Ken responded with the one word he could repeat for "welcome." This seemed to slightly surprise the alien, but it also appeared to please him because the smile on this face seemed to get just a little deeper. With the wave of his hand, he gestured them to go further inside the room. Baz whispered, "He is inviting us to follow him," to which HQ responded, "Be wary of any traps." They need not have mentioned it.

Visual Communication

There were four official-looking chairs where the alien beckoned them to occupy, and he occupied the fifth. The chairs were arranged in a semicircular pattern with a table in the center of the arrangement. Each was hoping that they would not be subjected to some kind of mind-altering hats like the last time. Having sat down, Ken was furiously trying to think of something to say, but this was a dead language. It had evolved into other modern-day languages, and the origins of the modern-day languages had been lost to the mists of time. All that remained on Earth were some stone tablets that archeologists occasionally unearthed and, with various degrees of success, deciphered them and related them to a language in existence today. Ken had learned a few such languages in the past. Coincidentally, some of these scripts spoke of people who had come from the stars, the star people. Ken suddenly had a thought. Were they the ones who had originally spoken this language and imparted the wisdom of writing to the humans of that time, six or more thousand years ago? Only time would reveal the secrets of these aliens. For now, they seemed to be amiable enough—unlike the ones in the pyramids.

The alien looking at Ken spoke first. Ken only understood a word or two, and even that he was unsure as to the meaning. However, with reference to context, Ken thought, his guess would be fairly accurate.

Nicole asked, "What did he say?"

Ken was deep in thought parsing what he could remember of the words that the alien had spoken. He looked up and excitedly said, "I believe this is a long-lost language. It is possible that six or seven thousand years ago, in the infancy of civilization, these people had come here and taught us this language. It sounds like it is a derivative of the Phoenician language. Some of the writings that were found speak of star people, known to us today as aliens." Ken, the consummate professor that he was, could go on for hours speaking about ancient languages.

The voice in his ear interrupted him. It was HQ asking the same question that Nicole had asked earlier. "Did you understand him?" HQ could hear the humans, but the microphone was directional, and any sounds other than the wearer's voice were, at best, muffled. So although they knew that the alien had spoken, they could not make out the exact words. So even if HQ employed the technology they had at their disposal, it would take time to process the words and isolate the muffled sounds and then decipher what was spoken by the alien. That particular avenue was closed. The only option to interpret was to rely on the humans, particularly Ken.

Ken answered very guardedly, "I could understand only a word or two. I think he gave me his name. Kesu. I believe his people are called Baan-russ. Sounds like a holy city in India where I stayed for a few months a long time ago. If I am not mistaken the name also sounds Indian. This method of communicating is not going to be easy. I only vaguely know the human version of the Phoenician language. Added to that their language is most likely different from the ancient Phoenician, although there may be some words that are in common. I will have to use those common words to make sense of what is being communicated. I am going to attempt to say something, and once we start speaking with each other, I will get some idea of how this will turn out."

Ken turned to Kesu and spoke some hesitant words, but what could clearly be heard was his name and followed by the names of the accompanying humans. He obviously had introduced himself and the other humans, which the alien seemed to understand.

Next Ken asked a question which clearly was not understood. He started writing imaginary words on the table with his finger, hoping more meaning would be conveyed that way. Seeing this the alien did something which lit up the table, and a screen materialized on its surface. The perfectly looking table had become, in the human parlance, a touch-sensitive tablet. Ken wrote out the words on the touch-sensitive surface. As soon as he was done, the words moved around by themselves. Certain letters changed and then reformed into a sentence, which presented itself in front of Kesu. He read the sentence and nodded and wrote something, at the end of which exactly the same thing happened, and the sentence presented itself in front of Ken. Ken noticed that this tabletop technology not only presented the words to Kesu and him, but it was also interpreting and changing letters to make the words meaningful to both of them. Briefly Ken wondered how it was accomplishing this task and how reliable it could be. Perhaps it was using modern algorithms and ancient information stored in their databases to convert what Ken and Kesu were writing. Whatever the technique it was using, Ken could not worry about that now. This was the best they had. He had to focus.

Kesu had written that the conversion would get better as the exchange continued, so they carried on for the moment writing and reading what each other had written. Ken was also speaking, narrating what he thought he understood, so that the other humans as well as the HQ could hear. A confirmation of what was being written was when a question was directly and accurately answered by the other person. The progress was slow, and they were there for what seemed like hours exchanging information.

One of the things Ken wrote was to confirm the alien's name and planet. As originally thought, he confirmed that his name was, in fact, Kesu and his planet was called Baan-russ. Ken then asked if Kesu was aware that they were referred to by Aten-Heruans as Garg-Ar. Kesu looked surprised, answered, "No, I was not aware." Then Kesu asked if the humans had managed to communicate with the Aten-Heruans. Ken answered affirmatively, which, judging from his expression, seemed to confuse Kesu.

Slowly the exchange was getting more substantive. Ken had asked where they had come from, but could not understand the answer. What had appeared on the screen in response to that question was a video of a galaxy, much like he had seen on the monitor in the pyramid. The image was from a different vantage point, but unmistakably a spiral galaxy and more than likely the Milky Way.

Then the image zoomed in, in steps till it got to a local cluster of stars. Then it zoomed further to a planet that appeared to be in orbit around a star and finally a closer image of the planet itself. As in the previous instance, the Earth was also highlighted, and to the person viewing this it appeared to be a great distance to travel due to all the stars and other galactic formation in between. As in the previous case, they noticed another planet orbiting the same star. It was of a different color to the rest of the myriad of stars, so it was a good guess that, that was the planet from where Aten-Heru came.

Ken relayed this information, making sure to state the fact that the galaxy was most probably Milky Way and the grouping of planets looked identical to the ones seen earlier in Aten-Heru's spaceship. The response from HQ was "Galaxy and star names and positions are relative to our viewing vantage from Earth. The names are what humans have coined, so no one but humans would understand what galaxies or planets our names represent. Similarly, we determine the positions of galaxies and planets relative to the position of Earth. Viewed from another planet, even if it is in the Milky Way, the positions of the same planets and galaxies would be different. What you saw was their view of our galaxy. It will be next to impossible to locate them with just that information. Even if you saw some of the same planets in that image that you may have seen from here, viewed from Earth it would look different. We can never understand their location unless we have a common reference point. Ken, you can table this for now and move on. We will try to get an answer on this when the communication is a little more fluent, and perhaps they can share the video with us."

The next logical question that Ken asked, almost reluctantly, was, "How did you travel all this distance?"

He was bracing himself to the possibility that the answer would be completely unintelligible to him. When he did see the answer, he was not very off the mark—he did not understand most of it. He relayed, "This is not much better than before. It appears that they use the Universal Force. It is their term. Whatever term Kesu used, it translated as Universal Force. There are four known forces. That is a scientific fact, and we humans know about them." As Ken was wondering what Universal Force was, HQ chimed in and instructed, "Ken, see if you can drill down a little further. Draw the four forces on the table. Draw gravity, the weak and strong nuclear forces, and the electromagnetic force. Improvise your diagrams. We are certain they will get it. Then ask the question about the Universal Force."

Ken complied with the instructions. The translation technology did not alter the diagrams too much. It was as if the processor knew when to interfere and when to abstain. The answer was only slightly more illuminating. Ken responded, "This appears to be beyond my range of comprehension. I am not a physicist. Let me try to explain Kesu's response as best I can. It appears that they understood the four forces that I drew for them. He explained the Universal Force with very few words but drew some galaxies and pointed to the spaces in between them. This tells me that the force is everywhere in intergalactic regions. The last thing he wrote was that they did not travel any distance, they only traveled in time. All this is very confusing to me. Perhaps the scientists back at HQ can figure out something from this exchange. It is time to change topic since I cannot get any deeper without being completely lost."

Then Ken wrote out the words in the ancient and now defunct language, as best as he could recall, "How long ago did you come here?" The answer was again confusing. The numeric translations were not easy since there needed to be precedence in order to be able to translate accurately. And numbers gave no margin for error—it was either right or wrong, no middle ground. Besides, even if the symbols representing the numbers were accurately deciphered by the humans, there was still the possibility of an error since they may not be using base ten Arabic system of numerals. It was obvious to Ken that this was also a question that they would have to revisit.

Seeing the confusion in Ken's expression, Kesu tried to elucidate further which Ken verbalized as, "They again say that they did not travel in distance but they traveled in time. They are from our past! I don't understand this statement although I think I am not too far off the mark. I will attempt to get this clarified."

A few minutes later Ken announced, "I think this is what Kesu said in explaining why they came to their future. If they travel to the future to perform unethical experiments, they could avoid any potential objections from their population. After all they were engaged in indiscretions. They did not want to leave evidence of any misdeeds. If they were to perform the experiments in their present time, the population would protest. If they went to their past, evidence could be unearthed. Whereas if they went to the future and kept things quiet, evidence could be mopped up easily without raising suspicion. If the atrocities had not taken place yet, the mind would be less willing to complain. This is why Kesu thinks the powers in Aten-Heru decided to do unethical experiments in the future. Look at it this way. We are all ashamed of some aspects of our history, the wars, genocides, and such. But if it became necessary for a nation to do something extremely unethical that would cause disgrace or shame, it is better to do so in the future and try to keep it as quiet as possible. Doing so in the past would open up the potential for many politically charged inquiries and possible retribution against the individuals who perpetrated these crimes. If the experiments were far enough in the future and, by the end, the entire experiment were destroyed, everyone would be none the wiser."

Ken saw that his human audience was processing what he just stated. He imagined the individuals at the other end of the radio communication were similarly digesting the information.

Getting conscious of the fact that the last few questions were not understood or possibly even misunderstood, the initial euphoria was waning. So Ken decided to ask a question, the answer to which did not need too much thought process. "Where did you stay during your last visit?"

The response was a map of the Earth which appeared on the screen—zoomed in to the present-day country of Turkey. Of course, there were no borders on the map since these aliens did not yet know the geopolitical breakdown of the various countries. However, Ken almost instinctively knew what the red dots on the map represented. He had often visited all the locations, touring and researching in his linguistics endeavor. In modern times this place came to be known as Derinkuyu, in the country that is now called Turkey. Below the ground in Derinkuyu, there is an extensively constructed cave system which has defied explanation. This cave system has been dated back more than eleven thousand years. This also partly helped answer the previous question. They were here on Earth at least once as long ago as eleven thousand years. Below Derinkuyu, there are as many as eleven layers of catacombs and labyrinthine passageways, a number of which still remain unexplored. No one is able to explain how, or even why, these living spaces were constructed. On seeing the locations Ken started to realize, Kesu's people were hiding in these cave systems, doing their own research on humans. Since they were hidden belowground, there was practically no chance of being detected, even if the Aten-Heruans knew of their presence on Earth.

Ken relayed this information via his communicator. In addition, in his inimitable way, he decided to add a lengthy discourse about the surrounding area, saying, "It appears they were at Tiahuanaco and Puma Punku in Bolivia and Petra in modern-day Jordan. But they were mostly in and around Gobekli Tepe and Derinkuyu, in Turkey. Derinkuyu is underground. The rest are kind of camouflaged. They are cut out of hills so they don't stand out. The cave was created by cutting through stone. This was done so precisely that even after so many years, none of the eleven layers has collapsed. There is a theme with all these locations. These locations and many others in the immediate surroundings have a number of stunning and seemingly impossible stone structures of varying sizes. Reputedly carved by humans with nothing more than stone tools, these structures still stand today and are generally popular tourist attractions. These structures are a testament to accurate and meticulous cutting. They could not be made using manual labor. It is not possible to get such precision without the use of machines to grind down these massive monoliths. Some of the locations have massive stone structures carved with such precision that two or more of these blocks would fit together and snap into place like a child's building block toy. No one has been able to explain how or why these have been done. And then they moved these structures into place so precisely that it is incomprehensible how simply manpower could have achieved the task. Now all these places are starting to make sense—" HQ gently interrupted and reminded him that there was a task at hand, to which he commented, "I tend to get carried away sometimes," and continued on with the immediate assignment.

Ken decided to ask why they had come here. Basically, the information Kesu gave corroborated what was already gleaned through several encounters with the Aten-Heruans. The two groups were at war and had been for a long time, longer than could be measured by generations on Earth. But the most shocking information was that these aliens also had a hand in the shaping of humanity as is known today. The communication was difficult to understand, but Ken proclaimed into his communicator, "I think Kesu said that they have also meddled with our DNA." Kristen and John, who were still in the pyramid, heard what Ken said. Kristen asked Atra-has, "Did you know that the other guests had also made changes to how we are made?"

To her surprise Atra-has responded, *Yes, but we do not know what the change is. Part of our mission is to find it and make the necessary corrections.* He said it matter-of-factly, almost condescendingly, as if the humans had no say in the matter. Kristen relayed that information to the others listening.

However, Atra-has was thinking that if he was able to get the answer from the humans, it would save them a lot of time that would otherwise go into investigating what was wrong. They could apply the fix straightaway. The same genes that they had so carefully designed a long time ago would again function as designed. If they did not have to take the human specimens back to their world to find out what was wrong, they would save an entire round trip. This could bode well for him and this trip and would more than make up for the lack of finding the shiny metal. Of course, this part was not relayed to anyone. Only Atra-has was thinking of this scenario.

Ken asked on the writing pad, "What changes did you make?" and also announced it on his communicator. The answer confused Ken at first, but he started to ponder on the answer. Everyone else was waiting, eager with anticipation. There was some more exchange and some more quizzical looks and further pondering. After a long time, Ken announced, "I am not sure what is written here, but it seems like they introduced a virus, which was not originally present in humans. From what is written this virus gives us a *soul.*" The last word he said slowly, enunciating every letter.

"What?" The exclamation came like a chorus. Kristen, John, and HQ as well as the other humans sitting around the table exclaimed all at once. No one could believe what Ken had just said. Ken responded, "I think this is what Kesu just said. I am trying to process this myself. But I think I am pretty sure that they introduced some kind of virus that gives us a soul. This was done, I believe, only to undermine the efforts of the other aliens, the ones that constructed our DNA. This is the same as giving us a conscience. This explains Lela's behavior towards us, that she wanted to help us and prevent succeeding generations from the fate into which she was forced. She displayed a high degree of altruism. This is not present in animals. This…" He was looking for words which eluded him for the moment. "This…nanotech virus gives us a conscience—a soul. I guess these guys succeeded—at least to some extent."

With that bombshell, Ken was lost for words or questions to ask. So the only thing that came to mind was for him to write, "Do you have any questions that you want to ask?" knowing fully well that these aliens, just like the others, knew more about human makeup than humans themselves. They were the architects of the genetic engineering process that made the humans what they are, albeit they were on opposite sides. Moreover, they would definitely not be interested in any technology on Earth. They were far too advanced, as it was patently obvious.

The response almost immediately was that they did not have any questions and that they did not mean the humans any harm. That their enemy was in the pyramids and that they were glad that the pyramid was captured. This alarmed Ken, and when he repeated what Kesu had said, HQ immediately asked Ken to inform them of the facts. They must have assumed that the pyramids were captured because they saw a couple of them that were already destroyed and a chopper piloted by a human come into view.

Ken wrote out the information, and as Kesu was deciphering and comprehending it, his expression visibly changed. It tightened up, his smile went away, and when he looked up, his eyes revealed a deep concern. He started to bark out orders to his crew, but it was too late. It was such a novice move to give up a winning position.

TENSIONS ESCALATE

Atra-has must have picked up from Kristen's mind what she heard Ken say as he wrote to Kesu that the pyramids were not under human control. As Kesu was barking the orders to his crew, Atra-has also issued orders to his crew. The cannons on the crafts captained by Kesu had not been aimed at the pyramids for a couple of reasons. Firstly, they thought that the pyramids were under human control, but more importantly, they could not fire at this proximity without obliterating themselves. This knowledge was not lost to Atra-has. He had to move fast and make the first move.

The lights on the monitors on Kesu's craft became red, indicating the engines on the pyramids were fired up. Within a second and with surprising alacrity, the six functional pyramids were airborne, and within a second after that, the pyramids were crossing the outer reaches of the atmosphere. This rate of ascent and acceleration would have crushed any organic life-form into a pulp, but Kristen, John, or the rest of the aliens did not feel any ill effects. In fact, they did not feel anything. If they were not viewing the monitors they would not have been aware that they had moved at all. There must have been some sort of a mechanism that provided antigravity assistance inside the pyramid. Fortunately, neither protagonist fired their weapons, either because there was no time to aim them quickly, or because they wanted to avoid collateral damage, or because Atra-has had orders not to engage enemy on Earth, or because of a combination of all the reasons.

Kesu, Ken, and the rest of the crew had started early in the morning; when the humans looked at the blank monitors that were, until recently, projecting images of the pyramids and the surroundings, they noticed that it was getting dusk outside. Although the humans did not know what the alien translation system was doing, the computer could carry on the interpreting indefinitely. However, the humans, and to some extent even Kesu, were starting to get tired. Besides, Kesu and his crew had other things on their minds. They had to assess the danger posed by the pyramids and make a decision of whether to follow them or to stay put.

HQ announced, "The pyramids are in orbit. They have not departed yet. Either they are waiting to ambush and fight these guys in space, or they are waiting for further communication from us. John and Kristen are still on the pyramids. We have to try and get them back, as well as the rest of humanity they have with them. In the meantime, we do not want you all to become unwitting prisoners of Kesu. Excuse yourselves and see if you can depart the spacecraft."

The humans who had accompanied Ken looked at him almost as if to encourage him to comply with the request from HQ. Nicole spoke, "We are all getting tired. We have been here for a while." Referring to Ken, she suggested, "Especially you, you have been focusing on the communication aspect. Before mistakes are made, we should take a break, and if necessary, return later."

Ken, who was in two minds of whether or not to break at this juncture since he was making some headway, allowed himself to be convinced with this line of argument. Although he did not see Kesu and his crew as a threat, he agreed that his concentration was wearing thin and could do with some recuperation. Maybe after some rest and analysis of the interaction, his efficiency would improve. There were some things to ponder, discuss, and analyze. Perhaps a plan to glean more information would make future communication more effective.

He wrote, "We are tired, and the pyramids are gone. We need to rest, and you probably have things to discuss. We hope you will stay. We will come back and discuss more. Two of our friends are on one of the pyramids, and we need to try to get them back."

Kesu had simmered down to an extent, and almost as calmly as before he wrote, "Yes, we understand."

It was not the complete answer that Ken was hoping. It was, however, evident that Kesu had other things on his mind and was almost glad that Ken and the humans offered to leave. They needed to figure out their next move. The choices were to pursue or remain where they are. If they pursued, the tables would be turned, since the pyramids would detect them ascending and take action, the consequences of which could be bad for Kesu and his crew. If they waited, there was a better chance of leaving Earth intact. But wait for how long? Also waiting and letting them go would mean letting Atra-has return with the items for which they had journeyed to Earth. Kesu had his orders. He was not sent here to admire the scenery. He and his panel of senior staff would need to brainstorm and figure out an optimal course of action.

RETURN TO THE
WHITE CATHEDRAL

Other than Ken, none of the other humans had any participation in the communication. It was only Ken who was able to read and write, aided by the intelligent computer system. It was with great relief that the others welcomed the chance to stretch their legs. When Ken stood up and announced that they could leave, they all stood up with a sigh of relief. Ken walked toward the exit followed by Nicole, Baz, Thor, Manny, and Greg. They exited Kesu's craft by following exactly the same path that they had taken to come in. They were escorted out by an alien being or a robot, they could not tell which, since the entire walk was in silence. Not that Ken could have said anything anyway. Without the aid of the computer, communication was impossible. When they came to the exit, the stairs materialized almost supernaturally, and they walked down. They all breathed a sigh of relief that they were out of the confines of a spacecraft operated by a vastly superior force. At the same time, in the back of their minds they knew that John and Kristen were not in an ideal situation. The area looked empty, without the black pyramids.

As they walked back to the vehicle that was waiting for them, Ken pondered the events that had taken place. Although outwardly Kesu was friendly, friendlier than Atra-has had been, Ken had a niggling feeling that something was not right. It could be a show, based on their initial assumption that the pyramids were captured. After it was revealed that the pyramids were indeed not under human control, Kesu's demeanor had changed in an instant. Perhaps it was a concern or perhaps his true personality was coming out. After all, it was Atra-has's people who had created the humans. Kesu's people had only introduced something, the sole purpose of which was to sabotage the hard work to get a step on the war being waged at their home.

HQ, which was monitoring everything through a video feed, came online as soon as they walked into the makeshift war room, which was actually a large tent.

"Ken, what is your analysis of the situation?" The makeshift war room was a large tent set up within eyesight of the alien spacecrafts. It contained some electronic equipment powered by portable generators. It also had a large table and some chairs. There were already some senior personnel gathered around the table. Thoughtfully there was some dinner on the table, the sight of which reminded the six that they had not eaten for at least ten hours, possibly longer. There was a speaker in the middle of the table and microphones at strategic ends of the table through which the audio communication with HQ could take place. Ken sat down and took a bite, then spoke, "Outwardly Kesu was friendly, but his countenance changed when he realized that the pyramids were not in our control." He took a moment to savor the food in his mouth that he was busily masticating. Then he inquired, "Are Kristen and John still on the pyramid?" He was hoping against hope to hear that they were on their way back.

"Confirm that, they are still on board and currently in orbit at about 22,000 kilometers from Earth" was the response from HQ. "Currently, we are in touch with them, and they are all okay. We are trying to determine Atra-has's next course of action. As yet it is undetermined. However, we have a theory about these guys not traveling in distance but in time. When Kesu mentioned that to you, it was very confusing to you as well as our analysts. They have been working away at various theories and have come up with the best possible one. We think, part of the problem with time travel is that if there is a significant natural event at the location where the time travel is taking place, such as an earthquake or a volcano, then the machine being used could get destroyed. If that machine happens to be in space and a comet or a meteorite passes by at the exact location of the time-traveling spacecraft, there would be a collision and the craft would get damaged or destroyed. So, we believe what these guys have to do is to go to a place where this is least likely to occur. Earth is in a less densely populated area of our galaxy, being about two-thirds of the way out from the center. Finding empty space is easier here than closer to the center where the stars and planets are more densely packed. Time travel here, closer to empty space, reduces their chances of an unexpected demise. So, cleverly they charted all the celestial bodies and projected their positions in the future and turned on their time machines. The Milky Way makes a revolution every 230 million years. What the analysts here at HQ are speculating is that they turned on their time machine and waited for the Milky Way to make its usual revolution. When Earth appeared, they stopped traveling—in time. This means that their home planet is about the same distance from the center of our galaxy as Earth, but it is a few years of revolution of the Milky Way. Unless we understand their numbering system, no one can tell how many the few years mean. It could be hundreds or even thousands of years. Since they are from the past they moved forward in time to get here—but did not have to travel much in distance—very ingenious."

Ken added, "That makes sense. Throughout our encounter with the aliens I have been associating our past knowledge—history and mythology, with present findings and information from the aliens. Things are corroborating so well, it is scary. So what I have to add is that the Hindu scriptures talk about a certain length of time. They call it yuga—or epoch if you like. It is approximately 430,000 to 450,000 years in duration, give or take a few thousand years. I have always wondered how they came up with this precise length of time. To be more specific, the scriptures speak of four yugas. We don't have time now to go into the details. But I bet you if I sat down and did come careful calculations, I could come up with some very interesting answers. The only concern is that we are in the fourth and last yuga. How the ancients got this knowledge is an open question, but current events indicate that the information may have come from our visitors. The Hindu texts also indicate that there will be a cleansing and rebirth after this Yuga. My point is, and it is a really scary thought, will the events unfold as predicted in the scriptures? Will Earth or its human population be destroyed? Was this planned all along many years ago, and is that how it became part of ancient texts? We humans make sure that we do not leave any traces of genetic experiments with plants or animals. We make sure that everything in the lab is properly discarded or incinerated, unless we are ready to cultivate them for consumption. Will we be cleaned up before they leave?"

There was a stunned silence in the war room as well as at HQ. After a while HQ spoke, "We cannot worry about that for now. Let's see what we have and see if we can get Kristen and John back."

Ken continued, "Right! First things first. Atra-has and his group altered our DNA to make us humans, who knows how many tens of thousands of years ago. At about the same time, Kesu and his group surreptitiously introduced something into our bodies, or maybe into our DNA. I am not sure what this is, but it was meant to sabotage Aten-Heru's war effort."

Kristen, who was listening in on this conversation from the pyramid, spoke, "Earlier I asked Atra-has what he thought Kesu's group had done to us. He said that he knew exactly what they had done. When I pressed him for some more information, he was elusive as usual, but gave me enough to indicate that it was kind of a virus...not a virus that makes us sick but a virus like a foreign entity that resides in the long-term memory part of our brains, in the hippocampus. He also said something about Lela which I could not understand."

"Nice to hear your voice. Hope you and John are okay," Ken responded. He confirmed what he had found out. "The information corroborates with what I was thinking. What you called virus is in fact what we label as soul. This is the only way I can explain it. If they wanted to sabotage something without letting the enemy know that they are working with compromised systems, you would want to do it in such a way that the enemy cannot detect it. Frankly, I think it is very clever, something that cannot be touched, seen, felt, tasted, or even detected by any instruments we possess. The change cannot be visible, and it must impact the parts that they want to use in the robots. It also has to be easy to introduce, without having to go through all the DNA manipulation that the Aten-Heru aliens performed. That only leaves one organ in our body, the brain! As for Lela, the reason she helped us, despite all the training she must have endured, is because I believe the virus works in a way where it introduces a filter to all actions that she might take. The virus makes you think, analyze, and figure out the consequence of your actions. This process is meant to inhibit the response to any instruction that may be received. Since it slowed down the response, the human brain did not act spontaneously or impulsively—such as animals do. This is probably all the advantage the Baan-russ aliens needed. But this is also something which makes us human. Most of us do not acquiesce to every emotion without due thought process."

Kristen responded, "Agreed, except for the part about detection. I don't know if they have instruments to detect the virus or soul, but Atra-has's associates have found a way to neutralize this modification. I still don't know how they will do it."

Ken said, "Whatever the virus does or does not do from the perspective of the aliens, it makes us human beings. We must stop them from making any changes. It seems unlikely they can make mass changes to so many humans from that far away. So logically, they must have plans to return."

That was a comforting thought to both Kristen and John. Without plans to return, they had no chance to get off the pyramid.

HQ interjected, "So what information do you have that positively identifies this virus that you mentioned?"

Ken took a moment to collect his thoughts. "Based on the writing we exchanged, I am very certain that they have introduced a virus. Atra-has also confirmed that with Kristen. Now that we have had a few minutes to consolidate the information I gleaned, I know Kesu wrote that they have tried to sabotage the human beings by giving them, I mean, us, a soul. Whatever we call it, soul or conscience, this is what was meant to stop us from becoming effective cyborgs. That is why Lela rebelled against them and helped us. Atra-has also told Kristen that the human population on their planet was not as effective as they had planned. Maybe they suspected foul play and thought that the humans in Aten-Heru were compromised in some way by their enemy. Whatever the reason, they came to Earth for more, a fresh batch of humans—hoping that the fresh batch would not be afflicted with the same problem. They probably never expected to make this return journey. Luckily for them, and us, they left their creation to run rampant on Earth. When they probably realized that the batch of humans in Aten-Heru was contaminated, they could have either destroyed them or did not allow them to reproduce. They figured that the humans they had left on Earth would be pure—and plentiful. This conjecture makes sense with the limited information we have. Why else would they travel at such expense just to pick up some humans? But think about this, if they strip us of our bodies and our soul, all we are left with is intelligence with no inhibitions—intelligence that can be molded into whatever they want us to do. No machine can duplicate this complexity."

John jumped into the conversation. "This means that they could make nearly perfect fighting machines, almost indestructible, and with the ability to accept and process any command without fear. The virus that is present must have caused them a lot of frustration, not to mention time and resources. Atra-has and his people must really be seething."

Ken weighed in again. "If you strip the body and soul away you are self-aware, but I am guessing you lose the self-preservation instincts. If you think about it in reverse, the soul is what makes us who we are." As he mulled over this thought, the concept struck him. He said, "Damn! This has been looking me right in the face, and I did not get it. Listen to this." He paused for a second, then continued, "The self-preservation virus also makes us introspective. It gives us meaning. If we can contemplate about ourselves we will be reluctant to fight. Strip that away and we become killing machines. We will probably even maim and kill each other."

There was radio silence for a few minutes when everyone was processing this line of discussion. Then HQ came online with a new question. "If that is the case, how is the virus propagated? We mean, from one generation to another generation? And also, Ken, could you please keep this short since we do not have time."

Ken answered as if he were already prepared for that question, "I asked Kesu as best as I could, and his response was something I could not understand completely. It is either through the umbilical

cord when the baby is still in the womb or soon after birth. I think
Kesu meant to say that the virus is transmitted when the baby is
still in the womb. This is why some societies celebrate the seventh
month of gestation, as that is when they think the fetus becomes
viable. By equating what we celebrate today as religious or cultural
events of significance with what I have recently gathered, I think I
am right with this hypothesis. It is a replicating virus. Therefore, it
never runs out, but once it reaches a certain density it stops so as not
to overwhelm its host. I also asked him how this virus, in the human
host, could help them. His answer was initially confusing. Now that
I have had a little time to think, here is what I think he said. I believe
there is significance to the shape of this structure, just like there is
significance to the pyramidal shape. This kind of structure, placed in
certain energy fields on Earth, will transmit the virus, and the information it contains, to their planet. The shape of this dome together
with the energy of the Earth intensifies the power. I could not understand what information gets transmitted. It could be something as
simple as the capability of a human brain. In situations of war what
else would they want to know? As a side note I want to say that this
may be the reason why we see today so many establishments with
the dome-like shape. Every major religion has this kind of structure.
I will ask him again to get some clarity, although I may not be very
successful."

There were more murmurings and then the question, "Did
you find out how they travel such large distances? And remember to
make your answer as fast as possible." HQ was trying their best to
make Ken answer as tersely as possible.

Ken answered, "I will try to make it fast." With that he addressed
the question, starting out at a rapid rate of speech. "I tried to get
that information, and with this I am less certain than with my other
questions. As best I could tell, they use energy that they said was all
around us. I am really out on a limb here when I say that I think they
could be referring to particles, what we call neutrinos. Or maybe
they are referring to dark energy. I am no expert in this area of science. All I know is about 78 percent of the universe is comprised of
this…stuff. I read somewhere that every second, trillions of neutri-

nos pass through our bodies. Just makes logical sense that something in such abundance is used to your benefit." He stopped to take a quick breath, then at a slower rate he continued, "Boy, we have a lot to learn. We don't even understand this thing that is speeding up the universal expansion, and here we have cultures that are using this to power their interstellar travel. From my unscientific perspective, all the stars produce some sort of magnetic fields and gravity, which is prevalent everywhere in the universe. They are experts in gravity as well as this universal energy and make use of it to their advantage. As a side note, Hinduism refers to the universal energy. Maybe ancient humans were referring to exactly this, without understanding it— not that we are any better off than them. These alien cultures are so advanced, they must have been around from countless years before mankind. They also alluded to panspermia, where there are many complex organisms around the universe. Needless to say, I could not get into the details. For all I know, it is these guys who are spreading life across the habitable universe."

Clearly, attempting to muzzle a loquacious professor was not very effective. There were some more murmurings while the experts and analysts at HQ discussed the next course of action. Ken welcomed this opportunity to make progress with his meal. He ate as quickly as he could, as did the others. Finally, HQ spoke, "Our primary concern and focus at this time is to get Kristen and John back, as well as the others who have been taken hostage. Ken and the rest of you will have to go back to the white cathedral spacecraft and try to ask them to leave. In the meantime, we can bait the pyramids to get back to Earth, which should be the first thing we do. On the ground, there are greater chances to get Kristen and John off the crafts. In space, we are no match. On Earth, too, we are no match, but we can use guile and trickery to give them a chance to get off the pyramid."

Ken was about to say that if they heard this conversation, Atrahas would know, but he was preempted. "We have shut off the communication to Kristen and John. They have not heard the last three minutes of our conversation. We will turn it on again, so as not to raise any suspicion, but remember not to mention any of this over the open wireless communicator."

As Ken was ready to acknowledge that remark, he heard HQ continue, "We are back online, sorry for the temporary glitch." This was solely for the benefit of Kristen and John, with the hope that the pyramids had not learned to interpret the conversation.

There was no time to waste. They had to try to at least make an attempt to rescue Kristen and John, impossible as it may seem at the moment. They finished the rest of their meal and headed back to what was now termed as the white cathedral, since this was how it looked from the outside. They, or specifically Ken, since he was the main communicator, did not know what to expect or say to convince them to leave peacefully.

A smaller unit was asked to go to the white cathedral this time around. Such a large group was not needed and would be an unnecessary risk. Ken was obviously needed. Nicole volunteered, and HQ thought it was a good idea. The final member was Baz. He was chosen from the four engineers for no specific reason, other than that he volunteered first. They needed someone with military training, and one individual would be sufficient. As they were heading back to the white cathedral, conversations were taking place between HQ and the astronauts on the pyramid. HQ informed Kristen, "Kristen, tell Atra-has—we can deliver gold."

Kristen said, "I think he can see through that."

HQ said, "Maybe so, but this is the only option we have to get you back."

Kristen said, "What do I tell him, that we have gold for them? How much gold do we offer?"

HQ said, "We don't know how you can tell them what weight of gold we will have for them since you cannot communicate weight. Tell him we will have some gold and if he asks how much, tell them it will be about your and John's weight in gold."

Kristen said, "Wow! You want to exchange our weight in gold for John and me?"

This was a rhetorical question. The conversation continued in this vein when Ken and his entourage arrived at the white cathedral. The stairs appeared as before, and the group knew where to go. As in the past, they were met at the stairs and escorted to the table.

Kesu started typing on the table, and Ken noticed that the translation was more fluent than before. What was translated was "You are back sooner than I expected."

Ken's responded, "Yes, we have much to discuss. I noticed that this has become faster and better."

The response which Ken almost expected was "Yes, this device has been working ever since we stopped. It has been analyzing the language you and I have used and has come up with a better way to translate. Our future exchange will be faster and better. Although, if we introduce a new language, it will be as slow as before while it learns."

Despite the urgency Ken did not want to seem too eager, nor did he have a plan to get Kristen and John out. He decided to ask a generic question, "How does your craft get energy to travel such great distances?" This question was on everyone's minds, although the current circumstances made the release of the rest of their team a priority. Ken figured this would be an innocuous question to ask. He did not want to reveal the desperate situation they were in. He had to somehow try to manipulate Kesu to make the pyramids to come down to Earth.

Surprisingly the answer was very lucid. The algorithms in the alien computers had done a very thorough analysis. Ken wondered how much computing power would be needed to perform this task and how long would an equivalent analysis take using Earth-based technologies. Kesu's response was "The star protects and eliminates a lot of forces that is present all around. When you go outside the influence, about the sixth-planet distance from the star, those energies are present everywhere. We use those energies."

Ken translated into his communicator, "Kesu said that when we reach the heliosheath, there are some energies that we on Earth do not see. That is why we do not know about it. If I am allowed a personal opinion, those energies are driving all the galaxies apart. I am not a scientist, but I recall Einstein postulating more than a hundred years ago that there are some energies present all over the universe. Possibly this energy that we cannot account for is what is making the universe expand. This energy is possibly the remnants of the big bang, or it could be new. Today we call it dark energy—because we do not know anything about it. If all the fundamental particles did not have a chance to coalesce into higher-level particles, they would be left over and float aimlessly in space. Maybe these regular particles and energy particles are what is making the universe expand. According to Hinduism and string theory, these particles are vibrations. When these specific vibrations called fundamental particles are combined together, they form protons and neutrons. Added with electrons, they can form atoms and ultimately the matter that we see and touch. If today, we are still at a point too soon after the big bang, then there is a chance these particles will ultimately form matter. Which means the current theories about a cold universe could be incorrect. We don't see these vibrations because we are protected by the sun. Can you believe the energy that gives us life, the sun, is also something that is keeping us from understanding the other energies—the strings? The sun is preventing us from understanding the fundamental principles of nature? Maybe we are lucky that the sun protects us as well as gives us light. Nevertheless, Kesu said that they use those energies to traverse the vast distances. Maybe some of the energy particles, if deployed correctly, can be used to traverse space and time. Maybe it is simple once you know how. Perhaps the pyramids also use the same forces. Can you imagine the amount of power they have if they can control the fundamental particles at will?"

HQ heard this. At this point it was just easier to let Ken continue in his usual loquacious manner. Trying to hurry him up was proving futile and wasting time more time in repeating the same request over and over.

Kesu asked some basic questions. Ken translated the questions for the others listening while typing out answers on the translator. These questions ranged from how mankind is organized to what motivates us on a daily basis. This led to discussion about how Kesu's people had altered humans. Ken wanted to find out a little more about the alteration that was done. However, the translator was not as accurate as he had hoped. Kesu answered that they had introduced some kind of thing, which Ken could not understand or translate. All he got was that it resides in the brain and is passed from the mother to the fetus. However, the new item of information gleaned this time was that they had experimented with having it transmitted to their planet. To enable this, they had built some devices in certain locations, to which he pointed on the map. Those corresponded to modern-day India, the Arabian Peninsula, as well as places in Southern America and Australia. Ken translated them as Dwaraka in India, Petra in Jordan, Puma Punku in Bolivia, and the Black Rock Mountain in Queensland, Australia. He added his own commentary that all these places were surrounded with mysteries that could not be explained by humans, and for the most part humans give these places a wide berth.

Ken endeavored along the same theme trying to get more detailed information. He announced on his communicator that due to higher energy levels registered at these specific places, their locations were found by Atra-has's people and had been destroyed. One of the objectives for Kesu was to reestablish these gates, as he called them. He continued translating, confirming that just like the pyramids for the other group, cathedral-shaped structures are the significant shape for the Baan-russ race of aliens. These structures, used with the Earth grid pattern, had the capacity to send and receive messages over interstellar distances. As to how they adjusted for the time variation, since it had to travel in time as well as an unknown distance, was something that Ken could not understand. However, he added, the shape of the cathedral-like dome was important in channeling the virus.

Ken added his thoughts, "I think that maybe they built these so that they could monitor this virus or soul without making the round-trip journey. That is why there are some man-made structures on Earth which resemble the cathedral-like shapes of these spacecrafts. Being placed under the dome enhances and intensifies Earth's magnetic forces and allows the virus to make the journey. Whatever is making this journey, it exists in each human and gets released upon death. So, within a short period of time after a person dies, our custom is to place the dead body in a domed structure. If the journey is not made, it just dissipates. If you think about it, the other guys

K. PAUL GOMEL

developed a being and these guys subtly modified it, so today we have a human being. This is ingenious."

Ken asked why the craft they were in was shaped the way it was. Earlier he had hypothesized about the shape but wanted to make sure he heard it from Kesu. He also tried to find out why the enemy crafts were in the shape of a pyramid. The answer was a confirmation of Ken's conjectures. That the shape of the cathedral was a means to efficiently send information from Earth to their planet about the virus that they had implanted into every human. These structures needed to be located at specific places where the Earth's natural magnetic fields could provide a boost to the virus to travel the interstellar distances. What was surprising was that the pyramids also had a similar effect; in this case it was with the thoughts, telepathy. If the thinker sat at the vertex of the pyramid, the thoughts could be boosted to interstellar travel. That is how, Kesu assumed, the Aten-Heruans left behind on Earth kept in contact with their planet, provided updates, etc. The person intending to communicate would sit in the vertex of the pyramid and initiate the thought transmission. However, the Aten-Heruans left behind their relatives, and all their progeny had died before they could establish themselves. Ken added that he saw a wicked glint in Kesu's eye when he wrote this. So he thought that it was Kesu's people who had ambushed and assassinated them all. The most surprising revelation of all was the fact that thoughts and the virus that they had introduced were also vibrations or particles. Due to the language barrier, Ken could not determine which one was the appropriate description. This was the biggest revelation thus far. Understanding this fact meant that thoughts could be picked up by machines and transmitted over great distances. Similarly, the information contained in the soul could also be transmitted, from Earth, over great distances. But what information could be carried in the soul?

In order not to reveal the utter shock of this news to Kesu, Ken downplayed the information and asked about their origins and found out from him that their mythology indicates that the Baanruss and the Aten-Heru people had a common source. For unknown reasons, the people from a planet far away were loaded onto two crafts and sent away, a long time ago. Kesu did not know why, but the two crafts had landed on habitable but separate planets, close to each other. Kesu and his civilization's quest was to find out what their source planet was and why they were sent away. They suspected the answer could be found on the planet occupied by the Aten-Heru civilization. The spacecraft that was used to evacuate the Baan-russ people had been preserved for posterity and had some of the information. Their quest was to find out about the other craft and see if it had some more information. But due to the length of time it had taken to develop the technology to travel interplanetary distances, the two civilizations had evolved independently. They had different languages, customs, cultures—indeed, everything was different.

So what started off as a quest to investigate the original craft on Aten-Heru had been misinterpreted and had escalated into full-scale war. That was several generations ago, but the war and multiple skirmishes persisted till today. However, the quest still remained the same. Kesu could not elucidate about their enemy whether or not they had a similar mission. The peace mission had not been possible due to lack of communication, and every peace envoy sent had been met in space and ended up being destroyed even before any communication could be established. Kesu admitted that they were as guilty of this as his enemy. Ken looked up after translating this larger-than-usual paragraph and took a sip of water that he had the foresight to bring with him.

This kind of exchange went on for a while with questions and answers from both sides when Ken had an idea. He came back to the question of transmitting thought and the information in the soul but could not understand the answer; either that the translator needed more time to interpret fully or Kesu was being understandably circumspect with his answers. So he asked a question that was answered earlier, "Have you thought of making peace with the other side?"

The response was the same as before, "We live on another planet, and we do not have any means of communicating. As soon as we send an emissary, even before the craft has a chance to land, it gets destroyed. I am sure we have done the same to the other side. Since we cannot get close and even if we do, we have no way of speaking with each other."

After this fact was confirmed, Ken's plan to get Kristen and John back started taking shape.

MEDIATION PLANS

Kristen had radioed that Atra-has now knew what was not quite right with the humans. They had a solution, which was alarming. They had analyzed some of the humans that they had picked up earlier and figured out what was wrong. This could not be done earlier on their own planet since they were not sure if this situation afflicted only the individuals they had taken earlier or it was present in the general human populace. When they figured out that the nature of the sabotage was in the form of a virus, their solution was to make genetic modification to counteract the change.

Kristen asked Atra-has in what she believed to be an alarmed tone, *How will you change the makeup of all the humans on our planet? Will we be going back to the ground to make the changes?*

Atra-has said, *We have analyzed your makeup from the samples taken earlier. We know Garg-Ar has put something in you. We can fix it. We do not have to go back. We can do it from here. As your planet rotates we will send beams that will fix everyone. We will have to come back later for the new supplies of your species. For now, we will work with what we have, although it will not be very efficient.*

Kristen had to think for a while. What did Atra-has mean by "beams"? She discussed various alternatives for the meaning with John. All this was being heard by HQ as well as Ken and his small group. Finally, it came down to two possibilities as John put it. "Either they will destroy the Earth with beams of energy such as we have seen in the recent past with their weapons, or they will alter the human genome by intense and specific radiation. The first alternative will serve no purpose to them because this planet will become barren, devoid of any human life. When he said, 'We will have to

409

come back for new supplies,' I think he meant the alteration will only take effect in future generations."

To confirm Kristen asked, *Will you destroy our planet?*

No was the answer. Unknown to the humans, Atra-has was slowly coming around to the idea that the humans were closer to his species than originally planned. He suspected that this is what his predecessors had eventually realized. In the throes of attempting to accomplish a time-critical mission one tends to focus solely on the job at hand and not consider the consequences. Atra-has was forced to interact with the humans, something that was not planned. This had slowly led him to realize that there is an organizational structure here, much like his home planet. The people taken from the earlier mission, who were kept in captivity, were never allowed to become human. Training started at an early age. He was starting to see that, left to themselves, the humans had an innate need to organize and develop. But if he did not destroy the planet, more humans would fall victim to him and his people. If he did destroy the planet, he would have a lot of explaining to do. In his mind, he would be murdering people similar to himself. He would have to see how things played out. It also depended on his enemy and their actions.

Kristen turned around to John. "He confirmed no, but he might as well destroy it since we will not recognize our offspring. No matter how accurate the beams are, if our children do not have a soul or conscience or whatever you want to call it, there will be a radical shift in society, culture, attitudes…" She did not have to say any more. Everyone knew it would be chaos within a generation. "No matter how foreign this virus was, it still made *Homo sapiens* into human beings. It gave us restraint. It is what Kesu's people wanted, but it is also what humans want."

Ken interjected, "Kristen, tell Atra-has that we can arrange a meeting with Kesu if he can return to Earth. Maybe this meeting can start some peace negotiations. I am sure they ultimately want peace. They have been fighting for generations. I will translate, although not very effectively, for Kesu, and you can translate for Atra-has." He did not have to provide a lengthy preamble to this request. Both

Kristen and John were listening to all the translation that Ken was providing to HQ.

Kristen was not too confident about this. "Ken, although I am more adept at this than anyone we currently know, I can only understand a small fraction of what Atra-has says. I can certainly not translate peace negotiations by interpreting imagery that seems to be the basis for telepathic communications between Atra-has and me. Besides, from what I gather you can only translate a small portion of what Kesu writes. It will be a stretch to attempt this. I don't think it will work."

Ken had to try to convince her. "But this is the best chance we have. They will see through any other ploy we devise. Unless you or HQ have a better plan this is the best course of action. What this meeting has, if it takes place, is that there is something for both sides. In fact, there is something in it for us too. If the pyramids come back, there is a chance we can free you and John."

HQ chimed in, "Kristen, this seems like a reasonable request. You can ask Atra-has if he wants to talk with Kesu. You will have to convince him."

John interrupted, "What about the gold we were about to offer?"

HQ said, "That could be an added incentive. Use that 'carrot' if they are not too certain about meeting their enemy."

Kristen responded, "Roger that."

With that, Kristen turned to Atra-has and said what was agreed. She said how Kesu had a translator and that Ken had learned to communicate using that device. She embellished a little by stating that Kesu had wanted to meet with him in order to try to negotiate peace, not just here on Earth but also on their planet. She also indicated that the best place to negotiate was on Earth where the two can meet in person. It would be convenient for the interpreters to set up the equipment on the ground outside the spacecraft, on neutral territory. Atra-has was picking up the communication with interest, and when Kristen finished, he did not say anything for a while. To Kristen and John, he appeared to be analyzing and evaluating.

To Atra-has this was a potential solution. Maybe end the war, not only here but also on Aten-Heru. He would have to think hard and make sure this was a successful meeting. He had to play out the various scenarios in his mind. He could not let the enemy get the better of him or his fleet. He would have to dictate some conditions to ensure the safety of his personnel.

In the meantime, Ken had communicated essentially the same information to Kesu. The only difference was that he, too, embellished by stating that Atra-has had wanted a meeting. The best place to meet was here on Earth where the two parties can meet with the respective translators. Kesu, too, had to make sure that there was no trickery. He had to think of the options and consequences and figure out what was safe for his people. At first glance attempting to end the war here appeared to be a good idea.

Atra-has left the control room and must have gone to consult with his senior officers. After what seemed like a quick turnaround, maybe fifteen minutes, he returned. Kristen wondered if the speed of communication was quicker because they were not using words, just telepathy. He spoke very matter-of-factly almost as soon as he took his seat at the controls. He turned to Kristen and communicated, *Yes, we can meet but on a few conditions. Firstly, no one fires at the other. All weapons must be turned off and de-energized. Secondly, we must meet in the middle. We cannot be closer to their craft or my craft. Lastly, their leader must come to meet me with no more than two officers on each side, and at least two humans must be present on each side.*

Kristen nodded and indicated that she would communicate these conditions to the other side. As she spoke, Ken took notes and translated as best as he could to Kesu. He could not get a few words such as "fires" or "weapons" or even the word "middle." But he improvised by drawing pictures and hand gestures where needed. Kesu seemed to understand and agreed to the conditions, adding one of his own, which was to request all the pyramids to return and for them to land close to their spacecraft. Obviously, there was a large element of distrust between Aten-Heru and Baan-russ. Ken mentioned this to Kristen, and the two acknowledged that the conditions were acceptable and that the pyramids were returning imminently.

Three aliens and two humans would meet the opposing three aliens and two humans, approximately in the middle. The weapons systems on both the alien spacecrafts were de-energized, and this was verified by each alien race.

As they were leaving Ken could not help thinking that this mediation could be momentous. Two warring aliens could come to a peace agreement, but Earth could end up being destroyed since it would not be needed anymore.

EMERGENCY RETREAT

The approaching clouds were almost black and heavy. It had not started raining yet, but the air was stifling. It was as if the atmosphere was already saturated with humidity. The Florida summer downpour was imminent. Minute by minute the clouds were getting thicker, heavier, and lower to the ground. The sun was almost completely blocked out with the dense clouds. Soon the clouds would need to relieve their burden. Since it was getting too dark to see, the military personnel were ordered to relocate the lights to the vicinity of the meeting. This was done in order to aid the communication as well as to make it easier for the cameras. They did not have to move the lights far since the meeting location was close to the previous landing spots. The stage was set. The pyramids landed, and John, who was with Kristen, communicated that they were about to egress the pyramid. He also indicated that Atra-has was very uneasy, possibly because he did not trust his enemy. Ken and Nicole did likewise, and they, too, indicated that Kesu was jumpy. Nevertheless, the two parties slowly approached each other.

The atmosphere, already thick with humidity, was made denser with foreboding. Just standing outside made one perspire. Everyone was soaked, and it had not even started raining. The tension only added to the discomfort.

Baz returned to the relatively safe confines of the rest of the group, since only two humans were required at the conflagration. As Ken and Nicole and the three Baan-russ inhabitants approached, Nicole said, "Nice to see you two. This place feels like a pea soup." Atra-has and his two lieutenants as well as Kristen and John were still on the litter and were about to disembark at the meeting point. This was a rare occasion where an Aten-Heru being would lay eyes on a

414

Baan-russ being, when one of them was not dead or trying to kill the other. Although it was daytime, the clouds had blocked the sun to such an extent that they could only make out the presence of one another as silhouettes.

John started to respond, "Nice to be back—" when he was violently interrupted with the loudest thunderclap that he had ever heard emanating from the low clouds. It seemed to make the heavy air and the Earth they were standing on shake. They were all rattled to their bones, especially magnified because they were outside and the clouds were very low. Coincidentally at the same time, to aid with the proceedings the soldier turned on the bright lights, brought in specifically for this purpose. The two events were almost simultaneous. The lights, the vibration from the thunder, and the noise that could be felt to the innermost core, all at the same time, made everyone outside hit the deck. No one had disembarked the litter. Atra-has picked up the panic in Kristen's thoughts and, thinking that this was an unprovoked attack, stood up with amazing alacrity and turned the litter around. Within seconds all five of them were on their way back to the pyramids. A similar thought went through Kesu. When he saw the litter heading back, so as not to be at a disadvantage again if the pyramids started ascending, he and his lieutenants grabbed hold of each human's arm and turned back toward the white cathedral. The grip on Nicole and Ken seemed to be like a vise. These aliens were physically very strong; their run back to the white cathedral was faster than any human could sprint, even with the weight of the human beings literally dragging along the ground. Fortunately, the distance was not great, and as soon as they had run up the steps and entered the cathedral, the crafts started lifting up.

In the distance, they could see that the pyramids also were lifting up. Kristen had tried to interrupt Atra-has several times in their hurried retreat. But Atra-has was single-minded, focused on getting out. He had built a wall around his mind, and no one could penetrate it. Once was enough. He would not be put in a compromised position again. Before long and with the same degree of speed, both crafts were ascending, albeit on a divergent course. The only saving grace was the fact that neither group fired at the other.

Atra-has had had enough of this. He was angry and somewhat let down. His mission was not completely successful. He was going to set a course for home, his home. The humans would have to come along. There could be various uses for them. If not they would be material for the next generation of harvesting. He gave the orders even as the pyramids were ascending, so they continued their ascent up and out into space.

Kesu was not going to let the pyramids out of his range. He had not fired, nor had they. Each had kept their word. But now, in space, all bets were off. The humans would be company, until all information could be gleaned from them, then they were disposable. He was not about to return just to let them off in case he lost contact with the pyramids.

John radioed, "I think we are going farther out in space than earlier."

Ken responded, "We are up in space, too, don't know where we are heading."

Kristen tried communicating with Atra-has, and a few seconds later, dejected, she told John, "We are heading to Aten-Heru."

John's initial euphoria abated immediately when he realized that this could be the last he would see of planet Earth. He immediately announced in his communicator, "We are heading out into space. I don't think we will be returning."

A few seconds later the communication came back from Ken. "Kristen, try to get them back. You will need to persuade Atra-has. Somehow you need to convince him. I will do the same here with Kesu." The message was getting fainter, as the distance from each other as well as from Earth was increasing. The distance that really mattered was the distance from Earth, since the relay was Earth based.

HQ heard everything. Given the hopelessness of the situation and lack of time to formulate an intelligent response, all they could say was, "Yes, please try to convince them to return and negotiate. Let them know that it was a weather-related coincidence. Keep trying. Offer gold if you have to."

Almost simultaneously HQ faintly heard from Ken, "This is wonderful," and from John, "HQ, what we are seeing is breathtaking, amazing does not begin to describe…"

HQ could not figure out to what they were referring. They had not left for very long, but the communication had rapidly become sporadic, and now there was complete silence. This was the last that was heard from either group. Either the distance had become too great for the tiny communicators, or something else had occurred.

HQ tried in vain. "This is HQ. Please report what you are observing."

NOTHING

"Commander John, report what you see."

Their communicators faintly picked up the pleading from HQ. But their response did not have the signal strength to carry all the way back to Earth—the distance had grown too vast in a very short space of time. Soon, even that was lost. There was silence at both ends. No one either on Earth or the humans in the alien captivity heard anything else.

Everyone at HQ had a forlorn look as they stood up trying to figure out what the next steps should be. Rescue was out of the question. The crafts were almost already out of range even to be detected.

BREATHTAKING SIGHTS

The people on Earth waited for what seemed like hours. Nothing was heard from Nicole or Ken who were now prisoners of Kesu or from John and Kristen who were prisoners of Atra-has. There was nothing Mission Control could do. The crafts were so far away that they could not even be detected with the instruments on Earth. No one on Earth even knew in what direction the alien spacecraft were going. Rescue was out of the question. The only hope for Earth was that the aliens would not come back with malicious intent in mind, as was gleaned from the aliens during the course of conversations.

The conversations Mission Control was having with the human prisoners were still being transmitted to the tents at the site from where the alien spacecrafts had hurriedly departed. Thor, Baz, Manny, Greg, and the military commanders were all listening to what was going on. Thor, almost with a need to break the deafening silence, suggested, "Maybe we can get up to the remaining dSEs and try to chase them down." Almost immediately Greg responded, "It is useless. They are much faster than us, and they have a head start. Besides, in which direction could we pursue them? Mission Control has lost track of them."

There was no argument from Thor. He and everyone else knew it was a lost cause. As a matter of fact, the spaceships of both the alien groups were capable of tremendous speed. Even if the humans could launch something immediately and knew in which direction to go, the dSEs were not capable of accelerating quickly enough to reach the speed required to pursue the aliens. Thor asked the obvious, "If they can travel that fast, why did they take so long to come here. We first saw them more than seventy years ago at the edge of the solar system?"

419

A male voice from Mission Control responded, "With all the data we have collected since your journey began, we think they were making many minor time adjustments to when they arrive here. They could not make few large time jumps for fear of crashing into something. We think they wanted to be at Earth at a specific time period with the hope that they would be able to gather their human cargo which was more developed and less prone to the problems they were having. At that time, they had not figured out what was wrong with the humans they had taken earlier."

None of the military staff in the immediate vicinity could argue this conjecture. No one within hearing distance of the speaker was scientifically trained. Thor meekly responded, "Thanks, over and out."

As a matter of fact, the spaceships of both the alien groups were not only capable of time travel but also of tremendous speed. That speed was needed to get to a safe location from where time travel could be launched. This was the intention of Atra-has. The cathedral-shaped ships were pursuing the pyramids to keep track of what their enemy was planning. Due to the unpredictable and possibly undesirable outcomes time travel can cause, both the alien ships had safety mechanisms built in so that upon return there would be no significant net gain or loss of time. Everyone on the ship would have aged almost identically to those left on their respective planets. Coincidentally, both the alien races had found out that this was an essential feature of time travel and had enacted identical rules, albeit implemented differently.

What the humans on the respective alien ships were witnessing was something no human had seen before and, due to the current lack of technology, would not be able to see for the foreseeable future. The spaceships had left the atmosphere of Earth and accelerated away at tremendous speed. As they got farther away from the gravity of Earth, they seemed to gather more speed. Then they engaged another drive mechanism which Kesu had referred to as Universal Force. This further accelerated the crafts in a short time to unimaginable speeds. The first one had left as fast as possible in order to get away from effective targeting range of the second ship. The second one was attempting to chase down the first one. Within a short space of time they were so far away that the Milky Way, in all its majesty, could be seen. The view from Earth, nestled between the third and fourth spiral arms of the Milky Way, is always the same. Looking up, one can see only one of the spiral arms. Even from orbit around Earth, there is no perceptible difference in the view. However, in these alien ships which had sped away from Earth, the human astronauts could see more than the spiral arm. They could see clearly into the center of the galaxy. The powerful equipment on Earth had picked up John's last words as more of the galaxy came into his view.

Now, a few hours from the hurried retreat, the entire majesty of the Milky Way galaxy was visible. John continued to speak into the communicator in a futile attempt to communicate with Earth. Kristen said, "John, we are too far away. If we cannot pick up the transmissions from Earth, they certainly cannot pick up our weak battery-powered signals."

John responded, attempting to be cheerful and not think of their immediate future, "At least we have some breathtaking views. No one from Earth has seen views like this, and I don't think anyone ever will, at least not for a few hundred years."

"Yes, let's enjoy the sights. Who knows when we will be able to speak with each other again", was the response. John looked quizzically at Kristen who was standing next to him, admiring the billions of stars from the window. She turned to look at him and noticed his puzzled look and responded, "I did not say that. It sounded like Nicole!"

Atra-has and his crew were busy. They knew the humans posed no threat, especially this far out in space. They were busy navigating the crafts, which were now in their familiar formation, minus two which were lost on Earth. On the monitors to the side some digits appeared and then some charts and graphs. After a myriad of charts, graphs, and digits, a point appeared on the screen with what looked like coordinates.

John suspected that these were calculations to go to a safe location before the time-travel mechanisms would be engaged. Then what little chance they had of returning to Earth would be gone.

In this hopeless situation, there was a reason for joy. John immediately shouted into his communicator, "Ken, Nicole, can you hear us?"

There was a simultaneous response, with both a male and female voice audible to John and Kristen. *"Yes!"*

John, with all his experience and the only nonscientist among the four, had to think fast. He immediately responded, "We can hear each other, but I suspect you, too, cannot hear Earth. You all must be close to our vehicles."

This time Ken responded, "They are tracking you. They don't have you on visually, but there is a point on the monitor here that they appear to be tracking. That point keeps moving away, and we appear to be moving toward it. There are a lot of calculations appearing on the second monitor. It is showing a lot of moving figures. I cannot tell what they are. It is moving too fast for me to read. But I think it is the calculation for them to return to their time. We may be getting ready for time travel."

John said, the urgency clear in his voice, "Ken, try to get Kesu's attention. Try to convince him to return to Earth." Then he turned to Kristen and said the same, "Kristen, try to get Atra-has's attention. Try to convince him to return." Ken and Nicole heard John's instruction to Kristen and knew immediately what John was thinking. This was their last hope.

Kristen closed her eyes and began her process to communicate through thoughts. Atra-has did not respond. It was that familiar voice—it must be her trying to distract him. John noticed that some of the others at the bridge turned around briefly, but they refocused their attention back to their jobs at hand. By that he knew that Kristen was successfully trying to get Atra-has's attention. Atra-has, however, was engrossed with his duties and could not be interrupted. After a while, Kristen opened her eyes and turned to John. "He is not responding. I heard him give stern instructions to the rest of the bridge to focus on their job."

Nicole came through on the communicator. "Ken has had some success in speaking with Kesu. They are currently sitting at that magic table exchanging some information. Briefly, from what I read, Ken said that you are trying to stop Atra-has and return to Earth. He said that the noise and flash of light was a freakish coincidence. It appears to be going over well. However, Kesu is focused on chasing down the pyramids."

John responded, "Yeah! Well, we are not having too much success. We will keep trying." Then looking at Kristen, he said, "Kristen, you heard that. Keep trying to get Atra-has's attention…What. I don't believe it! Nicole, we will get back to you. Something has developed here. Keep Kesu occupied."

Nicole responded, "Wait, John! What happened?" Ken, in order to focus on the communication, had taken out his earpiece, so he did not hear what John had said. Noticing the alarm in Nicole's voice he looked up at her as if to inquire what happened.

There was no response from John. "Ken, I will monitor the communication. You should keep Kesu engaged."

ACCOMPLICE

Earlier Kristen had noticed a robot which was moving around and doing something in the background. She had assumed that it was engaged in some relevant work. This robot closed in on Atra-has from behind and put its arm around his neck, as in a choking death grip. Atra-has was initially surprised, then he tried to lunge forward in order to reach the controls in front of him.

Kristen heard the thought conversation between Atra-has and the cyborg. *Don't do that. I am much stronger than you. You built us this way.*

Kristen and John immediately realized that it was not a robot—it was a cyborg. Lela had referred to the others in the contingent who were willing to help. This was the help that they needed—and not a moment too soon.

Atra-has responded, *One of the other can reach the pain switch.* He was referring to the switch which was used to control the unruly cyborgs.

The cyborg responded, *If the pain starts, I can crush your neck. When the pain starts, who knows what involuntary movement I could have? Believe me, I have experienced this pain many times in training as part of the training process. Limbs move uncontrollably. It is not something anyone should experience, let alone separate a brain from a body to be put in a machine. The power in these unnatural limbs could kill you instantly. Listen to me, just go back to Earth. Release these prisoners, including the ones in hibernation."*

Bewildered that the cyborg had crept up behind Atra-has without his knowledge, he asked, *How did you come up so close to me without my knowledge?*

The cyborg simply responded, *Lela taught us.*

Atra-has, like the others, could compartmentalize his thoughts. He could transmit or just think without transmitting. He started to wonder if this was some sort of a rebellion among the cyborgs. There were not many cyborgs on board, but if this knowledge was well-known among the humans at Aten-Heru, it would cause a tremendous amount of disruption. At this point, he was defeated, especially if they went back to Earth and unloaded the human cargo. He had no gold, no humans, and had been chased out by their enemy. It was a disgrace for him. At this time death was preferable to what was waiting for him back at Aten-Heru. He would be relegated to a lower rank and made to do menial work. It was pathetic. In the clutches of a cyborg, everything lost and dishonor to follow. He was too proud to have that happen to him. At least, if he issued the command, he would go down fighting, like a true soldier. The command to hit the switch was forming in his mind. In this extremely stressful situation, he heard a familiar voice in his head—someone known to him was calling via telepathy. But there was no one known to him in this ship.

When Kristen heard the conversation, she realized immediately that she should interrupt. *We are communicating with the enemy chasing you. They are willing to go back and talk.* She was hoping she could help sway Atra-has's mind into going back.

Both Atra-has and the cyborg looked at her. The cyborg spoke first. *My name is Meru. Lela was my friend, and she said I should help you. This is the first chance I had of providing assistance."*

Atra-has did not speak at first. He was still being held by the cyborg. Was it her thoughts he had heard? How could he mistake her voice. He came to a sudden stop with that line of thinking. It was her thoughts.

Kristen did not know the equivalent of "Thank you." She projected an image of gratitude while simultaneously bowing slightly.

The cyborg was overjoyed at this. *No one has done that to me. I am glad to be of help.*

Kristen then asked the obvious, *Are you like Lela, a female?*

Yes.

Atra-has was still compartmentalizing his thoughts, but his mind was racing. How could that be? How could he think her voice was familiar? Ever since she had spoken he thought he had an affinity for that thought transmission. But he could not place it and had put it out of his mind due to the work on hand.

Kristen then addressed Atra-has, *Garg-Ar is willing to go back and negotiate. If we go back, you can stop this war with Garg-Ar. You will be remembered as a great person on your planet. You will never have to make this journey again if you and Garg-Ar start talking with each other. We can help.*

Atra-has, still in the clutches of Meru, did not say anything for a while. It was obvious he was thinking. But unknown to anyone he was not thinking of what Kristen had just mentioned. He was thinking of why she seemed so familiar. All the lieutenants on the bridge were ready to jump to the control panel and hit the pain switch the second the command was issued.

After what appeared to be an eternity, he issued the command for his lieutenants to stand down. The humans on board breathed a huge sigh of relief. They had not realized that they had stopped breathing while anticipating an answer form Atra-has.

Kristen immediately spoke on the communicator, "Nicole, we have contact with Atra-has. It appears that he will cooperate. He has not said it yet, but things look promising."

Nicole relayed this to Ken who typed it out on the panel in front of him for Kesu to read.

ARRIVAL—AGAIN

The military personnel was instructed to dismantle all the considerable equipment that was set up temporarily at the location of the landing of the alien crafts. Item by item the engineers unbolted, unscrewed, and dismantled the equipment, folded them neatly, and packed them up in their custom-made containers. Then they loaded them onto the giant military vehicles. There was a line of vehicles arriving and departing. The vehicles all followed the same path. One arrived and one departed. There was no tarmac road to this forested clearing; consequently, the path was getting severely rutted. The excessive power of the military trucks was digging up the dirt as the deeply scalloped tires grabbed for some traction. The wet path, made damp with the downpour, was getting deeper with every passing vehicle.

There was only the last remaining tent and its ancillary support equipment remaining. That consisted of generators, speakers, lamps, tables, and the like. The high-ranking entourage on-site was still in the tents accompanied by the four astronauts who were not captured. The debate had shifted from attempting a rescue to what the possible fate would befall their colleagues and good friends who were now speeding away from Earth. They all realized that it was getting to be time to get up and let the other personnel pack up the tent.

Faintly there was a sound that came over the speaker. "Mission Control, do you read me?" Everyone around the table looked up and looked at one another. Manny said, "I must be hallucinating. I thought I heard John's voice."

Greg confirmed. "That was no hallucination. I also thought I heard John."

Everyone was silent for a while, everyone straining to hear the speakers over the din of the equipment that was clearing the site.

427

A few minutes later they heard a female voice, still very faint. "Anybody, can you hear? Please acknowledge."

Manny continued, "And I just thought I heard Nicole. What is going on?"

Baz jumped in, speculating, "What are the chances they would be returning? None of the humans on board the alien ships has the capacity to overpower the aliens, let alone navigate the crafts. But I did hear John and Nicole."

Then, speaking into the microphone, Baz asked, "Mission Control, are you picking up voices that appear to be John and Nicole."

Mission Control responded, "Affirmative. We are monitoring and verifying. Please stand by. We have tried to respond, but apparently, they are too far away. Our powerful equipment can pick up their signals, but their small communicator cannot pick us up. That is, if they indeed are John and Nicole."

A few seconds later Mission Control came on again and stated, "We will turn on the two-way so you can hear our continued efforts to establish contact with whoever it is that is transmitting." With that the channel opened up, and the people in the tent could hear all kinds of efforts to communicate with the source of the sound. At least, this cacophony would break the monotony of sitting around and waiting for something to happen.

A maintenance person responsible for packing up everything came in and wondered when the tents would be vacated. The local person in charge responded with instruction to leave this tent alone and load and move everything else. They could come back for these items the next day. After that, food was brought in. Everyone picked at it till it was too cold to eat. Then it was removed.

The speaker then came on loud to jolt everyone to attention. "Mission Control, this is John. Do you copy?"

Mission Control responded, "John, we hear you loud and clear. Give us your status."

The response heard was, "I will explain when we land. We are returning. The two alien parties want to proceed with negotiations. Prepare for our return."

That was tremendous news—everyone in the tent stood up, clapped, and cheered. They could hear through the speaker that there was the same reaction at Mission Control. Immediately Mission Control radioed to the departing trucks to turn around at the first possible opportunity and return to the original location. They could begin setting up the equipment as soon as they got there. Unsurprisingly, there were more than a few curses. Some of which were purposely uttered while still transmitting. The rutted roads would turn into a quagmire. One driver of a truck was heard saying, "We will need boats to get back." They were all military personnel. They did what was instructed. The trucks turned around and started heading back, slowly because traction was next to nonexistent by now.

When the cheering in the tent subsided, Mission Control responded, "Copy that. What about the fate of the human race?"

Atra-has had earlier instructed for the squadron to turn around and head back. He was still in the clutches of the cyborg. He could not tell the cyborg to release him since, unsurprisingly, it would not comply. It would be like this till they reached Earth. He had noticed that the Garg-Ar crafts had also turned around. Perhaps this was the best-case scenario. He had nothing materially to show for this trip. But, if the discussions were successful, he would have something more valuable—peace. Something equally valuable would be his dignity being intact. Given the situation he could not think of getting accolades for his efforts. He had finally figured out why the voice in his head was familiar. Once he was released from the clutches of Meru, his first action would be to check his own DNA with that of Kristen. It was highly likely she was related to him—separated by several generations, but related to him. It was clear in his mind that his brother, who had volunteered to be left on Earth with the others, had intermingled with the humans. For reasons unknown to him, the Aten-Heruans left on Earth had intermingled with the humans. These humans were now de facto Aten-Heruans. The genetic markers of his family, although diluted over the generations, were still showing in Kristen. He first had to make sure. That was easy. He was as yet undecided whether he should reveal the relationship to her, if there was a positive result, after he had performed the tests. From the corner of his eye, he saw Kristen looking at him sympathetically. Was she picking up his thoughts? She could not. He had made sure no one could. There would be others like her, part Aten-Heruans—maybe all humans had the DNA marker to indicate that they were descendants of the Aten-Heru ancestors. Based on local laws on Aten-Heru, if the humans could get there, they would have a right to live there. Only Aten-Heruans were accorded this right. He would have to get permission from Aten-Heru if they still wanted to destroy Earth. More than likely they would not allow that, knowing what they know now. Luckily for him, he would become the protector of Earth. Maybe he and some of his crew will want to stay back. He wanted to know more about Kristen, find out how much of her ancestry she knew. Maybe the perfect détente would be to leave the humans alone—without altering anything. Let the virus stay. That way no one could use the humans for any purpose.

John, who noticed the pensive Atra-has, responded, "We will have to cross that bridge when we come to it. That part is unknown for now. Our best bet is to get these two groups to talk, and hopefully, during the course of discussions, we can throw in the fact that they should leave us alone."

Not knowing what Atra-has was thinking, Kristen added, "In case the conversations are not proceeding as planned, we can always make sure that they do. Remember we are the mediators and translators. I don't believe the two alien parties are capable of communicating with one another. We can cleverly maneuver the conversations into something desirable."

While everyone was digesting that information, she added, "If things go really badly we will need to hide as many people as possible in bunkers capable of shielding them from radiation. This way at least a small portion of humanity will have its DNA and its soul unaffected by their weapons." After a brief pause she added, "Hope it does not come to that."

That was a sobering statement, but at least they were coming back, and there was hope as long as the enemies were willing to talk.

ABOUT THE AUTHOR

K. Paul Gomel was born in India and moved with his parents to England, where he attended boarding school. Going to the school library and reading books about real old-world expeditions and adventures was a way to avoid the cold, wet, and windy weather of Northern England. This pastime evolved into reading sci-fi adventures by many accomplished authors. Consuming these kinds of books, he discovered the parallels between exploring the unknowns on land and in space.

He completed his education in London, United Kingdom, earning a postgraduate degree. He moved to the United States and became a technology consultant, growing into the role of strategy and architecture. These positions involved writing and communicating to various levels of audiences. He wrote/constructed short commentaries/blogs about current issues and events that circulated among his friends and coworkers. The burning desire to write a novel was realized when there was an extended period of downtime. His life experiences in different continents have given him a unique perspective on life. He considers himself a citizen of the world and constantly endeavors to make it a better place for everyone.

He is interested in ancient cultures, astronomy, space technology, innovative puns, and fitness. He is an avid runner and has completed challenges like a half marathon and even a few triathlons. In his spare time, he likes to go on his own adventures, finding new trails to hike and bike. He currently lives on the East Coast of the USA with his family.

Despite his family's well-meaning contributions to this book, he managed to complete it. His words of gratitude, "Thanks a lot!"